DON'T
GET
CLOSE

Also available by Matt Miksa

13 Days to Die

DON'T GET CLOSE

A NOVEL

MATT MIKSA

CROOKED
LANE

NEW YORK

Copyright © 2022 by Matthew Miksa

Published in the United States by Crooked Lane Books, an imprint of The Quick Brown Fox & Company LLC.

Crooked Lane Books and its logo are trademarks of The Quick Brown Fox & Company LLC.

Library of Congress Catalog-in-Publication data available upon request.

ISBN (hardcover): 978-1-64385-900-2
ISBN (ebook): 978-1-64385-901-9

Cover design by Melanie Sun

Printed in the United States.

www.crookedlanebooks.com

Crooked Lane Books
34 West 27th St., 10th Floor
New York, NY 10001

First Edition: March 2022

10 9 8 7 6 5 4 3 2 1

For Mom,
who taught me to keep an open mind.

Nothing exists except atoms and empty space; everything else is opinion.

—Democritus of Abdera

PROLOGUE

*I*F HE FINDS *me, he'll stab me again, right through the belly.*
Sophie Whitestone pushed into the holiday crowds gunking up Michigan Avenue. She'd fold into the herd and disappear. When zebras packed in close, their stripes confused predators. Hadn't she read that somewhere?

Strings of lights wrapped around the tree trunks lining Magnificent Mile, the wires like green snakes, coiling up every crooked branch, reaching the raw tips where new buds wouldn't emerge for another five months. Each blinking bulb reflected off the carpet of fresh snow, where Sophie's rubber soles made glistening patterns—little lacy flowers. These boots were her favorite. Something about leaving trails of icy blooms seemed magical, like spreading winter wishes.

These were childish notions, she realized with some sadness, not the ideas of a young woman. A *college* woman, who just that morning had stamped those enchanting impressions across the University of Chicago's snow-covered quad, each oval evenly spaced and deep-set from a confident stride. Not hitched and staggered, like the damp shapes she was now marking on the downtown sidewalk.

He'll follow my footprints, Sophie thought. *Even if I'd lost him back at the L station, he'll track those kiddie sunflowers.*

Another drop of blood detached from the cuff of her coat and landed on the bright ground. Sophie winced and grabbed the sleeve, which was too long and hung limp past her fingertips. It wasn't actually her coat. It belonged to a forgetful businessman who'd sat beside her on the Red Line. Sophie had stolen it, in fact. That "S" word made her sound like a criminal—like a *thief*—but she'd only taken it because she *had* to. In any case, she'd ruined it (blood never came out completely), but it was still in better condition than her own coat, which now sat stuffed inside a trash bin with a hole punched through its Gore-Tex shell. A perfect, round hole that matched the one in Sophie's shoulder.

Even if he can't track the boot prints, he'll follow the dripping red trail. And if he catches me . . .

A woman screeched and Sophie's shoulder blades flinched, sending shoots of pain down her arm. She dared to turn and look, just as the shriek swooped into a clucking laugh and the woman fell into a handsome guy's embrace. He smiled through a graying beard. This man looked kind. It wasn't *him*. *He* was still out there, somewhere in the crowd.

Sophie pushed through the pain. She accidentally kicked the back wheel of a stroller—a double-wide couch-on-wheels built for two. The lady steering the monstrous thing glared, and the pair of tots strapped inside, bundled up to their gums, squealed like piggies.

"I'm sorry, excuse me," Sophie mumbled, and then regretted opening her mouth at all.

Shut up! she begged herself silently. *Don't speak. He'll hear you and then he'll find you and he'll take out that weird screwdriver, the one with the handle shaped like brass knuckles, and he'll add a few more holes in your body, or maybe more slash marks to match the ones from before, so please please please SHUT UP!*

The lady snapped, "Just watch where you're going, all right? Look, if you can't handle a crowd, you should turn around now. It doesn't get any better down there."

The wind whistled her words into an updraft and whisked them away, toward the lake, where barges were moving into formation for the midnight fireworks show. Sophie burrowed her chin into her collar, mashed a hand into her injured shoulder—applying pressure would stop the bleeding; she'd read that too—and turned east onto Grand Ave, into the thickening mass of humanity.

She passed a coffee shop, and a sushi restaurant, and a store selling fuzzy slippers for half off. "Only one shopping day left in the year," a sign in the window warned. She wanted to burst in and holler for the saleswoman to call the police before *he* found her again. But that would only put Sophie in more danger. A policeman couldn't protect her— not from *him*. He would track her all the way to the station if he had to, just like he had been following her around the city for weeks.

A month ago, Sophie had discovered fingerprint smudges on the glass of her second-floor dormitory window. Fingerprints on the *outside*, right beside a sticky smear that her roommate had guessed was probably semen. And just last week when she'd met her study group at the library, Sophie had excused herself to use the ladies' room and returned not six minutes later to find someone had tampered with her backpack. She was one hundred percent *positive* of this. Sophie always pulled the two zipper sliders to the far right side of her bag. She *never* closed them together at the top, not since Steve Barino had come up behind her in tenth grade, hooked his thumb into the small gap between the sliders and, in a single yank, spilled a week's supply of tampons onto the cafeteria floor. When Sophie had returned to her seat and reached for her backpack, she'd seen that the sliders were indeed at the *top*, not the sides. Irrefutable proof of tampering.

Her classmates swore they hadn't seen anyone touch her stuff, but Sophie couldn't take any chances. On the walk back to her dorm, she'd slung her backpack into the dumpster behind the library. The whole darn thing, with everything inside. Even her driver's license and credit card. She'd felt so stupid for leaving her bag unattended. *He* might've slipped something in there to track her. That was probably how he'd found her tonight too. He'd probably tucked a homing beacon into the lining of that ruined coat.

The crowd coagulated into a hard clot as Sophie neared Navy Pier. She squirmed through the tight gaps between men with potbellies and women with sharp elbows. Every bump against her shoulder sent another scream down her arm, into the bones of her knuckles. She pulled her hood over her forehead, down to her eyes, which scanned each face. If *he* caught up with her here, in this hardening tumor of bodies metastasizing at the base of the Ferris wheel, she'd have nowhere to run. He'd brush up against her, close enough to smell her hair, slip a hand around the small of her back, and run his screwdriver straight into her naval like it was a keyhole. Her legs would give out, but she wouldn't fall; the knot of other bodies would hold her up. She'd exhale her last foggy breath into the cold night and die standing up, pinched by the throng. The thought made her shudder. She wished she was home, in her pink bedroom above her father's study, listening to Celine and Mariah and Snoop Doggy Dogg (but only on her Walkman, so Daddy couldn't hear the songs with the *bad* words). Those days were over. Those *safe* days. Sophie was a woman of the city now, with important stuff to do. She was intelligent and fearless.

And she needed grow the eff up.

So, no, she wouldn't let *him* get her. Not tonight. She had safety in numbers, crammed inside the zebra herd with its dizzying, protective stripes. If you suspect you're in danger, or being stalked, find a crowd Mom had taught her. Perverts and thugs don't like a bunch of beady little eyeballs fixed on them. They operate in shadowy alleyways and backseats. *And sometimes university libraries too, Mom. Did you know that?*

The masses began shouting the countdown to a new year, a new beginning.

Ten . . . nine . . .

Sophie felt a surge of confidence, surrounded by the grinning, bubbly faces. She'd made it. She'd played the victim for too long, spent months looking over her shoulder, running from shadows. *No more,* she thought. *Let him find me. He can't stop me now. No one can.*

Eight . . . seven . . . six . . .

In the white space between *seven* and *six,* an older woman howled, "It's a bomb!"

The herd twitched, heads turned.

Turned toward Sophie.

She'd unzipped the stolen coat that smelled of men's cologne. Like a heavy blanket, it had concealed the messy puncture beneath her right collarbone, still oozing. It also had hidden the bricks of C-4 plastic explosives strapped to her bare stomach, just beneath the wire of her exposed bra. The coat fell away, and the cool breath of December hit her shoulders. *It's almost over.*

"What the hell is that on her back?" a man asked behind her. He'd seen the long, curved scar along her spine. Sophie lifted her pale arms, one hand gripping a detonator, the other with its fingers splayed.

Five . . .

Farther away, voices continued the countdown. Maybe they'd mistaken the screams on the pier for jubilance. *A new year is upon us,* Sophie thought. *They should rejoice. All of them. Even if they'll never know what the Sons of Elijah have done for them. What I've done for them.*

Four . . . three . . .

A guttural bark cut through the chanting rhythm of a thousand throats. *He'd* found her after all, and now he was ordering her to stop.

Sophie stared back at him, her chin raised. The man stood out, in that black cap with those three tall yellow letters beaming: "FBI." He yelled for people to let him through, but they had nowhere to go. Every inch of the pier had filled in with revelers. He tried to claw through, but the mob pushed back on him like a muscle. He still gripped the screwdriver—the one he'd snatched from a technician's work cart and jammed into the L train doors right before they'd snapped shut on his wrist. The tool had punctured Sophie's shoulder then, but now the man was too far away to hurt her again. Or to wrestle the push-button detonator from her grip.

Sophie smiled underneath the spinning shadow of the Ferris wheel, her arms straight as sticks in a high V for victory. She felt no pain now; the white-hot flame in her shoulder had blown out in a whoosh. Others were prepared to make a similar sacrifice. Sophie had made sure of it. They'd reveal themselves at the airport, the mall, wherever a large group had gathered. Even if the cops managed to round them all up, the Sons of Elijah would return. Sophie knew just how much depended on that, and she was proud to play her part. In this moment of triumph, death didn't frighten her. The thought of only one thing made her blood run cold: failure. The Sons of Elijah mustn't be stopped.

Sophie's eyes locked with the FBI agent's, and she mouthed a final warning: "Don't get close."

Two . . . one.

Click.

The horde pulsed. Arms and legs flung out from a center point, like a daisy blooming in fast motion. There were no more screams, just the rush of heat. A squeal of metal sang out, a regretful moan. The steel latticework of the massive Ferris wheel bent against its braces. Bolts popped. One of the gondolas snapped loose and fell more than a hundred feet. It smashed into skulls that were no longer connected to necks and rib cages that held in nothing but boiling pulp. A minute later, the whole affair collapsed, a pile of steel bones. The air filled with fine gray dust that smelled like bacon. Like crispy piggies. A half mile out from the tip of the pier, the floating barges launched their first battery of rockets over

Lake Michigan, right on schedule. Smoke from the fireworks mingled with the black pillar rising from the explosion on the pier. A damaged electric sign hanging high up on the terminal building sputtered its gleeful message:

"H PPY NE YE R 1995!"

TWENTY-EIGHT YEARS LATER

1

Miller: My feet were sweating. And my toes were sticky, practically glued together inside my sock. Is that gross?

Dr. Jacobson: Do you think it's gross?

Miller: I wanted to take off my shoes, but I knew my feet had to smell terrible, so I kept 'em on. But I had this itch, right on the arch, so I kinda kicked my boots together—you know, like when you're trying to knock off snow?

Dr. Jacobson: You were wearing boots? It was September in Alabama, right?

Miller: I always wore boots when I traveled. Still do, in fact. My pop taught me to wear steel toes at the train yard. All that heavy machinery—metal couplings and railcar loaders, the kind with the long, motorized belts for moving coal into those big cars. Plenty of ways to tangle the digits, he used to say.

Dr. Jacobson: This was a passenger train, was it not? It wasn't transporting coal. There wouldn't have been machinery like what you're describing near the platform.

Miller: A fella can never be too careful when it comes to his dingles and dangles. Pop taught me that too. I'm extra careful when it comes to fingers and toes, but I'm pretty sure Pop was also speakin' about his . . . you know.

Dr. Jacobson: I do. And your father sounds like a wise man. Did this particular trip happen when you were a child, Caleb?

Miller: Gosh, no. I was full grown by then. But somehow your old man's good sense sticks with you, even years later.

Dr. Jacobson: Yes, I suppose it does.

Miller: Well, anyhow. Do you still want to know more about my boots?

Dr. Jacobson: Do you have more to say?

Miller: Just that I didn't like the way this old lady looked at me when I started thumping my feet together, to get at that dang itch. She sat across the aisle, glarin' out of her side eye and curlin' those awful lips—so thin they looked drawn on. She musta took me for some junkie fightin' off the jumps. But I *never* went for drugs, Dr. Jacobson. Not in my whole life. Unless you wanna count that wad of chew Nicky Foulmouth made me try. His real name was Fullmont, but all us guys called him Foulmouth 'cause he dropped F-bombs like those murder drones the army uses.

Dr. Jacobson: Okay, Caleb. It sounds like this woman made you uncomfortable. What did you do about it? Did you say anything to her?

Miller: Wouldn't be gentlemanly. It would just be easier to move, I figured. Besides, I had to drain the radiator, as my pop used to say.

Dr. Jacobson: Drain the what?

Miller: I had to urinate, Doctor. I'd slugged a Big Gulp back at Union Station, while we waited for the mechanics to fix the air conditioning.

Dr. Jacobson: Oh, of course. What happened after you drained the . . . after you urinated?

Miller: Never got the chance. A big sign on the toilet door said "Out of Order." First the AC, then the john? Amtrak isn't what it used to be.

Dr. Jacobson: They've struggled with funding, I hear. But you said earlier that they'd already repaired the broken air-conditioning, back in New Orleans.

Miller: That's what they *said*, but we were rounding Mobile in the high heat of summertime, and the cars didn't feel any cooler. I raised my hand to the blowers and felt nothin' but hot breath. If you ask me, they lied about fixin' it up. Just kept us idling on the platform for an hour to make it look like somethin' was being done. Probably thought it would put people at ease, and we'd just forget we were roasting. Well, *I* didn't forget nothin'. My dang sweaty feet made sure of that!

Dr. Jacobson: Did you ever think about that problem with the AC, later on I mean? What if it hadn't broken down? What if the technicians hadn't delayed your departure from New Orleans?

Miller: No, I suppose I never did. But it does sound like terrible luck, now that you mention it. I suppose if that train had left on time, I wouldn't be sitting here on your couch gettin' my head shrunk, Doctor. Maybe a loose screw changed the entire course of my life.

Dr. Jacobson: Not just *your* life.

Miller: No, not just mine. That grouchy lady—maybe she'd still be alive if Amtrak had thought to buy better air-conditioning units. Maybe the jerk who cut Amtrak's budget is to blame. Yeah, maybe that bad bastard's responsible for all of them. All forty-seven souls who left the earth that night. [sniffles. weeping?]

Dr. Jacobson: We can stop here, if you'd like, Caleb.

Miller: No, sir. I wanna keep going.

Dr. Jacobson: Very well, but just so you know, we can stop anytime. If you don't feel comfortable—

Miller: Comfortable? I never feel comfortable. That's the point! I need you to *fix* me, Doctor.

Dr. Jacobson: Caleb, that's not—

Miller: [shouts] I need you to make it go away! Wipe my memories, or somethin'. I know you can do weird stuff like that. I've *heard* about it.

Dr. Jacobson: Typically, I help my patients remember their past lives, not forget them. I can't erase your memories, Caleb. And it wouldn't be productive anyway. Your experiences make you who you are.

Miller: Don't you get it? I don't *want* to be this person. I don't want to stay up until three in the mornin' watching infomercials for vacuums and jewelry cleaner because I'm terrified to close my eyes. 'Cause every time I do, I see those sparks spitting from the rails, and I hear those growls. Steel scrapin', scratchin'. And the train car twistin', then rollin', bodies slapping the windows like raw chicken thighs on a butcher's block. I see a baby sail from her mama's arms straight into the luggage rack, crack its tiny skull. Then we're all falling and falling. My knee crashes into my lip, and I taste pennies on my tongue. Eventually, I wake up from this nightmare, but only after we hit the river and water spills into the car. *Freezing* water. Sometimes that baby floats by, with a bone sticking out from its crooked neck. It winks at me. Then I'm fully awake, and the horror show blinks off, like flipping the channel. Now I'm in my La-Z-Boy and it's back to the lady selling the Shark DuoClean. That sucker can pick up a dang bowling ball, Doctor! Why do I know this? Because I—can't—fucking—sleep! [heavy breathing]

Dr. Jacobson: You're experiencing post-traumatic stress, Caleb. Similar to what soldiers experience after they return from deployment. It's difficult, I know, but we can work through it.

Miller: I should have died that night.

Dr. Jacobson: That was never a possibility.

Miller: You weren't there.

Dr. Jacobson: And neither were you. Not in the way you believe anyway.

[silence 00:15]

Miller: You don't know what you're doing. I shouldn't have come back here.

Dr. Jacobson: Caleb, you told me this same story last week and the week before that. I did some research. You've given a near flawless description of the derailment of the Sunset Limited. Earlier that day, a barge collided with the Big Bayou Canot bridge and knocked the rails out of alignment. When the passenger train hit the gap at seventy miles per hour, it jumped the track and fell into the Mobile River. It was the worst disaster in Amtrak history, and it was all over the news.

Miller: The *news*. You think I'm a liar? That I made it up?

Dr. Jacobson: I don't think you're a liar. Lying requires intent, Caleb, and I don't believe you intend to deceive me, or anyone, for that matter.

Miller: Then why don't you believe me? Why don't you believe that I was there, that I saw all of those people drown?

Dr. Jacobson: What would you say if I told you that the Sunset Limited derailed twenty years ago? What would you say about that, knowing that you were only eight years old at the time, not an adult man in a former life, as you claim you were in this vision?

[silence 00:22]

Miller: How do you know that?

Dr. Jacobson: The *Chicago Tribune* has digitized its archives going back fifty years. It's searchable online and publicly available. Your pop certainly was proud of his baby boy. He ran a birth announcement in the Sunday edition, December fourteenth, 1994. So, the day of that train crash, you would've been sitting in your third-grade classroom here in Chicago, safe and sound.

[cough, Miller?]

Dr. Jacobson: Caleb, you came to me for help. Now, I may not suggest the kind of treatment you had hoped for, but there are many effective methods for addressing what you're going through. If you trust me, I can help you put all of this behind you.

Miller: No, you're wrong, sir. I don't need to put this *behind* me. That's been the problem all along. I need to put it in *front* of me.

Dr. Jacobson: I'm not sure I understand.

Miller: The only way to stop this is head on, walk right up and punch it in the dang gut.

Dr. Jacobson: Let's just take things slowly, and—

Miller: There's no time for that. If you don't believe me now, then you never will.

Dr. Jacobson: I believe your pain is real. And I believe you can get better.

[rustling]

Dr. Jacobson: You're perfectly welcome to leave, but we still have twenty minutes left in our session. Have a seat and we'll talk about this.

Miller: I'm tired of talkin'. Talkin' won't fix this. It's time I did something about it.

[silence 00:27]

* * *

"What happened to the audio? It cut out. Did we lose the feed?" a woman asked.

"I dunno," came the reply. "The signal's at full strength. These bugs are finicky, though."

"Oh, crappo, there he goes."

FBI Special Agent Trainee Vera Taggart pulled off her headphones and slid open the van door. The afternoon humidity fogged her sunglasses, but she could still see Caleb Miller tromping up State Street with his hands shoved deep into his pockets. And she could see the scar on his neck, underneath his right ear. A pink infinity symbol etched into skin so pale the man's blue veins showed through. The mark was jagged and angry. The botched result of cuts made in the heat of passion.

Taggart quickened her pace. Her ear buzzed.

"Be calm, Tag. This is a simple practical exercise. Trail the subject, see where he goes, but for Chrissake, don't attract attention. Miller doesn't know we've been watching him, and I'm sure Butler would like to keep it that way."

She had no intention of getting on Butler's bad side. This was Tag's final field test, and she couldn't graduate the new agent training course without sign-off from the special agent in charge of her assigned field office.

"I'm closing the gap, one hundred feet. I don't want to lose my line of sight," Tag said.

"That's too close. This is a basic surveillance operation. Trust me, Miller's not sophisticated enough to evade us. Hell, even if he does, the guy's hardly important. We'll probably close his case file after we're done today. Besides, Butler's doing you a favor, letting you conduct your last test with a *real* subject before you've officially earned your wings."

"That's because I have such a terrific mentor," Tag snarked.

"Tuck that sass back into your britches, Li'l Miss. I've been sitting Q-babies ever since the white-haired president got blown in the Oval Office." Special Agent Joe Michelson, her training officer and temporary partner, let his smoker's cough crackle in Tag's earpiece.

"Q-babies? That's not how you're supposed to refer to your coworkers."

"When you wipe that Quantico 'Q' off your creds, I'll be the first to salute," Michelson said. "For now, just stick to the ops plan. Follow this skinny fuck for the next forty-five minutes, write up a shiny three-oh-two, and then you'll get your big boy pants."

"Again, not an appropriate way to speak to a female colleague."

"If I see someone who looks like a female colleague, maybe I'll change my tune."

Tag brushed off Michelson's sexist remark. She'd heard it all before. "Hey, what do you think Caleb meant by 'It's time I did something about it?'"

"Beats me. That sad sack has major self-esteem issues. Maybe he's finally going to sign up for a gym membership. Work on that bird chest."

"What if it's something else, Joe? What if he really is part of the Sons of Elijah? They could be planning another attack, and he could be helping," Tag said.

"The last time the Sons did anything like that, you were learning to write in cursive. Whatever members haven't already blown themselves up have probably died from teta-nus, the way they liked to carve those infinity symbols into their skin. And even if the group hasn't dissolved completely in the last thirty years, even if there's a den of dirty cultists holed up in a basement somewhere, having a circle jerk inside a giant pentagram, Caleb Miller is definitely not involved. He's just a skinny-ass mouse man with serious psychological problems."

Michelson had a point. Tag thought about the inconsis-tencies in Caleb's story about the train crash. He'd said it was summer, his feet were hot—but somehow the river water was *freezing* cold? Caleb claimed to have been on that train in a past life, but he had the time line totally wrong. Why would he lie about something like that?

"Maybe Caleb is a fraud," Tag said, "but for Agent Butler to open the case, there must have been some kind of evidence of criminal activity to predicate an investigation."

"Everyone makes mistakes, even the big boss."

It would have been one hell of a mistake. After six months of tracking Miller, the FBI hadn't picked up anything useful on his cell phone or on the bugs they'd slipped into the air vents in his apartment. Tag had read through the prior surveillance logs. The guy did the same thing every night. He went straight home after work, microwaved a frozen burrito, watched some TV, maybe a little porn—and not even the nasty kind—and then it was lights out by nine thirty. Not exactly the life of a religious cult member and domestic terrorist. Still, something about the guy gave her a brain itch. Maybe there was more to Caleb Miller, and everyone had missed it.

"We should bring him in," Tag said flatly, not convinced.

"Now, hold on, Elliott Ness. Butler would bust both of your gallbladders if you tried shit like that. You'd be on the first bus back to the Virginia forest and probably get recycled into the next training class, if you're lucky."

"*Gallbladder*. Singular. You only have one."

"What?"

"You said *both* gallbladders, but you only have one," Tag corrected. Expletive-laced mumbling filled her earpiece.

"Look, you're not testing arrest procedure today, last time I checked, so leave the little guy alone," Michelson advised.

"I don't mean we should *arrest* him," Tag explained, breathing harder as she sped up. "Let's just bring him in for an interview. I don't see the harm if Butler's done with him anyway."

Caleb had lengthened his stride, and the gap between them had widened. Tag worried she'd lose him completely.

"Hey, it's your exam—and probably your funeral. The boss said I wasn't supposed to help you."

"Agent Butler said that?" Tag asked.

"Well, if you plan to catch your mouse man, you'd better turn up the cardio because he's already across Wacker, and the light's about to change."

"Christ. Can't you keep it green, hold up the traffic until I cross?" Tag would draw too much attention if she began running. Caleb probably wouldn't notice; he hadn't lifted his eyes from the sidewalk since leaving Dr. Jacobson's office. Someone else could be watching the street, though, like the man in the expensive suit standing outside Peet's Coffee or the yoga mom letting her Pomeranian blow mud onto the grassy easement.

Tag smoothed her hair—a habit that began after she'd cropped it short her freshman year of college. Back then, she'd doubted she had the courage to do it, right up until the first black strands had floated to the bathroom floor. Even now, she liked to brush her hand up the back of her head, against the grain, to make sure it was still gone. Somehow the prickly sensation helped her remember important details, like the techniques she had learned from the droning Academy instructors counting down the days to retirement. Check for countersurveillance, they'd said. Tourists taking too many pictures, smokers flicking ash off unlit cigarettes, women pushing empty strollers.

Who would actually do any of those things? Tag thought. *How old was that advice?* Nowadays, *everyone* took too many pictures. It didn't mean you were a suicide bomber. And this was downtown Chicago, not a classroom. She would just blend into the hustle of the street and catch up to Caleb as best she could.

The stoplight flicked red as Tag reached the intersection. She could see Caleb walking onto the bridge ahead, crossing into River North. Once across the river, he could easily slip into a store or an apartment building. There were a thousand mouseholes in that neighborhood. Tag stepped into the street, searching for a gap in the flow of vehicles. A truck blared its horn and forced her back onto the curb.

"Gah!" she shouted, flicking up her middle finger at the driver.

"Don't sweat it. We've still got the tracker in Miller's backpack," Michelson said. "Besides, it looks like he's stopped."

"Stopped? Where did he stop? I can't see him anymore. Did he get across the bridge?"

"Oh, shit," Michelson's voice darkened. "You don't think—"

"He's going to *jump!*"

To hell with the red light. Tag pulled out her badge and gun and held them both high above her head. She waved them at the oncoming cars like magic talismans, commanding the metal beasts to halt. The FBI's OIC, Office of Integrity and Compliance, would probably censure her later. Drawing her sidearm in the heat of rush hour jeopardized her safety and the safety of those around her, they'd say. In bold, twenty-four-point font. They'd be right too. Pull out a gun in downtown Chicago and you're likely to get three more pointing back at you. At least that's how it had worked growing up on Tag's block.

A man riding a motorcycle didn't see Tag sprinting across the street until he'd nearly slammed into her kneecaps. His front wheel jerked sideways as he tried to avoid hitting her. A plume of white smoke sprayed from his back tire, and he tumbled onto the road.

"Oough. Sorry, man." Tag stepped over the motorcycle guy's back. He'd torn a hole in the elbow of his leather jacket, but otherwise he looked unharmed. Causing injury to a motorist—add that one to the list of infractions.

Once Tag reached the curb, she looked back to see if anyone had noticed. The entire intersection had jammed up with a snarl of cars wedged together at odd angles like a vehicular orgy. A Jeep Wrangler had smashed into the electrical box that housed the workings for the stoplight, which now flashed red. The blat of angry honks drew the attention of a hundred eyeballs up and down Wacker Drive.

"What's going on out there, Tag? Didja get hit?" Michelson asked.

"You don't exactly sound concerned," Tag said between huffing breaths. She ignored the chaos behind her and sprinted onto the DuSable Bridge that spanned the Chicago River. The concrete and metal drawbridge bounced to the rhythm of rolling tires. American flags whipped from poles positioned every ten feet along the railing. A small crowd had fanned out near the bridge's apex. Some of the spectators stood with raised phones, waiting for something to happen.

Caleb Miller stood on the railing with his chin pressed into his chest, looking down at the brown water. He swayed apathetically, except for the occasional jerk of his arm to regain his balance. The jagged scar on his neck was plainly visible now, and it pulsed purple. A woman yelped when Caleb lifted his right foot from the iron railing.

"He's definitely going to jump," Tag whispered. "He's going to hurl himself off the side of the bridge. He'll hit the water like it's a cement slab."

"Focus, Tag. Do not engage the subject," Michelson advised, all business now.

"Like hell. The guy's about to *kill* himself, Joe."

Tag wiggled through the human wall and climbed the railing. She stood beside Caleb, fifty feet above the flowing water. An open-top boat passed underneath the bridge. A guy on the deck was imparting architectural trivia through a bullhorn to rapt tourists. Then he shouted and pointed at Tag. The tourists' heads hinged back on open jawbones like baby birds awaiting a snack. Then more phones appeared. Everyone wanted a pic of the crazy chick on the bridge, clinging to a flagpole beside a young man who leaned into the wind with a dead look in his eyes.

"It's way higher than it looks, once you get up here," Tag said. The rippling river made her dizzy.

"Taggart, what in God's glory are you doing?" Michelson spat. He sounded genuinely angry now. Tag ignored him.

Caleb slowly raised his arms and squinted into the sun. Tag needed to get his attention.

"Yeah, so, this is a real rush, my dude, but I'm gonna be honest with you," she said. "Heights make me super light-headed—and sometimes nauseous. In that order. What do you say we hop on down and talk this out? Not that way, of course." Tag nodded toward the river. "We can sit right here, on the street, and just get into it. You and me. What do you say, Caleb?"

The young man angled his chin toward Tag. His bloodshot eyes spilled salty streams onto his flushed cheeks. Tufts of unwashed hair flickered around his temples like flames. "How do you know who I am?" he asked.

"For fuck's sake! You said his name, Tag. The subject's *name*. You've totally blown it," Michelson's voice crackled. "No way in hell Butler's passing you now. Get back to this van right—"

Tag pinched her earpiece and flicked it into the river.

"What was that?" Caleb asked.

"My earpiece," Tag explained. "My partner—my instructor, really—he wanted me to leave you to your business. You know, your *suicide in progress*. I disagreed with that idea, as you can probably see." Tag's stomach churned.

"Are you a cop?"

"Not exactly. I'm a trainee. You're my final exam, actually. Can you believe that? How am I doing, bud?"

"I don't understand." Caleb's foot slipped and his knee buckled. He threw his arms out, hands like blades, striking a tightrope walker's stance. The people on the bridge gasped in unison but settled once the young man restabilized.

"Listen," Tag said. "I'd really love to chat more, get to know all about your hobbies and favorite pastimes, but I'd really prefer to do that shit on the sidewalk, if that's okay."

"Talking and talking. There's nothing left to talk about," Caleb groaned.

It wasn't working. Tag had thought climbing onto the railing alongside him would make Caleb reconsider his options.

He'd realize that someone cared about him—a stranger he'd never met. He'd feel *seen*, and that would be enough to talk him down. She'd misjudged the root of his distress. Caleb didn't feel marginalized or rejected. Self-pity hadn't brought him to this moment. Something else had driven him to the point of self-destruction.

"Guilt," Tag blurted.

Caleb blinked and bit his bottom lip.

"All those people on the train died, but *you* got to keep on going," Tag continued. "You got to breathe and run and eat Mexican food and fall in love. By fate or luck, you swam out of that busted train car and crawled onto the riverbank. *Alive*."

"You're going to tell me that life is precious. Every day is a gift."

"No, I wouldn't feed you bullshit like that." Tag lowered her voice and leaned closer to the troubled young man. "It's not *cold* enough, Caleb."

"What?"

"The water down there. It's summer in Chicago. It would probably feel like slipping into a warm bath. Maybe even relaxing. Not like that churning current the day of the accident. That was *freezing* water, remember? That water was so cold it burned, didn't it? It locked up your arms and legs. The people who died, it turned their muscles into rocks, pulled them under. And when they opened their mouths, and that icy river water gushed past their tonsils and filled up their lungs, it probably felt like grenades exploding in their chests."

Caleb was sobbing now. Snot dripped from his nose.

"It won't feel like that for you, Caleb. Not on this sunny day. You'll go easy, peacefully. And all those people from the crash," Tag continued, "they'd be ashamed. How dare you pretend to know about their suffering? How *arrogant* of you."

Caleb crouched and gripped the railing with both hands beside his shoes. He looked like a swimmer on the starting block, about to spring into the pool. Except Caleb didn't spring forward; he stepped down, onto the walkway, and tipped onto his side with his knees pulled into his chest. Tag slid down the flagpole and lowered herself onto the sidewalk too, watching the open-deck boat drift farther downstream and navigate the gentle bend in the river. The surface of the water waved hypnotically. The gurgle in her belly grew into a rolling boil, and Tag leaned over the railing and puked.

The bystanders cheered and began spreading the news with their thumbs. Caleb blubbered in the fetal position with a yellow pool spreading under his hip. Tag wiped vomit from her lips and smiled. The young man would live another day. *Who doesn't love a happy ending?*

Agent Butler might not. The boss might fail Tag right out of the Bureau. Or maybe not. Either way, Tag felt a rush of satisfaction, watching Caleb suck in short breaths on the sidewalk. She'd saved a man's life. That was some superhero shit. Right then, she couldn't have predicted how she'd feel about Caleb Miller just a few days later. She'd think back to that moment on the bridge and realize the gravity of her mistake.

She should have let him jump.

2

"RECKLESS. UNPROFESSIONAL. JUST plain *stupid*, Taggart."
Acting Special Agent in Charge Gina Butler stood
behind her desk with one hip cocked inside her tailored
sheath dress. She pressed the heel of her hand into a stack of
folders with her fingers curved into slender arches, like she'd
trapped a spider before it could crawl to safety.

"I knew the moment I climbed onto that railing, I was
probably going to fail the field test, but—"

"Then why? What made you decide to throw it all away?
After everything you've worked for all year?"

"I can retake a basic surveillance exam, but I can't bring
a man back from the dead. He would've jumped, I know it.
That guy—something about the look in his eyes. I knew I
could save him," Tag explained.

"Caleb Miller is a dead end. He's a nothing subject who's
part of a nothing case. Guys like that snuff out their own
lives every day, and the world is hardly affected. But you,
Tag, we all had such high hopes for you. *I* had high hopes
for you."

"*Had. She said* had," Tag thought, and began chewing the inside of her cheek. She scrunched her nose and the skin between her eyes bunched. "May I speak freely? Is that okay?"

Butler sighed. "Why censor yourself now?"

"Since I returned from Quantico last month, you've blocked me at every turn. You made me retake my covert entry exam three times, even though no one performed as well as I did. I could plant a bug up a mobster's nostril without getting caught. You know this. Every one of my New Agent Training classmates has already been placed on their permanent squads, and I'm still in day care. And then, when I'm finally one measly exam away from finishing my field trials, you pair me with Joe 'Misogynist' Michelson, who probably thinks the Bureau went to hell in a Harley by letting women become special agents in the first place. And it just sucks—" Tag's neck flushed. "It sucks my ass, speaking freely."

Butler ran her tongue over her perfect, if a little too large, teeth. "You feel like I'm putting you through a gauntlet, and it's unfair."

"Yes, I do."

"And what do you think those other women went through? Susan Roley Malone, Joanne Pierce—the ones the Bureau *let* become the first female agents nearly a half century ago? Think about how many Joe Michelsons they had to contend with. Those women shoveled piles of dung so I could have my name on that door. And still, I'm only an *Acting* Special Agent in Charge, until someone with a penis frees up, probably. You know why they call the SAC job the *sack*? Because you've got to have a heavy set of balls to sit at this desk."

Tag grunted. "That's ridiculous."

"Not at all," Butler replied. "I've got a whole drawer full of them, in fact."

Tag stifled a laugh.

"Go ahead," Butler said, smiling through a ring of red lipstick. "We've got to laugh at this stuff. I smile every day, because I'm doing my part. I've got my blade, and I'm hacking a path through the Amazon. It's frustrating, sometimes demeaning work. I'm rounding out twenty-five years with the Bureau, and I still get called 'sweetheart' by the grayheads in Washington."

Butler sat on the edge of her desk and crossed her long legs. Her knees peeked out from underneath the hem of her dress. "But that's not the worst part. You know what sucks *my* ass, Taggart? The goddamn underbrush just grows back. Left alone, nature reclaims that little jungle footpath I've made and closes it right back up. That's why I can't stop. None of us can stop. More women must come up behind me and keep slicing at those vines and gnarly branches.

"Not all women are up for it—you must know this by now. Some see that the broad leaves have blocked out the sunlight, and they're simply too terrified that the dark, dark forest will swallow them up. But others . . ." Her voice dropped. "Other women grab their own machetes and go apeshit." Butler picked up a pen and stabbed its tip into the wood of her desk where it stuck there, rigid. "So, Agent Vera Taggart, are you willing to go apeshit with me?"

* * *

"What'd she do to you?" Michelson asked as Tag breezed past his cubicle. He swiveled in his chair, hands clasped behind his head and grinning under his walrus mustache.

"She gave me her case," Tag answered.

"The Sons of Elijah? That case is colder than a nun's teat. Five suicide bombings within the span of six months back in ninety-five, and then nada for almost thirty years. Whatever ideology that cult prayed to disintegrated along with their own flesh and bone. We lost three of our best agents during that shitstorm, some fucking great guys. Trust me, for years I wanted nothing more than to rip that terrorist cell apart with my own hands, but they beat me to it. The Sons are a relic. Butler is tossing you table scraps until she can get rid of you."

"It's not like that."

"Sorry, chickadee. Just watch. You'll get a transfer order to the forensic lab within a month, I promise. Probably spend the next ten years comparing pubic hair samples."

"No, Joe. The Sons of Elijah case isn't dead, it's just unsolved. Caleb Miller could help change that." Tag wrapped a pair of red headphones around her neck and slipped into her army-green fatigue jacket.

"The fuck are you going?" Michelson asked. He gnawed on the end of a toothpick.

"Where I should've gone days ago. I'm going to see a shrink," she answered, and spun away.

3

"'Since the soul is not found *without* body and yet is *not* body, it may be in one body or in another, and pass from body to body.'" Dr. Seth Jacobson removed his reading glasses and set them on the lectern. Tag sat in the back row of the university auditorium, beside a medical student with a thick neck beard.

The doctor's voice sounded different than it had during his session with Caleb that morning, when his velveteen timbre had seeped through Tag's headphones. That had been his therapist voice, she supposed. Now, in the cavernous lecture hall, Jacobson's baritone rang out, clear and deep. A grandfather clock marking time, commanding attention with rich musicality. The students leaned over their laptops and tablets, tapping away to the beat of every lyrical phrase.

"Sounds pretty tame, doesn't it?" Jacobson continued. "Well, not if you're the Catholic Church." He squeezed the remote in his hand, and an image projected onto the twenty-foot screen behind him. A mob of hunched peasants, many lifting wooden crosses, filled a piazza lined with ornate buildings. Priests in flowing robes and tall hats stood in a wide circle. In the center, a ladder rose from a nest of tree branches. A man was tied to the ladder's rungs, upside down and naked. A blue tongue flopped out of his mouth. The rubbery thing had been wrapped tightly with twine. The man's face glowed red, either from the blood rushing into his head or the flames licking at his scalp. Tag found the torture scene intriguingly horrific, but not surprising. Men reserved a special creativity for the monstrous things they did to one another.

"Baptism by fire—that's what the Roman Inquisition called it," Dr. Jacobson explained. "The condemned man you see here was named Giordano Bruno, and he paid the price for his heretical commentary, such as his inflammatory statement that I just read. And to think: when I write something contentious, all I get is a snarky op-ed by the *New York Times Book Review*."

The students laughed.

"It's worthy of mention that the Romans of the sixteenth century didn't typically execute their enemies in this brutal manner. As part of its spiritual purification campaign, the Church burned fewer than twenty-five heretics at the stake, and that's out of the thousands they executed, mostly using rather mundane methods. Bruno got special treatment, though. This inverted position you see depicted in the painting was a particularly devious innovation just for him. It's fair to say, Bruno really pissed off the Church leaders. Probably because he was one of them—an ordained monk." Jacobson paused and scanned the room with bright eyes that belied his age. "So, how does a man of the cloth get himself torched for proselytizing reincarnation?"

No hands went up. The plaque on the outside of the ivy-covered building had read "University of Chicago Department of Psychiatry and Behavioral Neuroscience." The physicians-in-training packing the hall likely hadn't prepared for a lecture in Renaissance-era history.

"Okay." Jacobson waved his hands in circles, as if to stir up the latent intellectual energy of the room. "If you were the Archbishop of Canterbury, you might say Bruno ignited a controversy simply because he wanted to become famous—a condition I've had some experience with and frankly wouldn't wish upon my most vile enemies."

More laughter.

"But Bruno was more than a hotshot provocateur. He threatened the Church's power. He believed in the Universal Soul, one that wasn't bound by flesh and matter. More controversially, a soul made of *divine* substance."

"So, we're all gods?" the neck-beard guy asked, his tone laced with cynicism.

"In a way. At least Bruno felt we all had *a part* of God within us. But this substance is impure, like gold ore before it's melted and refined. Purification takes time, he believed. Maybe even millennia. Ultimately, through a progression of human lifetimes, we can decontaminate ourselves. Same soul, different bodies. We learn and grow, until we have fully honed the divine substance within us and become one with God," Jacobson explained.

"Sounds a bit like Buddhism," a brunette said from the second row.

"Indeed, it does. Giordano Bruno certainly didn't invent this concept. He drew heavily upon the philosophies of others. The notion of enlightenment through reincarnation was, and still is, widely accepted among many Eastern religions. And a large number of early Christians also believed souls were reborn. By the fourth century, long before Bruno, reincarnation had grown in popularity, and that terrified the Church. If everyone got a second chance, and a third chance and a fourth, what urgency would they feel to convert to Catholicism today, in this life? The idea undermined the Church's monopoly on salvation."

A few of the students, rapt at the outset of the lecture, now thumbed through their phones. This metaphysical stuff wasn't their jam, Tag assumed.

"Look, I'm going to take a leap of logic here and assume none of you majored in art history or philosophy as undergraduates," Jacobson continued. "You're medical students, scientists. I get it. I was like you. Our existence is powered solely by the brain, I thought. And the brain can play tricks on us. Mental disorders have biological explanations. Neurotransmitters firing out of control, chemical imbalances. Hard science can explain anything, right?"

Dr. Jacobson walked around the front of the lectern. His loafers shone under the lights. "I'll be the first to admit: I have no proof that reincarnation is real. Can any of us truly know for certain where we go after we die? Of course not. But that's not the point. Frankly, I'm not so concerned with what's real or imagined, truth or fantasy, fact or faith. I'm not in the business of spiritual awakening. As a psychiatrist, I'm in the business of *healing*." He swept his hand over the sea of students. "That's the business you've signed up for as well, or else you wouldn't have taken on student debt up to your eyeballs just to be here."

Jacobson leaned against the table curving along the front row. Tag could see the gleam from his gold tie clip, pinned to his starched Oxford shirt.

"Now, somehow along the way, I became the foremost expert on past-life regression therapy. You may have heard?" Dr. Jacobson gestured to a stack of hardcover books at the end of the row, each plastered with the man's airbrushed face. The class tittered again.

"I help people access memories of the lives they claim to have lived *before* in order to alleviate their suffering in the life they're living *now*. For those who haven't read my books—and fear not, there's still time—allow me to elaborate. Under hypnosis, a patient of mine with chronic neck pain remembered being hanged for witchcraft in seventeenth-century Salem. He'd suffered for years before visiting my office, but after one session, he awoke the following morning totally cured."

"He?" a student asked. "I thought those accused witches were all women."

"Indeed, most were. But gender-switching is quite common. My patients have remembered former lives as men, women, children, criminals, priests, even a king or two."

"And you believe them?"

Dr. Jacobson bit on the end of his reading glasses. His smooth eyebrows arched. "Does it matter? However, if I *did* believe them, I'd have good company. Henry Ford, Benjamin Franklin, Tolstoy, Thomas Edison—they all believed in the reincarnation of the soul. In fact, according to a reputable study, one in every three Americans believes it too. So, maybe past-life therapy really does tap into our soul's retained memory."

"Well, then how does it work?" the brunette asked.

"No idea," Dr. Jacobson answered, and threw up his palms. Mr. Neck Beard snorted and shut his laptop.

"But I don't *need* to know, and neither do you. Giordano Bruno professed to have all the answers, and look where that got him." Jacobson gestured to the gruesome painting still displayed on the screen. "In Bruno's time, and in ours, quite honestly, the notion of reincarnation is divisive. I've been called a quack, a charlatan, even a con artist. I expected nothing less. Hell, that's precisely why it took me so long to come forward with my research. I worried: Would anyone take me seriously as a physician if I started telling tales about suspected witches reincarnated as insurance adjusters? It's weird—I get it. And I've paid a high professional price."

Tag squinted. She knew that Jacobson's last book had sold over ten million copies in forty languages. According to his FBI file, he'd purchased a four-story townhouse in one of Chicago's wealthiest neighborhoods for nearly eight million dollars. Just this year, Jacobson had appeared on *Ellen* and *Fallon. Saturday Night Live* had even parodied the psychiatrist, capturing his dramatic stage presence and blonde bouffant perfectly. Dr. Jacobson had reached celebrity status, with the bank balance and Twitter following to prove it, so Tag wasn't buying his nonsense about having paid a "high professional price."

"No matter the consequences," Jacobson continued, "I would never discourage you from pursuing any treatment that could heal a patient. Past-life therapy works, and that's good enough for me. But you should know the risks of following my path. It's 2023, and entertaining the possibility of reincarnation may not get you burned at the stake, like our friend Bruno, but sometimes the YouTube comments section can burn just as badly." Jacobson returned to the lectern.

"With all due respect," Neck Beard said, "most of us registered for your course to learn the specifics about your patients. You know, the *clinical* details? Can we at least get to the case studies?"

Jacobson smiled and every polished tooth lit up like he'd swallowed a string of LED lights. "We already have. I met Giordano Bruno about four hundred years after his execution. In fact, he was one of my first patients."

The lecture hall fell silent. Even the tapping of keys had stopped.

"All right, let's move on," Jacobson said cheerfully.

*   *   *

Tag lingered until most of the medical students had filed out of the lecture hall. The handful who had remained formed a line for Dr. Jacobson to autograph their copies of his latest bestseller, *Perhaps Another Time*. Tag imagined that by ten PM, most sixty-five-year-olds had finished their split pea soup and turned in for the night, but as the evening stretched on, Jacobson radiated energy. He beamed and shook hands with each adoring fan. Tag could practically see his ego swelling. Especially when a busty blonde student leaned in for a hug, the deep V of her blouse attracting his eyes like ants to a popsicle.

"Dr. Seth Jacobson," Tag said as she approached the psychiatrist and flapped open her leather-bound FBI credentials. "Special Agent Taggart."

Jacobson fastened the clasps of his worn bag. "I was wondering how long it would take you all," he said, waving to the blonde as she left the hall.

Tag nodded. "You've seen the videos online, then." The incident on the DuSable Bridge that morning had already made the rounds on social media. Some clips had picked up clear audio of Tag's words on the railing. Her inbox had filled with unread emails from the FBI's public affairs office marked "Urgent."

"In my forty years as a psychiatrist, treating the deranged and deluded, I've never observed behavior quite like that before," Jacobson said.

"Caleb's dealing with some pretty messed-up issues."

"I wasn't talking about Caleb," Jacobson replied. "I'm grateful that you intervened on the bridge, but for the record, I don't approve of your methods. That young man doesn't need any more scars."

"If I'd hesitated another second or two, the CPD Marine Unit would be scraping him off the bottom of the Chicago River right now. A little verbal motivation to coax him off the ledge wasn't so bad, given the alternative." The Twitter trolls had already upbraided Tag for the way she'd spoken to Caleb. *Another fascist foot soldier tramples over the mentally ill,* someone had written. People had even accused her of goading Caleb to jump.

The internet's cyberbullies had found their latest whipping boy—or girl, in Tag's case—and once they grew tired of lashing her, the FBI's lawyers would take over from there. And now there was Dr. Jacobson, a man in a perfectly pressed dress shirt who looked at her the way her father had when she was thirteen and he'd discovered her lower-back tattoo. His expression was one part disappointment, two parts disgust. Tag didn't need any more admonishment today.

Dr. Jacobson turned to leave. He didn't attempt to shake her hand. "It's been a pleasure to meet you, Ms. Taggart—"

"Special Agent Taggart," Tag corrected.

The psychiatrist nodded. "Of course. A pleasure, *Special Agent*. However, I must mention, the FBI has customarily scheduled our interviews in advance."

"I need to speak with you now. And besides, you're flying to London at the end of the week. You're speaking at the International Symposium on Parapsychology."

"You've done your homework. Very well, how about you walk an old man to his car, and I'll answer whatever questions you'd like."

"You don't look all that old to me, Doctor." Except for his fussy attire, Dr. Jacobson looked more like a svelte forty-five. He stood rail-straight, with his shoulders pulled back, and underneath the psychiatrist's tweed sport coat, Tag could see the contours of a defined chest and narrow waist. And she imagined that Hollywood smile could still charm a coed or two.

"Then I suppose looks can be deceiving," Jacobson said, checking his watch. "But I imagine you already know that, Special Agent." His eyes rolled over Tag's leather pants and wrinkled military jacket with the collar pulled up to her earlobes. Not exactly the standard-issue FBI uniform.

"Is he one of them? Is Caleb a member of the Sons of Elijah?" she asked bluntly.

"You certainly cut to the chase, so to speak." The psychiatrist squeezed the stiff handles of his bag. "But I don't speak about my patients without their permission. They trust me to protect their privacy."

"Even if it means others may get hurt? Is your professional integrity really more valuable than preventing a bomb from ripping through Millennium Park?"

Jacobson cocked his head. "Do you have specific information about a threat like that?"

"Would it matter? The argument is the same: if you have knowledge of your patient's involvement in a crime, you are ethically obligated to report him," Tag said. Jacobson couldn't hide behind doctor–patient confidentiality if he believed that Caleb posed a threat to public safety.

The doctor started up the center aisle toward the double doors in the rear of the hall. "The Sons haven't been active for three decades. I'm no federal investigator, but it's fair to assume that the world has seen the last of that particular organization."

"Is that your professional opinion?" Tag caught up to the doctor and matched his stride as they entered the building's foyer.

"Look, every couple of years, one of your esteemed colleagues reaches out and we have a wonderfully speculative chat about the Sons of Elijah. Were they nothing more than a handful of misguided zealots or an organized domestic terrorist cell whose remaining members went underground? We may never know, and yet the government continues to invest our tax dollars in seeking the answer. Personally, I object to such wastefulness, but I suppose I do understand the reasons for it. So, I'm happy to oblige and offer my perspective whenever federal agents come knocking, but please know that I have no special access to this group, if it even still exists."

"Sophie Whitestone and Gerald Cutter—two of your patients—were *both* members of the Sons."

"And they're both long gone, sadly. Sophie and Gerald's crimes happened well before your time, but surely the FBI has maintained extensive case files on them."

"Of course."

"And if you've reviewed them, then you must also know the FBI suspected that *I* was involved in their misdeeds," Jacobson said, and pushed through a wooden door that opened onto a grassy field. "They believed I had manipulated Ms. Whitestone and Mr. Cutter into committing those acts. The wise professor took advantage of impressionable minds—so went the theory."

"You must have expected some degree of scrutiny after the attacks. Two of your psychiatric patients—both highly educated with absolutely no criminal background—committed heinous murders. It's not hard to connect the dots."

Dr. Jacobson stopped, turned. "Dots. I like that. Yes, Special Agent Taggart, there are many dots, but I disagree with your assessment regarding the ease of their connection."

Tag grew frustrated with the doctor's vague manner of speaking. She'd read through binders of notes drafted by FBI interrogators who had interviewed Jacobson, dating back twenty-eight years, and she'd learned virtually nothing useful. The psychiatrist answered questions with questions (if he answered at all) and slipped into metaphors without warning. It was true, the FBI had obtained zero evidence implicating Jacobson in the Sons of Elijah attacks in the nineties, but that didn't mean the doctor was innocent. It only meant he was damn smart or slick as hell. Probably both.

"Why is that?" she asked.

"Before you can connect the dots, you must know where they are. And how *many* there are," Jacobson explained.

Tag perked up. "So, you admit there are more members of the Sons out there, ones we haven't identified."

"I admit nothing of the sort. A word like 'admit' suggests a confession. And as I have stated countless times—forgive my evident frustration with the matter—I had nothing to do with the Sons of Elijah's violence. But that doesn't make me naive, Special Agent Taggart. I accept that there's an indisputable nexus between my life and this radical faction. This fact has captured your imagination for reasons I won't probe into. But association alone does not complicity make. It has, however, made me a lifelong student."

"You're more than that, Doctor. You literally wrote the book on the Sons."

"And did you read it?"

"Of course," Tag lied. She'd only skimmed Jacobson's six-hundred-page tome, *Raising the Sons of Elijah*. This investigation had fallen into her lap barely eight hours ago, and immersing herself in Jacobson's FBI case file had consumed most of her afternoon.

"Well, that places you in an ever-shrinking clique. My life's work with reincarnation began with the Sons—it was the group's core belief, after all—but these days my publisher doesn't like when I bring up the terrorism stuff. It scares readers off, she says. She'd much rather I write about how past-life regression therapy helps housewives lose weight or addicts get clean, which it does, mysteriously enough. I see her point. Who wants to hear about a kooky religious cult that vanished without a trace a quarter century ago?"

"You still occasionally lecture on the Sons. I've watched a few clips online. If you truly believe the group has vanished, why not let it go?" Tag asked.

Dr. Jacobson cleared his throat. "I suppose I'd like to get the feds off my back—no offense. Someday I'd like to clear my name. All these years, the FBI has clung to the hypothesis that I sought out Sophie and Gerald. 'Why were you so interested in these troubled individuals?' your colleagues have asked. 'Why did you refer every other patient to other physicians in the department and choose to focus exclusively on those two?' It never seemed to occur to anyone that perhaps I had no choice in the matter."

"Are you saying someone forced you to treat Sophie and Gerald?"

"No, no. That's much too overt. 'Forced' implies coercion. I was no more forced to see those two than you were forced to come here and speak with me. It's the momentum of our lives—the invisible slipstream that pushes us into one another, diverging and converging again through time, like a braided rope. Make no mistake, Sophie Whitestone changed my life. My professional pursuits, my personal beliefs—she flipped the dinner table upside down and sent the fine china crashing against the wall. I'd always been a student of the mind, but after Sophie, I became a student of the *soul*. I've learned that these two concepts cannot be considered in isolation."

They reached a parking lot on the east side of campus. A black Cadillac Escalade idled at the curb. Dr. Jacobson pulled a handkerchief from his breast pocket and used it to grab the door handle.

"You said Sophie changed your life. Not Gerald. What was so special about her?" Tag asked. "And what was with the scars on her back? The giant infinity symbol cut into her skin, looping around her spine."

Dr. Jacobson sighed. "In all my years of teaching, some things never change." The SUV's passenger door popped open, and a small step folded down automatically. Looking over his shoulder he added, "Even the smartest pupils think they can skip the required reading."

"You said you'd answer all my questions," Tag said. "I'm not done."

"Read my book; don't skim it. Then we'll talk. Maybe I could even hypnotize you." Dr. Jacobson flashed his bone-white smile and pulled the SUV door shut. The Escalade rolled away.

4

Raising the Sons of Elijah
by Dr. Seth Jacobson

The Bishop

"HIS FINGERS SLIP underneath the neckline as he drapes it around his body. The yellow trim catches the light. I know the seamstresses spent weeks weaving the bright threads into the robe, which are made from real spun gold."

"What does the man do next?" I asked. We were twenty minutes into our third session, and Sophie Whitestone had never spoken about this man before. Nor had she mentioned these strange garments. She seemed to be recalling a specific memory, but of what?

Over the previous three weeks, Sophie had proven exceptionally receptive to hypnotherapy as a method for alleviating her anxiety, which had intensified as her coursework had piled on. She typically fell into a hypnotic state with very little coaxing. In these trances, the body relaxes, and the mind achieves marvelous focus. Patients like Sophie can tap into long-forgotten experiences from adolescence, or even earlier, and sometimes uncover a deep-seated reason for their mental distress.

Until today's session, Sophie had only shared a smattering of unremarkable details from her childhood. Quarrels between her parents, confrontations with schoolyard bullies—conventional dramas that affect American youths. But this particular description, of this elegantly robed man, felt like something completely distinct. I wanted to probe into it.

"His knuckles look like raisins, even though he hasn't touched the water yet. They dug the pool especially for the ceremony, and I heard they brought water all the way from the river in buckets to fill it up."

"Who, Sophie? Who dug the pool?"

"I don't know. I don't think it's important."

This notion would become a theme in our subsequent sessions: important versus trivial information. Sophie would recount scenes with such vivid detail but dismiss certain questions abruptly, deeming them insignificant. She'd become impatient, agitated. Almost as if the visions had an expiration date, and no time could be wasted on minutiae. In moments such as these, I learned to let my patient drive the conversation, and simply go along for the ride.

"It is purple, the robe. Bright purple with that glorious yellow trim. The man pulls it open and lets it fall to the ground. I'm embarrassed to look upon his nakedness, but the man shows no shame. His nipples droop from sags of skin that pull away from his chest and point down at his feet. A wilderness of silver hair covers his groin, and I'm thankful for how thick the curls have grown. I can barely make out the fleshy parts of his manhood, and my eyes are not tempted to seek—something God would surely punish me for."

"What does he do next? The man?"

"He moves toward the pool. An aide—a young boy—rushes to the man's side and grabs his elbow to guide him down the steps, but the man shrugs him off. He is old, but proud. He will descend the steps of his own power. This terrifies me."

"Why?" I asked.

Sophie's neck tensed. Her shoulders bunched up to her cheeks. This vision had raised her cortisol levels. Her body was beginning to demonstrate signs of a physiological response to emotional stress and I wanted to know why.

"Because if he slips, breaks his neck, dies in the pool, maybe . . . before I am finished . . ." Her breathing became short, labored.

"Keep going."

Sophie exhaled. "He doesn't slip. The man approaches me, submerged up to his navel. I am in the water too, and it sloshes against my waist. I just want to get this done. The man glares at me through sunken eyes. He wants it done too. In a swift motion, with one palm on his forehead and the other against the small of his back, I push him underneath the water. *Hold your breath, you miserable old bastard,* I think, but I do not dare speak the words. And then he's back up. Wet pearls slip over his neck, down his back, where I can see his spine pushing through spotted skin."

"He's alive?" I asked.

"Very much so. The man turns to me and for a flash, he's . . . *radiant.* His skin glows and sucks back into his frame, tightens. His shoulders broaden and pull back. The gray springs of hair on his chest blacken and thrust out of a swelling, powerful chest. The sagging sneer on his lips relaxes into a knowing smile. He looks exactly the way he did on that *other* day, many years before."

"What day, Sophie?"

Our hypnotherapy sessions rarely followed a linear chronology. Attempts to steer her back on track were almost never fruitful, so instead, if she snagged a new thread in her storytelling, I helped her pull on it.

"We are near the lakeshore. In a great hall with a checkered floor. The tiles are black and white, alternating. Like a chess board, but I don't think of that at the time. Still, the pattern is striking."

When Sophie would get stuck on a particular detail, like the color of the drapes or the temperature of the air, I could sometimes nudge her back into the flow. Were these minor descriptions relevant, the ones she'd dwell on? I thought no, at first, but later came to believe these were markers, like sign-posts guiding her through the vision. She could hook into a specific detail, like a checkered floor, and pinpoint a specific scene. She could jump there and immerse herself. Wayfinding details like this provided another utility too: they were often verifiable. In this case, as I would validate later through persis-tent research, Sophie was describing a room that existed six-teen centuries ago, twenty thousand miles away, in a picturesque town near Lake Iznik in modern-day Turkey—a country she'd never traveled to in her life. This was the first time I'd consid-ered the possibility that Sophie was recounting memories that were not, in fact, her own.

"The old man is there, in this room?" I asked.

"Yes, but as I said, he's younger now."

"Are you in the room as well?"

"Yes. I'm one of three hundred bishops. My name is Eusebius. We are standing as the man arrives."

"Why are you standing?"

"We stand for the emperor," she explained.

Now we were getting somewhere, I thought. "The man from the pool is an emperor? What is his name?"

"Constantine of Naissus, son of Flavius Valerius Constantius," Sophie said as confidently as if she'd order a grilled cheese sandwich from the Bartlett Dining Commons on campus. She'd just identified the powerful Roman emperor, Constantine the Great, by the ancient name of his birthplace. This nineteen-year-old girl from Illinois had no prior knowledge of fourth-century Mediterranean geography or architecture or customs, all of which she would go on to describe in detail over the course of our following sessions.

When I'd revived Sophie after our first hypnosis session, she'd had no recollection of what she'd recounted. She found it silly, and clearly doubted the veracity of my report. So I asked for her permission to record the sessions, and only when I played back the tape, and she heard the low drone of her own voice, did she finally believe me. Fortunately, Sophie allowed me to continue recording, but she refused to listen to any future sessions. They made her feel *oogey*, she said.

We continued the exploration of the remembered character we'd come to refer to as the Bishop.

"You said the emperor, Constantine, is there with you. And he is younger now?" I asked.

"Yes. He has passed the median of his life, but at this point he is still in good health and exudes virility. His skin sparkles, as do the jewels on his many rings. Two adolescent boys accompany him. They are nephews or maybe distant cousins—I don't know for sure. One is named Lucius, the fair-haired boy. Constantine is sleeping with him, but the other bishops don't know it."

"Then how do *you* know it?"

"The emperor trusts me. That's why he asks me to perform his baptism when he reaches the end of life. I know many of his sins, and I can wash them away before he separates from his earthly form."

Earthly form. Exudes virility. Median of his life. These were not common phrases for the average American coed, even among the hyperintellectual University of Chicago student body. I'd never heard Sophie speak this way before.

"What does Constantine do after he enters the hall, the one with the checkered floor?" I probed, hoping Sophie wouldn't lose the narrative.

"He sits in a golden chair. The bishops each place a hand over their hearts. I do this too. Constantine speaks and his voice is resonant. He says, 'This schism is far more pernicious than any kind of war. We will not depart until we have achieved common harmony.' He nods to Arius, who then moves to the pulpit."

"Who's Arius?"

"Arius of Baucalis. He's the reason for the trouble."

"The schism," I clarified.

"Yes. He believes that Jesus, the Son, was not made *of* God, rather he was made *from* God. The distinction threatens the emperor, and it has gathered popularity in certain sections of Alexandria."

"It sounds like trivial semantics. Why does this matter to Constantine?" I asked.

Sophie breathed slowly and continued. "If the Son was made *from* God—composed of separate, human material—and yet still achieved divinity, then all of mankind likewise could ultimately reach such a godlike state."

Sophie's hand lifted to her chin and caressed her cheeks. *Was she stroking a beard that wasn't there?* I wondered.

"Then what role does this leave the Church?" she continued. "Constantine wants to be the arbiter and sole grantor of salvation. This is the source of his power."

"He's the emperor. Can't he simply demand it?" I asked.

"No, because Arius's philosophy carries an implication that is even more significant . . . and dangerous. He believes that mankind's journey to divinity requires *cycles*. Rotations of earthly and spiritual form. Again and again and again, each time bringing us closer to our innate godliness."

"You're describing reincarnation, no?"

"Correct." More invisible beard stroking.

"And the emperor doesn't like this idea either. Why?"

"Simple. It gives people too much time. Why beg the Church for salvation when you can just cycle through again? Constantine's hold over his people requires a greater sense of urgency. He intends to squash Arius for good, today, in front of everyone. The entire council, ostensibly called to debate the matter, is a farce. I tried to warn Arius before, but he is stubborn. Let the emperor cut me down, before all of his bishops, Arius had said. That man enjoys the role of martyr. He welcomes the pain."

At this stage, I fully recognized the irony of Sophie, a college freshman, lecturing me on the obscure controversies that shook ancient Roman theology. She had never studied this material previously (I'd confirm this later). And yet the precision of her descriptions—the names, the places, even the attire of the men in the great hall—reached far beyond what she could have

absorbed from an Encyclopedia Britannica. Still, I retained professional objectivity, if not outright skepticism.

What happened next changed everything.

"It is late. I'm entering his bedchamber now," Sophie
explained. "The emperor's body sinks into the cushion. His hair
forms a fan around his head, and his is very still, but he is
alive."

We'd jumped ahead again, to the days shortly after the baptism scene that Sophie had described at the beginning of our
session.

"Constantine summoned me. He needs my counsel, and
he's running out of time."

"What does he ask you?"

"He wants to know if he has been liberated. In the emperor's
final days, he has come to believe an evil presence has infected
him. This must have terrified the man, who had always believed
his body to be a holy vessel for God Himself. He'd once con-
fided in me that God had spoken to him as a young boy, on a
pilgrimage to Gesoriacum. I'd asked what he'd learned, but
he'd refused to elaborate. He'd only said God had shared won-
drous knowledge no ordinary man could understand. But Constantine was far from ordinary, possibly even immortal, he'd
come to believe. Imagine the depths of his fear when sickness
finally ravaged his body. Most days, he can barely stand. The
man did not talk of immortality anymore. He had ordered the
baptism at the last possible moment to ensure he would pass
into the afterlife free from any contaminants."

"What do you tell him? Are you there to comfort him in his
final moments?"

"No. For decades, I feared this man. His power had swelled
to an inhuman volume. *Godlike* volume. But he looks so weak
now, withered. I'm wondering how he had ever frightened me
so much. So, I tell him the truth."

"Which is?"

"An evil spirit *had* corrupted him long ago. The emperor
should have listened to Arius, but instead he had allowed the

darkness to seduce him. He had caused immeasurable damage in the decades following that afternoon near the lake. I told him this, though I could hear my own voice quavering as I voiced the words. He deserved the rebuke and I prayed for the strength to deliver it assuredly. The emperor's foolish councils had nearly stamped out the last flickering flame of truth, that cycles of rebirth are real. Now, the Church will hunt down those who challenge its creed, execute them as heretics. It will take thousands of years to recover, and that is only if the few of us willing to defy the emperor risk our lives to nurture the handful of dying embers. I want the emperor to reckon with the damage he has caused. I want him to hear the devil's scraping laughter as he slips away. I want him to carry this crushing guilt to his grave—and beyond."

"I imagine that it took great courage to stand up to such a powerful figure. How did he respond?" I asked.

"He collapses further into the bedding. The blankets swallow him up. A great, puckered creature. His loose cheeks fold over his tortured face, and he mumbles a reply. I cannot hear the words. I approach the bedside." Sophie craned her neck, stuck out her chin. *Listening* to a voice that rang out only inside her mind. "He says . . . he says . . ." Sophie's lips moved but no sound came out.

"What is it, Sophie? What does the emperor say to you?"

Her eyes widened. "It's the message. The one he received from God on the road to Gesoriacum. It is . . . shocking! It is clear why he never revealed it. And if it is true . . ."

"You can tell me. You're safe here," I assured her. My own curiosity ached to know what secret she believed the emperor Constantine had shared on his death bed.

"Nolite propinquius venire!" she shouted so loudly the recording buzzed with distortion when I reviewed the tape later that evening.

"My face is hot. I pull the fabric of my robe away from my neck," Sophie continued. "Anger surges inside my belly. My lungs fill up with fire. I try to conceal my rage. I do not want the emperor to call out again. There is no one else in the room, and I do not want the guards to hear him yelling. He trusts only me with his message. I place a hand on his chest, lightly, and smile reassuringly. The all-powerful emperor, now a wrinkled mass of flesh, exhales through wet, round lips."

Sophie's own face had flushed, and her speech quickened. "I climb on top of the bed. My body is aged and fragile, like his, but I have a burst of strength. I lift my vestments and swing one leg over the emperor's body so that each of my knees push into his armpits. His mouth widens with concern, and I can see the puffy puss growing in the back of his throat. I slap both of my hands over his face and lower my full weight onto his ribcage. The bulb in the front of his neck shoots up and down. He gnashes his jaw, tries to bite me, but I feel only soft gums rub against my palms. His small hands paw at my back. His fingernail scratches my arm." Sophie panted as the words came fast now.

"A burning feeling fills my chest, and I am convinced it is God's own hand trying to push me away, or maybe guide me forward; I do not know. I am so confused—and so *frightened*. But I do not stop. I push down on the emperor's frame until I hear a cracking. It sounds like a tree branch splitting. A terrible snap. Now he is still. And wet. I am wet too. Dripping and warm. The pain strikes like white lightning. I look down and see a knife handle sticking from my abdomen. The rubies set into the knife's heel match the emperor's rings. The wound is surely fatal, but I am not afraid of death. What I see on my arm, the clear shape he's etched into my skin with his fingernail, horrifies me."

In the wingback leather armchair, positioned in a cozy corner of my office, Sophie began convulsing. With her eyelids mashed shut and her face screwed up like a twisted washrag, she clawed at her stomach, sending shirt buttons flying, revealing a wedge of skin, drawing blood. A scream roared from her throat.

Sophie appeared to be in extreme pain and still under a hypnotic trance. I needed to awaken her immediately. It took much effort—and some brute strength—to subdue the girl and raise her from hypnosis. Once lucid, Sophie's pain dissipated, but not her fear. She clutched her torn blouse and curled into the back of the chair. I was sweaty and breathless from the episode.

"What happened?" she whispered with a hoarse voice.

"You should rest, Sophie."

"What did you do to me? What did you *do*?"

Her ripped clothing. My flushed face. I knew how it must have looked to this young woman. Sophie didn't remember anything that had happened while under hypnosis, and admittedly, I began to worry about what she'd tell people about the session. For both of our sakes, she needed to listen to the recording.

"Absolutely not," Sophie said. "I don't want to hear those things."

I knew she'd feel worse if she left my office thinking I'd somehow taken advantage of her during her trance, that maybe *I'd* ripped her blouse. My duty to my patients was to heal old scars, not create new ones. It took some coaxing, but I convinced her to listen to the tape. Just this once.

Her screams captured on the recording upset her greatly. *Nolite propinquius venire!*

"What am I saying?" she asked. "I don't even understand it."

"It's called xenoglossy, although no one seems to have much of an explanation for it," I said. "There are a few documented cases of people suddenly speaking a language of which they have no prior knowledge. It's a rare phenomenon, to be sure. Many in my profession classify it as paranormal or even dismiss it altogether as a hoax."

In medical school, I'd learned about a case out of New York from the turn of the twentieth century. A respected physician had awoken before dawn, hearing murmuring from down the hall of his stately residence. He rose from bed and discovered his twin boys, age two, whispering to each other in their nursery. The toddlers weren't babbling or giggling the way children might when inventing funny words. They were *conversing*—nodding to one another in agreement, gesturing for emphasis—and yet the doctor couldn't understand any of the mysterious exchange.

At the recommendation of a colleague, the man brought his sons to Columbia University and asked them to demonstrate their strange vernacular for the foreign language department. The exhibition dazzled the faculty, and many agreed that it sounded like legitimate syntax, but none of them could identify the origin. The physician nearly gave up, when a professor of ancient history dipped his head in and said, "My word! Who taught these children to speak Aramaic?" The boys had been conversing in the now-dead language once spoken by Jesus Christ himself.

Since this notable case, researchers have documented a handful of patients who have demonstrated similar abilities, none with any reasonable explanation. Sitting across from Sophie, my pulse thumped at the possibility that I'd stumbled upon a new instance of authentic xenoglossy.

Sophie clutched her shirt tighter and turned away from the tape recorder. "It sounds like me, on that tape, but I swear I have no idea what those words mean. How do I know you didn't fake the recording?"

"I suppose you don't know that for certain, although I can assure you that I would have no motivation for doing so," I explained. "Or the means, for that matter. You spoke these words less than five minutes ago, just before you scratched yourself. Would you like a bandage for that?"

"I'm fine." Sophie's eyes glazed over. The shivering stopped and her chest rose with a long breath. Her eyes focused on the overhead light, and she stared at it unblinkingly. I could see her pupils constrict into pinheads. Was she remembering? I wondered.

"In the vision, what did the emperor do to your arm?" I asked.

"He scratched out a symbol." Sophie rubbed her triceps as if to assuage the pain.

"Do you remember what it was? Here," I said, handing her my pen and notepad. "Try to draw it."

Sophie scribbled a mark and then quickly handed the pad over, wanting to be rid of it.

"He did it right after screaming those words," she explained. "*Nolite propinquius venire*. What does it mean?"

"I'm not sure," I admitted. My Latin had rusted since university. I made a note and planned to research the translation after our session. Whatever its meaning, the phrase had upset Sophie. "What are you feeling now?" I asked.

"The same fear that I felt then."

"What are you afraid of?"

"That I waited too long."

"Too long for what, Sophie?"

She inhaled deeply again, then whispered, "I waited too long to kill him."

Sophie Whitestone, the timid teenager who held back her bangs with heart barrettes, was talking about having murdered someone. Surely this would do nothing to calm her troubled mental state. The girl already suffered from chronic panic attacks and severe menstrual cramps, and when medication hadn't worked, she'd finally scheduled an appointment with a psychiatrist, only to wind up believing that she'd killed an emperor. What had I done to this poor young woman?

I felt deeply responsible for exacerbating my patient's emotional distress, and yet her revelations under hypnosis fascinated me. Sophie had recalled vivid details of shockingly violent acts and had spoken Latin with the eloquence of a first-century scholar. She'd known the names and birthplaces of men who'd lived more than a thousand years ago. This knowledge had burst forth from her subconscious without warning.

This therapy session, in January 1993, marked an inflection point in Sophie's young life, and in my burgeoning career. For the first time, I had to consider that something had happened in my worn-out leather lounge chair that had no medical or scientific explanation. Sophie hadn't imagined the scene in the emperor's bedchamber; she had *remembered* it. My patient had accessed a memory from a former life.

Sophie zipped into her coat and left the ruined blouse on the rug. She fled my office, still rattled, and I assumed I'd never hear from her again. The experience left me with a hundred questions. I wanted to see what else we could uncover, but it wouldn't have been fair to my patient to push her if she wasn't comfortable. As spellbinding as the session had been professionally, I worried that the events of that afternoon may have actually compounded her trauma, ratcheted up her anxiety to eleven. Except they hadn't.

Sophie Whitestone called me a month later. She hadn't had a panic attack since our session, and her menstrual cramps had not returned. She sounded ebullient and hopeful. And she wanted to keep going. This news delighted me, but my excitement faded when I remembered that final Latin phrase she'd uttered after waking from hypnosis. I retrieved my notepad and flipped to the relevant page. In my terrible script, I'd written, *Nolite propinquius venire.* With the aid of a dictionary, I'd determined the meaning was an ominous warning.

Don't get close.

I'd printed the English translation just above Sophie's sketch of her scratch marks from the vision. With a fluid, unbroken stroke, she'd drawn an infinity symbol.

5

THE TRASHCAN OVERFLOWED onto the kitchen floor. A bowl of half-eaten spaghetti from last night's dinner sat on the countertop. The marinara sauce had crusted over, but that didn't stop the houseflies from gleefully buzzing around it. Tag opened her refrigerator, releasing a sour odor that may have emanated from any number of expired items. She flipped off the cap of a milk carton, sniffed, and took a swig. If it hadn't yet turned, it certainly would by morning. She poured the rest into the sink, watching the white swirls circle the drain.

From this spot, she could look upon her entire apartment, which had the offbeat vibe of a bohemian co-op. The sparse unit had a single gray couch that often doubled as a bed. Tag had pushed it into a corner to make room for her easels—four of them—which stood like the skeletons of stiff-legged giraffes on a wrinkled drop cloth. For the first time in nearly two years, the easels held no canvases. They were nothing but bare wooden bones, wasting away from neglect.

Tag had sketched and painted since the day she could hold a brush. Her father used to say she'd been born with bristles shooting from her fingernails, and the doctors had to trim them off. The old man hadn't been a bit surprised when the School of the Art Institute of Chicago had admitted Tag into its prestigious fine arts program by age seventeen. She'd flourished there for nearly a decade, surrounded by sculptors, fashion designers, and filmmakers—all the other crabgrasses and milkweeds who happily blemished the world's perfectly manicured lawns. Tag's talent burgeoned, as if she'd unlocked a box and watched blooming vines spring out and climb the walls. Her instructors had noticed something unusual developing in Tag's art, but even they didn't fully understand what was happening. The neurons of Tag's brain had thickened, somehow, like thirsty roots. She was *germinating*, and paint was plant food.

The past year had been different, though. Her diploma and portfolio of work should've taken her career to galleries and museums on a steam locomotive, but one spring night, a switch got thrown, and she'd veered onto a track that headed directly to an FBI recruiter's office.

Tag hadn't felt inspired to paint since returning from Quantico, and a nagging part of her wondered if she'd killed off her mojo. The long days bumping along in Crown Victorias beside black-suited dudes with buzz cuts hadn't exactly titillated her inner muse. A collection of unfinished ideas, mostly still pencil sketches, had been resting against her apartment wall for months and would probably remain there for many more. Still, Tag kept them out, just in case a drop of inspiration splashed into her eyes from the showerhead.

Her walls themselves were completely bare despite the stacks of paintings she'd produced in school. Tag had shoved the completed ones in the closet. Once she finished composing a painting, her obsession with it snuffed out, and the piece no longer interested her. For Tag, art was a cathartic process, a release. All of her energy and emotion went into the act of creation itself. Her finished works only looked like shadows, inert and immobile, like the echoes after a monster rockslide. She imagined serial killers felt the same way about their crimes. That's why they hid their victims' bodies. They weren't covering up evidence. They wanted to hide the pallid, dead thing that had resulted from such a passionate outpouring.

Art and murder—two sides of the same coin. That was how Tag saw the world, and for some reason, the FBI had taken an interest in her unique viewpoint.

Tag cracked a window, flipped on the ceiling fan, and removed her jacket, to let her skin breathe. The couch beckoned. Stretched out on her back, she watched the fan's spinning blades and drifted back to the evening that had turned her life into a runaway railcar.

*   *   *

"I'm supposed to make some kind of announcement, so here goes," Tag said. She stepped onto a wooden box that barely raised her height above the tallest attendees in the gallery. "Some insist that art is a solitary exercise," she began. "They say that only through lonely suffering can one produce something meaningful. Well, that's bullshit. This night would've never happened without all of you. I'm looking around and I see the faces of the friends who encouraged me when I thought I couldn't pull it off, and the instructors who kicked my ass to make sure I did. Thank you for coming. Really, I mean that. And please stick around, even after this terrible speech." The crowd laughed. "Anyway, you came to see my work, not to hear me babble, so let's get to it."

Ten oversized canvases, spaced at even intervals, hung from the gallery walls. Tag had rented the small space in Chicago's West Loop neighborhood to showcase her collection. She'd worked toward this night for months, and after it was over, she'd have completed all of the necessary requirements to graduate with an MFA from the city's top art school. She'd developed the series of paintings over the course of her final semester, under the tutelage of renowned adjunct professors—each one an accomplished artist in their own right—but none of them knew what Tag had planned for tonight's showing. The secret was part of the fun. Art should be unexpected and uncomfortable. Keep people on their toes, and then knock 'em off balance with a thwack to the kidney they'd never see coming.

Tag had insisted on covering the windows with dark felt and slathering the walls with black paint. She wanted her canvases to stand out like bright squares floating in a void. The subjects of her portraits—lithe young women with pastel skin and willowy arms—struck a variety of helpless poses. They draped themselves over upholstered chairs, slipped down curved staircases on their backs, hung upside-down over the edges of beds with their arms flung out. In each painting, the women's slender necks craned away from the observer, and they pulled at their swooping necklines, exposing doughy breasts. Tag's aesthetic approach had worried her adviser, who cautioned against such cliché representation of female vulnerability. "Enfeebled damsels went out with Henry Fuseli," he'd said. She'd assured him there was more to it.

Now standing with his back to the wall, squeezing his chin between long fingers, Tag's adviser looked as skeptical as ever.

"You came to see it," Tag said to him, "so open wide."

She nodded to the studio technician, who then flipped the light switch. The yellow overhead lamps shut off with a clack, and cool violet light bathed the room. Tag had installed special light bars along the floor so that the eerie hue would wash the black walls and diffuse into the space. Her once-muted canvases exploded with color as long wave UVA light revealed a flurry of hidden brushstrokes. The women's clothes now looked torn, the plush fabrics chewed away, leaving only frayed strips. Bright red slashes cut across their throats. Somehow, their supple bosoms had morphed into flatter, meatier plates. Their chins sharpened and hair sprouted from their armpits. Their groins swelled too—that bit really clinched the effect. With invisible, UV-reactive paint, Tag had transformed a collection of fair, powerless women into the murdered corpses of muscle-bound men. Most shockingly, blood dripped in long streaks down the gallery's black walls. Ceiling-mounted projectors created the slow-motion, oozing effect. The entire scene was quite immersive. And horrifying, Tag hoped.

After a choking silence, the small crowd applauded. Even her cynical adviser had to wipe his goatee off the floor. Tag exhaled with relief when the man finally nodded approvingly. With her hands folded behind her back, Tag allowed her guests to mill about her bleeding horror box. After a few minutes, a stranger approached her.

"A little on the nose, don't you think?" the woman asked. She wore a snug white dress that glowed in the UV light and purple lipstick that matched her eyes. "The butch lezzy takes down the patriarchy one slashed aorta at a time."

"Have we met?" Tag asked.

"But there's something I don't get," the woman continued, ignoring Tag's question. "Why the stiffies?" She nodded to one of the slain men gripping his bulging crotch. "Technically speaking, it's impossible for a man to hold an erection after death, what with his heart having stopped and all."

"Are you speaking from experience?"

The woman fondled her earring and raised her chin, displaying a stupendous jawline. "Do you find homicide erotic?"

"Of course," Tag answered without hesitation. "Sex and murder are mirror images. Both are at once carnal and violent. And powerfully stimulating. What arouses the senses more than having your soul ripped from your flesh and flung into oblivion?"

"Oh, honey. If that's what sex feels like to you, I'm afraid you're doing it wrong."

Tag smiled. "Maybe. But what do I know? I'm just a butch lezzy." She lifted two champagne flutes from a server's tray as it bobbed passed. "A toast to erotic homicide?"

"A raincheck, perhaps. I'm on the clock." The woman snapped open her clutch and removed a leather billfold. A quick flick revealed the letters "FBI" printed in tall blue capitals.

Tag squinted. "Is this a joke? Forgive me, but you really don't look like a federal agent."

"That's just the thing, Vera Taggart, artist extraordinaire. Neither do you."

* * *

Tag's roommate Chloe sat on their overstuffed couch with one bare foot digging into the crack between the cushions. She held the business card of Special Agent Gina Butler. "So, this lady tried to recruit you for the FBI? At your art show? Was she shitting you? Wait, are you shitting *me*?"

"She said the Bureau needs abstract thinkers, people who can see what others can't. Art is like a third eye or something. I know—it sounds dumb." Tag pulled a beer bottle from the fridge and pried off the cap with her pocketknife.

"It *sounds* like a salary. The way things are going, you may be the only one in our graduating class with a legit, paying offer. Plus, maybe you'll get to hunt down serial killers. Just think how much material that would give you for your next gore show." When Chloe laughed, her stretched-out shirt collar slipped down a shoulder.

"A buddy opened a bar in Queens," Tag said. "I'm going to head to New York and try my luck there. Maybe I'll get an internship at a gallery in Chelsea."

"And eat canned beans for dinner, like a true artist? It's ridiculous. You're brilliant, Tag. And creative. And fucking dark as hell." Chloe flicked the business card with a fingernail. "You'd be perfect for the FBI."

The intercom buzzed.

"Ugh, that horndog. Jacob sexted me another nude this afternoon—while I was at an *interview*, I should add. And there are only so many jobs for a graphic designer with zero office experience." Chloe adjusted her bra and straightened her shirt. "This dude thinks he can ride that rusty Schwinn over here whenever, and I'll drop everything and—"

Tag sucked on the neck of her beer bottle and batted her eyes.

"Oh, fuck you." Chloe flipped up two middle fingers and skipped to the door, all giggles.

*   *   *

That night, alone in bed, Tag grew bored of staring at the insides of her eyelids, so she picked a random spot on the ceiling to fixate on, knowing sleep wouldn't come easily. Chloe's headboard finally stopped banging against her bedroom wall around one o'clock in the morning. Whatever pills her Romeo had popped must've given him some kind of sex magic. Chloe's extravagant moaning had reverberated through the walls. Although Tag assumed her roommate faked most of those porno-movie sound effects. The woman was a bit of a showboat.

After the festivities in the adjacent bedroom finally wrapped up, a bar of light appeared in the crack of Tag's partially open bedroom door. Chloe skipped across the hallway to the bathroom, and she hadn't bothered with a robe. Tag should've rolled over, but her body refused to move. And her eyes refused to shut. They traced the smooth curve of Chloe's spine, from the woman's shoulder blades down to the small of her back, until her roommate disappeared into the bathroom.

A moment later, Tag heard the toilet flush and a rush of water from the sink faucet. Then Chloe stepped into the hallway and froze. She spotted Tag staring from her bed. Tag's throat caught. Before she could blink or bury her face underneath the blanket, Chloe smiled. She looked like Cleopatra, with the vampish curl of her lips and cock of her chin. Then Chloe did something strange. She pushed two fingernails into the flesh of her neck. She inhaled so deeply her chest swelled, and then she switched off the light. Tag was left to stew under her bedsheet with that glorious image of Chloe's lithe form burned into the thin membrane covering her corneas.

That was the last time Tag saw her roommate.

The apartment was stone-cold quiet the next morning. Tag opened her closet and chose a clean shirt from the neat row of hangers, arranged from light to dark, left to right—an idiosyncrasy that her roommate had teased her about, but one that made perfect sense to Tag's artist's brain.

Chloe's bedroom door was ajar. Her pillows were piled up on the floor beside her bed. A pink thong hung from her closet doorknob. In the kitchen, a jug of orange juice sat on the countertop, and someone had left the refrigerator open. Oddly, the apartment door's barrel bolt was still locked. The steel slider could only be latched from the *inside*. Tag checked the windows, and felt a little foolish doing so, since no one could've exited the tenth-floor apartment that way and lived to tell the tale. Chloe had probably just zipped off to breakfast with her boy toy.

And those spots of blood on her roommate's bedspread had just come from some innocent slap and tickle. Chloe liked a little nibble, she'd once confessed to Tag. *It might not even be her blood. Maybe she scratched that dude.* A nice thought, but Tag knew it was her roommate's blood even before the police later matched it to a DNA sample from Chloe's toothbrush.

"What was the young man's last name?" the detective asked.

Tag didn't know. She'd only seen Jacob one other time, and only for a moment before Chloe had yanked him into her bedroom. Tag strained to remember every detail: taller than average, athletic build, dark hair, blue eyes—or maybe green. *And when the man climaxed, he growled like a goddamn bear. Does that help?*

Apparently not. No one by that description with the name Jacob or Jake or Jack had enrolled at the School of the Art Institute, even though Tag could've sworn that's where Chloe had said she'd met him. The detective interviewed neighbors, friends, owners of nearby shops, but none could identify him either. Jacob could've been anyone or no one.

The police had other suspects in Chloe's disappearance too. After all, if Jacob had snatched her in the night, how did that barrel bolt get locked from the inside? The detective had grilled Tag after learning that bit, but she didn't care. She'd told him that she didn't know why the slider was still locked, and that was God's honest truth. She would've offered any detail she could squeeze from her brain, if it could've helped them find Chloe . . . if only she'd remembered something useful.

The dreams started immediately. Chloe as Empress of the Nile, a golden headdress, jewel-studded choker, tan breasts with swollen areola like purple buttons. *And those awful slithering things.* Tag began painting the haunting image from her recurring nightmare, mostly for therapeutic reasons but also with hopes of triggering a memory. She hadn't bothered laying a drop cloth, and when she finished, splashes of brown and black and red stained the parquet floor. Tag stepped back from the canvas and her heart nearly stopped. She collapsed and cried into her kneecaps, refusing to look at the horrid thing she'd created.

Then she called Special Agent Gina Butler of the FBI.

*   *   *

"An asp?" Agent Butler asked after arriving later that morning. She stood back, squinting at Tag's canvas. An olive-skinned woman lay in a stained bathtub, her arms draped over the sides, fingertips dripping. A nest of snakes crawled over her limp body, coiling around her thighs and neck. One of the serpents raised up from the woman's forehead, its hood flaring. "You think a snake bit Chloe King?"

"Not just any snake. An Egyptian cobra, also known as an asp. It's a controlled species in Illinois. You have to obtain a permit to own one. I read that online," Tag explained. "You could search the Department of Natural Resources database for anyone named Jacob with an active or expired herptile permit."

"Herptile?"

"Yeah. Snakes and lizards and shit," Tag explained. She shifted her weight nervously, careful to keep her back turned to the painting. She didn't want to look at it.

Agent Butler circled the living room, casually surveying the furniture, the photos on the wall, the paperbacks stacked on the bookshelf. Tag knew the woman would mentally catalog every detail. "Is that Chloe's bedroom?" she asked, pointing at a closed door. "May I?"

"Of course." Tag followed Butler and sat on her roommate's bed. "The police already took the sheets."

The FBI agent moved to the headboard and examined the chipped paint where the wood had slammed against the wall. Butler scraped off a flake and frowned.

"She likes the rough stuff," Tag said.

"You two were intimate?"

"No. God, no. Chloe likes men. A lot. She has a kinky side. Likes to experiment. She always tells me about it. Sometimes she has sex with her door open. It's an exhibitionist thing, I guess. Makes her feel dangerous."

"Dangerous? Like someone who would incorporate a snake into sexual foreplay?" Butler's violet eyes narrowed.

"I don't know. That sounds pretty risky, even for Chloe," Tag said. "Maybe if the dude had told her it wasn't venomous . . ."

"And then the animal bit her, stopped her heart. He panicked. An accident, perhaps?" Butler said.

"I don't know who *accidentally* brings their pet asp into bed, but check the permit database. Please. You'll find him."

Agent Butler turned to look back into the living room at Tag's artwork, still shiny in places with wet paint. She bit her lip and squinted again.

* * *

Tag hadn't expected Butler's call so soon. The following afternoon, the FBI agent's number blinked on Tag's phone screen.

"Jacob Kairo Marques," Butler said. "We found a grand total of thirteen snakes in his apartment. He kept them in glass tanks. He had permits for six of them. Said he used them for educational purposes, whatever the hell that means."

"And one was an Egyptian cobra?" Tag asked.

"With a middle name like Kairo, I don't see how he could've left that one out."

Tag didn't want to ask the next question. Somehow, she already knew the answer. But if she didn't vocalize the words, maybe she'd never have to confront the truth.

After a long pause, Butler said softly, "She was there too, Vera."

More silence.

The agent's tone lowered. "I'm sorry to have to tell you this—"

"Chloe is dead, isn't she? Snake bite." The words hardened in Tag's mouth.

"We won't get the toxicology report until tomorrow morning, but she had . . . marks. Under her jawbone. So, yes, we believe that was likely the cause of death."

"Thank you, Agent Butler, for letting me know. I just . . . I've got to . . ." Tag's voice broke up.

"Vera," Butler cut in, "do you want to know where we found her?"

* * *

The fan blades wobbled as they spun, as if they were smacking away the unwelcome memories of her roommate's murder. The FBI and the Chicago Police had called it an accidental death, but Tag couldn't accept that. Even now, a year later, she had few answers.

As she lay underneath the fan, Tag imagined the bolts holding the fixture to the ceiling would snap and the entire whirling apparatus would crash onto her face. They'd find her days later, smelling as toxic as her overflowing trashcan.

Dark thoughts like these used to distress her—especially as a child, when she'd imagine her parents roasting in a house fire or her brother drowning in the lake—but over time she'd begun to embrace them. She'd roll the terrible little ideas into sticky clots, push them through her veins, and then squeeze them out of her fingertips and onto the canvas. Her morbid imagination had become her superpower. Her third eye, as Agent Butler had said. Maybe Tag really could see what others couldn't. Maybe that's why she hadn't needed Butler to tell her the FBI had found her roommate's lifeless body curled up in Jacob Marques's bathtub. Tag's bristle-tipped fingers had already known.

"Don't take this the wrong way. I don't believe you had anything to do with Chloe's death," Butler had said when she'd called that afternoon with the news, "but I'll admit, the accuracy of your painting, the information about the snake, the tub . . . how could you have known these details?"

Tag had wondered the same thing. She didn't believe in psychic abilities or paranormal phenomenon. Chloe's ghost hadn't guided her brush, intent on revealing her killer through Tag's macabre artwork. That freaky shit was for the movies. Tag's inspiration for the painting—the one of Chloe snarled in a knot of scales and forked tongues—came from somewhere far less supernatural. It was the product of simple subliminal observation. Tag must have seen old puncture marks on Chloe's body when her roommate had stood naked in the doorway the night before her disappearance.

And the way Chloe had pushed her fingernails into her own neck with such an erotic hunger . . . Yes, she and Jacob had played with the snakes before, and one had already bitten her—not a venomous species, but one with a hard bite just the same. Its fangs hadn't done any harm except draw a little blood, and that was part of the thrill, wasn't it? So that night, even after Chloe's athletic romp with Jacob in her bedroom, she'd craved something more dangerous. She'd convinced the man to take her to his apartment for another round, and this time they'd add two or three snakes. She wanted to feel them slithering up her thighs. Possibly in the heat of passion, Jacob had mistaken the asp for one of the harmless species in his collection.

But what about the barrel bolt latch? The following morning, our apartment was still locked from the inside, Tag thought. She still struggled with this detail, but she had an explanation, as lame as it sounded. She must've heard Chloe and Jacob leave late at night, and she'd stumbled to the front door, half asleep, to lock up after they'd left. Tag had never done anything like that before, as far as she could tell, but it wasn't implausible. And that's how she'd known that they'd left together, to spend the night at Jacob's place.

And the tub? The bathroom setting just made the most sense. After his pet asp had accidently killed his girlfriend, Jacob would've freaked out. He would've wanted to get her body out of sight until he figured out what to do. He probably lived in one of the crowded downtown apartment buildings nearby—*Chloe had said he'd ridden his bicycle over, right? An old Schwinn wasn't great transportation for anything long distance*—so he couldn't have exactly thrown her body over his shoulder and hopped in the elevator. Someone would've spotted him, and those buildings have cameras everywhere. So, until he had a good plan—*and let's get real; does a dude with a tank full of snakes really ever have a good plan?*—into the tub she went.

"I guess the clues were all there," Tag had explained to Butler. "I was just too shaken up to remember. When I paint, though, it focuses my mind. Working on that awful piece . . . it must've rattled something loose in my subconscious."

Agent Butler's soft breathing had filled the phone's earpiece. "This may be a bad time to ask, but have you given my proposal any more thought?" she'd asked. "You have a gift, Vera. I'd hate to—"

"I'll do it," Tag had blurted. The words had tumbled across her tongue so effortlessly. "I'm in."

Now, alone in her apartment, Tag stared at the door to Chloe's old bedroom. Sometimes she still expected to hear those bubbly giggles coming from inside. She even missed the raw thumping of the headboard. Chloe was impetuous and fatally reckless when it came to men, but she'd been a solid friend, and Tag didn't exactly have a long list of those.

She pulled herself up from the couch, chose a blank canvas from the stack leaning against the wall, and positioned it on an easel. Agent Butler had cleared Tag's final training test and given her the Sons of Elijah case. It was time to focus on the present. The problem was, after nearly thirty years with no activity whatsoever, the Sons could be long gone.

Or not.

"Maybe the clues are all there," Butler had suggested in her office that morning. "Just like they were with your friend Chloe. No one else has been able to figure out what happened to the Sons, but no one else has your gifts, Vera."

Maybe Butler was correct and the answer was right in front of them. Tag just needed to rattle something loose again.

She spent the next three hours working at her canvas. By the end, a pile of rags and used brushes lay at her feet. She stood back and studied the image she'd painted.

Well, now, she thought, staring at the wet square, *this certainly changes things.*

Drained, Tag's body ached for sleep. She'd collapse on her bed and shut her eyes for an hour or two. At daybreak, she'd pay Dr. Jacobson another visit. If what she'd conjured with sweeping brushstrokes of resin and pigment had any ounce of truth, Jacobson knew more about Sophie Whitestone than what he'd written in his bestselling book. A lot more.

6

"I'M TAKING YOU up on your offer," Tag said from the stoop of Dr. Jacobson's four-story walk-up. She'd arrived shortly before sunrise, pleased to see that the windows of the psychiatrist's Gold Coast residence were still dark. When a man in a tailored sport coat had finally thrown open the curtains on the second floor, he'd immediately made eye contact with the young FBI agent peering up from below. Dr. Jacobson's thin eyebrows had arched, but otherwise his face expressed no outright irritation toward his early-morning visitor. Within moments, his front door had clicked open.

"It would seem the sun sets and rises with you now, Ms. Taggart. People may start to think we're becoming friends." Dr. Jacobson stepped into the orange morning glare and put on a pair of sunglasses that made large bug eyes above his pinched nose. Despite the early hour, Chicago's summertime humidity had already draped the city in a soggy blanket. Sweat sprouted from behind Jacobson's ears, which he blotted with a creamy handkerchief. The fabric came away discolored. *Is he wearing concealer?* Tag wondered.

"*Special Agent* Taggart," she corrected again.

"Ah, yes. You must forgive me. These days I tend to confuse anyone under the age of forty with one of my students. The esteemed Federal Bureau of Investigation recruits them younger every year, it would appear. If I may pry a little, did they snap you up right out of university?"

"Art school, actually," Tag answered.

"Well, now that sounds like a story." The doctor bounced down his townhome's front stairs. Tag hopped off the stoop to catch up.

"My first appointment begins in thirty-three minutes, and the walk to my office takes thirty-one. I would consider your company a privilege for the journey if you don't mind a brisk pace." Jacobson's mouth formed the shape of a smile, but the other muscles of his face hardly moved. In the sunlight, the skin of his temples looked stretched and pulled at the corners of his eyes. His smooth forehead reached back to a receding hairline that the man had attempted to obscure with a fluffy blonde pompadour.

"When can you do it?" Tag asked. "When can you hypnotize me?"

She hadn't shared her plan with her partner, Agent Michelson, or with Acting SAC Butler, for that matter. If she had, they would've objected. Neither of them seemed genuinely interested in digging any deeper into the Sons of Elijah case. Tag knew that allowing Dr. Jacobson to hypnotize her carried risk, but it would also bring her closer than ever to the psychiatrist's private world. The man had built an enthralling public persona, with sold-out seminars and ratings-busting television appearances, but these events were merely performances, expertly staged for an adoring audience. Tag wanted to peel back the veneer and examine the authentic man beneath. What better way than an intimate therapy session? Dr. Jacobson had offered, after all, even if he'd only made the invitation in jest.

"Last night, before you got into your car, you suggested it," Tag reminded him.

"I suppose I did." Jacobson smiled warmly to a passing young woman in yoga pants.

"Well, then, let's do it."

Dr. Jacobson scratched his Adam's apple, seeming to consider the prospect. "I'm thrilled that you're so willing, Special Agent. That's a good start. When patients open themselves intellectually to the experience, they achieve much better results."

"I'm not a patient. That's not the idea."

"Then what exactly *is* the idea?"

"I've read your case file twice. My colleagues have interviewed you sixteen times since the last Sons of Elijah bombing in the mid-nineties. The transcripts are long and boring as hell, no offense. Most of the men who questioned you I've never met. Many have retired by now. Some are dead. So I can't ask them myself."

"Ask them what?"

"Why they didn't give a shit," Tag answered. "It's obvious from their questions that they wished they were doing something else—anything else—other than speaking with you. And I'm assuming you felt the same way."

"My perennial conversations with the authorities often retread well-worn territory, I'll agree with that. And what eager young protector of society wants to waste an afternoon listening to the bygone recollections of an elder? But as I said, I'm more than happy to cooperate, no matter how many mornings such activities may consume."

"We've wasted a lot of your time," Tag admitted. "And ours. No one took it upon themselves to really understand what you do."

"But you're different, I gather. You want to dip your toe into the pool, so to speak."

"I want to dive into the deep end. In my experience, if you want to know about something, there's no half-assing it. You throw yourself in and swim for your life."

"I'm flattered by your enthusiasm," Jacobson said. "If a fraction of my students shared your zeal, the world wouldn't have such a dangerous shortage of well-trained psychiatrists. That said, hypnosis is not a parlor trick. When done correctly, it's not meant for entertainment."

"You don't make anyone flap around the room and cluck like a chicken is what you're saying."

"No, I don't. In fact, the process doesn't involve any form of mind control or suggestive manipulation, despite what Hollywood would have you believe. Just a lot of deep breathing and soft talking. I consider myself a humble guide."

"Fine. And where do you guide people?" Tag asked. She'd seen clips from Dr. Jacobson's seminars. He packed convention center ballrooms with starstruck fans who paid top dollar to witness his live demonstrations. The lucky ones got picked to join him onstage.

Maybe his volunteers didn't imitate livestock, but they certainly performed astonishing acts. At a seminar in Tucson, one middle-aged woman recalled when she'd tripped while hiking near the Grand Canyon. Under hypnosis, she claimed to *feel* herself plunging hundreds of feet toward the rock formations below. From a perfectly safe, reclined position in a lounge chair, she screeched and flailed her arms and legs. Tag assumed Jacobson had planted the woman in the crowd. The whole episode seemed set up for max shock value. Cutaway shots of the audience showed a crowd of New Age spiritualists clutching their crystal necklaces in astonishment.

Then, with a tap on the forehead, Dr. Jacobson calmed the lady. This disappointed Tag. She'd wanted to see what would've happened if he'd let her hit the imaginary rocks.

"I guide patients into their subconscious," Jacobson explained. "We remember everything that has ever happened to us. Most of this information we tuck away and hide from our conscious mind. Sometimes because it's irrelevant and would gunk up the system. Other times, we do this to protect ourselves."

"Protect ourselves from what?"

"From trauma. Painful memories that bring us emotional distress. If we carried around the weight of our most agonizing experiences, we wouldn't be able to function normally."

"Then why are therapists always trying to get people to dig up old shit that happened to them—arguments with family, child abuse, stuff like that?"

"Well, the subconscious isn't an incinerator. It's more like a lockbox. Just because we've stored a traumatic memory there doesn't mean it's gone. These things have a way of sneaking back into our conscious mind, and for some, this can cause severe mental stress," Dr. Jacobson said. "One patient of mine had a terrible fear of choking. He ate only soft foods and liquids, soup and the like. The problem began during his final semester of college, and by the time his graduation day had arrived, he'd lost fifty pounds. This troubled young man knew he would die if he couldn't overcome his phobia. He refused pills, too afraid they'd lodge in his windpipe, so standard pharmacological treatment wasn't an option. We turned to hypnosis and discovered he'd nearly suffocated in his crib in infancy. A wool blanket had fallen over his face."

"He remembered this? That doesn't even sound possible."

"Oh, but it is. As I said, the mind stores every memory," Dr. Jacobson answered, waiting for the light to change at the intersection across from his office building. "That's where the power of hypnotic regression comes into play. By bringing that very early memory of his near-death to the surface and integrating it into his conscious mind, he could effectively process the trauma and—*poof*—release it." Jacobson opened his fists in front of his face like two starbursts.

"And that helped him, remembering a near-death accident that had happened twenty years before?"

The doctor grinned again. "Oh, I didn't say it happened twenty years before. Try *two hundred*."

The "Walk" sign appeared on the traffic signal, and Jacobson bounded across the street, leaving Tag momentarily frozen.

"Wait a sec," she called to him. "This dude remembered suffocating in a past life? Because the brain stores everything—is that the idea?"

"Not the brain, Special Agent Taggart. I said the *mind*."

The two reached the lobby of the psychiatrist's office. Dr. Jacobson nodded to a security guard and proceeded to the elevator.

"So, it's not just the members of the Sons of Elijah who believe in past lives and reincarnation. You're onboard with that stuff too? You sure you're not just trying to sell books?"

"Believe me, it wasn't easy to accept. I'd published a dozen scientific papers on perfectly mainstream topics before falling into this genre. Quite accidentally, I might add."

"When you met Sophie Whitestone," Tag clarified.

Dr. Jacobson nodded. "You've been catching up on the required reading, I see."

The elevator doors opened, and they both stepped inside. Jacobson reached for the buttons, but Tag grabbed his wrist.

"There's only so much I can learn from your book, Doctor," she said. "Like you said, I'm open to this . . . intellectually. I want to experience it for myself." She released him, and he pressed the button for floor number four.

"Open, yes, I see that. But are you sure you're prepared? Past-life regression therapy typically goes one of two ways. Either you tap into the grand mysteries of your soul and gain an entirely new perspective on your spiritual journey—it's quite a beautiful . . ."

"Or?" Tag prompted.

Jacobson grew quiet and shook his head.

"Well, whatever it is, I'll be fine," Tag insisted. "I'm tougher than I look."

"My dear, what you look like here, in this elevator, on this steamy day in September, has nothing to do with it. Maybe it's best to go slow, get your psyche warmed up."

"That's BS, and you know it. You do this stuff with volunteers at your seminars all the time. You won't convince me that Diane from Waxahachie with her bedazzled denim jacket is somehow psychically *warmer* than me. You brought this on yourself when you offered to hypnotize me. So let's get this thing going, Doc."

Jacobson sucked in his cheeks and then opened his mouth with an unsettling kissing sound. "Very well. I'll have Justine set something up for next week."

"Next week? You're kidding. It can't wait that long."

"What's the rush? A week is a mere flash of time, cosmically speaking."

The elevator opened. A young woman sitting behind a reception desk waved a piece of paper at her approaching boss.

"There's a problem with your eight o'clock. His insurance card expired last month," she said. "He called to explain, but you know what I always tell them: no money, no honey. Needless to say, there's a full carafe of coffee on your desk beside the *Tribune*. You've got about an hour to kill, and I don't want you fartin' it away on Insta."

"Special Agent Taggart, this is Ms. Justine Curio, my faithful assistant," Jacobson said.

"Pleasure," Justine responded without looking up from her computer. Tag could hear the woman's nails tapping on her keyboard. "There's bottled water and soda in the kitchen."

"What luck. It appears you've got an opening this morning," Tag said, and breezed past the reception desk, into Jacobson's private office.

7

AGENT JOE MICHELSON licked runny yolk from his fingers. The undercooked egg had soaked into the bread, making his breakfast sandwich a soggy mess, but it was still a damn decent meal for three dollars.

"She went in fifteen minutes ago," he uttered. He had a pair of those stupid earpods shoved inside his ears. "Hasn't come out yet." From his table at Potbelly's on Wabash Avenue, Michelson had an unobstructed view of Dr. Jacobson's office building.

"And she didn't mention it to you?" Acting SAC Gina Butler asked over his earpods. "She didn't ask you to cover her while she went inside?"

"Nope."

"That's foolish. She doesn't know who she's dealing with. Does Taggart even know about Jacobson and Sophie? What he did to that girl?"

"No. But if Tag stays in there long enough, she's bound to get the idea." Michelson sipped his coffee, which nearly singed the tip of his tongue—just the way he liked it. "Do you regret your decision, to let out her leash?"

Silence. He tapped his earpods, which sputtered and spit. "Hello, Gina?"

"No," she said, finally. "I don't."

"You're a cold motherfucker," Michelson said. "And thank God for that."

"Stay on her. Text me when she comes out."

"And if she doesn't?"

"Don't be so melodramatic, Joe."

A soft beep let Michelson know his supervisor had ended the call. He plucked out the earpods and plopped them into his coffee. Maybe they'd improve the taste. Useless doodads. He slipped a Marlboro from his shirt pocket, leaned back in his chair, and lit up. He thought about Taggart. That little Q-baby had wandered off the porch and into the yard and fallen right down a well. Before long, he'd hear a tiny voice echoing off the stones, crying out for Uncle Joe to lower the rope. Yeah, well, maybe after another egg sandwich.

8

"I'M PLAYING DICE with two soldiers. They're nervous, the men, as daybreak approaches. I'd suggested the game as a distraction. The sky turns from black to pink to yellow, and the others still haven't returned. I'm worried too. A party of three dozen soldiers left two mornings ago, and some of the villagers went with them. The group didn't carry more than a meal's worth of grain; it was supposed to be a quick trip north and then back again."

"Where were they going?" Dr. Jacobson asked in a low voice.

"Avignonet," Tag answered. Her closed eyelids vibrated, but the rest of her body lay motionless, stretched out on Jacobson's recliner. "Three nights ago, a messenger arrived on horseback—a stable boy under the count's employ, but he's loyal to us. The boy told us that an inquisitor had arrived at the count's estate. The news sparked a fire within the hilltop fortress where we are taking refuge. We all know of this particular inquisitor, mostly by word of mouth. However, some of our kin have also known the tip of his longsword.

He has brutalized our people for months. After hearing of his arrival, there was no question about it. The men of our settlement wanted revenge, and they would have it."

"An inquisitor? What is the year, Special Agent Taggart? Do you know?"

Tag drew a slow breath and continued without acknowledging the doctor's question. "It was foolishly provocative. I had made my position clear. Scratch an itch and it becomes a raging rash. I couldn't order them not to go, but I'd hoped if I made the argument, reason would prevail. They'd stay put and forget about poking the bear in the eye. Perhaps I'm the foolish one."

"Your job is to protect them, I gather. To keep the others safe."

Tag nodded. "And to protect the treasure, the Capstone. We keep it hidden away in the cellar, in a small room behind where we store the meat. That's what I'm most worried about. I've started sleeping with my fingers wrapped around a dagger underneath my pillow. Last night, my wife shook me awake. She said I'd screamed so loudly she'd thought the walls would collapse and crush us in our bed."

"Are you a man, some kind of mercenary? Do they pay you with the treasure?" Dr. Jacobson asked.

"The perfecti I am protecting are quite wealthy. And yes, we have an arrangement." Tag's head twitched. "I hear the horses. The men have returned. A woman is calling to them. Her voice swoops with delight. She joins the men in song. There is clapping and stomping. A sentry has climbed the tower to ring the bell we hung there to use as a warning signal. Except he's not sounding the staccato *one-two-three* chime we'd designated for danger; the young man is simply clanging away, hanging half out of the belfry, bare-chested and waving his tunic with abandon. My companions drop the dice and embrace. The mood is euphoric."

"But you are not celebrating. Something still troubles you."

"The perfecti take pride in their nonviolent customs. They seek purity through the denial of earthly pleasures. They work the small plots and grapevines running up the hillsides with a punishing work ethic. They keep to a strict diet, and some even abstain from sexual intercourse. They claim this brings them closer to God with each incarnation of their soul, but I'll never understand what purpose such behavior serves. What good is life if it is not lived fully? The celebration this night is completely out of character, as if a single drop of bloodlust has tainted a lifetime of virtue. And yes, that troubles me greatly." Tag squeezed her hands together, pressing her thumbs into her knuckles.

"Describe what you see around you. Look carefully at the details. Breathe the air, listen to the smallest sounds."

Tag's head swished in lazy figure eights. "A donkey roams the courtyard, untethered. I grab its reins and guide it to the stables, where the creature collapses from exhaustion. I bring it water in a terracotta bowl, and it drinks. The trails tracking up the southern slope to the fortress are narrow and rocky, but they are the only passable paths to reach our high elevation. The donkeys know the way, so they are very important to us.

"I hear footfalls. My wife approaches. Corba. She's had wine, and her gown hangs loosely from her shoulders, revealing the bare nape of her neck and the space between her breasts. She's practically *nude*. Who else has seen her this way? Fire flashes behind my eyes at her indiscretion, and I whip around to take stock of the stable. We're alone. The heat of my rage travels from my eyes into my neck, breastbone, abdomen—lower still. And now the anger has transformed into something else—a boiling pot of lust that Corba stirs with the slender crook of her finger. Then she squeezes."

Tag's chest rose off the back of the chair with a gasp. Her chin pointed to the ceiling, and she exhaled slowly through a wide-open mouth. "I've joined them now. The revelers. The foolish ones. I loathe myself for lacking the strength to resist. How could I? Corba is a seductress. My greatest weakness and my eternal love. A rapture has consumed the fortress, and I'm swept into the hot updraft along with the others. Corba and I entwine, our flesh kneading into a single slick twist. The tendrils of her long hair swish across my skin as she trembles on top of me and sends warm shoots into my fingers and toes. My senses go blank, and I see and hear nothing except for that clanging bell, which fills my head as it explodes from my shoulders and rushes toward the heavens."

Sweat dripped from Tag's eyebrows. She drew in air like she was sucking through a straw, and then let it out again in one rushing mouthful.

"We'll regret it later, I know. The revenge, I mean. Our hunting party assassinated an inquisitor. That evil man deserved every blunt strike against his ribs, every pierce of his skin. Still, the Crown will bring a hammer down on Montségur—our home, our protection. The king will crush the fortress and grind the stones between his gold-capped molars."

*   *   *

When Tag awoke disoriented, she remembered arriving at Dr. Jacobson's office, settling into the warm leather chair, propping her feet up on the ottoman. She'd had no idea if it would work. As much as she'd tried to keep an open mind, hypnosis still seemed like a cheap carnival trick. Did all of those people at Jacobson's seminars truly believe the good doctor could lower the veil of their consciousness with a wave of his hand? Maybe some folks really were plants, or some were just faking it. The rubes who'd paid three hundred and ninety-nine dollars to watch wouldn't know the difference.

Though there could be some truth to it, Tag had admitted. Hypnosis wasn't exactly a new technique, and Dr. Jacobson wasn't the first practitioner to use it as performance art. But in the videos Tag watched, Jacobson's theatrics overshadowed everything else. Tag had wanted to strip away all of the bright lights and oohs and aahs from the audience and experience it for herself. She'd know if the psychiatrist was a fraud. She was no rube.

At the beginning of the session, Jacobson had asked her to count backward from sixty. She remembered listening to his voice and thinking about how it must've sounded twenty-eight years ago. Did he comfort Sophie Whitestone with those glassy tones? Did he make her feel safe, resting in his chair with her eyes shut? Or maybe he made her feel something else, if that scene Tag had painted of the two of them held any truth.

Now that the session was over, Dr. Jacobson stood near the window. He'd opened the blinds, and sunbeams made tiger stripes across Tag's legs. The lamp on Jacobson's desk had toppled over. Jagged pieces of a smashed bulb spat from its shade like broken teeth. A spilled teacup lay on the floor. The doctor avoided eye contact, but Tag could see his whites were spiderwebbed with red veins. He gripped a pinch of skin underneath his chin.

"My sincere apologies, but I'm afraid I cannot continue," Dr. Jacobson said. "It's best you go now."

"What?" Tag sat up and wiped the sweat from her forehead. "What the hell? This was your idea, remember? This isn't exactly standard investigative procedure. I'm going out on a limb to give this a try, Doctor. And you want to kick me out within a minute of starting? I haven't even finished your countdown. Are you afraid it won't work?"

"It *did* work. We've been going for almost two hours."

The wall clock confirmed the doctor's claim. Of course, he easily could've changed it. It was the ancient, analog kind, with a brass knob on the bottom to spin the hands. Jacobson couldn't fake the position of the sun, though, and those bars of light, slicing through the window at a high angle, backed him up.

"Well, what did I talk about? I deserve to know, don't you think?"

"In this instance, it's for the best that you don't."

Dr. Jacobson opened the door leading to the reception area. A cool draft whooshed against Tag's hot cheeks.

"You're kidding," she said.

The doctor looked older, tired. "Please. I never should have suggested this. You must trust me and just forget this ever happened."

"Trust you? Dr. Jacobson, I was passed out on your chair for most of the morning, with zero memory of what went down in here. What the hell is going on?"

"Hypnotic regression is a powerful tool. It allows a patient to peel back the layers of the psyche, to scrape away the hard shell. Underneath, we reveal the beating heart of our trauma. Whatever brings us grief or anxiety, we can usually treat it because we can *see* it. We can pluck it out and release the patient from its unearthly hold. Typically. But you must understand, sometimes that hard shell isn't meant to be cracked. Sometimes it's best *not* to see what lies beneath. It's best to trap it inside." Jacobson made a small cage with the fingers of his shaking hands. "This may be the case for you. I fear any further regression would only bring pain to you and others. We must stop. It's for the best."

Tag threw her arms into her jacket and rose from the chair. "Unbelievable," she said, and stomped into the hallway.

"I am truly sorry," she heard Dr. Jacobson mumble behind her, but she didn't turn around.

Once on the street, the fog began to clear from Tag's mind. She'd made a terrible mistake, putting herself in a vulnerable situation like that, especially with a man like Dr. Jacobson. The psychiatrist oozed authority and gravitas. He had such a dominant, yet reassuring, demeanor, even she'd felt herself peeling away her armor, submitting to his commands. Had Sophie Whitestone peeled away even more for him? The image Tag painted flashed in her mind: Sophie, her naked back pressed into Dr. Jacobson's bare chest, Jacobson's hands cupping her breasts. Not caressing them, as a lover would, but seizing them. *And his grin, those bright teeth all white and sparkling.* The painting made Tag shudder. She hoped there was no truth to it.

Tag pulled her phone from her jacket pocket. With a tap, she paused the recording. Whatever she'd said in Jacobson's chair, she'd captured every word. The man clearly didn't want her to know what had happened over the past two hours. *Well, tough shit,* Tag thought. She'd listen to everything, whether Dr. Jacobson wanted her to or not.

CHAPTER

9

Tag's stride wore down to a dull shamble, but she never considered taking the L or an Uber back to her apartment. The moment she stopped moving, she'd probably fall asleep—the hypnotherapy session had drained every ounce of her energy—and she needed to stay alert.

Another intersection, another step, another slow, dragging breath. She followed the stream of pedestrians, block by block, until the familiar guideposts of her neighborhood steered her up the steps of her apartment building. The crushing fatigue intensified. She didn't remember pressing the elevator button, stabbing the jagged tip of her key into the door lock, crashing face-first onto her couch. Those mindless activities could've happened any time, any day. Her memory had simply decided not to log them this time. Her subconscious had other priorities. The images it conjured up while she drooled onto her throw pillow required the dream factory's full capacity. And she'd remember those details.

It was hard to forget the smell of burning flesh.

* * *

A great splash and swirls of steam. A man emerges from the thermal springs, and his shoulders hit the cool air. Beads of water turn to mist before they have the chance to roll down his arms into the pool. How fragile those droplets seem. They will live again, the shiny pearls, taking the form of rain or snow; and yet, as they vanish, their mortality appears final, irreversible. The man imagines a bit of his own spirit seeping from his pores and lifting away from his skin with that water, entwining with the hot spring's dying breath.

He is called Ramon, but standing naked in this smoking hole, he is nameless flesh. Organic matter soaking in more organic matter. The water is too hot, his wife had warned. No one visits the springs in March. But Ramon prefers the near-scalding temperature; it is the only way to feel everything, everywhere. Tonight, more than any other night, he craves the sensations. They sharpen his thinking. He faces a weighty decision, and it seems unthinkable for one man to carry the burden.

The bath will cleanse me, and with a pure heart, I will make the correct choice, Ramon had told his wife. Another lie. Lies piled on lies, like bodies. The springs are not pure, far from it. They stew with muck. His toes squish into it, and it pleases him. In truth, he has come for the filth.

Ramon climbs out of the pool into the muddy bog. He claws on his hands and knees like a beast. Scooping the sludge, he smears his bare chest, neck, shoulders. He slathers his stomach until the mud drips in streaks. His groin and legs are next, then back and buttocks, and finally his face, which he covers with long wipes that paint his beard. He leaves clear rings around his eyes, but otherwise he is fully engrossed in the earth's essence.

He pinches his shoulder blades together, throws back his head, and opens his pink mouth to release something terrifically primal. Clarity overwhelms him at last. Yes, he has made his decision.

Ramon climbs the southern slope, following the narrow footpath known only to a few. He leaves his clothes and shoes behind; they are pointless now. The invaders will strip them all in the morning anyway. That is the proper way to punish a heretic, after all.

After Ramon announces his surrender, the French army will storm the fortress and march everyone to the pyre. The bastards have already built it, at the base of the mountain, according to Ramon's spies. It is large enough to burn an entire village—the women, the children. The heat of a thousand thermal springs will strip the hide from their skeletons, leaving behind smooth skulls grinning with all their thirty-two teeth. The Cathars will smile at death because the sacrifice will have been worth it. The soldiers and their families will be spared, though; those are the terms of the bargain.

Ramon reaches the fortress's soaring wall. The sentry standing watch points his spear at the brutish creature approaching the gate, covered in sludge.

"Stand down. It is I, Seigneur Perella," Ramon says with a raised palm. He sees the gunk from the bog has worked its way into the creases of his knuckles.

"Sir?" the young guard whispers and averts his eyes. "My apologies." He unlatches the iron bolts for Ramon to pass.

"I want you to deliver a message to the French. Leave your weapons so they see you are not a threat." Ramon tells him exactly what to say and sends him racing down the footpath.

Montségur's courtyard glows purple in the low light that leaks from the horizon just before daybreak. Smoke curls from a cooking fire along the western perimeter. An elderly woman stands outside her hut, shaking the dust from a sheepskin blanket. Somewhere deep inside the maze of hastily constructed wooden shelters, a baby cries.

A handful of Ramon's soldiers are collecting the shards of limestone that broke off the outer wall during the last attack. The French army has finally managed to position its trebuchets within range and has been pummeling the village for the past eight days. Stones the size of horses litter the vineyards to the east of the fortress. The heart of Montségur is still mostly out of reach of the enemy's weapons, so the entire community has crammed within its protective shell. Ramon admires the people's resilience. Each night, after supper, the perfecti—the elders—gather the families in the central courtyard and lead everyone in prayer and song. Candles and oil lamps bob in a ring of orange light. The children hold hands and dance, giggling. Satan's Synagogue—that is what the French call Montségur. *What damn fools,* Ramon thinks with sadness.

Corba approaches. She has been crying. "It's Clara," she says, taking no notice of her husband's unusual appearance. "It's happened again. Her thrashing woke me up. She'd rolled onto her stomach, and her head jerked back toward her feet, as if connected by an invisible rope. I thought she'd snap her own neck. I tried to calm her, pressed my hands to her cheeks, and—oh God, her eyes, Ramon!—they had rolled up to the whites. Our daughter is in so much pain. I don't know why the Lord punishes her like this."

"It's the water that's done it. It has turned," Ramon answers. "The first captain found rats floating in the cisterns. There's no way the vermin could've clawed up the sides. They are too slick. Someone tossed them in there. The count has spies inside our walls, no doubt. They have contaminated our drinking water, and the last of our meat couldn't fill a single pot. We've held out for nearly a year, but I'm afraid we've reached the end, my love."

Corba swallows, sending a ripple down her slender neck. She rakes her nails over Ramon's chest, scraping away flakes of dried mud, which have clung to the curls of his chest hair. The gesture is not sensual, but tender, almost maternal. "You've made your decision, then?"

Ramon nods.

"The perfecti believe this is the last stand. They won't denounce their faith. If that's what the French require, there's no possibility," Corba says. "Surrender means death, you must know that. Do you really believe you have the right to barter away their lives? Their family's lives?"

"No, I don't. And until this morning I'd never considered the option. It kills me to think about capitulating to those despots. At the very least, Inquisitor Ferrier has agreed to let the soldiers go. They are mercenaries doing a job. He takes no issue with them."

"You'll trade the Cathars' lives for those of your own men."

"That's not what I'm doing, and you know it," Ramon defends. "Even if that's how it looks."

"Bishop Marti won't allow it," Corba continues. "He still leads their church, and he has more sway with the perfecti than you."

"Marti pleaded with me to take the deal. I've opposed the idea for days. That's why I needed to visit the springs. I needed to clear my head, and now that I have, I see that he is right. There is something more importar.t at stake. His people are prepared to die to ensure their treasure stays safe and out of French hands."

"The Capstone," Corba whispers. She knows how important it is and what they must do next.

"Yes." Ramon turns to the east, where the sky radiates violet. "The agreement goes into effect at daybreak. The king's army will be at our door within the hour."

"Then we don't have much time." Corba removes her velvet cloak and wraps it around her husband's waist to cover his nakedness. He grabs his wife's hand. They'll wake Bishop Marti, but not before making another trip to the stable. Though this time, it won't be moans of ecstasy spilling from Ramon's mouth.

"Do you really think it will work?" Corba asks, once they've arrived and Ramon shuts the stable door. She pulls the ends of a pair of iron tongs out of a small fire. The tool's pinchers squeeze the sides of the Capstone, which glows like the devil's eye. Ramon turns away and crouches until his forehead presses into his knees. He shuts his eyes, but he knows that won't lessen the pain. He hears Corba's feet shuffling, moving closer behind him.

"Just do it," Ramon commands. His firm tone belies the dread brewing in his chest. The hairs on the back of his skull twitch. Bishop Marti hadn't only urged him to strike a bargain with the French; the man had beseeched him to make an even greater decision. Ramon had shunned the idea at first, but as Ferrier's troops chipped away at Montségur's defenses, the choice became clear, almost destined. In a moment, with Corba's help, he'd seal his fate.

"May God protect us," Corba whispers and presses the red-hot Capstone to the back of her husband's skull. Ramon howls but all he hears is the bubbling sizzle of his own scalp.

A moment later, Ramon awakens to Corba shaking his arms. "I thought your heart had stopped," she says, breathless. Ramon blinks and wipes a trail of blood from his neck. He stares into his wife's amber eyes and feels a brief moment of peace before all of the pain crashes over him. He yelps and lifts his hand to his head.

"Don't." Corba smacks his palm away. "It needs to heal perfectly."

Ramon curls up on the stable floor, whimpering.

"You need to get up now. Time is short," Corba says. Her voice is solid, but Ramon detects a slight quaver. She pulls on the straps of her dress and peels the fabric down over her breasts and past her stomach. Her skin is covered with gooseflesh.

"I can't," Ramon groans. His scalp throbs, and he knows that if he sits up, he will vomit and maybe pass out again.

"I'm afraid you have no choice, husband," Corba says. Ramon opens his eyes just wide enough to see that Corba is holding the iron tongs again. Her arm is stretched out so that the tong's handles point at Ramon's chest. She opens her other hand to reveal the Capstone, resting cool in her palm.

The shape of the carefully carved rock resembles the head of a regal lion, as dauntless as Corba herself. She straightens her back and juts her chest out proudly. "Take it," she says. "Before the fire dies out. It's my turn."

*　*　*

The leaders of Montségur had set the plan weeks in advance, even before the French catapults had finally found favorable angles and destroyed much of the eastern tower. Ramon has little to do but give the order, and a pair of young men, pre-selected for their outsized strength (and propensity for discretion), ready themselves for the operation.

"Anchor the cables there and there," Ramon barks. The young men obey. Ramon can see their hearts beating in their chests as they coil long ropes around their waists and crane their necks over the chasm, ready to rappel down the mountainside. With a wave, they are gone, and God's shining grace, which protected the impregnable fortress, fades like the last dying embers of a wildfire. Now nothing will stop the French dogs from scrabbling up the footpaths.

The sun's golden arc peeks above the mountaintops, marking the new day and sealing Ramon's agreement of surrender. The refugees of Montségur will have one final chance to renounce their faith and pledge allegiance to the Catholic Church, or they will suffer the wrath of the inquisition. Of course, Corba is right; the perfecti—the spiritual leaders of the Cathars—will never deny the truth and risk God's eternal punishment. So, they will all go up in smoke.

By sundown, Ramon's enemies will believe they've snuffed out a seditious sect and taken possession of a king's ransom, once they pry open the cellar door and discover the perfecti's gold and jewels. *But they'll be wrong*, Ramon thinks. The real treasure—the Capstone—has already slipped down the cliff face, in the pack of a swift-footed soldier. The Capstone holds sacred importance to the Cathars; they had hired Ramon to defend it, not to protect their own lives. Lives come and lives go. The Capstone possesses a sacred permanence that no flesh can replicate. Some call it the Holy Grail, but Ramon knows it's far more significant. Bishop Marti explained everything. The Capstone is the key to life, and likewise the key to life's undoing, he said. Only four perfecti safeguard the truth, and now Ramon and Corba have joined them, making the circle six. This isn't new, Marti explained; they'd always been linked. Sometimes those bonds weakened, but he'd devised a system to ensure the integrity of the group. Ramon feels the raised flesh on the back of his scalp, still tender. Marti has one too. All six now bare the indelible mark of the Capstone.

The French have posted a thousand soldiers at the base of Montségur. They salivate as a chain of Cathar prisoners winds down the rocky footpath, through the wooded valley, into a field of long grass. The captives move like work-weary mules, sure-footed but despondent, resigned to accept the sentence handed down by the king and the mighty Vatican.

In the center of the field, an inquisitor named Ferrier stands on a wooden box, gleaming in polished bronze armor. He grips a massive shield—brilliant blue dotted with golden fleur-de-lis. The coat of arms of the House of Capet. Ramon knows of this man. Ferrier isn't the warrior he pretends to be, but the inquisitor enjoys the fervent loyalty of the French soldiers, the Crown, and the Church, and that makes him the grand master of the Occitan region.

Ferrier had severed Montségur's supply lines. He knew that eventually, the heretics would slink out, the purity of their faith betrayed by their growling bellies. The inquisitor was wrong, though. The Cathars would've starved to death, if necessary. Suffering only brings them closer to God. This morning, they will suffer a great deal. And Ramon—not a Cathar himself, but a humble mercenary—will be made to watch.

One by one, the French soldiers drag the men, women, and children to Ferrier's feet and demand that they deny their belief in reincarnation and pledge allegiance to King

Louis and the Church. And one by one, they refuse. A pair of soldiers with arms like tree branches strip the prisoners and flog them until black welts rise from their naked backs. The torturers slam their boot heels into the men's groins. One soldier slices off the purple head of a perfecti's penis and tosses the wrinkled meat onto the pyre. With each Cathar heretic finally strung up, some bound two and three to a stake, Ferrier surveys the scene. A gust of wind whisks away the prisoners' whimpers, leaving behind an unsettling silence. A child coughs and the sound echoes for miles, like the first crack of a great avalanche.

Ferrier stares on, sneering. No one breathes a whisper. Then a voice, clear and high, resonates in the cool air. A woman is singing. Her dry lips vibrate with every note. A deeper, male voice joins her, and a beat later the entire line of prisoners becomes a chorus, belting the melody from their stakes like a human pipe organ, bewitched.

"Car mais val mortz qe vius sobratz," they sing: *"Better to die than let him conquer."*

Ramon recognizes the tune, but he doesn't lend his own voice to the death choir.

Inquisitor Ferrier turns to his men; his eyes are white diamonds. He raises a fist to signal a French soldier to light the pyre. The prisoners' song is replaced with howls as the fire grows. Their bodies are candles, skin falling away from bone like melting wax. Their blood pours into the fire, hissing. The flames swallow it all.

One of the stakes cracks and topples. The ropes break apart and a prisoner rolls into the soggy soil. He is still alive, but the fire has eaten a hole in his throat. Ferrier approaches the man with a dagger in his fist. Ramon prays he will show the prisoner mercy, drive the wicked blade through his heart and end his suffering. Instead, Ferrier squats and uses the tip of his knife to carve out the man's eyes. He squeezes them like swollen grapes and flings them into the fire. They pop in the heat.

"Now do you see the wrath of God?" Ferrier shouts at the blackened husk writhing at his feet.

Ramon's stomach rolls inside his abdomen. He spits into the grass, and it tastes sour. The French troops arrange Ramon and the other mercenaries into a line and force them to face the pyre, which spews a black pillar into the sky. The heat stings Ramon's cheeks. He has fed the Cathars to the Beast. To *Ferrier*. Will God judge Ramon any differently because he didn't light the woodpile himself?

"Bring them out," Inquisitor Ferrier shouts.

Ramon's men fight against their binds at the sight of their wives and children marching into the grass. Some of the women wear torn strips of cloth that had once been dresses. Most of the children have no shoes. Their feet are cut from the trek down the slope. They wince with each step like mewing kittens.

"To your knees," Ferrier orders, having returned to his box. The soldiers don't need to force the women to the ground; most collapse from exhaustion. The little ones cling to their mothers.

"You belong to these men," Ferrier says to the women and children, gesturing to the line of mercenaries. "Like obedient servants, you followed them here. You served them—your husbands, your fathers—as faithful subjects of the Church." The inquisitor springs from his box and approaches the huddle. "But it is a *lie*. Some of you are *not* faithful. Some of you have assumed the dirty, sinful beliefs of the disloyal dogs now burning on that pyre." Inquisitor Ferrier unsheathes his sword with a metallic squeal. The women yelp at the terrible sound. "Who among you will confess? And I will remind you, if you renounce your heresy, you will be spared. Rise now, sinners!"

None of the women stand.

Ferrier smiles. "Now, now. You need not worry, my dears. We have a deal, after all. God has charged me with the great purification of this land. I extinguish heretics, not Christian mercenaries or their kin. What is the value in that? Confess your misdeeds and all is forgiven, in the eyes of God and the Church. This is my sacred word."

Ferrier holds a gloved hand against his heart. Still, no women rise to their feet. They only sink into one another, hardening their resolve as one solid mass.

"What should we do?" a French soldier asks.

Ferrier extends his arm and presses the tip of his blade against the breast of one of the women. It is Corba. Her eyes reflect the flickering bonfire. She looks at Ramon, and for that split second, he sees the young woman he married more than twenty years before. She has not aged a day, and the flame of righteousness inside her belly still burns brightly. Ramon has never met anyone with such conviction and fortitude, man or woman. He nods to his wife, for a moment unafraid and swelling with pride. Corba raises her hands and squeezes the blade of Inquisitor Ferrier's sword until blood streams down her forearms.

Ramon growls, but the soldiers hold him back and stuff his mouth with rags. His eyes lock onto his wife's. Despite her pain, her eyes glint with a small smile that only Ramon can see. He watches Corba's mouth form soundless words. Without hearing her voice, he knows that she is repeating the same reassuring phrase that she had said to him on the day they met: *"I will find you again. I will be there when it counts."* The message should have sounded odd coming from a stranger wandering an unremarkable Langeudoc fruit market that summer afternoon so long ago, but somehow Ramon had understood its significance, even then. And he understands Corba's message now too. He feels waves of love coming from his wife. They are in this together. A matched pair.

"Kill them all," Ferrier barks. "God will recognize his own." He kicks Corba's sternum, knocking her backward. Then he approaches Ramon. The Inquisitor wipes his sword on Ramon's tunic, smearing the cloth with Corba's blood.

He leans in close and whispers, "Except you. I've got other plans for you."

This wasn't the deal. Ferrier had agreed to release the mercenaries and their families in exchange for the Cathars. Ferrier brings his lips to Ramon's and kisses him. Ramon stares into the man's eyes—two black channels with no end—and his chest fills with fear. Ferrier cocks his head and opens his mouth so wide his jawbone must disconnect. He will swallow Ramon whole and then work him down his throat like a snake. Ramon sees an unusual black splotch on the back of the man's wriggling tongue. It's hooked, like a reaper's scythe. Then a terrible buzzing comes from Ferrier's gaping maw and Ramon recognizes it as the voice of the devil himself.

*   *   *

Tag's phone chattered on the coffee table. She swatted at it, knocking it to the ground, cracking the screen.

"Shit," she hissed. The phone vibrated again, and that grassy valley at the base of the rocky slope in central France evaporated from her mind. The awful smell stuck around, though. The rich stench of cooked meat clung to her nose hairs.

I'm smelling the bodies. From the dream. The rotten, smelly dream, she thought.

Tag groped for her phone. "Yeah," she answered, her voice box coated with mucus.

"Godammit, Taggart. Have you been sleeping under a rock?" Joe Michelson asked.

"What?" Tag swiped to her news feed. "Holy sh—"

"Yeah, holy Father who art in heaven, along with about two dozen unlucky fucks who joined Him about thirty minutes ago. Someone delivered a package to Tang Dynasty restaurant on Wentworth. Wrapped up a bomb like a fuckin' Christmas present. Big red bow and all."

"Is it a hate crime? Racial targeting?" Tag asked.

"Dunno. That's gonna be your job to figure out."

"*My* job? I mean, of course, but this is obviously an all-hands kind of thing, Joe. Butler will stand up a special response team, a command post."

"Tang Dynasty had one of those doorbell cameras. The manufacturer sent us the video clip before we even had to ask for it. That present had a big ol' fuckin' tag on it, clear as day on the video. It's an infinity symbol."

Tag felt a stinging in her throat (*from inhaling that black column of smoke*). "I'm on my way," she said, and hung up. She inhaled deeply and instantly regretted it. A big gulp of that suffocating corpse-stench slipped across her tongue, into her body.

An infinity symbol on the bomb, she thought. *Just like the one Sophie Whitestone had carved into her back.* Dr. Jacobson was wrong; the world hadn't seen the last of them.

The Sons of Elijah were back.

10

O SCAR PEREZ, THE FBI's incident commander managing the scene of the bombing, lifted a yellow barrier tape for Tag to duck under. "The suspect carried the package under one arm, so we know it wasn't too heavy," he said. "Here, put these on before you go inside." He handed her a pair of protective shoe covers and a hard hat. "My guys just finished sweeping the interior for secondary devices. The place is clear, but chunks of the ceiling are unstable, so I'm limiting access."

"Where's Joe?" Tag asked.

"He's combing the alleyway out back, behind the restaurant."

Good, Tag thought. She wanted to evaluate the scene without distractions. She'd only conducted one other bomb investigation, and it hardly counted. The victims had been crash test dummies, the blasted-out building a staged barn in the backwoods of the FBI Academy campus. The procedural checklists from the field manual flashed in her mind: Secure the premises, check for survivors, identify witnesses.

A pair of EMTs emerged from the restaurant, carrying a man on a stretcher. At least, Tag assumed it was a man. He was missing part of his lower jaw, and a pink tongue hung out from the pulpy void. The techs loaded him into an ambulance.

"How many survivors?" Tag asked.

"Don't know yet. We're still clearing away debris. There may be more people trapped underneath the rubble. We're sifting through it as fast as we can. The place is littered with body parts. I hope you've got an iron stomach."

The explosion had ripped the front door of the Tang Dynasty from its hinges. Fragments of a sign clung to the eave over the entryway. Tag pulled a face mask over her mouth and stepped inside.

Fine particulates filled the air and coated everything with a layer of dust. It would be difficult to collect latent prints on any of the surfaces. Splintered tables and chairs jutted out from piles of broken dishes, chunks of the crumbling ceiling, and iron light fixtures. Tag's boots crunched over broken glass—from the windows, probably.

"I want to document every person who accesses this site. In and out. Names and times," Tag said to Oscar. "I don't want to contaminate the scene any more than necessary. And I'll need the final list of survivors and where they're being treated. Joe and I will need to interview the witnesses." *At least those with intact jaws and working tongues.*

"Yeah," Oscar said with some irritation. "That's all standard procedure. The Bureau's bomb squad knows what to do."

"Right, of course. I'm just thinking out loud." This wasn't a training exercise, and the dismembered arms and legs and the torsos split open with their ribs poking out like bony fingers weren't from stuffed dummies. Tag was standing inside a real bloody heart, slick and dripping. She worried that she'd need to vomit, but the urge never came. Instead, she felt an electric thrill, standing amid the carnage. This was what she'd signed up for.

"Where's the bomber's body?" Tag asked.

"Didn't Michelson tell you? This was a drop and run. The bomber didn't stick around for the main event," Oscar explained.

"The Sons of Elijah are suicide bombers. They go out in a blaze of glory. That's their MO. I studied the cases from their streak in the nineties—Sophie Whitestone and the four bombers who came after her. None of those attackers survived. What's changed?"

Oscar shrugged. "I'm just in charge of the cleanup crew."

* * *

The metal door to the alleyway smacked against the side of the brick building when Tag flung it open. She peeled off her latex gloves, then threw them at her partner. "You never mentioned the bomber fled the scene," Tag said. "I asked you for a rundown on the phone. You didn't think that detail was important?"

Agent Michelson flicked ash from his cigarette. "I would've told you, but you didn't say 'please.' Besides, you *assumed* a suicide attack, and I'm not responsible for your faulty assumptions."

Michelson was right. The world had changed since the Sons of Elijah last terrorized the city, and it was logical to assume the group's methods would've changed with it. Or the whole thing could've been the work of a cowardly copycat. Still, Joe was an ass for withholding critical information. How were they supposed to work together when he was hellbent on sabotaging her?

"Besides, not *all* of those fuckheads killed themselves back then," Michelson added. "One disappeared, remember? Gerald Cutter. Probably ran off to Mexico with some chickadee. You're not the only one who's read the case files. Some of us actually wrote a few of them, you know. And some of our colleagues even lost their lives chasing the Sons. So try to show some respect."

"The doorbell cam—the one that captured the bomber carrying the package," Tag said, changing tracks, "show me the video."

Agent Michelson unclipped his phone from his belt. Tag snatched it and cupped her hand over the screen. She eyed the growing crowd at the mouth of the alleyway, just beyond the security barrier. A few reporters rotated the barrels of their telephoto lenses.

In the video clip, a skinny man approached the restaurant's entrance, toting a bulky package. He'd pulled a hoodie over his head and wore dark sunglasses. His whole vibe screamed lone-wolf bomber, Tag thought. He paused in the vestibule to let an elderly couple enter first. Then, the bomber reached for the door handle and turned his head. Tag noticed it immediately.

"Fuckaroo," she said. Joe hadn't just withheld the part about the bomber escaping; he'd left out something even more important. Now, watching this video footage, Tag knew why. Men acted like children when someone proved them wrong. Goddamn egos. She reached out and pinched the cigarette dangling from Joe's lip and took a long drag.

Michelson huffed. "You really should've let the little shit jump. Not such a hero, now, are you?" he said.

Tag slid the video back a few seconds. She watched again as the bomber's head turned, revealing the small scar on his neck.

Caleb Miller.

"How long did he stay inside?" Tag asked.

"Forty-six seconds," Michelson answered. "The bomb went off about five minutes later. Plenty of time to get outta Dodge."

"He's still out there. We need to find him before he hurts someone else." *Or himself.*

Tag should've trusted her instincts. Just as she'd suspected, Caleb *was* a member of the Sons of Elijah, and she should've brought him in when she'd had the chance. After the incident on the bridge—when Tag had talked him down from the railing—the FBI had referred Caleb to social services for a mental health evaluation, and then discontinued surveillance. He hadn't threatened anyone or broken any laws, and since the FBI had failed to uncover any evidence that connected him to the Sons, dedicating valuable resources to tracking Caleb's movements had seemed wasteful, even to Agent Butler. Now, the Bureau, the Chicago Police, and the Illinois State Police would launch a full-scale manhunt to find him.

Caleb could be anywhere. The dude was a skinny needle in a hulking Chicago haystack. Tag needed a solid lead if she hoped to find him quickly. She immediately thought of one person who likely knew more than he'd let on: Dr. Seth Jacobson.

"Finish up here. I'm going to follow up on something," Tag said, and spun away.

"This is serious shit, Taggart. Where the hell are you going?" Michelson asked.

"I'd tell you, Joe, but you didn't say 'please.'" She took another drag off Michelson's cigarette and flung it into a puddle. Her phone bounced in her jacket pocket as she jogged to the street. She'd confront Jacobson—threaten him with obstruction of justice, if necessary. But first, she'd listen to her secret recording from her hypnotherapy session. She slipped on her headphones and cranked the playback up to double speed. The psychiatrist was definitely hiding something, and Tag didn't have much time to figure out what.

11

Taggart: In the distance, the flames on Bidorta Summit bloom like a rose. This brings me a great sense of relief.

Jacobson: Relief? Even with the French soldiers licking their chops?

Taggart: The inquisitor—Ferrier—he doesn't care about heresy—not really. He's after the Capstone, and he'd kill a thousand good Christians to get it.

Jacobson: This Capstone, is it at Montségur?

Taggart: No, not anymore. They lit up Bidorta as a signal. It means the men who rappelled down the cliff face before dawn have made it to safety.

Jacobson: Where is it now?

Taggart: That's what *he* wants to know too. Ferrier. He thinks he can beat it out of me. He's chained my wrists to a cross beam supporting the stable roof. I'm hanging and there's just enough slack for my toenails to graze the ground. My shoulders are on fire. It feels like claws have torn into the muscles of my back, but I know it was the bite of Ferrier's whip. Blood streaks

my legs. It pools in the grout between the cobble-
stones. So far, he has spared my genitals, but I know
that's next. And for that part, he'll trade his whip for a
blade. I've heard the stories. If Ferrier fails to extract a
confession through beatings, he castrates his prisoner
and then feeds the man his own swollen testicles.

Jacobson: Do you fear he'll do this to you?

Taggart: I fear nothing. I watched as my wife—my
Corba—and my daughter burned on that pyre. I
heard their screams.

Jacobson: Are you going to tell the inquisitor what happened to the Capstone?

Taggart: No. And he knows that I won't, no matter what
gruesome torture he tries.

Jacobson: Will he kill you?

Taggart: He doesn't want to.

Jacobson: Why not?

Taggart: Because then it begins all over. He's searched for
the Capstone for the last four hundred years, and he's
never come this close before. After he kills me, he'll
find me again eventually, but he doesn't know where
or when. He won't be Ferrier, and I won't be Ramon,
but our paths will cross again.

Jacobson: You'll meet Ferrier again. In a later life?

Taggart: It will become a twisted game of sorts, with a
prize more valuable than the royal jewels. I will hide
it; he will seek it. I'm not even sure he'll know what
to do with it if he ever gets his meaty hands on it. I
imagine he'll clutch it to his chest, really squeeze the
thing, so he'll know it is real. And maybe that will be
enough. Just the power of knowing what he *could* do
will satisfy him.

Jacobson: And what's that? What harm could he do with
this . . . Capstone?

[silence]

Jacobson: You said a pair of soldiers escaped the morning of the surrender, and they carried the Capstone away from Montségur.

Taggart: Yes, that's correct.

Jacobson: You don't want Ferrier to know, but will you tell *me*? Where did they take it?

[silence]

Jacobson: You do *know* where they took it, don't you?

Taggart: Yes. I mean, I think so. The room is hazy now. I'm above myself, looking down on my naked, leaking body. Ferrier is kicking my kneecaps. I've thrown my head back. I'm howling. I don't want to feel it, so I float. I still hear everything, though. The cracking bone. I want to float far, far away. Until it all fades.

Jacobson: No. You can't do that. Not yet. You're sinking now, seeping back into the flesh below you.

Taggart: *Oh, God. It hurts. He's killing me.*

Jacobson: You feel no pain. You are only observing.

Taggart: *Christ, the Glory of God, I'm dying.* He's got a blade now, the one I've heard the stories about. It feels like ice between my legs, drawing blood. Oh, I want to *die*. He's pressing. He won't stop until I tell him. I'm trying to think of Corba, how she shook inside that red-hot flower. How her skin separated in black flakes and flew up into the trees. Her pain was worse than mine. I'm ashamed to pray for death, but I can't endure the lighting in my groin, *the slicing, sawing.* Please let me *die*!

[screams]

Jacobson: You can't die now. Not before you tell me. Where did your men take the Cathar Capstone? Free yourself of your guilt and shame, and tell me.

[silence]

Jacobson: Ramon?

Taggart: Oh, my, my, Doctor. I had a feeling you were up to something.

[laughs]

Jacobson: You're not Ramon. Who are you?

Taggart: Ah-ah. You only get one more question today, mister. How about I answer the one you're really interested in, hmm?

Jacobson: Yes, I'm listening.

Taggart: Not now, silly. Not until you do something for me.

Jacobson: It's really you. What do you want?

Taggart: It's not time yet, but I need to know that you'll cooperate when the time comes.

Jacobson: I don't know if I can make that promise if I don't know what you want.

Taggart: But you must. The Sons of Elijah will soon return. And when they do, they will need your help. Just like before. Let me explain . . .

*   *   *

Tag flew past Justine's desk on her way into Dr. Jacobson's office. "You're a goddamn liar!" she announced as she entered the room. The psychiatrist stood by the window, watering a collection of potted plants on a low shelf.

"You were part of it back then," Tag continued. "You helped the Sons of Elijah decades ago, and you're *still* helping them now."

Jacobson turned. "The bombing this morning, I heard about it on the news. It's a tragic event. Do you have reason to believe the Sons of Elijah were involved?" Dr. Jacobson asked, ignoring Tag's accusation.

"It was Caleb."

"Oh, I see." He looked back toward the window. "And you still think Caleb is a member?"

"We have him on camera. There was an infinity symbol on the explosive device."

"Is he . . . ?"

"Dead? No, Caleb suddenly realized his life was worth living," Tag spat.

Dr. Jacobson set his watering can the edge of his desk. "Special Agent Taggart, in light of this afternoon's unfortunate events in Chinatown, I am of the mind that my obligation to maintain patient confidentiality no longer extends to Mr. Caleb Miller."

"Got that right. Did you know? Did he tell you what he'd planned to do? Because if he did—"

"No, of course not," Jacobson said defensively. "Caleb suffers from depersonalization disorder. Specifically, he believes he's trapped inside a stranger's body. The sensation can be quite upsetting, like you're living in the wrong place and time. Any trained psychiatrist could competently treat him, but it's no mystery why Caleb came to me. I'm an expert on reincarnation—the idea that the soul can travel from body to body throughout time. To Caleb, this explanation helped him make sense of his . . . confusing emotions. He wanted me to regress him to his former lives, to help him understand why he felt so out of place here and now."

"You get a lot of requests for treatment. Why did you agree to see Caleb?"

"Ego, I suppose. Caleb has studied all of my books. And not just mine; he's read hundreds of publications on reincarnation. He's latched onto the Sons of Elijah. Specifically, he's obsessed with the secret that the group seemed to be protecting."

Tag remembered her terrifying dream and the strange words that she'd spoken on the recording. "The Capstone," she said.

Dr. Jacobson nodded. "This . . . item, the Capstone— whatever you want to call it—it shows up everywhere, in nearly every incarnation that my former patients, Sophie

Whitestone and Gerald Cutter, remembered under hypnosis. Caleb even found references to a mysterious 'treasure' and a 'hidden knowledge' in countless cultures, going back centuries, always connected to the concept of reincarnation. For a mostly uneducated, simple Midwestern boy, Caleb is rather clever."

"Clever enough to build a bomb?" Tag asked. "Or did he have help?"

"I'm afraid that's your department. However, it's my professional assessment that Caleb was wrong."

"About what?"

"He desperately wanted to unearth his past lives. I attempted to regress him on four different occasions, but he never recalled anything beyond his childhood in Illinois. We were both disappointed. I'd hoped I could help him, the way I've helped countless others. Just a glimmer of a remembered life would've given him such wonderful relief. Instead, the failed therapy only deepened Caleb's psychosis. He slipped into delusions, inventing remembered lives he couldn't possibly have lived, if not for the simple mechanics of timing. If that young man is linking himself with the Sons, I'm almost certain he's fabricated such an association."

"Caleb is a copycat. That's what you're saying," Tag reasoned.

Dr. Jacobson reached out with both hands, fingers spread. "And I had absolutely zero foreknowledge of his intentions. I'll submit to a polygraph examination if you'd like. I've got nothing to hide."

Acid gurgled up from Tag's stomach. "Like hell." She held up her phone. "I recorded our session. I heard everything."

"Oh, I see," Jacobson said. He moved behind his desk and let his weight drop, rather indelicately, into his chair. He paused, staring at a row of framed photographs for what felt like an uncomfortable amount of time.

"And what did you hear, exactly?" he asked finally. "You heard a doctor speaking to his patient, following her lead.

Hypnotic regression is complicated. My job is to probe and guide, not to contradict. It's counterproductive."

"Bullshit," Tag shot back. "To me, it sounded insane, but you knew *exactly* what I was talking about. And at the end of the session, the thing I asked you to do . . . to *sleep* with me . . . you weren't phased by it at all. It was almost as if you'd expected it. And then to *agree*? What kind of sick son of a bitch agrees to do *that*? Maybe I'm sick too, just for asking."

Jacobson rubbed his eyes. "I can explain."

Tag thought of her painting of Jacobson gripping Sophie's nude body. "Did you sleep with Sophie Whitestone? Did she beg you for sex, under hypnosis, just like I did? Did you . . . trick her somehow?"

The psychiatrist swiveled his chair to face the window and sighed. He rubbed the waxy leaf of a houseplant between his fingers.

"You know what? You can explain at the FBI field office," Tag said, exasperated.

"Do you plan to arrest me?"

Jacobson leaned back in his chair. Tag stood still, chewing her lip.

"No, you don't," he went on. "If you had planned to arrest me, you wouldn't have come alone. My office would be crawling with agents. Isn't that how these things work? So, why, then? That's the important question. You played back a recording of our session—one that you created without my permission, but that's another matter. And you were outraged. That wretched old man brainwashed you, you thought. He somehow used mind control to make you say those terrible things. How *dare* he? Is that right, Special Agent Taggart? Is that what you thought when you listened to it?" Dr. Jacobson leaned forward on his forearms. "Ah, but then something unexpected happened."

Tag glared at the psychiatrist. His smug grin needled her. She wanted to leap over that oak desk and drive her thumbs into the pressure points behind his ears. Instead, she squeezed her hands together behind her back. That man in her dream, Ramon, and the stone fortress, high on the cliff— everything had seemed so *real*. She could still taste the ash swirling around the pyre. She could still hear the screams ringing in her ears. *Corba's screams.* She'd never dreamed like that before.

"On the recording, you agreed to my . . . request," Tag said. "But then, after you woke me up, you practically threw me out of your office."

"You told a sensational story under hypnosis. Some might say you have a shocking imagination."

"Not you," Tag said. "Your reaction wasn't shock. It was something else."

Dr. Jacobson traced the woodgrain of his desktop with the pad of his finger. "The brain remains the most mysterious organ of the human body. There's much we don't know about how it works. I'll be the first to admit, after a lifetime of research, I'm still mostly clueless. One thing we do know, however, is that the brain operates in compartments." He tapped his blonde bouffant. "This bit controls motor function; this bit reminds you to breathe. The neocortex and thalamus control imagination. If you slip someone into an MRI machine and ask them to tell a bald-faced lie, these regions light up like Christmas." Dr. Jacobson tapped the top of his head. "Hypnotic regression doesn't do this, though. When patients fall into a hypnotic trance, they are accessing their hippocampus."

"Okay, so what does the hippocampus control?"

"Memory." Dr. Jacobson's voice darkened. "The story you told about a remote hilltop in Southern France—it wasn't fiction. And the same goes for that dream I suspect you had afterward. You didn't imagine that place or the events that occurred there. You *remembered* them."

"That's ridiculous," Tag whispered. She didn't want to believe it, but something fluttered in her chest as the doctor spoke. Something was waking up.

"What you're feeling now is completely normal. Not everyone can successfully regress into such memories—less than ten percent of people, according to my research. For those who can, it is often an intense experience. I assure you, with the passage of time you'll begin to feel even more connected with the memories you've now unlocked. You'll shed the fear, and you'll be left with only the knowledge. The dreams are part of this process. It's like a purification or a filtration. Like a miner panning in a stream, the sand will fall away, and you'll reveal the gold flecks within. I've seen it happen a hundred times."

"You really believe it, don't you? This past-life stuff? So, I was a mercenary in medieval France—is that what I'm supposed to believe? All because I conjured that horrific scene?"

Tag wondered what Dr. Jacobson would think if he were to see her artwork. Conjuring horror was kind of her specialty.

"It's not so difficult to imagine," Jacobson said. "You have sharp instincts. You're not intimidated by hazardous work. Even in this life, you've assumed the role of protector. I imagine that's what compelled you to pursue a career in law enforcement. Your natural talents make this field a good fit. Tell me, how did you score on your very first firearms test?"

"I hit fifty-eight out of sixty targets at twenty-five yards."

"And had you any prior experience with handguns? Did your father ever take you hunting, for example?"

Tag snorted. "My father's a florist. And no, we we're not a gun family. I'd never even held one before Quantico."

"Perhaps not in this life. But if I had to guess, I'd say you've accumulated a wealth of experience with weapons of all kinds over your past cycles."

"You think I was a sharpshooter in a previous life, and I somehow retained that skill? If this were possible, Doctor, don't you think there would be evidence?"

"But there is. Researchers in my field have studied this phenomenon of inexplicably retained knowledge for decades. Children make particularly good subjects. Adults have had years of subconscious media exposure to all kinds of information, but a child—say one under the age of six—hasn't had the opportunity to acquire many specialized skills. And yet, psychiatrists have documented cases of children exhibiting remarkable abilities. One girl from Indiana repaired the alternator of her family's minivan. She'd never worked on engines before."

Tag waved a hand. "She got lucky."

"It's difficult to explain it with luck alone. Just as it's difficult to explain how a boy from Vienna named Mozart could compose a symphony at age five. Is it so unreasonable to think that maybe he'd tapped into a wellspring of experience from a prior life as a musician? When describing Mozart, the composer Joseph Haydn claimed the world would not see 'such a talent again in one hundred years.' And maybe, eventually, it did. Maybe Mozart still composes today, in another body, in London or Culver City.

"A post-grad in my parapsychology seminar at the University of Chicago is conducting a fascinating study on this phenom effect—extraordinary talent that reaches near-inhuman levels of achievement. Reincarnation could offer an explanation. Humanity's most advanced souls may return over and over, each time soaring to new heights. Did you know that Isaac Newton was born just eleven months after Galileo's death? Both men fundamentally changed the way we understand the universe. Could they have been the same soul? It's astonishing to consider!"

Tag squinted. "That still doesn't explain your reaction to my session yesterday. If you've done past-life hypnosis with a hundred patients, why did you act so damn spooked when I told you a story about some guy named Ramon Perella and an obscure fortress called Montségur?"

"Because, Special Agent Taggart"—Dr. Jacobson's hands shook now, though from excitement or fear, Tag couldn't tell, and he clasped them as if to conceal the tremors—"everything you told me I'd heard before."

12

Raising the Sons of Elijah

by Dr. Seth Jacobson

Call Your Mother

ONE NIGHT IN medical school, after a grueling week of exams, I went to a bar with a group of students from the program. We'd walked there, so no one had to worry about collecting car keys at the end of the evening. It was a good thing too, because by midnight, my friend Billy had stacked a tower of empty shot glasses so high we'd begun taking bets on when it would topple. Billy liked to let loose, but remarkably he'd abstained from alcohol all semester. Apparently, that night the man felt it was high time he broke his dry streak. The rest of us, having taken a more conservative approach to the end-of-term festivities, sipped our Manhattans and old-fashioneds—drinks preferred by men of sophistication (so, by our fathers).

No one thought twice when good ol' Billy scooted out of the booth and stumbled toward the men's room with an urgency we'd all experienced once or twice in our collegiate careers. When our friend returned, his face had drained of all color, and his eyebrows had traveled so far up his forehead, I thought they'd burrow into his hairline. I assumed he'd just vomited a pint or two.

"Better out than in, Bill," I said, and clapped a hand on his shoulder. I felt the muscles underneath his sweater, the ones running up the back of his neck, the trapezius. They bunched under my touch.

Normally, Billy would throw a playful jab at my belly, pulling the punch just in time so all I'd feel was the bounce of his knuckles. Then we'd laugh and clink glasses. But not that night. He inhaled noisily through trembling lips and blinked rapidly.

"What the hell happened to you?" one of the other men asked.

"The phone," Billy said. "The one next to the restroom. It rang, so I answered it."

"Okay, so was it Ed McMahon telling you you'd just won a million bucks? Because you look pretty damn rattled," I said.

"It was my mom. She told me not to drive tonight. Said she loved me very much, and I had a lot left to do, so I shouldn't drive because I've had too much to drink, and it wouldn't be *safe*. That's what she wanted to tell me. I should stay safe and do the things I need to do."

Billy was weeping now, and I pulled my hand off his shoulder. He'd started to make the rest of us uncomfortable. We were men, and it was the 1980s, and our fathers—the same ones who drank old-fashioneds and taught us to shave and how to make a proper fist—had made it clear that such an outpouring of male emotion was strictly reserved for ballgames and battlefields.

"Fine. Geez," one of our friends said. "The dorm's across the street. We could roll you the whole way there on that beer belly of yours, if we had to. Tell your old lady no one's driving anywhere."

"She's not old," Billy said, his voice wavering. "And I *can't* tell her that."

"Why not?" I asked.

"Because my mother died when I was in the eighth grade. A trucker fell asleep at the wheel, drifted across the yellow line. She was forty-three."

If Billy had told the truth about forgoing alcohol for the last few months, even a couple beers would've sent his liver into overdrive. Then, pile on the stress of the program—it was Yale, for heaven's sake—and the resulting surge of cortisol. Plus, it was supremely late, nearly two in the morning, and the bar's music was loud and the air smoky. Undoubtedly, these stimuli could've had a deleterious effect on Billy's neurotransmitters, triggered certain immune-histochemical alterations. Any number of environmental or medical conditions could've explained Billy's auditory hallucination.

We said goodbye to our friends, and I walked Billy home. He was still pretty shaken up, and then he told me something else. His girlfriend was returning from an overseas business trip in the morning, and he had planned to drive to her apartment that night after leaving the bar. She'd given Billy a key, and he'd wanted to be there when she got home, to surprise her. Now, after that weird phone call, he'd changed his mind. This decision gave me great relief; Billy couldn't have tied his shoes, let alone drive. I left him to sleep it off, and my relief quickly turned to dread. Either this man—whom I'd greatly admired—possessed terrible judgment or was suffering from something else entirely. Maybe something really bad was worming around inside his brain.

That worried me the most. One of our program's star med students seemed to have experienced a psychotic episode. What if he became a surgeon, someone people trusted to operate on their heart or brain? Physicians made life-and-death decisions routinely, and this responsibility required sound mental capacity. How could anyone feel safe with a doctor who speaks to dead relatives on bar pay phones?

When I returned to my own dormitory, I sat at my desk and composed a letter to the dean of Yale Medical School. I described the events at the bar and expressed my strong recommendation that Billy be removed from the program. I did this because at this stage of my life, my mind was closed. As far as I knew, Billy would follow a ruinous path, fraught with increasing cognitive atrophy, maybe even full-bore psychosis. He'd need treatment and medication and, eventually, constant supervision. Healthy brains didn't invent phone calls from the deceased.

I never sent the letter. Not because I'd changed my mind. No, I held back for much more selfish reasons. I'd consumed three or four drinks myself that night—a fact any inquiry would surely uncover—and I worried the scrutiny would cast suspicion on my own suitability and judgment. Billy was a friend, yes, but he was also a rival. We often traded turns at the top spot in our class. A cynic might have suspected me of sabotage. So my decision to withhold the letter was purely out of craven self-interest.

Eventually, Billy went on to serve as the chairman of the Department of Immunology at Mount Sinai Medical Center in Miami Beach, Florida. And then as the director of the Centers for Disease Control and Prevention. He led the effort to contain the recent West Nile virus outbreak in New York. That contribution to public health alone likely saved hundreds of lives.

Now, looking back at that night in the bar in New Haven, I'm ashamed of myself. I nearly destroyed a brilliant man's career and wrecked what would ultimately grow into a thriving friendship, all because of a two-minute conversation that I couldn't explain. This was *my* shortcoming, not Billy's.

Did the phone in that bar really ring? Did he actually hear his mother's voice through the handset? Not necessarily, but even if these things occurred only in his subconscious, that made them real to him. He'd received a vital message from someone he'd loved dearly and who'd loved him: his late mother. That was all that mattered. I see this now because my mind is no longer closed; it's wide open.

And it was Sophie Whitestone who opened it.

* * *

Seven years ago, I'd just finished lunch at Alumni House on the north side of the university campus and decided to take advantage of the cool afternoon with a stroll. There's a charming pond just outside the school of zoology, and I watched the most elegant swans glide across it, pecking at the reeds. All around me, white flurries filled the sky, but they weren't the birds taking flight; they were sheets of paper. A young girl chased after them, clapping her hands in a poor attempt to collect the swirling pages. I ran over to help, and together we captured a half dozen while the rest snagged in the trees or landed in the pond. The girl thanked me, but her wet, puffy eyes showed her devastation. Students spend days, sometimes weeks, researching and writing academic papers. The University of Chicago is particularly demanding. To know a semester's worth of work had just become swan food would've hit anyone hard. I looked at the pages to see if I could help determine the order, and what I saw shocked me.

They were blank. Every page was a rectangle of pure white nothingness. Still, Sophie clutched the papers to her stomach and fell to her knees.

"I don't understand," I said. "You've lost nothing. You haven't written anything on these."

"No, but I was about to," she said through choking sobs. "I was about to fill every inch with the most beautiful words. Strings of them, spilling off the edges. I could *see* them. And I was about to write them down, all of them, but now . . ."

"You still can. There are reams of blank paper in the library just waiting for someone to come along and scribble away." I smiled to make light of the young woman's seemingly minor misfortune, hoping she'd smile back. She didn't.

"No, you don't get it. I needed *those* pages. Those pages were *A* pages. I can't use anything else. It's too risky. I'm here on a scholarship. I can't afford a *B* or worse. It's happened before, when I used the wrong paper or when that blue pen dried out and I had to switch to a different one, even when I *knew* it was the wrong one. I knew then, and I know now. It's all so *wrong*."

She looked up, eyes bloodshot, cheeks pink and puffy. "Oh no," she mumbled and brought the fistful of crumpled paper to her mouth to catch a fountain of vomit. Orange chunks splashed onto my shoes. "My stomach—it's spasming. I think I need a doctor."

As it would turn out, I was the doctor that this girl, Sophie Whitestone, needed—but not right away. That afternoon, she required a surgeon to remove the peptic ulcers clinging to her duodenum. I visited her in the University Medical Center to gauge her recovery. Physically, she healed quickly, as most young people do. Psychologically, Sophie faced more difficulty. She obsessed over her academic performance. I'd seen similar behavior before in our population of over-achieving undergraduates. Students who fixate on grades often suffer from exhaustion after too many all-nighters or become addicted to stimulants like Adderall or, occasionally, cocaine.

Sophie believed that her own success, however, wasn't so much a product of extreme effort. She held obscure superstitions. The phase of the moon, the temperature of her coffee, the exact weight and color of her notebook paper—these details could make or break her academic marks, she believed. Since most of these factors were completely out of her control, they caused her extreme stress. Enough stress to produce ulcers that had perforated her stomach. I urged Sophie to allow me to treat her, and she agreed. We met the week after the hospital discharged her.

At this stage in my career, I was the chairman of the psychiatry department—a rare honor for a thirty-four-year-old physician. I taught medical school courses on pharmacology and ran our research lab, which at that time focused exclusively on executing clinical trials of new psychiatric medicines. There's an expression: To a hammer, everything looks like a nail. This adage applied to many of my esteemed colleagues when it came to treating common psychiatric disorders like depression and anxiety, and it applied to me too. I prescribed Sophie a series of pharmaceutical concoctions designed to rebalance her brain chemistry. I was committed to rewiring her neurotransmitters, using all of the science and expensive education I'd acquired over my relatively short lifetime.

To my great frustration, nothing worked. Sophie suffered unpredictable mood swings—soaring highs and dark, murky lows. She'd begun tugging her hair out, strand by strand, to the point that she started wearing a baseball cap to cover the growing bald spot. It pained me to see how mental illness was affecting this young woman, so full of potential and exuberance, yet crippled by a brain out of equilibrium. And I suppose my ego had taken a hit as well. The youngest department chair in the history of the university was out of his depth, I worried they'd say. I will admit, the possibility of professional failure weighed heavily on me.

The holidays arrived, and Sophie planned to return home for the two-week respite. We met the afternoon before she left, and she told me she was considering staying away for good. She was ready to throw out all her hard work and take a part-time job at her hometown library. The orderly procedure of alphabetizing and reshelving books would comfort her when not much else could. Still, the suggestion of this mundane future for Sophie appalled me. I instructed her to mentally untangle herself from the demands of her coursework while on break. Visit childhood friends, read a novel, go dancing—anything to give herself a reprieve from the agony she'd been struggling with.

I took advantage of the winter hiatus too. I needed to reset and take a fresh look at Sophie's condition. A colleague invited me to a professional conference in Boston. Psychiatrists from all over the country had gathered to discuss the promise of hypnotherapy. As a man of science, I had generally categorized hypnosis as a form of paranormal hocus-pocus, more fitting for New Age gurus and carnival psychics. These men and women in Boston took the practice quite seriously, however, and swore by its potential to treat the untreatable.

One physician from Colorado, named Gloria, performed a demonstration. From the stage, she asked the attendees to raise a hand if they suffered from a chronic health condition. A man from a prestigious East Coast university (I'm withholding his identity as well as the name of the university to protect him from any judgment, as our profession is still quite squeamish when it comes to hypnosis) took the stage and sat opposite Gloria in a puffy chair.

She looked at him with a confident gaze. "Go ahead, put your feet up. Get cozy," Gloria instructed. "I promise I won't bite."

The audience laughed, except the man in the chair, who cringed and wrung his hands. I imagined he was reconsidering his willful participation. Things always look different from a stage. I could tell he felt vulnerable.

"So, what ails you, Doc?" Gloria's voice had the rasp of a chain smoker.

"Asthma. I've had it since I was a boy. No family history. I just drew the short straw, I suppose."

"Okay, honey. Let's see if we can get to the bottom of this." Gloria pressed her palms together, and her bright pink fingernails glinted under the lights. She inhaled deeply and then followed a rigorous procedure, encouraging the man to visualize every muscle of his body relaxing. "A white light, pure and clean, is descending from the ceiling, right above your head," she said in her husky tone. "It's inches from your face now, and you can feel its heat. It calms you, the light, and you want to feel it. The ball of brilliant white touches your forehead and spreads over your face, your neck, shoulders, chest. It's seeping into your muscles, circulating through your veins, filling the spaces between your cells. Your eyes fill with the light, and everything is white. White and bright."

The man's body visible relaxed. His head fell loosely to one side. The tension in his hands released, and a faint smile formed on his lips.

"There's nothing in this white room," Gloria continued, "but just ahead, there's a door. Do you see the door?"

"Yes, I see it," he whispered.

"Good," Gloria said. "I want you to approach it. Reach out with your hand, grab the knob, and open it. Now, walk through the doorway. Where are you? What do you see?"

"I'm on my back, staring at the ceiling. It's dirty. There's a brown water stain on one of the tiles."

"Tiles? Like one of those industrial ceilings with acoustic tiles and florescent lighting?"

"Yes, exactly. The lights flicker. This bothers me." The man's voice sounded higher-pitched, softer. "I'm wrapped tight, can't move my arms or legs, but I don't mind that. I'm warm. A woman leans over me. Her face is enormous, and she has a thousand eyelashes."

"Is this woman your mother?" Gloria asked.

"No, she's a nurse. My mother is in the bed next to me. I can smell her. I want to be with her. The nurse puts something on my head. It's a hat. It feels fuzzy."

"You're a newborn," Gloria said. "You're remembering the hospital room, the day of your birth."

The audience murmured. I'd never heard of someone retaining memories from infancy. A baby's brain is nowhere near developed enough to do so; the notion was absurd. This man was obviously imagining the visualization, I believed.

"Something's wrong," he said. "I hear a gurgling. It's getting louder. The nurse spins around, looks up at that spot above me, on the ceiling. It's not brown anymore; it's turned black and it's spreading. An ugly black circle growing wider and darker, directly above me. A terrible crash fills my ears, like banging two garbage can lids together. The ceiling tile breaks apart and water gushes out. It barely misses me, but I can feel the steam. There's dust everywhere. The nurse backs into my bassinet and I roll away—it must be on wheels. I'm even farther from my mother now. I hear her screaming. More scalding water pours through the open ceiling.

"A man wearing gray coveralls bursts through the door and immediately slips in the growing puddle. *'It burns! It burns!'* he cries. The room is jungle-hot now. The air is thick, and when that florescent light flickers, I see large pieces of dust floating around my bed like volcanic ash. It's getting into my mouth. I'm coughing, trying to turn my head, but I can't. Just coughing and gasping."

The man on the stage tore at his shirt collar. The cords on his neck stood out as he fought for air. He was having a genuine asthmatic episode and needed his inhaler. Gloria didn't appear concerned. She just scratched her nose with the points of those long pink fingernails.

"You're safe now. You can breathe easily," Gloria said. "The air is pure. The muscles of your neck are loosening. You are breathing slowly and deeply now. The air feels good, doesn't it?"

The man relaxed again. He sat with his hands folded in his lap.

"Now, I'll count backward from three, and on *one*, you will awaken." Gloria thumped her knuckle on the man's forehead, right between his eyes, with each count. "Three . . . two . . . *one*."

The man sat up. The audience clapped. We were relieved that he seemed unharmed.

"Well." Gloria slapped her knees. "That certainly was exciting. How about we take five, yes?"

I visited the men's room during the break, and when I came out, I saw the man from the demonstration, using a pay phone in the hallway. His speech hitched with soft whimpers. He hung up and turned to me. We didn't know each other, but he looked right at me and beamed with such a cosmic charge, I imagine he would've yelled out to anyone within earshot.

"It's true," he said. "All of it. A hot water pipe burst in the ceiling of the hospital room where I was born. The staff had to evacuate the entire maternity ward. I coughed like hell for an hour, from the dust, but then I fell asleep."

I'm not sure why, but I reached out to touch the man's shoulder. Somehow, I felt drawn to him. The emotional resonance of his experience was powerful, alluring. Even those of us in the audience could feel that. Then he hugged me—one of those big bear hugs.

"How do you know all of this?" I asked.

"I called my mother. She never told me about the busted pipe. It wasn't important, she said. No one was hurt, and the hospital moved her to a larger room with a better view, so she never thought twice about it."

"You'd never heard the story? No one ever spoke about the incident?"

"No one," the man confirmed. "My mother had sent my dad out to get tacos right before the ceiling collapsed, so he wasn't in the room when it happened. By the time he'd returned, the hospital had already moved my mom. Strangely enough, she never even mentioned it to him. She was too exhausted from giving birth and too preoccupied with her new baby. So my father just learned about this too, when I called home a minute ago!"

Gloria, the psychiatrist from Colorado, claimed she'd regressed this man to his earliest memory—a rather traumatic experience, from a baby's perspective. The fear of running out of air, choking on the dust, had made an indelible imprint on the man's psyche, she claimed. His asthma wasn't genetic or even a physiological problem; it was a psychological one. The man had uncovered the root of his trauma and thus taken the first step toward healing.

I returned to that conference the following year, as I have every year since. The man from the demonstration came back too. I approached him, not far from the very spot where we'd first met, and we embraced again. He reported no issues with his asthma since that afternoon on stage with Gloria. In fact, he'd stopped carrying his inhaler altogether. Gloria had cured him.

This man and I are now good friends. He runs a major hospital in New Jersey, but only his close friends and family know the full truth about his life-changing experience at the Boston conference. Regrettably, many doctors, like my friend, are afraid to accept the possibility of such inexplicable events. They are even more reticent to practice hypnotherapy themselves, although I know this man does, albeit with great secrecy.

I didn't have a clue how it worked, but after his twenty-minute hypnosis session with Gloria onstage, I could tell this man had had a major breakthrough. I thought of Sophie. Maybe hypnotherapy could help her when everything else had failed. What did we have to lose? We could spare twenty minutes and give it a shot, couldn't we?

Our first hypnotherapy session lasted forty-five minutes. Within a month, we were going for two to three hours at a time. That's when something finally clicked in Sophie, and I met Eusebius the Bishop. From that day forward, nothing would be the same. For either of us. Unlike that grateful man in Boston, however, hypnotherapy didn't help Sophie Whitestone in the end. No, it made everything much, much worse.

CHAPTER

13

"I READ YOUR BOOK, cover to cover. And, no, I didn't skim this time. There's no mention of Montségur," Tag said. "So what do you mean when you say you've heard this story before?"

Dr. Jacobson stood and turned to the bookcase behind his chair. His fingers danced as they scanned the shelves. He plucked a hardcover and slapped it on his desk. Then another and another, until he'd made a tower six or seven volumes high. Tag tilted her head to read the spines. Some had French titles, but a few were in English: *Montségur and the Mystery of the Cathars, The Treasure of Montségur,* and *St. Louis and the Albigensian Crusade.*

"It's fair to assume you've never read these books, correct?" Jacobson asked.

Tag picked one up and wiped the cover. "So, it's real," Tag said. "The ancient castle on the hilltop. All those innocent people were burned alive."

"Not all of them were innocent."

"Ramon."

"Yes, Ramon Perella was the seigneur of the fortress," Jacobson explained. "He protected Montségur from the royal army for more than a year, but when the food ran out, so did his options. He negotiated a deal. The French could have the Cathars, the heretics he'd been hired to protect, and in exchange, Ramon and his men would walk free." Jacobson sat on the edge of the desk and brushed lint from his knee. "Nice fella, huh?"

"But they killed him anyway. Not on the pyre, but later, in prison. An inquisitor . . . Ferrier, I think . . . he broke their agreement. I saw him in my dream."

"And it served Ramon right, don't you think? How arrogant must a man be to consider his own life more valuable than the lives of hundreds? There were *children* living inside that fortress. You must see why I didn't include this particular recollection in my official record. It would have destroyed her."

"Her?" Tag asked. She sat on the doctor's recliner. Her palms turned clammy. She pulled her jacket tight across her body, trying to close herself off.

"Yes. Sophie Whitestone sat in that very chair and described this entire scene to me almost thirty years ago. It was our ninth or tenth therapy session. By then, she'd already recalled four past lives with remarkable accuracy. Ramon was the fifth."

"Why should I believe you? If this really happened, you would've included the story of Montségur in your book. It establishes a pattern. Sophie believed she lived as Ramon— a man whose actions resulted in the deaths of hundreds of innocent people. Then she commits her own mass murder on Navy Pier. Children died too, the night Sophie blew herself up. Doesn't this prove—"

"That Sophie was delusional, like Caleb? That she harbored homicidal fantasies? That's one conclusion, yes."

"It's the obvious conclusion."

"No, it's the *easy* one," Jacobson said, his voice modulating with irritation. "I do not for a moment believe Sophie was psychologically ill. The events on the pier—"

"The *bombing*," Tag clarified.

"Yes, the bombing. There was something much more complex at play. Sophie had her share of idiosyncrasies, but they were mostly byproducts of an incredibly sharp intellect. The young woman wasn't impulsive; she was careful and calculated. Just like Ramon in the thirteenth century, Sophie struggled with her decision to take those lives. It tormented her. Ultimately, she came to understand that her suicide, and the deaths of others, would serve a greater purpose."

"So, she's some kind of martyr?" Tag asked.

"Perhaps in her own mind."

"And what evidence do you have?"

Dr. Jacobson moved to his filing cabinet. "I need to play something for you. I recorded nearly every hypnotherapy session with Sophie."

"And the FBI already analyzed the tapes—at least the ones they seized during their search. Did you withhold evidence from the investigation?"

"Not at all. I've always cooperated fully, turned everything over. That doesn't mean your analysts knew what to listen for. And forgive my presumptiveness, but I assume that not many of your FBI colleagues possess a working knowledge of medieval French poetry."

"What are you talking about?"

"Here it is." Jacobson lifted a miniature cassette tape from his cabinet. "Justine keeps threatening to have these digitized, but the new recordings sound so lifeless." He inserted the cassette into an aging Sony stereo system. A woman's voice filled the office. Her tone was lyrical and pleasant. She was singing:

E qand er en l'estor intratz,
Chascus hom de paratge
Non pens mas d'asclar caps e bratz,
Car mais val mortz qe vius sobratz.

"That's Sophie?" Tag asked, recognizing the song from her dream.

"Yes, and her pronunciation was impeccable, I'm told. A friend of mine graciously translated the recording. He was a professor of medieval history who specialized in the works of the troubadours. Those were the poets and songwriters of the day, and they shared many affinities with the Cathars. This particular verse you're hearing comes from a piece written by Bertran de Born, one of the more controversial troubadours."

"This is a real song?"

"Hard to believe, I know. A far cry from Bon Jovi. As obscure as Sophie's melody sounds to us, it was a smash hit about eight hundred years ago. Think of it as thirteenth-century pop music," the psychiatrist explained.

"Are you going to tell me what it means?"

"Well, I won't sing, if that's what you're asking." Dr. Jacobson grinned, but Tag sat stone-faced.

"Okay, there are a few ways to crack this, but I've been assured the best translation is as follows:

And when he enters in the lather
Let each noble brother,
Think only arms and heads to shatter,
Better to die than let him conquer.

"Sounds ominous," Tag said.

"Most certainly. I felt sick to my stomach when I first heard the translation. By this point in our therapy, Sophie had begun to demonstrate signs of distress. Something weighed on her. That last line: *'Better to die than let him conquer.'* And the reference to 'each noble brother.' Sophie believed something bad was about to happen. She had a responsibility to stop it, and, ultimately, she sacrificed herself."

Tag scratched the back of her head. "She never told you what she wanted to stop?"

Dr. Jacobson shook his head and bit his thumbnail.

Tag snorted. The psychiatrist was hiding something. She'd have to draw it out of him.

"Sorry, but you can't recast a suicide bomber as a hero," Tag said. "Not in this country."

"I don't take any special position on the morality of Sophie's actions. I can only offer my professional assessment of her mindset at the time. That young woman had considered the consequences of inaction and then did what *she* believed would serve the greater good."

"No one will buy that bullshit."

"I know." Jacobson sighed. "Which is exactly why I omitted Sophie's recollection of Montségur, and my resulting assessment, from my book. It's a counterintuitive conclusion that would have hurt the families of the victims. The press would've accused me of sanctioning violence—which I don't, for the record. That said, Sophie's true motive for the bombing on Navy Pier is the single most important mystery surrounding the Sons of Elijah. And it remains totally unsolved."

Yeah, and you're not exactly helping with that problem, Tag thought. "When did you record Sophie singing this song?"

"The night before she killed herself. I've always thought of those verses as her suicide note." Dr. Jacobson settled into his desk chair, nibbling on that thumb again. "There's still a critical question you've left unasked."

The psychiatrist was right, but Tag dreaded the idea of asking. The chilling words on that tape. Sophie's clear voice ringing out in strange-sounding French. *And that nasty little earworm tickling your brain, right in the back, in that itchy spot,* Tag thought. *The worm that wriggled its way in long, long ago, from the time when you last heard that song.*

"Sophie Whitestone had never studied French or medieval poetry or the history of the Pyrenees region. Yet she sang the lyrics written by a long-dead troubadour, word for word," Dr. Jacobson said. "She *remembered* that song from a past life on this earth.

"In the Middle Ages, while the crusades swept Western Europe, Sophie lived as Seigneur Ramon Perella," Jacobson continued. "And now you've put the pieces together, at least judging by the complete lack of color in your cheeks. You, too, lived this life, Special Agent Taggart. And perhaps more importantly, you—"

"You think *I* was Sophie Whitestone?"

Tag yanked a handful of her hair into a shiny, black spike. She tried to inhale through her nose, even though her lungs had crystalized into ice blocks. How could any of this be true? Maybe she'd seen the books on Jacobson's shelf. Maybe she'd learned about the tragedy at Montségur in high school and had just forgotten, or maybe she'd fallen asleep with the History Channel on. She'd subconsciously pieced together this fantastical story: *the product of simple subliminal observation.* And Tag couldn't eliminate the possibility that Jacobson had simply lied about Sophie recounting a similar experience. What evidence did he have really? Some spooky French song?

The same song the Cathars were singing that morning, strung up above the pyre. They belted out that familiar, haunting tune, remember? Their notes floated to heaven before the fire ate them up. Yes, that's where you've heard it before. You recognized it immediately, didn't you?

No, Jacobson was manipulating her. This man, this so-called doctor, had gotten inside her head. He'd planted those false memories somehow.

But the dream had seemed so real. It had *felt* real.

And that smell . . .

Dr. Jacobson pulled a bottle of water from a mini fridge under his desk. "Put this against your forehead. Take a sip, but don't guzzle."

"I might need something stronger."

"Well, Uncle Sam may frown upon that if you still plan to arrest me. Do you? I'm more than willing to comply." Jacobson held out his wrists.

"I need to think. There's so much that doesn't make sense."

"And yet, it *all* makes sense. You've begun to remember. Hypnotic regression can do that. It opens up portals in the mind to memories we've locked away. Mystics once believed our souls contained hidden knowledge that we could only access through meditation and spiritual enlightenment. You've begun this journey, and now you'll recall more and more," Jacobson said. "Details—the salty taste of a meal, the way the sun warmed your skin, how the air smelled. These sensations will flood your parietal lobe. That's exactly what happens when you dream too. If I hooked you up to an EEG right now, we'd see your brain shooting sparks. Believe me, I've done it. I've run every test you can think of. The data is always impressive, but it offers no satisfying conclusion. I've stopped trying to measure this phenomenon. Now I focus on recording it, documenting it, learning from it. That's what I recommend for you too. Those ancient mystics would say you've awakened. So, open your eyes. Look around."

"It's not good enough," Tag said. She held the cool bottle against her neck. "I need evidence. Some kind of proof."

Dr. Jacobson shrugged. "No, you don't. But I get it. I thought this stuff was pretty kooky myself. Initially, I'd diagnosed Sophie with delusional disorder, possibly schizo-phrenia. The stories she told while under hypnosis were entertaining and remarkably accurate, but I did not immedi-ately jump to reincarnation as an explanation. I was a fiercely analytical man—still am, in fact. We know very little about the subconscious and even less about the brain. So, at first I believed Sophie's memories were nothing more than mani-festations of physiological abnormalities."

"What changed your mind?" Tag asked.

"Ah." Dr. Jacobson removed his sport coat, walked around his desk, and sat in the chair opposite Tag. "My fiancée con-vinced me to see things differently."

Tag eyed the doctor's bare fingers. "I didn't know you were married."

"I'm not. The love of my life—an incredible woman named Dayella—died about a month before our wedding."

"I'm sorry to hear that."

"This was many years ago. Besides, she's fine." Jacobson waved a hand.

"You just said she was dead. How do you know she's fine?" Tag asked.

"Sophie told me."

14

"THE WORLD PSYCHIATRIC Association had invited me to address their global conference in Paris on the topic of plant-based biotoxins," Jacobson explained to Tag. "The shamans of certain Amazonian tribes still brew leaves from the *Psychotria viridis* shrub and the *Banisteriopsis caapi* vine to facilitate psychedelic visions. They believe they can drink the tea and reveal invisible elements of the spiritual world."

"Just like your hypnosis trick," Tag said.

"Not at all. The shamans are wrong. The plant biotoxins trigger chemical reactions that trick the brain into seeing things that aren't there. Seeing may be believing, but that doesn't mean it's actually real."

"And this plant stuff was newsworthy?"

"Plants are remarkable organisms. Some are powerful enough to kill a man with a single seed or cure a debilitating disease. In the case of the shamans, the biotoxins weren't just tricking their brains; they were reconfiguring them. I thought, with a few more years and maybe a shot of grant money, I'd develop a cure for schizophrenia or Alzheimer's."

The psychiatrist shrugged. "The point is that to me, at that stage in my life, the brain was merely a biological system, a machine of sorts. Visions, vivid dreams, hearing voices—these experiences were side effects of bugs in the wiring. All you had to do was tinker with the hardware."

"Sounds like you were a rising star, even back then," Tag quipped.

"Well, my peers thought so. No thirty-year-old had ever delivered the keynote to the Association before. I wanted Dayella to see me up there on stage."

"She didn't want to go?" Tag asked.

"Airplanes made her nervous. I'd give her a pill for short hops, but the thought of crossing the Atlantic terrified her. But she knew how important the conference was to me—to my career—and in the end, I convinced her. Our flight path arced over the southern tip of Greenland, and we hit rough air. More than rough air, actually. The chop bounced the jet so hard, one of the passengers, an older lady, fell into the aisle and broke her arm."

"Did the flight attendants ask for a doctor? Did you help?"

"No, but Dayella did. She was an orthopedic surgeon. Probably explained her acrophobia, her fear of heights. She'd treated one too many kiddos who'd slipped off the monkey bars and grandmas who'd tumbled down a flight of stairs. Ribs snapped like toothpicks, she used to say. Her work made her appreciate just how fragile the human body really is. So yeah, Dayella reset that woman's arm and jiggered a sling from a T-shirt. By the time she'd finished, the plane had descended to smoother air.

"I loved watching her work. Dayella had locked into healer mode. Caught up in the moment, she'd completely forgotten to panic. And the adrenaline flush had exhausted her. She slept with her head on my shoulder the rest of the way to Charles de Gaulle. When she awoke, I hugged her and thanked her again for making the trip. She'd endured an upsetting flight, and it meant a lot to me. She smiled and said, 'Tomorrow is a big day for you, Sethescope. Don't screw it up or I'll break every bone in your body. Trust me, I know where they all are.'"

"Sethescope?"

"Her pet name for me," Jacobson said. "Don't ask."

"So, you made it to Paris. You gave the big speech, and look at you now, Doctor." Tag gestured to the array of framed photos hanging on Jacobson's wall. The psychiatrist was in each of them, standing shoulder to shoulder with some celebrity or world leader.

"I never gave that talk. And Dayella was right: we never should've boarded that plane."

Dr. Jacobson removed his reading glasses and wiped the lenses in quick circles. His bottom eyelids looked red, swollen.

"We checked into our hotel that evening. It was a historic building undergoing a rather extensive off-season renovation, but the construction noise didn't bother us. Besides, our room was stunning. We had a view of the Champs-Élysées. The trees lining the street looked like fireworks, frozen mid-explosion. There were so many lights. They drew me to the balcony. I threw open the double doors and let the fall breeze waft into the bedroom. The night air smelled like fresh-baked bread. I wanted Dayella to join me outside. I thought she'd refuse given we were six stories up, but the magic of the moment swept her up too. She grabbed my hand so tightly that my fingertips glowed, and then she stepped onto the balcony. The hotel staff should've locked that door, but someone had neglected to do so. The construction crew had draped plastic sheeting over the iron railing and posted a sign for the workers in French that I couldn't read. Neither of us noticed the red warning symbols, not with such a stimulating scene before us.

"We absorbed the city, inhaled its perfume. I'd never seen Dayella look so beautiful. I wanted to skip the speaker's dinner that night and wrap up with her in the sheets. Just hold her and listen to the lullaby of the street sounds. We kissed and then the phone rang. The shrill clatter broke the spell and made me remember why we'd traveled across the world in the first place. The dinner, the conference, the black-tie cocktail hour where I'd clink champagne flutes with luminaries in my field—that weekend would catapult my career. I was already dreaming of the prestigious teaching position I'd secure by year's end. I darted to the phone, leaving my fiancée alone on the terrace."

"She must've freaked," Tag said.

"Her fear wasn't simply psychological; it manifested physically, in the form of severe vertigo. She likely felt disoriented, nauseous, light-headed. I lifted the phone receiver and turned back toward the balcony. The sheer curtains framing the doorway caught the breeze and snapped like silken whips. Dayella's eyes rolled up into her skull and she collapsed into the railing. The bolts had rusted, and the work crews were scheduled to replace the railing the next morning—that's what the sign said, apparently. After Dayella struck the iron with the full weight of her body, I heard an awful metallic growl, then a crack. And then . . . she was gone."

Jacobson sounded sincere. His spine bowed and forced his shoulders into hollow caves. In the span of the ten minutes it took to tell this story, he'd aged ten years.

"Your fiancée died that night," Tag said.

Jacobson nodded.

"That's awful." Tag blinked. "Before, when you said that Sophie told you Dayella was all right, what did you mean by that?"

"About an hour into an early session, Sophie had fallen into a deep hypnotic trance. She'd recounted memories from childhood, happy ones—long winter walks with her father, jigsaw puzzles with her brother—and then something truly odd happened. Sophie sat bolt upright, wiped her bangs away from her face, and said, 'Tomorrow is a big day for you, Sethescope. Don't screw it up.' She smiled and then flopped back into the chair. The next day, Sophie returned, and we resumed our therapy. And that was the first time she regressed into a past life and I met Eusebius the Bishop."

"Okay, so your deceased girlfriend sent you a message from beyond the grave through the ramblings of a hypnotized college coed." Tag rubbed her eyes. "It's time for that drink."

"Fair enough, but let's go with coffee. I don't need any more trouble with the FBI." Jacobson retrieved a spare mug from a high cabinet and poured from a carafe on his desk.

"Dayella never used that nickname in public," he continued. "She knew it embarrassed me. There's no way Sophie could've known about it, and then to repeat my fiancée's exact words from the airplane . . . I had no logical explanation for it."

"Sophie must've heard it from a ghost, of course." Tag threw her hands up. "Mystery solved, Doc."

"I didn't exactly believe that either. Not at first. But Sophie's outburst made the first small crack in my otherwise impenetrable rationality and then pried it open an inch or two more. It was enough to make me more receptive to what I'd observe over the next year while treating her. I now believe that was Dayella's intent."

Tag rubbed the back of her head to get at that persistent itch. The smell was back too, singed and ashen. *It's in the room. It's coming from* him.

She sipped the coffee and inhaled its aroma, hoping it would mask the stench.

"Special Agent Taggart, that's why you had that dream about Montségur. It has made cracks in *your* rationality."

Tag closed her eyes, just for a moment. She didn't believe Dr. Jacobson, and she certainly didn't trust him. But a dull nagging in the folds of her mind suggested there was something more at work. What had they taught her at Quantico? Go where the investigation takes you. Whoever came up with that advice probably hadn't considered cracks in rationality, whatever the hell that meant.

"Well, then I guess there's only one thing we can do about those cracks," Tag said. She propped up her feet and folded her hands over her stomach. "Let's blow them the fuck open."

CHAPTER

15

"WHERE THE HELL is Taggart?" Acting SAC Butler asked. She marched down the top-floor hallway of the Chicago Field Office, shoulder to shoulder with Special Agent Joe Michelson.

"I haven't seen her since she flitted off from the crime scene about . . ." He looked at his watch. "That's over two hours ago now."

"Is she running this investigation, or am I?"

"Tag's not answering her phone, but the counterterrorism analysts said they have something urgent. We can't wait until she's decides to pop in. We've got to hear their briefing now."

"Agreed." Butler pushed through the conference room door. A handful of men rose to their feet. "For the love of Christ, sit down." She put her hands on her hips. "Tell me you found that little shit, Caleb Miller."

The intelligence analyst, a handsome young man named Declan Walsh, with broad shoulders and a crooked necktie, shook his head.

"For fuck's sake. Then what did you find?"

The analyst tapped his laptop keyboard, and an image filled the flat screen TV mounted to the wall. "We believe we've identified Miller's next target."

Butler's left eyelid twitched as she studied the screen. She smoothed her eyebrow to hide the stress tick and then pulled out a chair. "Gentlemen, it seems it's going to be a long night. But before we get too far down the road with this, tell me— do any of you brainiacs have an advanced degree in particle physics?"

16

"You want me to hypnotize you again? Dr. Jacobson asked.

"If I lived as Sophie Whitestone in a past life, as you seem to believe, then theoretically I'd know the identities of any other members of the Sons of Elijah," Tag said. "We know she recruited at least four others—five if you count Gerald Cutter—and maybe there were even more. Maybe they're still out there. There could be a sleeper cell of cult members waiting to blow themselves up. I want to know their motives, their strategies, anything that could lead us to Caleb. Hypnotize me again. If you're right about this, you should be able to regress me to my life as Sophie."

Jacobson frowned. "You think I'm lying. You're trying to call my bluff."

"Yep."

"It's not that simple," Dr. Jacobson said.

"None of this is simple. Just see if you can do it."

"What if you don't like what you see?"

"I don't know. But I'm convinced the Sons are still around and they're going to strike again. I've got nothing to lose." She paused and stared into the overhead light. "Last time, when I awoke, I felt foggy, like I'd been drugged."

Jacobson blinked. "Special Agent Taggart, I assure you—"

"I didn't mean it that way. It felt like someone had rubbed one of those giant pink erasers over the last two hours of my life. I couldn't see words or letters, just a gray smear. That can't happen again. I need to remember this time."

"Unfortunately, I'm not in control of what you'll remember after a session. Some patients recall every detail, but many do not. They report feeling content but empty. A few have described the experience as cleansing. Nevertheless, the mind captures and stores it all. Memories often surface later, like in that dream you had. When riding on a bus or watching TV, something may trigger a meaningful event we uncovered during regression. The senses may activate, and you may hear and taste what isn't really there. It's quite powerful, I'm told. Bottom line: your mind, your rules. I am not in charge here."

Tag removed her phone from her jacket pocket. "In that case, mind if I record this?" she asked, watching Jacobson's reaction carefully.

"How considerate of you to ask this time."

"Not being considerate, Doctor. I just don't trust you."

Jacobson's smile faded. "Then, by all means, please, go right ahead. Close your eyes, try to relax, and let's get started."

Tag felt anything but relaxed. She'd saved a troubled young man from leaping into the Chicago River only to have him commit mass murder the very next afternoon.

"You should've let the little shit jump."

Butler had already investigated Caleb for months before Tag came along. The acting SAC hadn't linked him to the Sons of Elijah, but something had still felt odd about the dude. Tag had felt it in the pit of her stomach. Yet she'd *saved* him. What had compelled her to talk him off the bridge?

Caleb had to be the key to this. If she could find him, he'd lead her to the Sons.

"I want you to rest your hands on your chest, just below your sternum," Dr. Jacobson said, his voice like thick caramel. "Feel the warmth emanating from your heart. This is your center, the core of your essence. Imagine a ball of light growing there, in that spot, swelling, getting warmer, brighter. It's traveling up your spine, relaxing every muscle in your shoulders, your neck, your cheekbones. The light is behind your eyes now. It's filling your mind with its brightness, shining through the top of your skull. The ball has absorbed your spirit, and it's floating above you now. All of your thoughts and feelings float up to the ceiling, weightless. You can see yourself from above, lying in the chair. You look peaceful. Do you see?"

"I see a woman wearing my clothes, with my face, but she doesn't *feel* like me," Tag said.

"You're not connected to your body anymore. The body is matter, and you are something more. You are energy. Energy is free. Never created, never destroyed. Immortal."

"Yes, it's clear to me." The muscles in Tag's neck relaxed, and she smiled contentedly.

"Good. Our bodies are vessels. We inhabit them the way water inhabits a glass. You've had many bodies, all shapes and colors." Dr. Jacobson cleared his throat. "I'm going to count backward from three, and on *one*, I want you to return to your last body, the one that you inhabited just before this lifetime: Sophie Whitestone's body. Are you ready?"

"Yes," Tag whispered, her voice ragged.

"Three . . . two . . . you're going back, finding Sophie . . . one. *Go now!*"

Tag inhaled through her nose.

"What do you see?" Jacobson asked.

"White. I love the first snow, how it clings to the bare branches. There's no wind, so the flurries float like goose feathers. The path ahead is a sheet, untouched, even by the animals. My dad knows I like to make the first footprints. We always walk together, just the two of us. None of my brothers gets to come. Daddy wears his puffy red parka and huge black gloves. They make his hands look like bear claws. Mine are so small compared to his."

"You're a little girl."

"Yes. There's a letter stitched on my jacket. It's an *S*."

"Where are you going with your father?"

"Nowhere. We just walk in the woods. The sun's about to set, but we don't turn back. The moonlight will reflect off the snow and light up the forest, Daddy says. He knows about these things."

"Is there anyone else around?" Jacobson asked.

"No, but it's not quiet. City people think the woods are silent, but it's not true. I hear owls hooting overhead and squirrels dashing through piles of dry leaves. A few branches snap under the weight of the snow. Some of the trees are dead and break easily. Even though they stand tall, they're only husks and very brittle, like glass statues. After the trunks fall, the animals hollow out the rotted parts and make homes, Daddy says. The idea of living inside a rotten, smelly log makes me laugh. Daddy stops and lifts a finger to his lips. 'Do you hear it?' he asks."

"What does he hear?"

"A low grunting sound. Off in the thick part of the forest, near a hill, away from the trail."

"Is someone hurt?"

In the chair, Tag tilted her head as if straining to listen to some faraway sound. "It's some kind of animal. I'm frightened, but Daddy's already climbing the hill. I don't want to follow, but once he disappears over the crest, I'll be alone, and that's worse. I rush after him. My feet slip in the soft mulch. I grab at tree roots looping up from the ground, to keep from sliding down.

"Daddy never brings a flashlight on our walks. Our eyes will adjust to the night, he says. I hope he's right, because the forest is so black. It's like I've thrown a wool blanket over my head. The sounds of Daddy's footsteps guide me. I catch up, out of breath. He points into a gully. Another grunt, like a dry bark, and then I see it, lying on its side. Its body has blocked a stream cutting through the gully, and a pool of water has collected along its back. The moonlight seeps through the bare branches, just enough to trace the animal's muscular form with a deep purple outline. The beast's antlers rise from its head, sharp and crooked, like a witch's fingers. The buck moans again and kicks its front legs."

"It's injured. Has the animal been shot?" Jacobson asked.

"No, it's pinned down by a massive trunk. One of those dead ones. The tree's weight has crushed its spine, Daddy says. The poor creature won't survive. We can't just leave him! Alone in the dark, in the cold. To *die*!" Tag shifted in the recliner. Her chin pulled back into her neck. "No, Daddy says. We won't leave him like this. He approaches the buck, palms out and knees bent. The animal is twice his size, and I imagine it breaking free and spearing Daddy with those antler points. It brays and groans, kicking harder. The log shifts and sheds some bark. Daddy keeps moving closer. He's not afraid of anything. He'll lift the log, and we'll watch the buck bound into the woods. It'll survive with just bruises. But the closer Daddy gets, with his hands now curling into claws, I know I'm wrong. The buck is in terrible pain.

"Don't, please, I want to yell, but can't. Daddy grips the animal's antlers, sets into a deep stance, and rotates his entire body like he's swinging a baseball bat. There's an awful crack. The grunting stops."

Tag sobbed quietly and wiped her nose with her sleeve. "'Why, Daddy?' I ask. 'Why did you have to kill it?' He turns, walks right up to me. Shadows stripe his face. 'Sometimes killing is for the best, Hunny Bunny,' he says. He leads me back to the path. A cold sleet has begun falling, and it's leaving pockmarks in the perfect snow blanket. I nearly slip and

Daddy reaches out to grab my hand, but I pull it away before he can touch me. We don't talk the rest of the way home."

"Do you want to talk about it now?" Jacobson asked. "Do you want to tell me how you felt?"

A long pause, then: "No. Daddy is right. I understand why he did it. Sometimes killing really is for the best." Tag's breathing returned to normal. Her cheeks relaxed.

"Do you want to continue?"

"Yes."

"Then I want you to move forward. Leap ahead in time, to a day you were with the other members of the Sons of Elijah. The ones you recruited into the group. You were in Chicago, at university, yes?"

"Yes, but I only see shapes. People moving through a thick fog, colorless," Tag said.

"I'm going to put you deeper into your hypnotic state. In a moment, you'll feel three taps on your forehead," Jacobson explained. His voice sounded tinny and distant. "On the third tap you'll float above your body, just as you did before, and you'll observe yourself. It will feel like watching a movie. Everything will appear perfectly clear. Ready now? One . . . two . . . three. *Look.*"

Tag lay still. Her eyes darted underneath closed lids. She was seeing something new now. She felt her heartbeat in her palms. Jacobson's voice faded away to a whisper, no louder than the rustling of the fabric of his trousers as he shifted in his chair. Tag's lips parted, but she didn't speak. She couldn't form words to describe what she was seeing now, and even if the words had come, she wouldn't have dared to utter them. Not with Dr. Jacobson in the room. This new vision seemed important, and it was none of his damn business.

The scene unfolding in her mind turned dark green, and the air snapped with electricity, the way it gets outside before a thunderstorm. This wasn't Chicago—far from it. She saw a woman curled up, her face pressed against cold cobblestone, surrounded by young, menacing faces. A temple, built in a

distinctively Chinese architectural style, rose from the courtyard. Tag knew what was coming next, but she didn't want
to watch. The choice to look away wasn't hers to make. It
was as if someone had stapled open her eyelids, strapped her
to a board, and wheeled her right into this bleak square. The
woman screamed, first with fear and then from pain as the
young people struck her repeatedly.

Is that me? Tag wondered. *It will feel like watching a
movie,* Jacobson had said. *No, it doesn't feel like that at all.* She
looked at her arms and legs, which remained immobilized,
and blooms of purple and blue spread across her skin: bruises,
developing like a photograph in a darkroom.

Tag felt pressure on the bridge of her nose. A thumb,
Jacobson's thumb, pushing into the bone. Heat filled the
mask of her face. Her ears popped from the crackle of fire,
and finally her eyes snapped open to let out wisps of smoke.

"What the hell was that?" she asked, breathless. She put a
hand against her side and then lifted her shirt over her belly
button to check if those bruises really covered her stomach.
Her torso felt tender for a moment, and then the muscles
hardened again. There were no marks, no discoloration.

"You tell me. You haven't spoken for over twenty minutes. I couldn't allow it to go on. You were writhing, and
it looked like you were experiencing severe pain. I had to
awaken you." Dr. Jacobson's forehead glistened. Sweat had
pooled in the fine creases. His reading glasses lay on the floor,
one lens cracked. A bright pink line ran along his cheek. He
had blood in his beard stubble.

"Did I . . . *scratch* you?" Tag sat up, still foggy.

"It's nothing. These sessions are often intense. A woman
in her eighties once kicked me right in the lips. I don't take
it personally."

"It was so real. What I saw . . ."

"To your mind's eye, it *was* real. After all, what is sight
but a series of electrical signals—a code deciphered by the
brain? You don't need eyes to see, or ears to hear. Just access

to the right signals. Signals in the mind." Jacobson stood. A dark, wet stain ran the length of his back along his spine. "What you experienced is for you. I would never expect you to share unless you feel comfortable doing so. However, as a psychiatrist, I may be able to help you."

"You already have," Tag said. She put on her jacket and retied her boots—the laces had come loose somehow.

"I have? How's that?" Jacobson asked.

Tag grinned. "Like you said: my mind, my rules."

Unlike the first session with Dr. Jacobson, she remembered everything, including that unspeakable scene at the end. *Who were those people standing over me, holding broken broom handles like billy clubs?* She hadn't ruled out the possibility that Dr. Jacobson had somehow suggested the ideas, but now she had a way to put his hypno-magic to the test. If the images she saw while lying in his chair were indeed authentic, she'd be able to verify them. And she knew exactly where to start.

Tag stood and almost tripped on her way to the door. She looked at her feet and saw that her laces hadn't just come untied; her boots were now on the wrong feet.

17

A TWO-STORY COLONIAL—white clapboard siding, black shutters, lavender hydrangeas sprouting from beds lining the stone walkway. An American flag fixed to the wrap-around porch, jutting out patriotically. Two wooden rocking chairs, painted blue. An iron lantern swaying from a chain above the front door. And a bell mounted to a brass pole, with a showy red yoke and big bowl body, the kind that a pioneer woman would ring at suppertime to summon the kinfolk from the fields.

None of it looked familiar. Of course, Tag had seen similar houses before, lacing the cul-de-sacs of Chicago's suburbs, but she'd never seen this *particular* house.

She climbed the porch steps, two at a time. Before she could knock, the front door opened. An older woman wearing a white apron, gold sandals, and a permanent frown beckoned Tag inside with urgent snaps.

"Bees," the woman said. "They've gone mad for my garden this year. Hurry inside before the whole swarm sets up shop in my pantry." She grabbed Tag's sleeve and pulled her into the foyer before slamming the door shut and turning the deadbolt.

"The bees figured out the locks too?" Tag asked, amused.

The woman wiped her hands on her hips. "Force of habit. I get plenty of no-goods creeping around, even after all these years. Came home from the supermarket to a broken window once. I reported it, of course, but the police don't seem too interested in *my* safety. The way they treat me in this town, you'd think I set off that bomb myself. People forget that I lost someone too." Her eyes flicked to a picture of a young girl in a prom dress hanging in the entryway, beside a silver cross.

"Mrs. Whitestone, as I said over the phone, I'm not here to judge you or accuse you of anything."

"Isn't that what the FBI does? Judge and accuse? Gah, I'm finished fighting with you people. You might as well get to it, ask me all the same things all over again. Let's see now. Did she have a happy childhood? Yes. Ever notice signs of abuse? No. Drugs? Probably—she was an American teen. But she never messed with the hard stuff, if that's what you're wondering about. How about animals? Your daughter ever hurt an animal on purpose? That one always turns me out. Did you know, when Sophie was seven, she cried for a week when her pet goldfish died? It's buried in the back somewhere near the zinnias. She even made a little headstone, scratched out a heart on it and everything. Why in God's name would a girl like that torture an animal?"

Maybe for the same reason she blew up four hundred and thirty-seven people on Navy Pier, Tag thought.

Tag followed Mrs. Whitestone into the kitchen. The smell of bread baking filled the room. "Were you aware that your daughter was seeing a psychiatrist? Before the . . . incident, I mean."

"You're talking about that self-absorbed scamster who wrote that filth about Sophie."

"Dr. Seth Jacobson," Tag clarified.

Mrs. Whitestone opened a can of tuna and placed it on the floor. She made wet kissing sounds until a white cat scampered though a flap in the back door and dove for the fish. "Tell me this, Agent . . . whatchamacalled again?"

"Taggart."

"Tell me, Agent Taggart." She waved the can opener with a limp wrist. "Do *you* think my daughter was the Queen of England or Napoleon Bonaparte in a past life, or some other crazy business like that? Because I only know of one person who rose from the dead to live again, and that's our Savior Jesus Christ." She kissed a crucifix hanging from a chain around her neck.

"I never had the chance to meet your daughter, and I wouldn't claim to know anything about her," Tag said. "I've only read the other agents' field notes; articles in the *Tribune* written around the time of her death; Dr. Jacobson's book, of course, and to be honest, it's—"

"Tragic, that's what it is." Mrs. Whitestone pulled a wooden spoon from a drawer and began stirring something gooey in a large bowl.

"I was going to say *puzzling*. You have a nice home in a nice neighborhood. Just looking at the photos on these walls, I can tell that Sophie was loved. Why does a girl like that end her own life?"

Mrs. Whitestone stopped stirring. "You're the first person to come by here who put it like that. The others, they all fixate on the people who were on that pier, the victims. I get it: my little girl hurt a lot of innocent folks, but she died that day too. No one has ever cared about Sophie's life." With sturdy hands, the woman screwed off the lid of a mason jar and poured a thick amber liquid into the mixing bowl. She licked her fingers. "Never could bake with honey back then. Sophie was allergic."

"So, you agree. Her involvement with the Sons of Elijah—it *is* puzzling."

"Nope, nothing puzzling about it. That man, Jacobson, brainwashed my daughter. She was practically a child. He has a thing for young women. It's disgusting. I bet you didn't know there were others."

"Other girls?" Tag asked.

"Oh yeah. The University's kept a lid on it. He's their star. Ask them about that, why don't you? Ask them how many girls they've paid to shush up."

Tag thought about how Dr. Jacobson had smiled at the medical student attending his lecture. His expression had had a lecherous quality that made her shiver. *And don't forget that racy painting of yours, that possessive pose.* Tag made a mental note to look into any complaints of sexual misconduct with the university personnel office. If Jacobson had harassed any other women, she'd find them.

"Not that you'd have to worry about such nonsense from a nasty old man like Seth Jacobson." Mrs. Whitestone eyed Tag's haircut with a mother's judgmental gaze. "Shame—all the young ladies shearing their locks. Sure sends a signal. Men don't like 'em butch. Not all the fellas are dogs like that doctor, you know."

Mrs. Whitestone sprinkled a layer of flour onto the countertop. "This dough has got to rise for the next hour, but I wasn't planning to spend it picking at old wounds. Do ya mind if you get to it, Agent Taggart? Why is it you came here?"

"Mr. Whitestone," Tag started, "your husband—is he home?"

"No," the woman answered abruptly. She lifted the dough from the bowl and slapped it onto the counter, diving in with both hands, kneading with the heels of her palms.

"Oh, I'm sorry. I didn't know he'd passed."

"Guh," she grunted. "That old coot will outlive me, even if it's just to spite me. And to drain our bank account. Mr. Whitestone is up at Sunrise Memory Care on Washington Street. I'd visit more often, but he usually doesn't recognize me when I do, so why bother? I betcha think that makes me a cruel old biddy."

"I wasn't aware that he was in poor health. I'm sorry to hear that." Tag felt a strange surge of surprise and sadness, even though she'd never met the man.

"You're off track anyway if you're thinking about Sophie having daddy issues or something clichéd like that. That man has given me hell for fifty years, but he adored his little princess. He never touched her."

"Do you have a picture of him? One from Sophie's childhood, when she was around eight years old?"

Mrs. Whitestone pressed into the dough and eyed Tag suspiciously. "That would be around when we moved down to Illinois from Michigan. Let's see, 1982 or thereabouts. Yeah, that was the year John bought me a Nikon for Christmas. I took a bunch of photographs in the old house before we packed up. Pass me that washrag, would ya?"

Tag reached for the towel and handed it to Mrs. Whitestone. The woman took it, and her lips nearly formed a smile.

"A lefty, huh? My Sophie was left-handed. Her dad, too, until the nuns beat it out of him in grade school. That's the devil's hand, they said." She ran her sticky fingers under the faucet and dried them on the towel. "Let me get you that album," she said, and disappeared into the living room.

Tag scanned the kitchen. A pair of dirty coffee mugs were stacked in the sink. A carafe sat on the counter, still half full. Gurgles came from the running dishwasher. An untouched loaf of bread, probably homemade, rested on a cutting board near the stove. Tag opened a cabinet. It was filled with more mason jars brimming with honey. Dozens of them.

Mrs. Whitestone returned with a dusty binder. Its cover, made of that plastic that was supposed to look to like leather, peeled from age. "Eighty-two," she said. "This is all I got."

"May I?" Tag asked.

"Don't get fingerprints on the photos." She scowled and began to wipe up after her baking project. "Looking for anything in particular?"

"No," Tag lied. "I just think to really know someone, you've got to know the home they grew up in, the family that raised them."

She flipped through pages of fading pictures. Sophie opening a present. Sophie playing with a small dog with curly fur. Sophie building a fort out of cardboard boxes. These were the mundane moments of an eight-year-old girl's life, captured in stills, frozen in time. And completely useless.

Tag thought she'd reached a dead end, and wasted the bulk of an afternoon, until she flipped another page, and there it was. Her temples pulsed. It was a yellowing photo of Sophie walking up a driveway covered in snow, her small hand gripping her dad's sleeve—the *red* sleeve of a puffy parka. It was the coat from Tag's vision. Her mouth went dry.

"Could I trouble you for a glass of water, Mrs. Whitestone?"

Tag guzzled the entire glass and felt her head clear a bit. There had to be a thousand men with red parkas in Michigan in the eighties. This forty-year-old photograph proved nothing. *But the black gloves, the ones that make his hands look like bear claws. He's wearing those in the picture too. You can feel the leather against your palm, can't you? Soft and slick. They're the same gloves.*

Tag could visit Mr. Whitestone at Sunrise Memory Care and ask him about the buck—the injured one that Tag dreamed he'd killed to spare it from a long, torturous death—but if the man was suffering from dementia, he might not recall that evening. Sophie's mother might know about the incident, but Tag doubted her daughter would have mentioned it. There had to be something else. Another way Tag could verify her supposed memories of Sophie's life.

"Guh, dang it!" Mrs. Whitestone peered out the window over the sink. "They're back at it. Dang dumb bees." She snatched the hand towel and rushed out the back door, into the garden.

Tag was alone in the house. Her eyes flashed to the stairs and then back to the window, where she watched

Mrs. Whitestone scampering in the grass, cracking the rag over her head. Tag's opportunity to search the house unsupervised wouldn't last long. She backed out of the kitchen and ascended the staircase.

Tag found Sophie's old bedroom immediately. The door still had a sign hanging from it with the girl's name, written in pink bubble letters. A heart dotted the *i*. The bed was made up as if Sophie would peel back the comforter and crawl inside that night. Faded posters of Luke Perry plastered the walls. A makeup table with a gold-framed vanity sat beside the window. On the mirror, someone had written the words *SENIORS '92* in plum lipstick and then kissed the glass. A layer of dust had formed on the sticky color. Tag wasn't surprised that Mrs. Whitestone hadn't scrubbed it off. The perfect lip print of her dead teenage daughter, the ridges and dimples of her soft skin preserved in Mac's Mulberry Myth, immortalized Sophie's memory.

Tag moved to the closet. A dreamcatcher hung from the doorknob. She inhaled sharply when she opened the closet and looked inside. Sophie's clothes hung neatly from evenly spaced hangers. The blouses and pants and jackets were organized by color, from lightest to darkest, left to right, just like they were in Tag's own closet. *A coincidence,* Tag thought. Anyone with an eye for design would understand the efficiency of arranging clothes in this way. A neat row of shirts did not prove Tag had once lived in this house, in this room.

Still, in the obsessively tidy space, something looked out of place. A bulky wooden dresser was pushed against the back wall of the closet. Tag had an odd feeling that the oversized piece of furniture didn't belong there, although she couldn't explain why. There were scratches in the wood floor near the dresser's legs, made from scooting it into position. Tag tuned her ears to the silence of the house. From the bedroom window, she could see Mrs. Whitestone was still in the yard, spraying her roses with a garden hose. It seemed the woman had won her battle with the bees. She would come back inside the house soon.

Tag stepped into the closet, gripped the edge of the dresser, and pulled with all one hundred and five pounds of her body weight. The behemoth didn't budge until she leaned her back against its side and planted her boot on the door jamb for leverage. With a series of unnerving scrapes, she slid the dresser a full foot to the right. *Is this how Sophie had moved it too?* Tag wondered.

Tag smiled when she saw the electrical outlet that had been hidden behind the dresser. It was positioned unusually high and off-center on the back wall of the closet—sloppy work for any licensed electrician. Probably a DIY job. She flipped open the blade of her pocketknife and turned the screws. The plastic cover fell away, along with the socket, which wasn't actually connected to any wiring. Tag stared at the hole in the drywall. Somehow she knew that when she reached into that dusty cavity and felt around, she'd find an object taped to a stud. Even before her fingers wrapped around its cold plastic shape, she *knew* it would be there.

With a twitch, Tag detached the thing and pulled it out. She hadn't seen anything like it except in movies. A small, three-inch plastic square with a fat metal slider along the top and a white label on the front. It was an obsolete piece of technology from the days of AOL and dial-up modems: a floppy disk. From the markings on the label, Tag knew exactly who it had belonged to.

A thud came from somewhere inside the house. *Mrs. Whitestone,* Tag thought. *She'll find the kitchen empty and raise hell.* Fumbling with the screws, Tag managed to secure the electrical outlet and faceplate back onto the wall. She leaned against the dresser and pushed. The floorboards groaned as it slid back into place. Tag gently closed the closet door and shut her eyes, listening.

Nothing. If Mrs. Whitestone had heard the sound of Tag moving the dresser, maybe the woman had thought it was simply the house settling. Or the cat had knocked something over. Or maybe the old lady's eardrums had blown out years ago, and she hadn't heard so much as a squeak.

Tag surveyed Sophie's bedroom one final time. Her eyes wandered to those lips on the mirror. She approached the vanity and leaned closer until her own puckered lips lined up with the purple print.

"Sophie! My sweet Sophie," a voice called from behind. "I've been waiting so long."

Tag whipped around. An elderly man with white wisps growing wild from his eyebrows stood in the doorway to Sophie's bedroom. The skin from his neck hung so loose, it looked as if it might drip off in globs. Worse, he was stark naked. Greenish liver spots speckled his chest. A network of purple veins striped his arms and legs. Dark liquid dribbled from his genitals and made glossy dots on the floorboards.

The man approached, arms outstretched. Tag backed into the makeup table and knocked over a perfume bottle. It broke, sending up a cloying scent of cotton candy. The nude bag of staggering flesh grew closer.

"Stop," Tag warned. "Keep your distance."

The man's bare feet stepped onto the broken glass from the bottle, but he showed no sign of discomfort, inching forward, stamping the floor with red footprints.

"I need you," he said, weeping. "I need you to take me away from here. You've come for me, I know it. Take me with you, Hunny Bunny. I'm *ready*."

Tag dodged the man's clawing hands. She fled into the hallway and down the stairs, her heart thumping in her ears. When she yanked on the front door, it didn't budge. *That batty old woman has me trapped,* she thought before remembering the deadbolt. Tag finally got it open and nearly ran straight into a figure standing on the porch wearing a wide-brim beekeeper's hat with a gauzy veil obscuring her face.

"Find what you were looking for?" Mrs. Whitestone asked from behind the mesh.

"You told me your husband wasn't here," Tag barked.

"That man hasn't *really* been here for years. Not as far as I'm concerned. His mind took the midnight train to Georgia, along with our retirement savings."

"It's a federal crime to lie to the FBI. I hope you're aware of that."

The hat tilted. Tag imagined the old woman's thin lips pulling back behind the gray veil. "Oh, Agent Taggart. Do you think you can simply ask your questions and people will serve up perfect little answers? At least the others who came before you understood the challenge. Besides, isn't it better to exhume the truth for yourself?"

"Sophie's bedroom—you haven't changed it. Why?"

"Oh, I dunno, dear. Maybe I'm still waiting for her to come home one day. Just . . . pop in." Mrs. Whitestone raised the mesh over the brim of her hat and Tag could see that the woman was indeed grinning. Every tooth jutted from her gums, making a ragged row of yellow stalactites.

Tag rushed for her car.

"Come back anytime," Mrs. Whitestone called out from the porch. "If you're looking for honey, I've got plenty to go around."

Tag started the Crown Vic's engine. She gripped the steering wheel so hard she thought it might snap off. Mrs. Whitestone had deceived her. The pair of coffee mugs in the sink, the absurd amount of freshly baked bread on the kitchen counter—it should've been obvious that someone else was in the house with her. Why had Tag believed that woman about her husband living at Sunrise Memory Care? *A facility for the confused, the cognitively disabled.* Mr. Whitestone *was* confused, wasn't he? He'd mistaken Tag for Sophie, his deceased daughter. How could he have made such an obvious mistake? In pictures taken of Sophie shortly before her suicide attack, the girl had a blonde braid to the middle of her back, chubby cheeks, and shiny eyes. Sophie had looked nothing like the spiky-haired, scrawny federal agent whom

Mr. Whitestone had just caught snooping in his daughter's bedroom. *But he'd seemed so sure.*

Visiting Sophie's parents hadn't brought the clarity Tag had hoped for. Between Mr. Whitestone's advanced dementia and Mrs. Whitestone's blatant deception, Tag had learned nothing.

"Isn't it better to exhume the truth for yourself?"

The old woman had a point. The answers Tag needed were long buried, tucked away. *Hidden inside a wall, taped to a stud, perhaps?* Sophie hadn't been the picture of suburban innocence that her mother had framed and hung above the mantle. That girl had kept secrets.

Tag felt the floppy disk in her pocket. Maybe the trip to the Whitestone residence hadn't been so useless after all. She pulled out the disk and dropped it into the cup holder. On the disk's label was a pink kiss, marked in Mulberry Myth, planted right over a single name scribbled in purple ink.

Gerald.

18

Raising the Sons of Elijah

by Dr. Seth Jacobson

Something Rotten in the Attic

GERALD CUTTER LOOSENED his tie and opened the top button of his dress shirt. He wanted to show me the marks on his neck. I used a penlight to examine the skin just underneath his Adam's apple, where I saw a ring of indigo splotches. A wave of dread washed over me when I considered if this man—a rising, twenty-five-year-old accountant—could have attempted hanging himself. As a psychiatrist, I had treated people with a number of phobias, anxieties, and mental disorders. I'd had patients threaten suicide before, and one who'd made a serious attempt involving a bottle of Windex. If Gerald had considered harming himself or others, I would have been obligated to take certain steps.

Upon closer inspection, I noticed the uniformity of the contusions. Blue-black ovals spaced at regular intervals all around his neck. A rope or a sheet wouldn't have made those marks.

"She started making me wear a collar," Gerald explained. "It has these metal studs. They're not sharp, but they still hurt like hell when she jerks on it."

"Jerks on what?" I asked.

"The leash."

Gerald's relationship with his wife, Linda, had deteriorated over the year that he'd been coming to my office. He'd explained how she criticized him incessantly for minor domestic infractions like forgetting to remove his shoes or falling asleep on the couch with the TV on. Despite his success at work, she still berated him until he felt inadequate. Until this particular therapy session, I'd had no idea this abusive dynamic had extended to the bedroom.

"She makes me wear her panties. They're so tight, sometimes my legs go numb," he said. "And I've been wearing the collar for a while now, but the leash is new. Linda leads me around the house like an animal, makes me lick the bottoms of her feet."

I understand that many couples enjoy some form of bondage and role-play, but it's crucial that both parties are on the same page regarding boundaries. Gerald's experiences went to the extreme and veered into nonconsensual exploitation. His wife's domination had taken an emotional toll on him, but I had an even greater concern. My patient *enjoyed* it. Deriving pleasure from humiliation or abuse is dangerous. He was a towering, athletic man with arms thicker than my own thighs. If he'd wanted to stop his partner, he could have easily done so. Instead, he welcomed the mortification.

"Has she ever hurt you physically?" I asked. "Beyond the bruising from the collar?"

Gerald picked at his nails. He sucked in large breaths through his nostrils and stared at my shoes.

"This office is a bubble. We're protected from any outside negativity," I assured him. "You can share anything you'd like in here. When we're done, we'll simply open the window and let it all float away into the atmosphere."

Finally he spoke. "Earlier this week, a package arrived. The empty box sat on the kitchen counter. I didn't know what she'd ordered, but I didn't think anything of it. That night, Linda stripped me and clasped the collar around my neck again.

Instead of her panties, she slipped a pair of stockings onto my legs. Red ones. I got down on all fours and she climbed onto my back. She wrapped a necktie around my eyes. She'd never done that before. I couldn't see anything."

"Did you ask her to stop?"

"No, the silk felt nice against my face. Linda had something new in mind and it . . . excited me."

"Sexually, you mean. This aroused you. Did you get an erection?"

"Yes," he answered. "It felt like my entire body was throbbing with anticipation. I asked her what she wanted me to do."

"Were you nervous?" I asked.

Gerald kept picking at his fingernails, pushing the cuticles back. "Not until she got behind me. She pushed my knees apart and knelt between my legs. I yelped when she grabbed my testicles. Not too hard—it just surprised me, that's all. Then she . . ."

"What, Gerald? What happened?"

"She . . . penetrated me."

Linda had purchased a sex toy—an artificial male appendage. It had metal studs like the collar, Gerald said. When Linda finally tore off his blindfold, he saw the thing. Slick and red.

"The doctors did some scans. They think the tears will heal on their own. I'll just be sore for a while," he said.

"Gerald, this is getting dangerous. You could have suffered serious physical injury. What did you finally do to make her stop?"

His eyes puffed up and his nose dripped. "I didn't stop her."

"Then what did you do?"

"I ejaculated," he whispered.

*　*　*

Even at his young age, Gerald managed the annual auditing of a multimillion-dollar client of his father's firm. He supervised a team of seven. With broad shoulders and a keen intellect, the man dominated the corporate class, physically and mentally.

And, as I'd come to learn, he derived sexual satisfaction from pain and suffering.

Over weeks of therapy, I'd learned that he'd slept with as many as thirty or forty women before meeting Linda, and he'd never assumed a submissive role before. More strangely, Linda didn't have a history of sadomasochistic practices with any of her past sexual partners either. Gerald's dynamic with his wife was unusually oppressive, and we needed to get to the root of this toxic relationship.

I thought about my experience with Sophie earlier that winter and how our hypnotherapy sessions had helped her. After some persuasion, Gerald agreed to undergo hypnosis. I guided him into a trance state, and within minutes he accessed a disturbing memory that explained everything.

*   *   *

"My cheekbone is soft. It's spongy, doughy, when I push my fingers into it. It hurts, but I've stopped thinking about the pain." Gerald reclined in the chair with his eyes closed and his hand touching his face. "There's a wooden table in the center of the room, with bowls and cups stacked on top. I'm breaking the stems off carrots. Afterward, I'll wash them and cut them into disks. There's a cutting board and long knife beside me. My hand hurts from chopping all afternoon. We're expecting guests from across the valley, and the lord has ordered a feast. I've probably chopped a thousand carrots already." He wiped his brow and neck, blotting behind his ears.

"What's wrong?" I asked.

"I'm sweating. I'm working next to an enormous oven. A boy has just added an armful of logs onto the fire, and he's prodding them with an iron poker to get the flame up. He's one of the stable grooms who sometimes does chores for the head cook. I don't like how he looks at me. I want to go to the cellar until he finishes his task, but I'll fall behind on the vegetables. Most of the others are setting up the Great Hall, so in the kitchen it's just me, the boy, and the cook, who has her back turned.

The boy is leering, licking his lips. He moves closer and I feel my body collapsing into itself. Then he reaches out and grabs my breast through my apron. I slap his hand and he runs off, back to the stables, I suppose. He'll brag to the other grooms about what he did. I'm worried they'll try to grab me too."

Gerald had regressed to a past life as a French scullery maid named Lucie. Later in the session, we were able to discern the year: 1794. His subconscious had chosen to recall this moment, this location. I wanted to know why.

"Is this stable boy the one who hurt your cheek?"

"No, he is harmless. He feels entitled to touch me, but he's a servant, like me."

"Then someone of higher stature assaulted you," I reasoned. "The head cook or—"

"He's here," Gerald whispered. His voice turned black and dull. "I know it's him. He has a . . . a scent. Like a wet weasel. A long shadow spills across the floor. I move away, but my leg is caught on something. I hear a clanking. My ankle burns."

Gerald flexed his right foot and tried to pull his knee up to his chest.

"Are you still in the kitchen?"

"Yes, I'm still chopping carrots," Gerald explained.

"Why does your ankle burn?" I asked. "Is it also injured?"

Gerald attempted to lift his leg again, but kept jerking it back down. "I'm chained to the wall," he said. "I tried to run away. The chaplain caught me hiding in the apple orchard. If one of the soldiers had spotted me, he'd have dropped me with his musket. I thought I was lucky, until the chaplain brought me to *him*."

"Him—it's a man who beat you."

"The wet weasel, yes. His name is Jean-Lambert Tallien. He's a prominent politician in Paris, and he's come to the estate for the night's gathering. I know him from his previous visits. He never comes down to the kitchen unless it's for me. I don't know why he singles me out. I'm so plain."

"You're afraid of him, of Tallien."

"Everyone is afraid of him. He has . . . an intensity, like the crackling fire. He's in the kitchen now. I want him to leave, but I know he won't. He peels off his navy tailcoat and tosses it over a chair with his cravat. His eyes meet the cook's and she nods knowingly, wipes her flour-coated hands on her apron, and leaves. Now I'm alone with him." Gerald gasped.

"What's the man doing now?" I asked.

"He sweeps the table clean. The carrots roll along the floor. He snatches the bonnet from my head and grabs a fistful of my hair. In a blink, I'm on the table, and he lifts my dress over my bosom. He presses the center of my naked chest and grins. The iron cuff around my ankle cuts into the skin. The chain is stretched taut, pulling my leg to the side. Tallien climbs on top of me and opens his trousers. His lips are shiny with lust. He wants to enter me, but his . . ."

"He's impotent. Is that it?"

Gerald nodded. "It's happened before, and that's when he beat me." His breathing grew rapid. He tugged on his ears.

"You are simply observing this experience. You'll feel no pain, only understanding," I reassured him.

"Oh, God. He's reaching for the fire iron. Its tip still glows," Gerald said. "He's ripping my undergarments. He's going to use the poker."

"Relax and breathe deeply. Witnessing the moment of a prior death may seem frightening, but it can have extraordinarily therapeutic value."

"No, I'm not going to die. Not this way. I won't let him kill me." Gerald's head snapped to the side, his eyes still squeezed shut. "My chopping knife is still on the table. It didn't fall to the floor with everything else. I don't think he sees it. Tallien puts his face against mine and growls, 'You know what I want.'"

"He wants to rape you."

"No, that's not it. Not this time," Gerald said.

This confused me. The scenario sounded all too familiar, unfortunately. A powerful man sexually assaulting a vulnerable subordinate. "Then what does he want from you?"

"Information," Gerald answered.

How bizarre, I thought. What information could a scullery maid—a woman of the lowest position in the household staff— offer this man? I probed for details. "Is this information of significant value to him?"

"Oh yes. He's looking for something. He's wanted it for centuries."

"And you know where it is?"

Gerald nodded. "He has come close in the past, but I've never said a word."

"You've encountered this man before? Not just in this lifetime, but in previous lives as well?" I asked. The idea of relationships spanning centuries fascinated me. Could it be that our souls are drawn to one another, life after life, like spiritual magnets?

"He's squeezing my throat, making me cough. His mouth is so close. That weasel breath covers my face. I shut my eyes. He doesn't like that. 'Look at me,' he barks. I obey. I can feel the heat radiating off the poker between my thighs, inches from my skin.

"'Where is it, you cunt?' he demands. I try to keep his eyes fixed on mine so that he won't notice what I'm doing. I reach back, above my head, groping. My hand slips around the knife's handle. It's like an extension of my arm. I bring it down with such force, I hear my wrist snap upon contact. Tallien howls. I see something black growing on his tongue. He raises me up by my neck, then slams my skull into the tabletop. Pain explodes behind my forehead. The blade clatters on the stone floor. I'd sliced through the sleeve of Tallien's linen shirt. Blood soaks the fabric. He peels it off, hissing."

Gerald rubbed his head, which had lolled to the side.

"Remember, no pain. What's happening now?" I asked.

"The cook has returned. She must've heard him yelling. Her eyes grow wide when she sees the blood. 'I've injured myself. Clumsy, I know,' he says. 'This young lady kindly offered to clean me up.' He dismounts me and turns to face the cook, giving me a good look at the bite the knife took out of his upper arm. *Oh . . . oh no.*" Gerald gripped the arms of the lounge chair. "It's . . . *oh God.*" He began to gag.

"What is it, Gerald?" His reaction to whatever he'd seen in his trance state had affected him so viscerally that I needed to wake him immediately. When Gerald opened his eyes, they swirled with terror. I felt a surge of panic. I had intended to alleviate my patient's suffering, but this man looked traumatized.

"The wound on his arm. From the knife," Gerald whispered. "It's the same. It's exactly the same."

"You recognize this injury?"

Gerald nodded.

"Where have you see this mark before?" I asked.

"She has a birthmark on her arm, just below her shoulder, in the same place. She's self-conscious about it, never wears sleeveless dresses."

"Who, Gerald? Who has this birthmark?"

"Linda," he answered. "My wife."

I allowed Gerald to rest in my office. I suggested a simple meditation exercise to calm his mind and help him integrate the revelation he'd just had. We sat in silence as a peaceful smile formed on his face. Over the following weeks, Gerald came to believe that he'd known his wife in multiple incarnations. Sometimes their genders had swapped, as they had in his remembered life as a scullery maid. Other times Gerald and Linda were both men or both women. Linda had been his wife, his son, his father. The details changed, but one thing remained constant: Linda's vicious hostility toward Gerald.

Now that he knew his acrimonious relationship with his wife had a long and tragic history—that she'd beaten, raped, and assaulted him in countless lives before—Gerald began to approach his marriage differently. His confidence and self-worth returned. He stood up to Linda when she belittled him, but more importantly, he made a genuine effort to understand the root of her hatred. Over the course of various lifetimes,

Gerald had withheld something from her, information of such immense value to Linda that she was willing to use torture to obtain it. For Gerald, this knowledge held such great importance that he was willing to endure indescribable abuse. I probed deeper into the secret that my patient had guarded so closely, but no matter what we tried, it remained locked away inside his subconscious. Nevertheless, I kept trying. If Gerald could figure it out, he and his wife could finally resolve this ageless conflict. I could help them save their marriage.

That's what I thought, right up until the morning they found Linda's body in Gerald's attic. He'd tied her to the rafters, head angled down. Inches from her nose, he'd placed a glass of water and a bowl of oranges. The medical examiner believed she'd survived for days, staring at that ripe fruit and water, before dying of thirst. Linda was most likely Gerald's only victim. His sexual submissiveness had given way to red rage directed specifically and exclusively at his wife.

Despite the gruesome nature of his crime, I didn't believe Gerald was a danger to society. This was my professional opinion, and I would have testified to this in court if a trial had ever taken place. My assessment would've held little sway, probably. If the police had apprehended him, a jury would've sentenced him to life in prison, no doubt.

Of course, Gerald never slept a single night behind bars. By the time the Merry Maids had let themselves into Gerald's spacious estate, and smacked face-first into an acrid smell seeping from the attic, Gerald was long gone. The authorities searched for weeks, pursuing a trail that first led them northeast, to the forests of Bangor, Maine, and then into America's Deep South. He'd liquidated a variety of assets and lived off cash, the police assumed, making Gerald a tough fellow to follow. Even today, I don't know if my patient is living somewhere in Georgia, under a false identity, or if he's even still alive.

Selfishly, I hope Gerald Cutter hasn't yet left this earth, because we never did uncover the nature of his secret—the one Linda had tried to squeeze out of him over centuries of lifetimes. I shouldn't have fixated on this so much; many psychiatric patients withhold information that they feel is too personal to reveal. However, I became haunted by this shadowy omission. It was the last missing piece of an unfinished jigsaw puzzle. In all of our hypnotherapy sessions, I only elicited a single clue from Gerald. Perhaps it was the reason he'd never revealed more.

"It's not my information to share," Gerald had said dreamily while in a hypnotic trance. "The secret belongs to the group of six sacred guardians." This he told me during his final session. I never saw Gerald Cutter again, so I couldn't dig deeper into the meaning of this strange group that he'd never mentioned before. It turned out not to matter much. Over the course of the next month, Sophie Whitestone would explain plenty about these guardians.

19

"I FUCKED UP," TAG said. She'd arrived at the North Side Diner about five minutes earlier, and in that short time, she'd already dumped the little packets of artificial sweetener onto the table and arranged them by color. The dinner crowd was sparse, so Tag had picked a quiet spot near the back, where she could keep an eye on the front door.

Special Agent Joe Michelson approached and set down his briefcase, strewing the sugar packets, before sliding into the booth opposite his partner. His head bobbed with an irritating swagger.

"You don't have to look so happy about it, Joe."

He tipped an empty coffee mug toward the waitress working the counter. The woman, who looked like she'd spent the last fifty years locked inside a tanning bed, wiped her hands on her apron and came over, a coffee pot in her raisin-wrinkled hand.

"I'm not happy, just not surprised," Michelson said. "But who am I to judge? I spent the first five years of my career at the Bureau with one hand up my ass." The waitress filled his mug, and Michelson made a kissing sound to express his gratitude. "Tell me that's not decaf, hon. I'm gonna need the high-octane stuff to keep me going all night."

"It'll do the job," the woman answered, with an epic eye roll. "How about you, love?" she asked Tag. Her breath smelled like green mouthwash and cigarettes. "Getcha somethin'?"

"Uh, a plate of French fries, please," Tag answered.

The waitress nodded, her frizzy ponytail swishing. "Good choice. Our fries are a chef specialty. Besides, you only live once, right?"

She galumphed away, and Tag turned back to Michelson. She reached into her jacket pocket and pulled out the floppy disk that she'd found inside Sophie's closet.

Michelson's grin faded.

"I went to Sophie Whitestone's house this afternoon. I spoke with her mother," Tag said.

"And she gave you this?"

Tag shook her head. Under the table her knees bounced nervously.

"Christ. You found this in the old lady's house and—"

"I took it," Tag admitted. "Yes."

"That's a major no-no, Taggart. You can't just lift shit from people's houses without a warrant."

"I know. I didn't have a lot of time, and I made a snap decision. I found it hidden in Sophie's old room, inside the drywall."

"Inside a goddamn *wall*? Why are you bringing me into this? I've got less than eighteen months until I can punch out and spend my golden years on a beach somewhere, slurping tequila from some chickadee's bellybutton."

"There's something important on this disk."

"What? What's on it?" Michelson asked, rubbing his receding hairline. "Something worth losing your job over?"

Tag bit her lip. "I don't know. Maybe."

"Fantastic. This keeps getting better."

"I bought a remote drive, but the disk is password protected. And I can't send it to the tech guys because—"

"Because you stole the fucking thing."

"Right. What should I do? I'm pretty sure Mrs. Whitestone doesn't know that I have it. I could just get rid of it, throw it into the river."

Michelson clinked his wedding band on the side of his mug. "No, don't do that."

"Anything we find on here is inadmissible. I know that. Fruit of the poisonous tree, and all."

"I'm glad you paid attention to *something* at New Agent Training."

The waitress returned with Tag's fries. "Ketchup and mustard's on the table. Holler if you need me," she said, and swirled away again.

Michelson snatched a fry off Tag's plate and gnawed the end. "There are ways around that legal mumbo jumbo. Especially when there's intel about a legitimate terrorist threat."

"What?"

"It's been a hell of a day back at the ranch."

"Did we find Caleb Miller?"

Tag cringed at the sight of Michelson's expression—one of righteous indignation. His disdain wasn't unfounded, Tag knew, and that's why her intestines had tangled into knots. She had been so preoccupied with Dr. Jacobson, and then with Mrs. Whitestone, that she'd lost focus on the target of the investigation: Caleb.

Was that Jacobson's plan? Tag thought. *Distract me with a fantastic theory about past lives to throw me off?* Just like on her first day at Quantico, she was a girl out of her depth, and the crushing weight of a dark ocean was enveloping her.

"No, the little prick is still at large, but we searched his shithole apartment."

Tag chewed the inside of her cheek. "I should've been there for that."

"Hey, kid, you can't be everywhere. You've got leads, I've got leads. But at some point, maybe we should start running them down together instead of saving the bombshells for date night."

Tag nodded. "So, what did you find?"

"Turns out that pansy-ass porn Caleb watched every night wasn't just to facilitate a little midnight squirt. He had established quite a library of dirty downloads, most of them encrypted," Michelson explained.

"The porn vids were mules?"

"You got it. We fired his entire stash off to the nerds at the lab. They cracked the encryption and found reams of documents buried in the files. Scientific stuff. It went way over the heads of our analysts, but even I was smart enough to notice the logo in the header of most of the docs." Michelson held up his phone.

"Fermilab?" Tag asked. "That's the particle accelerator just west of the city. It's a Department of Energy facility, right?"

"Yeah, and from what I know, they're in the business of smashing weeny bits of the universe at warp speed."

Tag stirred a circle of ketchup with a fry, like a brush in a blot of wet paint. "Sounds dangerous."

"It's sounds like a pretty sexy soft target for a domestic terrorist," Michelson said. "You know they don't even restrict access to the laboratory campus out there? There's a goddamn public bike path running right through the heart of it."

Tag squinted. "The forensics team found these scanned documents on Caleb's computer? That—"

"Doesn't make a lick of sense, does it? He had us all thinking he was a silly bumpkin from the briar patch."

Tag hadn't thought that about Caleb. On the bridge downtown, the light behind the young man's eyes had shone brighter than most. Tag had always sensed that there was more to Caleb. Still, papers on particle physics disguised as softcore porn? Who was this man?

"Why attack the Chinese restaurant?" Tag asked. "If Fermilab is the real target, why tip us off with something so small scale?"

"Small scale?" Michelson leaned forward. "You need to get your head screwed on right. Miller killed two dozen people with that Chinatown bomb."

Tag blinked. "You're right. I didn't mean to sound insensitive. It's just, back in the nineties, the Sons of Elijah typically went for the big numbers. High body count. They targeted dense crowds."

"So, it was a test. Whoever is running the Sons now gave Caleb a job to prove himself. The South Side gangs do that shit all the time. Cartels too."

Tag didn't buy it. The Sons of Elijah weren't a gang or a Mexican drug cartel. Loyalty wasn't a question. According to Dr. Jacobson's book, the group's members felt an ancient calling—a responsibility they believed they carried lifetime after lifetime. A secret they'd sworn to protect. This particular club didn't accept new members. You had to be *born* into it.

"What the hell is that?" Michelson asked, wiping grease from his mouth.

"What?" Tag looked down at the smears on the table. Ketchup still dripped from the soggy French fry pinched between her fingers. Without realizing, she'd painted sticky red letters onto the Formica. It looked like something from a horror movie when the murderer scrawls out a warning in his victim's blood.

She pushed her plate aside. "Give me your laptop."

"Yeah, sure. No prob." Michelson pulled it out of his briefcase, and Tag yanked it away before he could set it down. She removed a remote disk drive from a Best Buy shopping bag and inserted its cord into Michelson's USB port.

"Whoa! Don't stick that hot potato in *my* hole. I'm already fucked just knowing about it."

Tag ignored her partner's protests and clicked the metal plug into place. Somehow, sitting in the booth, talking with Joe, the password to crack open Sophie's secret floppy disk had bubbled out of her subconscious. She'd painted the single word on the tabletop in tomato gore. Tag typed it into Michelson's computer and froze.

"Don't tell me there's porn on that disk too." Michelson said. "I can't afford a third strike."

Tag surveyed the diner, which was still mostly empty. The rough-skinned waitress was leaning into the kitchen, chatting with the line cook.

Tag had opened the only file saved to Sophie's floppy disk—a JPEG. She spun the laptop around so Michelson could see the image on the screen.

"Holy Mother of Satan," he whispered.

"How many people do you think someone could kill by triggering an accident at a particle accelerator?" Tag asked. "You know, the thing that smashes weeny bits of the universe at warp speed?"

"I don't have the slightest clue, but we'd better get our asses over there pronto. This shit's gonna be bad."

The waitress approached again. Coffee sloshed in her pot as she walked. Tag slammed the laptop closed.

"You all right, love?" the waitress asked, concerned.

"Tag, your neck. It's breaking out in a really disgusting rash," Michelson said. "You got some kind of allergy?"

Tag felt the bumps on her throat, which had dimpled like the skin of a basketball. It began to itch. "These fries," she said. "What exactly makes them a chef specialty?"

"Oh, Sam back there in the kitchen just calls them his specialty 'cause he thinks it makes 'em sound fancy. The old showboat just adds a spurt of honey to the oil, is all," the waitress answered. "Maybe you got a touch of reaction to the pollen protein in the honey. I have a cousin like that. Nothin' serious—should clear up in an hour with a glass of water and some fresh air." The waitress tilted her head to read the password Tag had written in ketchup on the table. "Who's Caleb?" she asked.

20

A PETITE WOMAN RAN toward the Crown Vic at top speed just as Tag and Michelson pulled into a parking space. Directly ahead, Fermilab's main building rose from the earth like a concrete volcano. Gray storm clouds laced with pink morning light billowed up from the Illinois plains, creating an ominous plume around the imposing edifice. Raindrops speckled Tag's windshield.

"Hurry! You've got to come inside," the woman shouted. She flapped her arms with each bounding stride like a goose struggling to lift off. Tight springs of black hair made a magnificent, bouncing halo around her head. If not for the woman's wall-to-wall smile, Tag would've considered reaching for her sidearm. Instead, she opened her door and stepped into the drizzle.

"We've got eight minutes, max. Let's go, I don't want you to miss this," the woman said.

"We're here to meet Dr. Alex Torres," Tag said.

"Yep, you're looking at her. And I know who you are too, but we can slap palms and bump gums later. Let's boogie."

"You're the director of Fermilab?" Michelson asked. "I expected—"

"A man?"

"Someone older," he clarified.

"The most powerful tech company in the world was started by twenty-year-old man in a cheap hoodie. I'm a thirty-year-old woman in a very *expensive* hoodie, and yet I can't tell you how many times I've gotten that reaction. Now, come on—we can still make it if we scoot."

Before Tag could respond, Dr. Torres had already begun fluttering back toward the building. Trotting along in her oversized hoodie (which didn't look all that expensive to Tag), Torres appeared like a child racing through the schoolyard during recess. And Tag noticed that Torres wasn't wearing shoes. One of the nation's leading particle physicists had just sprinted through a soggy parking lot barefoot. Tag grinned at her partner, and they followed the woman inside.

The swooping sides of Wilson Hall converged at a glass ceiling, resembling a futuristic cathedral. Inside the soaring atrium, fifty-foot oak trees grew from a maze of brick planters. Birds chirped in the lush canopy. A wiry man with silver sideburns met them at the door. He held out a pair of well-worn black flats.

"She can win the Nobel Prize, but she can't keep track of her own footwear," he said with a vaguely European accent that Tag couldn't place.

Dr. Torres's glasses fogged in the air-conditioned space, and she wiped them clean with the back of her wrist. "You're a lifesaver, Max." She hopped on one foot to slip on each shoe. "Have they started yet?"

"No, but it's just a routine diagnostic test. Another dry run. Dare I say, nothing to get excited about."

"There's nothing routine about smashing protons, my friend." Dr. Torres scrambled across the tile, waggling a finger above her head. "We've been waiting six months for this."

Max turned to Tag and Michelson. "You'll each need one of these to access the lab." He handed them yellow ID badges printed with the word *Visitor*. "An escort is required at all times while you're on the premises. My schedule is impossibly full, so you'll have to do your best to keep up with that one." He nodded to his boss, who was already rounding a corner up ahead. Tag thanked him, and the two FBI agents jogged to catch up to the physicist.

"We just need a few minutes of your time," Tag said as Dr. Torres pushed an elevator call button. "Can we sit down together somewhere private? Your office, maybe?"

"Fermilab *is* my office. And for the record"—she punched the button again, even though it had already lit up—"I don't sit. Boo, these simple machines are so painfully slow. Someone's idea of irony, I suppose. Sometimes I like to think if you stare intently enough at the doors, they'll slide right open."

On cue, the elevator arrived, and the trio stepped inside. The director clicked her tongue, marking the seconds as the car descended.

"Are you always this . . . rushed?" Michelson asked.

"Protons are immensely rude particles," the physicist explained. "They don't wait around for anyone." She winked at Tag. "Not even cute FBI agents."

"What experiment are you working on? May I ask?" Michelson folded his hands behind his back. Tag knew he did this to appear less threatening, but Dr. Torres didn't seem like someone who was easily intimidated. The young Mexican American woman had excelled in a field that prized the achievements of old white men. Joe Michelson's hairy knuckles weren't going to spook her.

"Of course, you can *ask*, but I won't tell you," Dr. Torres answered.

The Department of Energy operated Fermilab, but Tag knew how secretive the US government could be, even within its own ranks. "I suppose it's classified," she said.

"No, not at all. We're not like the other DOE labs. And by that, I mean we don't make warheads here. We're working to explain the nature of the universe. That knowledge should belong to everyone. Fermilab is the most open and generous collective of international scientists on the planet."

"Then why don't you start by telling us why you're in such a hurry to get wherever we're going?" Michelson pressed, showing his own impatience.

Dr. Torres leaned over and whispered in Tag's ear. The woman's curls tickled her cheek. "Don't you love watching the boys squirm?" she asked. "Why tell you when it's more fun to just *show* you?"

Tag smiled. Her partner glared at her. The elevator doors opened to reveal a long concrete tunnel. Parked steps away was a golf cart plastered with bumper stickers with phrases like "I was Plancking before it was cool."

They piled in, and the cart streaked through the tunnel at an impossible speed. An inadvertent jerk of the wheel would've launched them into the thick ceiling, skull-first. Dr. Torres seemed unphased.

"One of my guys modified the engine," she said. "We like fast things around here."

"Do you also like vomit in your hair?" Tag asked, only half joking.

"Our new particle accelerator clocks in just under one hundred and eighty-six thousand miles per second. That's 99.9 percent the speed of light." The physicist pulled a granola bar from the front pocket of her hoodie, steering the mini rocket ship with one hand. "This is nothin', sister."

They parked at the end of the tunnel in front of a locked door. Dr. Torres opened it with her ID badge. Tag and Michelson followed the woman into a cavernous room with steel crossbeams painted orange and blue. A massive cylindrical machine sat in the center of the space. It had to be three stories tall and looked like the barrel of a gigantic six-shooter, fully loaded.

"What is it?" Tag asked.

Dr. Torres closed her eyes and raised her hands above her head. "My idea of God Herself. Big Bertha, she's called. It took seven hundred physicists over eight years to put this groovy gal together. She's the paramount of perfection. My all-seeing eye."

"You didn't exactly answer my question."

"It's a particle detector. Best in the world. We use the accelerator to smash protons into things, and then she tells me how it all turned out. Isn't it poetic? It takes a full-bodied lady like her to observe the most minuscule particles that make up all matter."

"What are you looking for, with your all-seeing eye?" Michelson asked.

"The meaning of life, among other idiosyncrasies." Dr. Torres whistled through her bottom lip. A bit of granola flew from her mouth. "Yo, Antonio," she called out to a man perched at the top of a thirty-foot scaffolding.

"I didn't think physicists were typically so philosophical," Tag said.

"Yeah, most scientists hate that shit. Plenty of geeks only go for the hard stuff. But those of us who kneel at the temple of quantum mechanics don't have that luxury. We're philosophers by necessity."

The engineer—Antonio, Tag surmised—climbed down the steel latticework and approached. "It's going to be another month before this particle detector is up and running again. Our maintenance crew is working around the clock, but we shouldn't rush it. She can be a prissy lady."

"Yeah, I get it. You can't exactly bang on the hood of a billion-dollar machine to jangle it back into shape," Dr. Torres said. "Well, keep at it. You're doing the Lord's work."

"I thought you were running a test today," Tag said. "Is this delay a major setback?"

"Heck no! I misspoke before. I said Big Bertha was the best in the world, but that's only true for about another"—she tapped her watch—"eight minutes and fifteen seconds. The real star is another mile underneath our feet. *Bigger* Bertha. Although, I don't like to mention *her* in front of you-know-who." Dr. Torres ticked her head toward the particle detector. "Enough chitty-chat—we'd better get downstairs."

"We're taking an elevator a mile underground?" Michelson sounded concerned.

"Nah, the control room is only one floor down. We'll take the stairs. It's faster than waiting for those cursed metal boxes. Plus, we could probably use the exercise, yes?" She playfully patted Michelson's midsection with the back of her hand.

Within minutes, Tag, Michelson, and Dr. Torres were bathing in the cool blue light of a hundred digital screens. Ten other scientists had crammed into the control room with them, which could comfortably accommodate three or four at best. Dr. Torres blotted moisture from her forehead with a crumpled napkin. She unzipped her hoodie and draped it over the bent arm of a pudgy man with a hint of stubble on his chin. "Hold this, Patrick."

Dr. Torres had the physique of a twelve-year-old boy. Boxy hips, flat stomach, and long noodle arms. She wore a black T-shirt that had a graphic of a cat sitting on a cardboard box underneath the words "Don't even think about it."

"Are they on track to fire the first volley?" Dr. Torres asked Patrick.

"Thirty seconds," he replied.

"Until what?" Michelson asked.

"When a star explodes, it spits out these funny little particles called neutrinos. You'll find them in nuclear reactors too," Torres responded, offering no further explanation.

"Okay, so what happens in thirty seconds?" Michelson pressed.

"A high-energy beam of neutrinos is going to crash into us." Torres adjusted her glasses. "And now it's happening in twenty-one seconds. You might wanna grab onto something."

"You're shitting me."

"Shh. Just hold your breath and clamp your sphincter," Torres advised. "This won't hurt a bit."

Patrick counted down. "Three . . . two . . . one . . ."

The computer beeped and the handful of scientists in the room whooped and hollered. Dr. Torres launched a double high five into Patrick's waiting palms.

"Look at that! The detector is flaring up like she's having machine-gun orgasms," she chirped. "Fan-freakin'-tastic, fellas! What are they seeing in South Dakota?"

"Green across the board. All systems performed beautifully," Patrick answered.

"Did you say South Dakota?" Tag asked.

"We use Fermilab's accelerator for short-distance experiments, but long-distance tests are much more revealing. The farther the neutrino beam travels, the more chances it has to interact with other types of matter. There's another accelerator in the Black Hills National Forest. That's where these neutrinos came from," Dr. Torres explained.

"From South Dakota?" Tag squinted.

"Eight hundred and three miles," Torres confirmed.

"You built an underground tube that's eight hundred miles long?" Tag knew an undertaking like that would've been difficult to keep under wraps, if not impossible.

"Nope," Dr. Torres answered. "Neutrinos can pass through almost anything, even lead walls. We call them 'ghost particles.' Our buds in SD just fired them right through the earth's crust. No tube required. Then, Bigger Bertha's job was to gobble them up, and it looks like she did fine work of it."

"Wait, so the test is over? I barely blinked an eye," Michelson said.

"Actually, we could've run the test eighty or ninety times before your eyelid made even one pass over your cornea. Like I said before"—Torres smiled—"we like things fast around here."

"So, am I going to grow a third arm now from radiation exposure?" A line of sweat had formed above Michelson's eyebrows.

"Nah, I was just tugging your junk." Dr. Torres clapped the man on the back. "Neutrinos are completely harmless. In fact, about a hundred trillion pass through your body every second. They're literally everywhere, buzzing around us all the time."

"Forgive my ignorance in matters of particle physics, Dr. Torres, but if these neutrinos are so commonplace, why go through all of this effort to study them?" Tag asked.

Patrick chuckled in his chair. Dr. Torres scrunched her nose in a manner that Tag found instantly adorable. "That's exactly the point. It's their ubiquity that make neutrinos so mysterious. The universe loves balance. Actions and reactions, that sort of thing. The Big Bang, in the first moments of the universe's birth, should've coughed out an equal number of neutrinos and antineutrinos. These two types of particles are opposites, the building blocks of matter and antimatter, and they should've cancelled each other out and produced a fat bag of nothing. But that's not what happened, is it? We've got skateboards and garden hoses and donuts and moody teenagers and foxy federal agents." Dr. Torres clucked her tongue again. "A whole armful of sweet, juicy matter. So, we've got more neutrinos than antineutrinos, and thus matter won the day. Something tipped the scales, some kind of unknown force."

"And you're looking for this unknown force with your massive detector," Tag reasoned.

"Bingo," Dr. Torres said.

"Neat," Michelson said. "But kind of a waste of time. Not to mention the American taxpayer's money. Why does it even matter?"

The physicist snorted. "Why does it *matter*? Get it? Joking aside, this matters very much. If we figure this out, we'll know the very reason we exist."

"The meaning of life," Tag said. "You weren't exaggerating."

"A helluva cool job, dontcha think?" Dr. Torres grinned with a glint in her eye.

Tag smiled back and felt a rush of heat behind her ears. The young physicist's enthusiasm was magnetic.

"You're a scientist," Tag said. "You must have a hypothesis. What do you think it is, the invisible force that made the universe happen? If you built an eye this big, you must have an idea of what you're going to see."

"Yes, I do." Dr. Torres blew a coil of hair out of her face. "I'm going to find human consciousness."

"Excuse me?" Michelson said. "The ghost particle thing was a little cool—even though I'm not entirely sure what just happened here—but now I'm officially lost."

"Human consciousness. Like, your spirit or soul," Dr. Torres said casually. "I'm going to light it up, take a big ol' picture, and hang it above my fireplace."

"No offense to your Nobel Prize, but that sounds like some New Age bullshit." Michelson rubbed the bristles of his mustache.

"Hogwash. There's nothing *new* about it. For thousands of years, people have suspected the mind and the body were two different things. Annoyingly, classical physics doesn't allow for this duality. Supposedly, the thoughts running through your mind are simply electrochemical signals—just neurobiology. Baloney, says I! Quantum mechanics has really fudged things up for the old guard."

"You mentioned before that in your field everyone is a philosopher by necessity," Tag said. "Is that because others have also tried to prove a link between consciousness and the physical world?"

"No, it's more incredible than that," Dr. Torres said, smiling. "They already have."

"Here, at Fermilab?"

"No, in England. Over two hundred years ago. Except that guy didn't really know what he'd stumbled upon. It took another hundred years for scientists to figure it out, and that time it was a couple of dudes from right here in Illinois."

"I can't imagine that anyone had access to a machine like this a century ago," Michelson said.

"They didn't. But you don't need a billion-dollar detector to prove the existence of consciousness. You can do it with a piece of paper with two slits cut into it. Well, plus an electron gun, but those are a dime a dozen."

The trio returned to the golf cart, and Dr. Torres gestured at the wheel as if to say, *"You wanna drive?"* Tag grinned, but Michelson grabbed her elbow and shook his head. They'd come to gather intelligence, not to play with the toys. Tag yanked her arm away from her partner's grip and climbed into the passenger seat.

"Don't worry, I reserve turbo speed for science emergencies only. Anyhow, it works like this. Let's pretend you fire a single electron—a teensy-tiny particle—directly at a sheet of paper with two identical vertical slits cut into it. Then you repeat. Fire one more. And then again. Let me ask you: How many times do you predict that the single electron will pass through the slit on the left, and how many times will it scoot through the one on the right?"

"I suppose half the time it's the left one and half the time it's the right one," Tag answered. "Kind of a fifty–fifty split."

"Sort of. But it's way spookier than that. What happens to the electron depends on if you are *watching* it or not."

Tag squinted. "So, if I'm not looking at it, the electron will always choose the left slit or something?"

"No, if you're not watching, this single particle will actually pass through *both* slits simultaneously. But"—Dr. Torres waggled that finger again—"if you *observe* the little booger, it must pick one or the other. The very act of consciously watching *creates* the outcome. In quantum mechanics, we call this the measurement problem, but it's more like a measurement clusterfuck. We've proven that a particle, like our teensy electron, actually exists in all possible positions until an observer forces it to choose just one."

"This officially makes no sense," Michelson said from the back seat of the buzzing golf cart.

"That's what Einstein thought too. And Schrödinger. Remember his famous cat?"

"Like the one on your shirt?" Tag asked.

"Yep, Schrödy thought this idea was all bull dung. He wanted to demonstrate the absurdity of the measurement problem. Put a cat in a box along with a radioactive atom and a Geiger counter, he said. Then add a vial filled with hydrocyanic acid—poison—and a little hammer. Imagine the atom has a half-life of one hour, meaning there's a fifty–fifty chance it will decay within sixty minutes, and if it does, the Geiger counter will click and trigger the hammer to smash the vial. Poison is released. Dead cat. But if there's no decay, the vial remains unbroken and our kitty lives."

"That seems excessively complicated," Michelson said.

"Welcome to physics. Stay with me," Dr. Torres said. "I promise, it will be worth it. So, let's say we rig up Schrödy's contraption, close the lid, put our feet up, and watch a *Star Trek* rerun. *The Next Generation*, not that Captain Kirk foolishness. When we return to the box, there are two possible outcomes, right?"

"Dead cat or alive cat," Tag answered.

"Yeah. Except quantum mechanics says *both* outcomes exist until observed, so Miss Kitty would be both alive and dead at the same time."

Tag nodded. "Until someone opens the lid and sees which it is."

"That's right. Which is totally bananas. A cat can't be both alive and dead simultaneously. Schrödinger thought he'd illustrated the fatal flaw with the whole idea, and everyone could just go home."

"But I'm assuming he was wrong," Tag said.

Dr. Torres nodded. "When it comes to particles anyway. Jury's out on cats. Thing is, if anyone could actually replicate Schrödinger's wackadoo kitty-in-box scenario, accounting for a bazillion different variables, it might actually work. Who knows?"

"This guy didn't try it himself?" Michelson asked.

"Hell no. The cat thing was a thought experiment. A theoretical cat. Personally, I like *real* pussy." Dr. Torres flipped her hair dramatically, and it brushed against Tag's cheek.

Michelson laughed. "Now you're speaking my language."

"Let's take Schrödy's thought experiment even further," the physicist continued. "What if, when you open the lid to his box, you don't just *see* what happened to the cat, whether it lived or died? What if, as a watcher, your consciousness actually *creates* the outcome? Just like when the electron passed through the slit."

"So, we can kill cats with our minds," said Tag. "It does sound absurd."

"Thank you." Michelson threw up his arms.

"Well, I'm oversimplifying the situation for educational purposes," Torres admitted.

"I appreciate that," Michelson shouted over the hum of the cart's motor. "But it's still a little hard to swallow."

"It's all theoretical anyway" Dr. Torres continued. "Only an experiment will prove if I'm right."

"That's what you're preparing for, isn't it?" Tag asked. "Here at Fermilab."

Torres picked her teeth. With one hand on the wheel, the golf cart drifted toward the wall before she corrected its course. "You think I'm cuckoo. I've seen that look before."

Tag laughed and held up her palms. "There's no look, I promise. This is all so . . ."

"Batshit?"

"Yep, that's the word," Michelson answered.

"I was going to say *unusual*," Tag corrected.

"Well, then I must be doing something right. I didn't go into science to seek out the *usual*." They reached the end of the tunnel, and Dr. Torres stopped the cart. "Bottom line: I hypothesize that human consciousness is a force that's been around since the very beginning—billions of years before human bodies even existed. That means our consciousness is completely separate from our biological brain, with properties we do not yet understand. It has the ability to influence matter and maybe do even more than that." Dr. Torres's dark eyes grew intense as she spoke. "No one has ever detected it before, but that doesn't make it any less real. And until we find it, the scientific establishment will just continue to explain it away with lame theories or, worse, ignore the phenomenon, as they have for the past century."

"What if you're wrong?" Michelson asked. "How can you be so sure consciousness really exists as a force if no one has ever found it?"

"That's how particle physics works. We can prove something exists even if we can't detect it directly. Okay, here's another scenario. No cats this time, don't worry. Imagine you're watching a tennis match for the first time, and you have no idea how the game works. Except in this version only the players can see the ball. It's invisible to you and the other spectators. The players are swinging their rackets and grunting like hogs, darting around the court. It's obvious they're smacking something back and forth across the net, and if you're crazy enough to watch this madness long enough, you'd start to figure out where the *thing* is that they're hitting, and probably how fast it's traveling. You would never have to actually *see* the fuzzy green ball to know it existed. Think of my neutrinos as the tennis players smacking around invisible particles."

"But you said neutrinos can pass through anything, like ghosts," Tag said. "How are they supposed to smack into something?"

"I said *almost* anything. We've observed neutrinos interacting with some forms of matter, in the way many other particles do. That's what led me down this path in the first place. Then a few years ago, I discovered something super strange. My neutrinos—these so-called ghost particles— were bouncing off something that all other particles seemed to ignore. Totally the opposite of what you'd expect. This invisible . . . thing pushes back on them, like our tennis racket. It's gotta be another undiscovered particle. One that's as powerful as it is elusive. That's what I'm looking for."

"How long does it take to find an undiscovered particle?" Tag asked.

"We knew about the Higgs boson particle for fifty years before scientists finally found it in 2012. Those boys called it the 'God particle' but, man, they had no idea Big C was out there."

Tag cocked her head. "Big C?"

"That's what I'm calling the force of consciousness—my elusive particle. Other scientists have looked for it too, but no one has even come close to nailing it down."

Michelson scratched his chin. "You really think you're going to find something that none of those guys could wrap their hands around."

Dr. Torres whipped her head to face Agent Michelson, who was spread out in the backseat. Tag put a hand on the physicist's shoulder as if to say, *"Pay no attention to the oaf in the cheap suit."*

"Those *guys* can't find the graviton either," Torres snapped.

"What the hell is a graviton?" Michelson asked.

"The hypothetical particle that explains the phenomenon of gravity. No one's ever detected it, but we're pretty sure that one's real too. Wanna come up to the roof of Wilson Hall for a demonstration?"

Michelson smirked. Tag knew how much he loved getting under people's skin. *Under women's skin.*

"Your work sounds fascinating, Dr. Torres. We appreciate the explanation," Tag said, and glared at Michelson. "*Both* of us."

"It's just the beginning," Dr. Torres continued, cooler now. "There are still plenty of scientists who think my entire theory is wrong, that Big C is just a myth. That's why I want to find it. I want to stare it in the eye, measure it, and put it in a glass case for all to behold."

Tag inhaled, considering whether or not to ask the next question. Finally, she said: "Out of curiosity—"

"I'm familiar with the concept. Shoot." Dr. Torres touched Tag's knee. The gesture filled Tag's stomach with a warm jelly feeling.

"Could this experiment explain where we go . . . after we die?"

Tag immediately felt foolish for broaching the topic. Michelson groaned.

Dr. Torres, however, considered her question carefully. The physicist fished another granola bar out of the cart's glove box. "I'm no priest, so I won't claim to have the answer to that one, but I can say this: if our consciousness is an energy force carried by a subatomic particle, one that's truly distinct from our brains and our physical bodies, then it's possible this particle would endure after what we know as death. Energy is neither created nor destroyed, or so our laws tell us. Maybe the body dies and the Big C particle just floats away, off to find another host."

"So we're immortal?" Tag asked.

"Probably," Dr. Torres answered before biting off a generous end of the granola bar. "But like I said, I'm no priest."

Tag weighed the possibility. Maybe a soul or spirit, or whatever you wanted to call it, could live independently of the body forever. The notion would seem to explain why Dr. Jacobson's patients claimed to remember living before as other people in other bodies. Dr. Torres's research could fundamentally alter the way people perceived the human experience. Religion, physics, medicine, philosophy—her discovery would fuse everything. That would definitely piss some people off.

People like the Sons of Elijah? Do they want to stop Dr. Torres by sabotaging her experiment?

"Dr. Torres. My partner and I came to Fermilab for information, and you've offered more than I could have hoped for . . ."

"Sure, no problem," the physicist said.

"But we also came with a warning," Tag added.

Dr. Torres's cheek twitched, and she straightened her glasses. "Okay, what's going on?"

"The FBI has reason to believe a known terrorist organization may be targeting Fermilab. Your experiment, and possibly your life, may be in danger."

21

"So, this particle accelerator is going to go haywire and create a miniature black hole? Punch through the space–time continuum? Is that it?" Acting SAC Gina Butler asked. She fussed with the silk scarf tied around her neck, turning it a notch to get the decorative knot in just the right place. With her hair twisted into a tight bun, she looked like a no-nonsense flight attendant.

"Nothing like that," Tag said. She leaned forward and the office chair squeaked. "The accelerator whips subatomic particles through a four-mile circular tube until they crash into a solid target, like graphite, but I'm told that's really nothing compared to the speed of the particles that naturally hit the earth every day."

"Apparently exploding stars on the other side of the universe are raining shit down on us constantly," Michelson clarified.

"Congratulations on learning something new today, Joe," Butler said. "If the accelerator isn't dangerous, then what? How is Caleb Miller going to attack the lab?"

"Everyone on the task force is focusing on the accelerator because smashing protons at top speed sounds scary," Tag explained. "In reality, it's the massive detector we should be concerned about."

Butler drummed the table with her pen impatiently. "What the hell is a detector?"

"It's the thing they built underground to keep track of the smashing," Michelson said. "The fucker's five stories tall and longer than four football fields. Plus it's filled with liquid argon."

"Seventy thousand tons of liquid argon," Tag added. "The particle detector is an enormous piece of electronics built into a carved-out pocket of the earth, a mile deep. It's like a ship in a bottle."

"A cold-ass ship." Michelson leaned back with his hands behind his head.

"Yes, argon is a cryogenic liquid. They store it at negative one hundred and eighty-four degrees Celsius," Tag reported.

"And argon," Butler said, "is flammable. That's the issue?"

"No, actually," Tag answered. "To keep it cold, they use liquid nitrogen kept under pressure. A *lot* of pressure. And if that pressure were suddenly released—"

"Our ship explodes and breaks the bottle," Butler reasoned.

"Except in this case, the *bottle* is the Central Plains of the United States," Michelson added.

"You're kidding." Butler adjusted her scarf again, a tick back to the right. "It's buried so deep underground, though. Wouldn't that contain the explosion?"

"The depth is actually the main problem. We consulted with seismologists from the US Geological Survey this afternoon. Hypothetically speaking, they believe an explosion releasing that much energy at that specific underground location would trigger a catastrophic earthquake. They estimate it could hit a magnitude of nine-point-five on the Richter scale. That's equivalent to twenty-five thousand nuclear bombs."

"So, Chicago is fried," Butler said.

"And Indianapolis, Columbus, Detroit. The shocks could even reach the East Coast," Tag said.

"What's the estimated damage here?" Butler asked. "Give me the body count."

"Ten to twenty million, maybe. That's just from the initial damage. Then there would be widespread homelessness, chronic medical conditions, suicides."

"The Midwest would be one big hellhole," Michelson added.

"I get it, Joe," Butler snapped. She ripped off her scarf completely and shoved it into her pocket. Her eyelid had begun to twitch again. "Okay, call a meeting of the Sons of Elijah task force. We'll regroup in the command center. We're going to figure out how to catch this son of a bitch Miller and whoever's been feeding him those engineering documents. It's got to be someone working on the project. We'll need personnel records of everyone with access at Fermilab."

"Already requested," Tag said. "We'll have them within the hour. Dr. Torres is fully cooperating with our investigation, even though she doesn't seem too concerned herself."

"A terrorist is plotting to obliterate her lab, and she's not worried about that?"

"We showed her the docs we recovered from Caleb's computer. Dr. Torres says they're decades out of date, almost like digitized photocopies from the archives. Most of that tech was scrapped years ago."

"Well, I'm glad the director is such a cool cucumber, but I don't have the luxury of being so dismissive." Butler pushed back from the table. "Round up the team. We'll meet in fifteen."

Agent Michelson slipped a pen behind his ear and stood. His shirt had come untucked in the back. "Great, cause I gotta do a wee."

He left the conference room, leaving Butler and Tag alone together.

"There's something else," Tag said.

"You've just told me that a madman is plotting to spoon America's greatest city right out of the crust of the earth. What else could there be, Agent Taggart?"

Tag removed a piece of paper from a folder. She'd printed the image saved on Sophie's floppy disk.

Butler examined the page. "You've got to be shitting me," she murmured.

"It seems there's more to Caleb Miller than we'd thought."

"Dr. Jacobson had to know about this. He concealed this from us."

"I agree," Tag said.

Butler popped her lips. "Tell you what. Joe can handle the ops planning with the rest of the task force. Find Jacobson. Figure out what the hell this is about."

"Yes, ma'am."

Butler tossed the printout onto the table and marched out of the room. The acting SAC would take charge, lead them through this. Tag admired the woman's ability to perform under pressure.

She reached for the page. On it was an image of a woman's hand holding a black and white photo. Printed in boxy letters at the top of the photo were the words "PATIENT: WHITESTONE, SOPHIE." Scrawled along the bottom, in Sophie's purple handwriting, was the name "CUTTER, CALEB," right underneath a sonogram image of a fetus in utero. Caleb was Sophie's son. And his birth name wasn't Miller. It was Cutter.

Gerald Cutter, Dr. Jacobson's *other* murderous patient, was Caleb's father.

22

Tag left the conference room and ducked into a stairwell. Each footfall on the aluminum steps echoed off the concrete walls. On TV, the interior of FBI offices looked so sleek and modern—all glass with digital screens ten feet tall, like fighting crime from the bridge of a starship. Hollywood didn't dare capture the reality: the rare window, completely blacked out to prevent nosey Russians from sneaking a peek; the wilted ficus in the corner, crying out for a ray of something other than green-tinted fluorescent light; and don't forget the cadaver walls. That's what Tag had noticed first, after swiping her ID badge and stepping into the bleak world of federal law enforcement. Walls, ceilings, *and* doors—painted a particular gray as pallid as a three-day-old corpse.

The color often triggered a memory from her first day at New Agent Training, when an instructor had passed around an infamous three-ring binder. The Barf Book, he'd called it. It contained police photographs of especially gruesome scenes—decapitations, oozing stab wounds, a woman with her red intestines spilling from a smiling slit across her belly.

And some recruits *did* actually barf. The instructors knew to keep a close eye on those.

The bloody gore hadn't bothered Tag. The few images in the book that had disturbed her deeply, however, were the drowning victims. Pulled from an icy river or scraped off some slimy lakebed, these puffy bodies lacked any color at all. Cadaver gray. Just like the FBI's death walls.

Tag reached the second floor and entered the analyst wing. Keyboards chattered from within the maze of padded cubicles. It sounded like a nest of clicking beetles. Tag had no doubt that if she peered into any one of the cubes, she'd see a pair of black, glassy eyes blinking in the blue glow of a computer screen.

Declan Walsh's workstation sidled right up to the wide oak door to the supervisory intelligence analyst's office. This drab corner was the second floor's center of power, if such a thing even existed, so naturally a man like Declan had insisted on locating his desk there. One could always find the largest beetle flitting around the brightest lamppost.

"I need your help," Tag announced, approaching Declan's cube. The man wasn't huddled over his terminal, scrutinizing FD-302 interview reports like his cohorts. He sat on the edge of his desk with one foot perched on the armrest of his swivel chair and an unlit cigar gripped between his teeth. And he was wearing a tuxedo. "Did I miss something?" Tag asked.

"What? Only agents can solve crimes in black-tie attire?" Declan asked.

"You look—"

"Like a fuckin' stud; you can say it, Taggart. It's okay to admire, even if you bat for the other team." Declan's grin spread so wide Tag could've counted his every tooth. "I'm only bustin' your balls. Just got this bad boy back from the cleaners and wanted to take a little test drive," he explained, smoothing his silky lapel. "The Black and Blue Ball is tomorrow, or did you forget?"

The Black and Blue Ball was the annual event at which senior FBI leadership and the Chicago Police Department's top brass rubbed elbows in some downtown ballroom. Rookie agents weren't invited to such festivities—not that Tag gave a damn. She had no appetite for shiny dresses or small talk, both of which were requirements at these soirées. Not to mention the shameless brownnosing.

"You know I'm not going to that. You've got to have at least three letters preceding your name to even get a seat."

"Well, that's typically the case, I suppose. Butler's reserved an entire table this year, right beside the stage. She selected a few of us to attend as her special guests. You know: her top performers. Rumor has it they're promoting her to the big job, and the director is flying in to make the announcement at the gala. It's going to be a helluva night." Declan slid open a drawer and produced a stainless-steel flask. "Something to toast to," he continued, and then took a nip from the stubby neck. "Want a swig?"

Tag scowled. "No," she answered with contempt. "Drinking's not allowed on duty."

"A lot of things aren't allowed on duty. But I didn't think that stopped someone like you, Tag." There was that grin again—roguish, bordering on wicked.

Sure, Tag had had her issues with compliance, but she didn't subvert the rules just for the hell of it. Men like Declan seemed to take joy in the sheer act of defiance, like a toddler testing his parents to see what he could get away with. Sadly, in Declan's case, it was a lot. Tag had heard the stories, about how the man had actually begun his FBI career as a special agent. He had risen to the head of his Quantico class, and he would've led the graduation procession if the director of the Training Division hadn't discovered that Declan had slept with a half dozen of the female recruits. Fraternization on the FBI Academy campus was prohibited, even when it was consensual. The Bureau had threatened to expel Declan from the program, but he'd hired a high-profile attorney and sued, claiming sexual discrimination. None of the women had been reprimanded, he'd argued. The FBI had settled quietly, and the public affairs office had managed to keep the matter out of the press, but everyone in the building knew the dirty details. Declan would remain employed, the agreement stated, but he would not serve as a special agent. Instead, the Bureau made him an analyst. A fate worse than termination, by some people's standards.

Unfortunately, he was also the best analyst in Chicago, and she needed answers.

"You've been following the Caleb Miller case?" Tag asked.

"Not until about two days ago. I wasn't assigned to the task force, but Butler pulled me in. She said she wasn't getting results from the team."

Tag glowered.

Declan smirked. "Hey, I'm just reporting the facts. We've all had our turn under Gina's thumb. You're nobody special, Taggart. Just let me know how I can help."

He held out his flask—his version of an olive branch, Tag supposed. Why hadn't Butler mentioned that she'd added another intel analyst to the team? She listened to the swishing alcohol lapping at the steel, and caught herself looking over her shoulder, considering an illicit taste. Declan bit down on his lower lip, and his cheekbones raised into chiseled points. He was daring her to take a drink and declare herself a phony and a hypocrite.

Tag shook her head and returned to business. "Miller had confidential documents from Fermilab on his computer. I need to know how he got them."

"Someone at the facility fed them to him, probably. An insider."

"That's my thought too, and Fermilab's security office is looking into it, but—"

"But you don't trust them," Declan said. "Smart girl. I wouldn't either. A breach of security would trigger a very public audit of the lab. Congress might even freeze federal funding until the issue was resolved."

"The lab's director is in the midst of a breakthrough experiment," Tag explained. "She doesn't want this investigation to cause any delays."

"A terrorist attack would certainly fuck up her time line. More than an audit would."

Tag nodded. Dr. Torres certainly understood the threat that Caleb and the Sons of Elijah posed, but she'd likely weighed the risks with the benefits. Her experiment could have a profound impact on the world's understanding of human sentience, and Torres had sounded so determined to succeed. Would that mean she'd purposefully stifle Tag's investigation, hold back personnel records of staff with access to the type of documents found on Caleb's hard drive? Tag hoped not. Dr. Torres seemed trustworthy. Still, Tag couldn't rely on Fermilab to help her find the leak. Butler wanted results, after all.

"The techs have already combed through Caleb's laptop, cloud storage, email, and social media accounts. We have a handful of leads, but nothing looks too promising," Tag went on.

"So, you've got to trace the info itself. Who wrote it, read it, shared it, jerked off to it in the shower—shit like that. It could be hundreds of people. It would take most analysts an eternity."

"Most analysts, sure," Tag said. "But you're a fuckin' stud, right?"

Declan groaned, "Oh for Chrissake. Climb off my jock before I blow a load, will ya?" He held his cigar to his crotch like a stiff finger and ran his hand up and down the shaft. "I took Sheppard's Quantico course on ego manipulation too, you know. That BS won't work on me."

"But you'll help?"

"Fine, whatever," Declan answered. "But only because I hate terrorists more than I hate that stupid smirk on your face." He hopped off his desk and stepped out of his cubicle.

"Where are you going?"

"If I'm going to be digging around for moles, I don't want to get my tux dirty," he replied over his shoulder. "Don't touch my hooch while I'm changing in the john."

Declan disappeared into the men's room, and Tag's eyes flicked back to his flask. The arrogant asshole had left it sitting beside his keyboard in plain sight. *Unbelievable.* Though if anyone walked by and spotted it, would they even say a word? Tag could never get away with such flagrant flouting of the Bureau's rules.

Or could I? she thought.

She peeked around the cubicle wall. The entire floor was quiet except for the soft crackle of computer keys. Tag eyed the flask, which reflected the glow of Declan's screensaver. She reached for it, her hand moving autonomously now, even as every fine hair on her arm raised like little warning flags, urging her to stop.

A lot of things aren't allowed on duty. But I didn't think that stopped someone like you, Declan had said.

Someone like me, Tag thought. *And who is that exactly? Someone who needs to buck up and take charge of this case, that's who. Take charge of her* life. *Rules be damned.*

With a swoop of her hand, she swiped the flask, unscrewed its cap, and pressed it to her lips. The liquid ran cool down her throat. She took a hearty guzzle, but it didn't burn. Because it wasn't liquor. Declan had filled his flask with tap water.

23

"SPECIAL AGENT TAGGART?" Dr. Jacobson answered the door wearing a navy-blue robe with silver buttons. A wedge of tan skin peeked out from the neckline. "You're soaked. Please, come in."

The soft warble of a woman's vibrato dribbled from speakers in the ceiling. Orange lamplight coated the walnut-paneled walls. The psychiatrist's lips were purple. A wineglass sat on a brass console in the foyer, nearly empty.

"I considered calling, but you probably wouldn't have answered your phone this late," Tag said. She wiped rainwater from her face. Her spiked hair had listed to one side like a sad puppy's droopy ear. "I'm just glad you're home."

"You deemed it too late for a phone conversation, yet you assumed I'd answer my front door?"

Tag shrugged. In truth, she had given the idea to drop in on Jacobson unannounced a fifty–fifty shot of working, and that was only if she went alone. If she'd showed up with Michelson, as a pair of federal agents flashing their FBI creds into the peephole, Jacobson would've popped in earplugs and made a note to ring his attorney in the morning.

Tag had taken a chance, and it seemed she had sized up the man well enough. Despite his swollen ego and tasteless vanity, Dr. Jacobson had a healer's heart. He wouldn't ignore a young woman standing on his porch in a downpour. Just as he wouldn't have suspected Tag of shoving her umbrella into the neighbor's manicured shrub just before tousling her hair and climbing the psychiatrist's front steps.

"It's important," Tag said. "Otherwise, I wouldn't have disturbed you."

"Are you here on America's business or your own?" Jacobson asked tentatively.

"I'm not sure how to separate the two anymore," she answered. A puddle formed around her feet. "Geez, I'm dripping all over your really nice marble."

"It's fine. You're shivering. Let me get you a towel."

The doctor returned moments later with a plush white bath sheet monogrammed with his initials.

"You live alone?" Tag asked, rubbing her head with the towel.

Jacobson frowned. "It's nearly midnight. Evidently you have something on your mind, or you wouldn't have appeared on my doorstep looking like you'd just crawled out of Lake Michigan. You knew no one else was here before you arrived. Just like you knew I was awake. I'm fully aware of the parade of dark sedans that have suddenly found my street such an appealing place to loiter. So, with all due respect, let's just get to it. Why did you come?"

"I met with the director of Fermilab out in Batavia. Dr. Alex Torres. She's conducting a . . . controversial experiment," Tag said.

"That's the best kind, if you ask me."

"She believes human consciousness is a kind of force, like gravity, and it exists independent of the brain."

"Not exactly a revolutionary idea."

"No, but with this experiment, she expects to prove it," Tag explained.

"And I imagine this effort has cost—what? Five, ten billion dollars? An army of government scientists is now expending vast resources to verify what my research has demonstrated for nearly thirty years. The question is: Will it matter? Do you think people will believe this Dr. Torres any more than they believe me just because she uses fancy machines, whereas I use a lounge chair?"

"She's a very accomplished—"

"Accomplishment has an entirely different standard in the modern world," Dr. Jacobson interrupted. "The great minds of the past—Newton, Einstein, Freud—pursued science to explain the nature of human existence. They were philosophers as much as they were disciplined technicians. Somewhere along the way, that changed. Science became exclusively about the objective observation of our environment. It's ridiculously narrow-minded. That's exactly why we've missed so much. Try to publish an academic, peer-reviewed paper about consciousness or the soul, or whatever you prefer to call it, and suddenly you're classified as a mystic. Thrown in with the tarot card readers and astrologists."

"But if Dr. Torres succeeds, if she detects a consciousness particle, don't you think—"

"I think she'll sell a truckload of books. They'll fly off the shelves of the New Age and Spirituality section."

"Is she right, though? Do you think consciousness can be detected, even *measured*—that it's like electromagnetism or gravity? It sounds like science fiction, but could it be possible?"

Dr. Jacobson sighed and turned away. "Let me get you a drink."

Tag followed him through a hallway decorated with more framed photographs of the psychiatrist grinning, shoulder to shoulder, with a parade of celebrities—A-list actresses, Olympic gold medalists, three former US presidents. Jacobson fit in comfortably with the rich and famous.

They entered a study with soaring bookshelves that rose two stories, the top shelf accessible by an iron ladder that slid on a metal rail. A stately desk, carved from a single block of wood, sat in the center of the room. The only light emanated from two brass lamps resting on opposite corners of the desk. Dr. Jacobson gestured to a tufted leather Chesterfield sofa that was flanked by two windows looking out onto the misty East Scott Street.

"Wine or whiskey?" he asked, businesslike, while retrieving a pair of glasses from a bar cart.

"I don't think I should," Tag answered.

"If we're going to discuss matters of the universe, we'll need some creative lubrication, Special Agent Taggart." He turned and flashed his toothy whites. "It's practically required."

The truth was, a drink sounded spectacular, and even though Tag had fully intended to elicit intelligence from Jacobson, she didn't want to give him the impression that she was officially on the clock. The doctor had stuck to his careful script during all prior interactions with FBI agents. None of them had cracked his seal. *Maybe because none of them was reckless enough to try a social visit to his home in the middle of the night,* she thought. *None of them drank hard liquor with the man while he paraded around in a silk bathrobe.* Whatever she'd gotten herself into, it was too late to back out now. Tag felt stress knots in her shoulders and exhaled.

"Whiskey, then," she answered.

"Atta girl."

Dr. Jacobson handed her a generous serving of what had to be the most expensive whiskey she'd ever tasted. Complex and dignified, yet dangerously intoxicating.

"So, are you going to answer my question?" Tag asked. "Is it possible that consciousness is actually a physical force?"

The psychiatrist pulled heavy curtains across the windows and then sat on the arm of the sofa. He swirled his glass, squinting pensively. "In the 1980s, there was group of researchers working in the basement of a Princeton engineering hall," he said. "They toiled down there for years. It was called the Princeton Engineering Anomalies Research Lab—the PEAR

Lab. They ran simulations on these machines that were pro-
grammed to generate random patterns, like endless coin flips.
These machines produced mathematically random results,
flip after flip. Heads or tails, heads or tails. The researchers
sat people down in front of the simulators and asked them
to focus on the computer-generated coin and think 'heads.'
Just stare at a screen and imagine the flipping coin landing on
heads. No keys or buttons. No physical interaction with the
machine at all. Just pure concentration. *Heads. Heads. Heads.*"
Jacobson flicked the side of his glass with his fingernail with
each repetition of the word. "After thousands of tests with
hundreds of subjects, do you know what they found?"

Tag shook her head.

"Indeed, the supposedly randomized, computer-generated coin landed on heads more often than it should have.
Quite a bit more often."

"That's impossible."

"Wait—it gets better." Dr. Jacobson took another sip,
pausing for suspense, Tag presumed. "These tests were boring as hell for the participants. They took a long time to
run, and the subjects would get burned out. So PEAR experi-
mented with ways to spice things up, mostly using pictures
instead of coins. In one version of the test, they superim-
posed two images on top of each other. Both images were
filled in with about half of their total pixels, so if you looked
at the screen, you'd see both pictures faintly. The random-
izer machine would then begin filling in the missing pixels,
slowly bringing both images to completion at an equal rate.
The observers were instructed to pick their favorite image
and concentrate on its pixels filling in more quickly, effectively blotting out the other one."

"And you're going to tell me they could do this too? Just
like the coin flip, the test subjects could will one image to
develop faster just by thinking about it?"

"No," Jacobson said. "Not this time. Of the forty pictures
the research team tried, most yielded nothing interesting.

The pixels filled in at the same rate for most of these images, no matter how hard the observer concentrated."

"You said *most*."

"That's right. Most were duds, but not all. *Six* of the images consistently beat out the others when people focused on them."

"What made those six so special?"

"All six of these winning images contained Christian iconography, and all of the participants who willed them to fill in faster were Catholic. The conclusion was stunning. The observers' ability to influence the supposedly random process, to tip the scale in favor of their preferred image, was amplified when the target of their concentration held emotional significance. Simply put, if they *cared* about the picture, it juiced their brain power."

"So, we're the X-Men. We can control machines with our minds. Neat."

"To some very small degree, yes, that appears to be the case. According to a bunch of Ivy League eggheads with a lot of free time, at least."

"You were right about the whiskey." Tag took a healthy swig. "If this is true, why doesn't everyone know about it? It's kind of incredible."

"Like I said, when you start talking about the metaphysical power of human consciousness, let alone spend decades studying it, you're dismissed as a quack. PEAR was an embarrassment to the entrenched scientific establishment at the prestigious Princeton University. No reputable grant would give them a dime, and almost no academic journal would publish their findings. The lab survived off private, anonymous funding until the University finally shut it down."

"Dr. Torres's experiment at Fermilab could corroborate everything PEAR found," Tag said.

"And everything I've found too. Perhaps physics paired with psychology will solve the greatest mystery of humanity." Jacobson leaned over the couch. His breath smelled like freshly mowed grass. "And then do you know what will happen?"

Tag wiggled on the couch, attempting to get a little space.

"Everyone will dismiss Dr. Torres as a kook too," the doctor whispered. He rose and ambled back to the window, peering out of the slit between the drawn curtains.

Or she'll get her own multimillion-dollar book deal and wall of celebrities, Tag thought. "Not everyone will dismiss her. Some people are pretty damn worried about what Torres is working on. They'll try to stop her."

"People like the Sons of Elijah?" Jacobson asked. "That's obviously what concerns you. It's why you came here tonight."

Tag nodded. "I still don't understand their motive. The Sons believe in reincarnation of the soul. They claim to have lived over and over again as different people, going back centuries."

"That's right. And based on my sessions with Sophie and Gerald, I tend to believe they did. I spent almost two years researching their remembered lives. I catalogued over three hundred verifiable details between the two of them—things they should have no information about, like the clothing of medieval cult members or the names of fourth-century bishops."

"But for the Sons' ideas about reincarnation to be correct, the mind or the soul would have to live on after the body dies. An immortal substance. Dr. Torres's experiment could *prove* this. Why would the Sons of Elijah want to stop her?"

"On its face, it's counterintuitive. I agree." Dr. Jacobson sat at an arm's length from Tag. His robe spread open another inch. "In many of Sophie's remembered past lives, she'd fought against those who'd attempted to stamp out the concept of reincarnation. Sophie, as Eusebius the Bishop, murdered Constantine—the emperor who tried to erase reincarnation from Christian doctrine. As Ramon Perella, the seigneur of Montségur, she attempted, and failed, to protect the reincarnation-believing Cathars from the French Inquisition. In both cases, Sophie stood up against powerful, oppressive forces, all to ensure the survival of this simple idea of rebirth."

"The Sons should embrace Dr. Torres's project, not try to sabotage it. Finally, it could vindicate everything they believe in," Tag said.

"Not necessarily. Transmigration of the soul was a deeply spiritual experience to the Sons of Elijah. The human spirit moves from body to body for a specific purpose: to purify itself. This progression through lifetimes brings us closer to God, they believed. If modern science somehow determined that consciousness was a *physical* force, not a spiritual one, the entire event of reincarnation becomes rather mechanical, don't you think? The soul is reduced to something as mundane as an electric current, and the body is merely a lightbulb. If one burns out, screw in a replacement. The current doesn't change at all. It just . . . exists. And what's worse, in this rather bleak paradigm—"

"There is no God," Tag interjected. "We're all just particles governed by the rules of physics. Dr. Torres's experiment could explain life, but in so doing, it could strip it of its very meaning."

Dr. Jacobson finished his last swig of whiskey. "The Greek philosopher Democritus warned us, 'Nothing exists except atoms and space; everything else is opinion.' A particle physicist like Dr. Torres might agree, but those are fighting words to a group that's worked for millennia to protect their spiritual truth."

Tag set her empty glass on a coffee table. "I guess that's motive after all."

"Perhaps." The psychiatrist stroked his Adam's apple. "But there's something about the Sons of Elijah that I've always found disturbing."

"More disturbing than the suicide bombings?"

"Those attacks were horrific acts of violence, but like you said before, it's the group's lack of a clear motive that baffles me. Take Sophie Whitestone. I've never figured out what triggered her. I believe she felt completely justified, that the attack was for some greater good, but I just don't see how it had anything to do with protecting the spiritual concept of reincarnation. Same goes for Gerald. He murdered his wife, Linda, because she abused him in her quest for information. But what was it? Hypnotherapy had worked wonders for them both, but in those final days, fear consumed them."

"The suicide bombings were acts of desperation. They were protecting something," Tag reasoned.

"Sophie and Gerald had achieved a remarkable sense of awareness. It was as if someone had handed them a book filled with pages explaining every life they'd lived on earth. They felt a weighty responsibility; I could sense it."

In Tag's dream, Ramon had sacrificed the men, women, and children of the Cathar village to prevent the Capstone from falling into French hands.

Not just any French hands, Tag thought. *Inquisitor Ferrier's hands.*

Ramon had been terrified of that man. A dark obsession had driven Ferrier. The inquisitor had desperately wanted something only Ramon could give him. Gerald Cutter had described Jean-Lambert Tallien the same way in his remembered life as a scullery maid, at least according to Dr. Jacobson's book.

"He's looking for something. He's wanted it for centuries," Gerald had said, explaining the nature of Tallien's bloodlust. And hadn't Gerald believed that his wife, Linda, was the reincarnation of this ruthless French politician?

Ferrier, Tallien, Linda. Maybe they all represent the same soul, traversing a string of bodies through centuries of time, gripped by the same obsession in every incarnation: to find the Capstone. It sounded insane, and Tag felt embarrassed for even considering the possibility.

No, it's not embarrassment you're feeling, Hunny Bunny.
(Ferrier, Tallien, Linda.)
It's something worse.
(Ramon, Sophie, TAG.)
It's shear dread.

Tag pushed the unsettling thought from her mind. She just couldn't accept that she could be a domestic terrorist reborn as an FBI agent. It sounded like the plot of a ridiculous horror movie. There had to be another explanation. Jacobson undoubtedly knew more than he'd let on. She needed to determine exactly how the psychiatrist was involved.

"Do you think Sophie and Gerald committed those acts of violence to protect an ancient secret?" Tag asked.

"I don't know. I can only speculate, but I've always assumed the Sons of Elijah constituted a guardianship of sorts. What they've guarded for the past two thousand years, I can't be sure. It must carry great significance, or they wouldn't have gone to such great lengths to keep it hidden."

Tag watched the psychiatrist's eyes. His lids, heavy from the alcohol, blinked slowly. *Does he know about Caleb? What is he hiding?* She pulled her shoulders back and straightened her spine. "Why didn't you tell the FBI about the baby?" she asked.

Dr. Jacobson's wine-stained lips parted. She could hear his lawnmower breath leaking from his throat. The tips of his ears darkened. "What?"

"Sophie gave birth to Gerald's child. A boy."

Tag waited for Jacobson to respond. He set down his empty glass and fidgeted with his robe, pulling on the belt. "I'd promised I wouldn't tell. Her family didn't know. There are strict laws about revealing a patient's confidential medical information. Especially if doing so could put her at risk."

"Your book pretty much spilled the beans on everything else. Besides, Sophie's dead."

"Yes, but Caleb isn't."

There it is. He knows all about Caleb. What else had Dr. Jacobson lied about? Was Caleb's depersonalization disorder a complete fabrication? Was the psychiatrist making excuses for the young man's violence, setting up his defense?

"I'm going to ask you this once, so I suggest you take all the time you need before answering," Tag said soberly. "Do you know where Caleb Miller is now?"

A fireball churned in her stomach, and it wasn't from the whisky. *Don't fill the dead air. Let the subject speak first.*

"No," Jacobson finally answered through dry vocal chords. "I only met Caleb a few months ago. I knew about him— that part's true—but a family in Oak Park had adopted him shortly before Sophie's death. I had no idea that he knew any- thing about his birth mother. When Caleb approached me, I wasn't entirely sure it was him at first. Although he has her eyebrows; I noticed that. As his doctor, I was able to request his medical history, and that's how I acquired his adoption records and verified the identity of his birth parents."

"Why did he seek you out?"

"My book, probably. Like I said, Caleb is obsessed with the Sons of Elijah. It makes sense. He never knew his mother, other than what he'd read about her attack. It's a difficult thing to come to terms with: your mother gives you up so she can explode herself on a crowded pier. He wanted to know why she did it. He came to me looking for answers."

"That makes two of us." Tag pulled her sleeves up her forearms and pressed her elbows into her knees. "Caleb is a dangerous man. He's about to do something that will make his mom look like Gandhi."

"I'm not sure how to help," Dr. Jacobson said. "But trust me when I say I'd like to try."

Tag couldn't believe what she was about to say. Her idea, if it backfired, could do irreparable harm to the FBI's inves- tigation into the Sons of Elijah and potentially destroy any viable attempt to prosecute Dr. Jacobson, if the man was indeed involved. However, if Tag could better understand the relationship between Sophie and Gerald, and what had driven those two seemingly normal people to commit such violent acts, it might shed light on what Caleb was planning. It might help Tag find him—and stop him.

"I need to go back," she said finally. "If I really was Sophie, you need to help me remember everything about her lover, Gerald Cutter."

24

Raising the Sons of Elijah

by Dr. Seth Jacobson

Making Revolution

"*SLEEP*," I COMMANDED, and rapped my knuckle firmly on the center of Gerald's forehead.

"I can't," he said. Gerald had never had trouble reaching a deep state of hypnosis before this session. I wasn't sure what could be causing the blockage. My frustration had begun to show.

"Why, Gerald?" I asked. "Why is it difficult to sleep today?"

"I'm trying," he whined. "I'm curled up against the window underneath my jacket, but three others have squeezed into the same row. Another student has crawled on top of me. He's a boulder on my back. With every bump of the train car, he presses into my ribs. I can't get much air, and when I do manage to breathe in, I only inhale the stench from his armpit. None of us has bathed in six days. Not since we left Chongqing."

Ah, so Gerald has regressed after all, I reasoned. In our previous sessions, we'd already uncovered two prior lifetimes, but this particular experience didn't sound familiar. I was eager to learn more.

"Are you somewhere in Asia?" I probed.

"I'm traveling to Beijing. I was fortunate to get onto the train. I ran alongside the tracks as it rolled through my village. The cars moved slowly enough that I climbed through an open window easily. There's no operator collecting tickets onboard; passage to the capital is free for us. But the trains are so crowded, just finding room to sit is almost impossible. Students sleep in the aisles or folded on top of one another in every row. The fat fellow lying on me shifts, making my bladder scream. I haven't peed since morning. The lavatories are always packed with more students. The toilets are being used as beds too." Gerald's face wrinkled with discomfort.

"You feel no pain," I assured him. "You are only observing this life. Allow yourself to be aware of the emotions without them affecting you."

His chest rose and fell more calmly. "Yes, I'm better now. I managed to wriggle free. I peel down my trousers and urinate out the window. I feel bad for the girls. They either wet themselves or just go on the floor. That's why it's so sticky."

"I want you to advance through time to the next significant event in this lifetime," I instructed. "What happens after you arrive in Beijing?"

Gerald's eyelids fluttered. "The city buzzes. Students are marching through the streets, punching the sky with their fists and singing."

"What are they singing?"

"Revolutionary songs. The ones we learned in primary school. I join them. We're a sea of gray and brown. I'm wearing my uncle's old uniform from the war. It's baggy and faded, but that's actually better. The kids with newer uniforms have had to slash their pant legs and sleeves. Tousle them a bit. Better to make them look beat up. New clothes are decadent."

"You said that you're marching with this crowd of young people. Where are you going?"

"There's a massive square in the center of the city, at the doorstep of the old imperial palace. We're all headed there to see the Chairman. I've got his little red book in my back pocket. I'm trying to memorize as much as I can, in case someone steals it from me."

I took vigorous notes. I wanted to capture every detail of the colorful scene unfolding before me. Gerald was recalling his former life as a student in China, which I determined with very little effort after our session. In the late 1960s, millions of students migrated from the countryside to Beijing as part of a radical campaign directed by Chairman Mao Zedong. This event in history occurred when I was a child, and I had little foreknowledge of the specifics. Gerald's account, rich with gruesome depictions, shocked me.

"What happens when you get to the square?" I asked.

"A woman hands me a red scarf with gold characters embroidered on it. This delights me, and I quickly wrap it around my sleeve, over my bicep. I'm filled with pride. I want to get closer to the rostrum. That's where the Chairman will appear." Gerald beamed in my recliner. "He's taken the stage now. I'm so close, I can see the mole on his chin. His cheeks are round and flush. He radiates raw masculine energy. A girl beside me shrieks with pleasure and drops away into the crowd. She's fainted. I'm holding my breath, waiting for the Chairman's words, for his *instructions*."

"What does the Chairman tell you to do?"

"He says, 'Class struggle is a struggle to the death,'" Gerald said. "The old ways are venomous. Old ideas, old culture, old customs—these are all just old habits of exploiting classes and oppressing the workers and farmers. We're going to tear it up! Chairman Mao is the greatest revolutionary who has ever lived!"

The hairs stood up on the back of my neck. I'd never heard Gerald, a measured corporate professional, speak with such fervor. He buzzed with the idealistic zeal of youth. It was difficult to picture the man I knew blindly adopting such incendiary populist rhetoric. "Let's advance a bit further," I said. "What happens in the days and weeks following the rally?"

"The organizers send me to Shanghai with about ten others. We're called Red Guards, and we're planning to make revolution in the city."

"And what does that mean exactly? How do you make revolution?"

The words poured from his mouth. "We rip down signposts and replace the street names with proper ones. The Bund becomes Revolutionary Boulevard. It's so clever! These small acts bring me much satisfaction, as if I'm helping to recast Shanghai in the Chairman's image, but the others grow bored with symbolic measures. They want to go after the intellectuals, the teachers, the university professors. An older boy in our group has heard about a wealthy woman who lives in the Nanshi District, in the Old City. She collects vases and dishes from the Qing and Ming dynasties. These things are illegal now. They represent China's feudal past, when the peasants toiled under the thumb of landlords. The older boy wants to smash them.

"We follow him to the woman's home, a *shikumen* lane house. It doesn't look like a place a rich person would live. Strings of apartments are jammed up against one another, their doors opening into narrow alleyways. A screech shoots from a second-story window, followed by a crash. Another group of Red Guards has found the woman first. The older boy in my unit grins wickedly, showing a set of pointed incisors, and rushes inside to join them. Then, more crashes and deep thuds, like heavy furniture toppling down a flight of stairs. A high window breaks and bits of glass rain down on me. My cheek is bleeding. Smoke spirals from the window. I hear the crackle of flames eating at wood.

"The older boy flies out of the front door, dragging the woman by her hair. She's wailing. The boy pushes her to her knees and unsheathes an angry, five-inch blade from his belt. He slices off the woman's silver braid. Another Red Guard, a girl about sixteen, grabs the severed hair and stuffs it into the woman's mouth. It does little to stifle her cries.

"One by one, a stream of Red Guards pour out from her house, carrying dishes, paintings, hand-painted vases, jewelry, books, a golden Buddha two meters tall. They hurl the illicit objects into a pile and douse them with kerosene. Someone lights the pile, and it goes up with a *whoosh*. The older boy breathes through his wide open mouth. I can tell that he's quite aroused by it all. He yanks his shirt over his head, and his bare chest heaves. Then he runs his blade lightly across his own bicep, drawing a dripping, red line. He smears the blood into a stripe, painting a grisly arm band with the gore.

"The doorway of the lane house coughs smoke. Another Red Guard emerges, rubbing his eyes and waving a pamphlet. It looks like a playbill. He shows it to the older boy, who growls and thrusts it into the lady's face. He leans in close and gnashes at her, like he's planning to bite off a chunk of her neck with those sharp teeth. His tongue is black spotted and dead looking. She turns away at first, but the older boy strikes her across the cheek. With a trembling finger, she points north, toward the theater district. The boy hurls the pamphlet onto the bonfire, but I get a look at the cover before it blooms into a hundred blazing petals. I'm right; it is a playbill. There's a picture on it of a young actress dressed as a Buddhist goddess. Such things are prohibited now."

"Plays or goddesses?" I asked. "Which is prohibited?"

"Both," Gerald answered. "Only revolutionary plays are allowed, and the only deity permitted in China is the Great Chairman Mao. By possessing this playbill, this wealthy woman, this *capitalist*, has committed an unforgivable crime against the Party."

"What happens to her?" I asked after Gerald finally fell silent.

"The students rip at her clothes. Someone splashes black ink on her face and then forces her to drink the rest. The boys take turns kicking her stomach. Her vomit is yellow-black, from the ink. The bonfire rages in the alleyway, growing taller. Its hot fingers tap on the windows next door, seeking more traitors to the Chairman's noble cause. I look up and see faces."

"Faces?"

"On the rooftops. Many faces, flickering orange. More Red Guards. They came to watch. I'm watching too. Just watching, too frightened to stop it."

Under hypnosis, patients often remember the events of their past lives that have had the most profound impact on their psyche. With countless incarnations over centuries, I'm always fascinated by the specific memories my patients recall in our sessions. This particular incident, in an alleyway in Old Shanghai, had traumatized Gerald, and he'd carried the guilt into this lifetime. It would haunt him until he allowed himself to separate from it. I could help him incorporate the lessons from his time as a Red Guard and move beyond the pain, into the present. However, he wasn't ready. I suspected his experience in Mao's China held more secrets. I allowed Gerald to rest briefly, and then we dove back in. To this day, I regret that decision. I wasn't prepared for what came next. Neither of us were.

25

S PECIAL AGENT JOE Michelson strained to see in the low
light of Decadence, an exclusive French restaurant on the
open-air rooftop of the Chicago Athletic Association. His
frumpy brown suit, with its long-set mustard stain on the
lapel, drew the probing eye of the hostess.

"Reservation?" the petite woman asked. She wore a black
dress made from stretch fabric that looked painted on.

"I'm with management," he answered, and flipped the
cover on his FBI creds. In his younger days, he could've collected a pile of panties with that leather-bound piece of plastic. This chickadee hostess seemed unaffected.

"My apologies, but we are quite booked tonight," she said.
"Perhaps I can schedule your party for tomorrow night?"

"Not necessary. I'm meeting someone."

Michelson breezed past the young woman and entered
the dining area. Even with a thin layer of clouds blotting
out the moonlight, he could see the million-dollar view of
Millennium Park. The trees shook their full leaves in the
breeze. Directly below, at the edge of the park, the Crown

Fountain displayed an LED image of a woman's face on a fifty-foot wall made of glass bricks. A group of children splashed in the stream of water spitting from her mouth.

Men in dark suits (without mustard stains) and women wearing shiny earrings filled every table on the patio. Michelson spotted her immediately, with her blonde hair slicked back behind her ears, sitting alone at a small table along the railing. She was the only patron who had rotated her chair so that her back faced the park. She didn't care about the view; she preferred to watch the door. An angry gnarl appeared on the skin between her eyes when she noticed Michelson approaching.

"Hoping for someone else?" Michelson asked. He pulled out the empty chair across from Acting SAC Gina Butler and roughly dropped into the seat. "So, what's good here? Frog's ball sack, or someshit?"

"Where's Agent Taggart? Why aren't you watching her?" Butler asked.

"Redman's taking a shift tonight. He reported in twenty minutes ago. Taggart is visiting with her new beau."

"Dr. Jacobson," Butler said. "Good. Then he's begun the process."

"Yes. We're picking up mostly terrible opera music from the bugs in his house, but we heard enough to confirm that he's working Tag over pretty good."

"Just like the others?"

"Not exactly. The others weren't bean flickers like our girl. His charm may not have as powerful an effect on her."

Butler frowned and swirled the cherry wine in her glass. A waiter wearing a snow-white apron materialized at the tableside. "Is everything all right, ma'am? Something for the gentleman?"

"He's not *the gentleman*," Butler answered. "We're fine for now." With a swat of her hand, the server vanished.

"How can you even afford a meal at a place like this? They bump you up to the SES pay scale, even though you're just *acting* as the SAC? Must be mighty nice." Michelson leaned back in his chair, lifting it off the two front legs, nearly tipping. "Might-*tee* nice, indeed."

"Has Jacobson asked Taggart about the Capstone or not?" Butler snapped.

"Yep, but he's not pressing too hard this time. He's learned his lesson."

"He won't wait too long. Not if he's already had multiple hypnosis sessions with her."

"She trusts him," Michelson assessed. "She'll fall under his spell, and then he'll turn up the heat, melt her like a candle."

"Don't underestimate Taggart. She's sturdier than you think."

Michelson shrugged. He reached for Butler's glass and took a swig of her wine. "Blech. I can't stand this fruity shit." He tried to hand it back, but Butler rejected it with a palm. "Have you thought about what we're supposed to do if this whole thing goes tits up?" he asked.

"It won't."

"The director barely green-lit this nutso idea. He's got his twitchy hand on the kill switch. I don't blame him either. Christ, that girl actually thinks she's running this investigation," Michelson said. "We sent her to Quantico, for fuck's sake."

"It's our best shot, Joe." Butler pressed a fingertip against her eyelid. "And so far, it's looking pretty swell. Has Jacobson brought up the China stuff yet? About the Red Guards?"

"No."

"That's the trigger. That's when we'll know things are getting serious."

Michelson noticed a shadow fall over the white tablecloth. A young man in a tailored suit had come up behind him. Michelson watched Butler's eyes for signs of distress, but she smiled and offered a cheek to the approaching man, who leaned over and kissed it.

"Sorry I'm late, babe," he said. "The parking garage was totally jammed."

"It's no trouble," Butler responded coolly. "Next time you'll valet, won't you?"

"Joe. I didn't recognize you," the man said. It was Declan Walsh, the broad-shouldered counterterrorism analyst who'd briefed them on the threat to Fermilab. "Will you be joining us?"

Butler smirked and fingered a button on Declan's oxford shirt. "He's not invited," she answered.

"I gotta hit the road anyway," Michelson said. "Nice seeing you, bud."

He offered his seat to the young man, who grinned like a kiddie unknowingly wading into shark-infested waters. The boy had no idea what he was getting into, tangling up with a woman like Gina Butler.

On his way out, Michelson winked at the hostess in the tight dress. She turned away and pretended to straighten a stack of menus. He looked back over his shoulder. Butler had leaned in close to Declan. Under the table, her foot was trailing up the guy's pant leg. The feeding frenzy had begun.

26

Raising the Sons of Elijah

by Dr. Seth Jacobson

Timeless Encounters

"HIS NAME IS Zhang Boda, the older boy with the pointy teeth and black tongue. They put him in charge of the revolutionary committee in Shanghai," Gerald explained. We'd returned to his lifetime as a Red Guard.

"How do you feel about that?" I asked. "About having to take orders from him?"

"Zhang breathes out an energy that lives deep inside his core. He's the spirit of Mao's revolution. He's terrifying but captivating. Sometimes his methods disgust me, but I admire his commitment to the cause."

"Have you killed anyone in this lifetime?"

"Not yet," Gerald answered. "I might if Zhang asks me to. I don't know. The city is teeming with counterrevolutionaries and capitalists. Zhang assures us that history will mark these as the days China finally shed the dead scales of its past and emerged as one powerful, rippling dragon. No one will judge the violence. Violence awakens the soul the same way it awakens a nation."

"What has Zhang asked you to do?"

"The playbill from the old lady's house, it came from a Buddhist theater troupe performing out of a temple in the Putuo District. Zhang wants me to stop it." Gerald paused. "And then punish the players. Let us make an example of them, Zhang says."

"I want you to advance in time to the next significant event," I instructed. "Do you go to the temple? Does anyone go with you? What happens there?" I hurled the questions quickly—a result of my impatience. We'd returned to this particular past life three times already, and I still wasn't sure why.

My research had placed the rally that Gerald had attended in Beijing in 1966, just twenty-seven years prior. Gerald himself was only twenty-five. That meant two things: one, Gerald's past life as a Red Guard had ended shortly after these recollections; and two, this was most likely the life he'd lived just prior to his rebirth as Gerald Cutter. The circumstances of his untimely death in China had to reveal something of significance. I was eager to advance him to the end of this remembered lifetime.

"I smell incense burning. The main hall of the temple is dark and smoky. At least fifty statues line the walls. The detail on the figures is impressive," Gerald continued.

"Is anyone else there with you?" I asked.

"A monk, dressed in robes, watches as I enter. He's old and hobbles, gripping the jade handle of a cane for balance. He bows and moves on, into the tucked-away halls. Probably to warn the others. My red arm band is unmissable. He knows why I've come."

"Keep exploring the temple. Go deeper."

"I hear babbling water. There's a small pond in the center of an open courtyard. Bright fish swim just under the surface. The sun glares off the water. I look away and then I see her."

"Who?"

"The woman from the playbill. She's young. I did not think any young people believed in Buddhism anymore, not since communism became the national religion. She's lying on a bench, resting on her side, with a hand propping up her head.

Her other hand smooths the wrinkles of her gown, tracing the curves of her hip. A tree planted in the courtyard shakes its leaves, which rain over her gently, like rose petals."

"She's attractive."

Gerald inhaled through his nose. "Yes, she is. I can't recall ever seeing such a beautiful woman. And she's looking at me."

I wondered why this woman appeared so relaxed with a Red Guard inside the temple.

"Is she afraid of you too?"

"No, she sees me clearly, but it's more than that. She *recognizes* me."

"This was your first trip to the coast, you'd said. Is it possible you'd met this woman before? Somewhere near your village?"

"No, nowhere near there. I met her long ago, when she wasn't a woman, but just as bewitching," Gerald said.

Gerald had already recalled knowing people from his current life in previous lifetimes. His wife, Linda, for example. Perhaps this woman in the temple could be the previous incarnation of an ex-lover or an old friend from Gerald's time at university.

"Yes, I'm positive now. Her eyes are the same. I recognize her too, and I'm filled with love. 'So, you've come looking for me, I suppose,' she says."

"Who is she, Gerald?"

"Eusebius," he answered incredibly. "She's Eusebius of Nicomedia."

My stomach dropped. For a full minute, I'm not sure I took a single breath. Eusebius was the name of the fourth-century bishop, described in detail by Sophie Whitestone not two months prior. I had never mentioned Sophie to any of my other patients, nor had I discussed her remembered life in ancient Greece. And yet, remarkably, Gerald Cutter, an ordinary corporate accountant, had just claimed that he'd known one of her past incarnations.

The implications were astounding. If Gerald and Sophie had met in Nicaea in 325 AD, and then again in Shanghai in 1966, had they also met during other lifetimes? Both patients had come to me separately for help with completely different issues, but now I couldn't help but wonder if some cosmic force had drawn them to my practice. I fought the urge to awaken Gerald and tell him everything I'd learned from my sessions with Sophie. A woman he'd remembered from a past life lived in the same city where he resided now! They'd occupied the same room, the same *chair*, within hours of each other.

My heart raced from the revelation and then ached from the acknowledgment that I could never share what I'd learned about the inexplicable connection my patients shared. The strict rules governing doctor–patient confidentiality prevented me from telling either Gerald or Sophie. Still, my own curiosity wouldn't allow me to dismiss the extraordinary discovery. I wanted to dig deeper. I was determined to learn as much as I could about the nature of their ageless relationship—a passionate and devastatingly tragic one, I'd come to learn. Their ill-fated story had spanned millennia.

And left piles of bodies in its wake.

27

Tag put her feet up on Dr. Jacobson's couch and closed her eyes. She could sense the psychiatrist hovering over her. She crossed her arms under her breasts, as if to protect herself. Hypnosis still seemed like a strange power that Jacobson had mastered.

"Relax your arms at your sides, please," he said. Tag didn't want to comply. What did it matter where she rested her arms? Still, she moved them, almost involuntarily. At his command.

"I'm going to take you back now, before this lifetime," Dr. Jacobson continued. Just like before, he guided her down the stairs inside her mind, to the door outlined in white light. "Reach out for the doorknob, but don't turn it yet."

Tag felt the muscles of her arm respond. She couldn't be positive her hand had actually extended, but the sensation felt real.

"In a moment, I'll instruct you to open the door and step through it. A young woman waits for you on the other side. She's you, in a previous lifetime. This time, you will not merge with her. I want you to simply observe. Float above her and look and listen, like you're watching a movie. Ready?" Dr. Jacobson asked.

Tag nodded her head and felt a prickling heat dance across her cheeks.

Jacobson's voice lowered. "Perfect. Now, turn the knob."

*   *   *

The tiger rushes at Rae Yin, and all she sees is dizzying black bars striping fire fur. And those ivory tusks for teeth. The incisors are grotesquely oversized so that the audience can clearly see them and imagine them puncturing their own stomachs, the way they appear to puncture Rae Yin's. Most nights, the young man in the tiger costume presses too hard. Accidentally, Rae Yin had thought originally, until he kept doing it. He wants the attack to appear real, she reasoned, so Rae Yin might enliven her performance with a convincing yelp.

Tonight, the snarl on the young actor's lips makes Rae Yin think he's got other reasons for being so aggressive onstage. He's a monk, assigned to the temple and devoted to aestheticism, to chastity, and yet he's still a man—primal and ravenous. How long has it been since he's pierced a woman's soft parts, and not with fake, elephant-bone fangs?

The tiger-man scoops an arm around Rae Yin's waist and presses into her, belly to belly. He's strong, like an acrobat, and practically nude underneath the faux tiger pelt. The man's hand slips inside her robe secretly, at an angle imperceptible to the spectators. Rae Yin feels the tickle of his finger across her nipple. How dare he! Her rage seems to boil all of the liquid inside her cells. She opens her mouth and roars into the lecherous monk's face. A hot-steam scream, plenty convincing.

The young man rushes her across the stage, heaving, growling as a tiger would. He's a frustrated lust-rocket.

"I deliver you to hell, Princess Miaoshan!" he shouts. "Let Yama, the ruler of this dark place, eat your soul, if he can stand its bitter taste."

The young monk drops her hard onto the stage, rather vindictively, and leaps away. Rae Yin expects he'll return, after nightfall perhaps, to her bedroom, those tusks in hand and the same snarl on his lips. She'll handle *that* problem later, after dealing with the fabled King of Hell.

Yama, portrayed by an older and fortunately less stimulated monk, emerges from the wings. He requires the assistance of a cane to walk, a detail that irritates Rae Yin. Why would the ruler of the underworld have bad knees?

"I have done harm to no one. I have lived a lifetime of service and gratitude. Although it is not your nature, I beseech you to spare me," Rae Yin wails.

"You've lived graciously? You've satisfied your filial duties, have you?" the monk playing Yama grumbles. "Then why do I find you here, in my glorious, dark hole, prostrating yourself to the God of Death?"

"Because I refused to marry. I wished to devote myself to the path of enlightenment. This angered my father, but he allowed me to join the nunnery." Rae Yin conjures tears. "I thanked him, but it was all a nasty trick. Father torched the nunnery. All five hundred nuns burned up."

"And you won't find a single one of them here. Those women respected their fathers' wishes, unlike you. For that, you will not cycle, Miaoshan. You will not be reborn, but will waste away down here."

Rae Yin, as Princess Miaoshan, rises and stares down Yama, her courage hardening. "I have already lived many lives. I have lived just and virtuous lives, cycle upon cycle, accumulating good karma. It flows within me and into this ground, into these cave walls, and into you, Yama." Rae Yin lifts her arms. "Yes, you can feel it, can't you? You can feel the good that I've done. It burns like acid on your skin."

In the rafters directly above her, a stagehand tips a bucket of lotus petals. The old monk shrieks under a pink shower. He squeezes the jade handle of his cane so tightly the veins in his arm stand out.

"I release the souls you have ensnared, O God of Death," Rae Yin sings out. "They will fly into newborn babies, to be reborn on Earth. My essence will destroy your realm." A handful of women in flowing white robes skitter across the stage, souls returning. Their savior—pure, benevolent, selfless Princess Miaoshan—turns to face the audience and bows deeply to the sound of tepid applause. The stage lights extinguish with a crack.

*   *   *

One of the saved souls, a pale girl from Wuhan named Li Na, approaches Rae Yin in the small chamber the women use for dressing. "He handles you too rough," she says.

Rae Yin wipes a layer of makeup from her cheek with a wet rag. "The tiger boy? Oh, he just needs a nice girl to sink his teeth into. Too bad for him, I'm not a nice girl. Hell, I'm not even Buddhist."

"You're not?"

"The abbot plucked me from an opera in Beijing last spring. Good thing, too. The Party shut it down back in July. The play was counterrevolutionary, they said. I don't know how a melodrama about a minister from the Ming dynasty is so controversial. Besides, I thought the Chairman loved it. It was his wife who closed the doors on that one. Such a jealous shrew."

"I've heard rumors here in Shanghai too. The Party bosses are reviewing the plays. Even ones that have nothing to do with politics are coming under scrutiny, especially religious ones. What if they shutter *Princess Miaoshan*?" Li Na asks.

"Listen, hon. If the authorities come after our little show, it's only because it's a dreadful production. A half-naked monk draped in a wild animal carcass? Sheesh. It's all eye candy, not real art. The middle-aged ladies packing the front row are probably soaking their panties by the third act."

Li Na blushes at this remark. She removes Rae Yin's headdress and begins to brush the actress's hair in long, attentive strokes. "*Princess Miaoshan* isn't about lust, forgive me for saying. It's about love and grace. Her purity releases thousands of suffering souls from hell. She grants them the gift of rebirth. A second chance to redeem their past sins. Is that not beautiful?"

Rae Yin rubs at her eyeliner. "It's gorgeous, love," she says. "About as gorgeous as the bulge in that tiger boy's loincloth."

"I thought you had no interest in him."

"I didn't say that." Rae Yin slips on a delicate silk robe. "It's just that offstage, I'm no man's prey. I much prefer the role of predator."

Rae Yin pushes Li Na's brush away. She stands and floats out of the bed chamber.

The temple's interior courtyard is empty except for a stunning jade sculpture of Buddha, lying on his side. The pose looks remarkably feminine, even sensual. Rae Yin sits on a bench opposite the figure and positions her body similarly. Man and woman. Mirror images.

Footsteps draw her attention to a visitor who has just entered the temple. He's tall and handsome, with sloping shoulders and the puffed-out chest of a young man who has yet to know failure. But his eyes, their shape, color . . . they tell a different story.

Rae Yin sits up. Her pulse quickens. *Is it possible? Is it him?*

"So, you've come looking for me, I suppose," she says. Her robe is sheer. It slips around her body as she walks to him. The man's gaze drips down her neck, shoulders, bosom. His lips open, showing a flash of wet tongue. *Yes, it is him!* Before he can speak, Rae Yin presses her mouth into his, and they are connected once more. From the halls of Nicaea to the unforgiving Pyrenees, still spitting ash, to the Jade Buddha Temple, they entwine yet again. Curls of smoke from the incense surround them with oaky perfume. Li Na watches from the doorway, her worried eyes fixed on the man's red armband.

* * *

Rae Yin's bedroom curtains ripple. The summer current wafting up from the street below is warm, even at night. The handsome Red Guard has shed his homemade uniform—and his childish ideology, with any luck—and lies nude under a thin sheet in Rae Yin's apartment. His name is Chen Wei in this lifetime, but she knows so many of his names from times before. Keeping track is difficult—and unnecessary. Names have little meaning. Naming a body is like naming a cloud. Blink and it's changed its form.

Rae Yin traces a fingernail down the centerline of Chen's torso, crossing through a lion-shaped birthmark. The ruddy splotch is the only physical constant, cycle after cycle, but she hadn't needed to see it to recognize this man. The light behind his eyes gave him away. She wonders if he remembers her. A powerful magnetism drew them together, and behind the closed door of her tiny bedroom, without so much as a whisper, they'd made love like wild animals in a full moon. Sometimes, that's when things come rushing back. All of the history and knowledge surges to the surface, erupts.

Rae Yin glances at a music box resting on her dresser. When she's sure that he remembers, she'll tell him about it. Not before. She won't take that risk.

Rae Yin presses against the hard muscles of Chen's chest with amusement. She remembers when they were soft mounds, modestly covered with tendrils of brown hair spilling down milky shoulders. She remembers lying on her back in a dark stable as that feathery hair brushed across her neck in rocking pulses. Yes, how the clouds change. His current shape is fun too, though. She slides a hand lower under the sheet.

Chen jumps, but not from Rae Yin's touch. A loudspeaker blares outside the window. Car horns blat in response. Then there's the crack of glass breaking.

"What's going on?" Rae Yin asks, and pulls the sheet up to her chin. "It's so loud, I can't even understand what they're saying."

Chen leaps from the bed and whips the curtains aside, exposing his nakedness to the street. Red taillights coat his bare skin. "It's propaganda from the revolutionary committee. A call to arms. They're encouraging the people to destroy the old ways."

"More Red Guards? They're like ants."

"Zhang Boda has whipped up a frenzy. No one can control him." Chen picks his pants off the floor and pulls them on. "The temple is in danger. I've got to go."

"That temple is centuries old. It's an organ of this city, as essential as a liver or lung. The Red Guards won't touch it."

"That's *exactly* what they'll do. Temples, chapels, mosques—they're all threats to the revolution. The Party is the only acceptable religion now, and Mao's *Little Red Book* is the Bible," Chen explains. "I'm so sorry. I should have told you."

"Relax," Rae Yin said just as her own shoulders bunched with tension. "Maybe those boys are content enough to spout revolutionary poetry into those speakers. How do you know they'll harm the temple?"

"Because that's what Zhang ordered *me* to do," Chen answers. "That's why I came this morning. He wanted me to shut down the heretical play, as he put it."

"*Princess Miaoshan?* Heretical?"

"It's a fable about rebirth, right?"

"It's Buddhist. So, yeah," Rae Yin answers. "At the end, Miaoshan transforms into a goddess. She returns to Earth and vows to remain until every soul has been delivered."

"The Chairman doesn't like that."

"Most powerful men don't, as I've learned. The Chairman probably believes only Mao Zedong Thought will deliver humanity. But the Chairman's not here. He's probably bobbing in his pool at the Summer Palace."

"Zhang Boda is the Party boss in Shanghai, and he's committed to carrying out Mao's orders," Chen says. "He commanded me to close the temple."

"Where would the monks go?"

"A factory, I guess. To work. I don't know."

"You're being naive. Monks don't work on assembly lines. The Party would ship them off to reeducation camps." Rae Yin's cheeks flush.

"I won't let that happen." Chen Wei buttons his shirt, which hangs wrinkled and loose over his taut frame. A torn flap of fabric winks on his elbow. *So the reformed hero will swoop in and stop the marauding zealots. Ridiculous,* Rae Yin thinks.

"I'm going with you," she says.

"It's too dangerous," Chen begins to argue, but he stops when Rae Yin rises from the bed.

"Don't you dare preach to me about what's dangerous." Her eyes flick to the music box. *I'll tell him, but now it will have to wait.*

Chen nods, and in a minute they are both dressed and flying down Anyuan Road, a modest thoroughfare soon to be renamed Red Guard Road.

A crowd of Red Guards has gathered on the wide steps leading up to the entrance of the Jade Buddha Temple. The building's pagoda-style roofline swoops up at the corners like angry eyebrows over the gaping doorways. A bonfire crackles in the plaza at the base of the steps.

"What are they burning?" Rae Yin asks.

"Books," Chen answers. "I've seen them do it before."

A shirtless Red Guard emerges from the temple. He bares his pointed teeth like a wildcat.

"That's him?" Rae Yin says.

"Zhang Boda, yes," Chen replies.

Li Na follows Zhang, carrying an armful of statues, the ones that lined the entrance hall. There are sixty in total, one for each year of the old Chinese calendar. Li Na only manages to carry ten or so. They look wooden, but Rae Yin knows they are made of glass. Her friend handles them with the gentleness of a mother cradling a newborn. They hold special meaning for Li Na, a devout Buddhist. Rae Yin has seen the girl light an incense stick before the canine statue nearly every morning before rehearsal, to commemorate the year of the dog, her birth year.

Now we're all dogs, Rae Yin thinks. *The Chairman's dogs.*

Zhang Boda pushes Li Na to the ground and instructs her to place the statues in a pile. She stands them up delicately. The young Red Guard sticks out his chin and hands her a hammer. Li Na quivers but takes the tool.

"That bastard! He can't make her do this." Rae Yin starts for the steps, but Chen grabs her waist, pulls her in.

"Don't," he warns. "He'll hurt you. They're only statues."

"Not to her."

Wailing, Li Na lifts the hammer high above her head, hesitates for a beat, and then chops into the figurines. One by one, she smashes them, sending shards flying across the steps. When it's done, she drops the hammer with a clank and holds her face in her palms. Zhang leans over and whispers. Then he points down the stairs toward the square, where the other Red Guards are raising their fists in the firelight.

"What is he making her do?" Rae Yin asks.

On her hands and knees, Li Na begins crawling across the broken bits of glass. The spaces between her fingers pool with blood.

"I'll kill him," Rae Yin spits out, and breaks away from Chen's hold. She races across the square and up the stairs, her black ponytail whipping. If Chen is rushing behind her, she doesn't know. She doesn't spare a second to look back.

Zhang Boda sees her charging. For a moment, he seems to smile, until Rae Yin slams her fist into his eye.

She's immediately tackled. Heels and knuckles and elbows batter her ribs. She flails, trying desperately to ward off her attackers. Both of her shoes fly off, but the assault continues. In the peeks between the crush of arms and legs, she sees Chen Wei help Li Na to her feet and usher the bleeding young woman away from the bedlam.

Rae Yin rolls onto her side, but someone kicks her onto her back. She looks up and sees dark spots float across the moon. Clouds—the sinister kind. A circle of black fringe shudders and jerks overhead. The boys are letting the female Red Guards have a turn. They're bent over her, swinging broken broom handles. Then, one by one, the girls peel off, like molars ripped from the gums of a terrible mouth. Rae Yin hears a man's deep bark.

"Get away from her," he shouts. *"Beasts!"*

It's Chen Wei. He rushes to her and lifts her head onto his lap. She smells his sweat. It's such a familiar scent.

"Do you know me?" Rae Yin asks weakly. Her lips are swollen. "From before . . . please tell me you remember."

Chen Wei cradles her body—a broken doll draped over his knees. He squints. "I do. I remember now." He follows Rae Yin's eyes to his red arm band. In a quick motion, he snatches it off and flings it away. "They want to stamp out the truth. I almost *helped* them. I'm so sorry."

Rae Yin coughs and splatters Chen's shirt with bright blood. Words crawl down her throat the wrong way. She shakes her head in frustration.

Chen Wei's eyes widen. *He understands,* Rae Yin thinks. *I've got to tell him.*

"Where is it?" he asks. "I'll keep it safe. I promise. They will never get it."

Rae Yin swallows hard to clear her mouth. She's lost feeling in one of her arms below the shoulder and the other is weak, probably broken. She reaches out and pulls Chen's collar toward her until their lips nearly touch. "The music box," she murmurs, thinking of the sacred Capstone hidden inside it. Her chest shudders, and then she becomes still.

*   *   *

Tag's eyelids flew open, and she gulped a powerful breath, as if shooting out from underwater. She shook out her arm, thankful that it wasn't really broken. She searched her skin for those blooming bruises, just as she had after her earlier session. Dr. Jacobson's hypnotherapy had brought her to that same courtyard outside the Jade Buddha Temple, twice now. Both times she'd relived a brutal beating that had left her dying on the cold stone. Now Tag knew why.

"She gave it to him! She hid it inside a music box, and she told Chen—or Gerald, I guess," Tag said.

"Hid what, Sophie?" Dr. Jacobson asked.

"The Capstone. The secret that the Sons of Elijah have been guarding. The one you've been searching for."

Jacobson's eyes flashed. "That's incredible. What did he do with it? Where is it now?"

Tag had an idea of where the Capstone might be, but she didn't want to say. Dr. Jacobson looked at her with unnerving intensity. She thought his lips might lift into a horrid grin. She'd seen that look before. It was the one men wore when their fingertips brushed up against their greatest ambition. *The look Zhang Boda had on the steps of the temple,* Tag thought. *And Inquisitor Ferrier . . .*

"Do you realize what you just said?" Tag asked.

"What?"

"You just called me Sophie." Tag gripped the chair's armrests. "And I didn't flinch."

And there it was, that wolf grin. Peeling back from Jacobson's pink gums.

28

TAG DESCENDED THE stairs to the underground Red Line station. A cool draft rushed against her damp clothes, and she suddenly remembered the umbrella she'd left jammed inside the boxwood bush near Dr. Jacobson's townhome. She would send a Staff Operations Specialist to retrieve it before sunrise.

The revelation of her latest hypnosis session haunted her. *A music box.* The secret of the Sons of Elijah was tucked inside some oak cube (*no, it's rosewood—Bolivian rosewood*), hiding underneath the twirling feet of a ballerina (*carved from ivory*). Where was it now? How was she supposed to find it?

If Rae Yin gave it to Chen Wei (*to Gerald*), then maybe the reformed Red Guard had kept it in his family, like a treasured heirloom. So, Tag was supposed to fly to Shanghai and start knocking on doors?

Tag rode the L train to the Loop, where the track emerged from the belly of the city and clanged along the elevated track. She'd missed two calls while traveling underground. Before she could tap her phone's screen, it buzzed in her palm.

"Special Agent Taggart," she answered.

"Thank God you picked up," the voice said. "You were right . . . about our security problem. I don't want to say any more on my cell. Can you come? I know it's late. I don't know who to trust."

It was Director Torres from Fermilab, and she sounded frazzled, not like the confident, professional woman Tag had met that morning.

"Are you in danger? If you are, I can send—"

"No, don't. Please, don't send anyone," Torres interrupted. "I'm being silly. Maybe your visit just got me a little spooked. It's all right. Have a good night."

"Wait," Tag said. "You wouldn't have called me three times in three minutes if everything was fine. And you don't strike me as a silly woman, Dr. Torres."

Tag heard a long sigh through the earpiece. "Look," she said. "I'm just a few blocks from my car. Tell me where to meet you."

"Thank you, Agent Taggart."

"Vera," Tag replied, the word sounding strange slipping from her mouth. No one used her first name, not even family, and she had never suggested that anyone do so.

"My house, Vera," Dr. Torres said. "Something's not right about it. Someone may have been *inside*."

* * *

After assuring Dr. Torres—*"Call me Alex,"* she'd insisted—that she'd come straightaway, Tag considered checking with the home office. If someone had entered Alex's home without the director's permission, it might have been Caleb, or maybe just a jazzed-up teen hunting for coke money, or a jilted ex-lover. However, those weren't the first possibilities that coursed through Tag's mind. *Did Butler order a covert search of Dr. Torres's residence? Were we, the FBI, the ones inside her home today?* Tag knew Agent Butler believed someone on the inside had fed Caleb technical schematics of the lab, but did she actually suspect Dr. Torres? If Butler had ordered a search, she'd kept Tag in the dark. *No surprise there.*

FBI search teams didn't always cordon off the block with yellow crime scene tape and swarm a place in their gray wind-breakers. Sometimes they took a stealthier approach, especially if tipping off the subject could harm the investigation. In these situations, they worked meticulously and left no trace. Tag had heard about one FBI team that had brought baggies of fine powder on a covert search, so they could replace any dust they'd disturbed on shelves and countertops. If the subject found anything out of place, the jig was up.

Still, even the most experienced agents made mistakes, and sometimes subjects took countermeasures—hidden web-cams or even the old-school strand of hair across the doorway. Dr. Torres was certainly smart enough to come up with clever ways to detect entry into her home, but why would she? Did the director have something to hide? Tag didn't think so. Torres had staked her entire career on the Big C experiment. If someone damaged her billion-dollar detector, she'd be devastated.

The approach to Fermilab's campus looked even more pastoral at night. The two-lane road cut through an expansive ranch where dark mounds rose from the prairie grass like boulders. Breathing, hairy boulders. *Bison.* The entire area surrounding Fermilab was part of an ecological restoration project, Dr. Torres had explained on the tour that morning. A herd of native buffalo grazed the land directly above the most powerful particle accelerator in North America.

Dr. Torres lived at Fermilab, figuratively and literally. Sixty years before, the lab's first director had built a modest residence onsite to stay close to the action. His successors had maintained the tradition, including Director Torres, who slept a short bike ride from her office in a rustic, two-story farmhouse. Tag piloted the Crown Vic into the driveway. The house was completely dark. In fact, the only light that evening came from a fingernail moon and Wilson Hall, rising proudly from the fields like a gleaming cement erection about a half-mile away.

Tag spotted Dr. Torres sitting on a white Adirondack chair on the wrap-around veranda.

"I cut the power to the house so I could listen for any buzzing or beeping. Or maybe I'd see one of those little red lights in an AC vent. You know, from a surveillance device," Dr. Torres said.

"And did you find any?" Tag knew without a radio frequency detector or a nonlinear junction detector, Torres wouldn't turn up anything. And if the FBI had actually bugged the home, even the best surveillance sweeping toys probably wouldn't find squat. The Bureau was that good.

The director grimaced. She'd fixed her black springs of hair into a pinch behind her head, taming their exuberant bounce. "I started thinking about all the gifts. Scientists visiting from overseas like to offer little tokens. A Russian fellow from the Institute for High Energy Physics gave me a pair of brass bookends. They felt strange . . . hollow, maybe. I tried to smash them open with a hammer, but I only dented the metal."

"Where are they now?"

"In the duck pond behind the farmhouse," Torres answered.

Tag's eyes widened at the thought of Dr. Alex Torres, Nobel Prize winner, hurling a bookend into the night. "The *pond*?" Dr. Torres chuckled, and that sent Tag into a full belly laugh.

"I know—it sounds so stupid saying it out loud," Torres said. "I almost ripped the entire frame off an original Yayoi Kusama too."

"Oof, you would've burned in hell for such a crime." Tag's eyes watered from laughing. She sat in an empty chair beside the director, and the two women caught their breath. "Just don't tell me you tossed your Nobel in the pond too."

Torres filled her cheeks and blew out a puff of air. "That's probably where it belongs."

"It's the top recognition in your field. Isn't it an honor?"

"I thought so, at first. I fought for that damn thing, thinking it would prove something, like I belonged. Only four women had won for physics before me, and I was the first woman of color. And gay, too, for bonus points. I thought I'd feel validated, but winning the Nobel Prize was like getting a jock strap for your birthday. It wasn't made for you, and no matter how much you want it to, it never fits quite right."

They sat in silence for a full minute, but the quiet moment didn't feel unpleasant. Despite their different career paths, they were still two queer women, battling for relevance in professions dominated by straight men. They both understood the struggle and the crushing sense of inadequacy that sometimes accompanied it.

Finally, Dr. Torres said, "Let me show you why I called," and led Tag inside.

The home was respectably furnished and clean, even if nothing matched quite right. Tag suspected the residence had undergone several rounds of patchwork remodeling over the decades. The light switches gave it away. They were different in every room, and some even had funny knobs.

Dr. Torres padded on bare feet, hugging herself inside her zip-up hoodie. Tag followed her into the kitchen. Cereal boxes, bags of chips, and half-eaten bread loaves littered the countertop, along with an assortment of other obscure items. Pink sugar packets, vinegar, a bottle of Merlot, a set of chopsticks. And naturally, about six boxes of granola bars.

"I got home later than usual. Came in here to grab a bite before jumping in the shower, and that's when I found this," Dr. Torres held up a green kernel, pinched between her fingers.

"Is that a Lucky Charm?" Tag asked, fighting back a smile. "You found a marshmallow and called the FBI?"

"You don't understand. I found it on the kitchen *floor*. I switched to Captain Crunch, like, forever ago. I haven't eaten Lucky Charms since March. Fermilab pays for a housekeeper, and Sandy cleaned this place tip to toe just yesterday."

"Maybe the maid's got a sweet tooth, helped herself to a little snack?"

"I considered that. But here's the other thing." Dr. Torres picked up the box of Lucky Charms from its open flap with just her thumb and index finger, the other three fanned out as if to preserve the evidence. "Check the date. This went bad before last winter's snow had even thawed from the porch."

"You've had expired cereal in your pantry for six months?" Tag asked.

Dr. Torres reached into the box and scooped out a handful of the sugary bits. "Go ahead, try some." She held her hand under Tag's chin like a dealer coaxing a preteen to pop her first pill. *Try one—they're magically delicious!*

Tag laughed. "I'm not going to eat your old-ass cereal."

"Suit yourself," Torres said, and shoved the entire handful into her mouth. She crunched noisily and then raised an eyebrow with vindication.

"What? What does that prove? You likely just poisoned yourself with a moldy marshmallow unicorn."

"Imf haut moaly." Dr. Torres held up a finger, finished chewing, and swallowed dramatically. "It's *not* moldy. It's crunchy and yummy. Meaning—"

"The cereal inside the box is not stale," Tag reasoned. She bent down to examine the floor for more bits of marshmallow.

"Someone was futzing around in my pantry and accidentally spilled the Lucky Charms. They wanted to cover their tracks, but they couldn't just sweep up the spilled stuff and pour it back in; there'd be cat hair and shit stuck to it. So, they refilled the old box with fresh charms. Why would someone do that unless they didn't want me to know they'd been inside my house, inside my *pantry*?" Dr. Torres's breathing accelerated, and her cheeks flushed as she shared her conclusion. She pulled the zipper of her hoodie halfway down the front, stopping between her petite breasts. The physicist wasn't wearing the black T-shirt underneath anymore. Or a bra. Tag began to feel hot inside her own jacket.

"Who would do this?" Torres asked. She grabbed Tag's hand and stared into her eyes expectantly. Tag immediately thought of that FBI covert search team and its vials of dust— *to replace anything they disturbed*. It was silly to imagine the agents toting baggies of replacement cereal, but it wouldn't have been difficult to send someone to the nearest Jewel Osco to buy some after an accidental spill. And if the FBI had entered the director's home, then the place was most certainly bugged. That meant the Bureau had heard everything they'd just said.

Tag listened to Dr. Torres breathe, and felt the warm air from the woman's lips breeze across her neck. She tried to ignore the director's low zipper, which just hovered there, glinting in the moonlight, creating a deep *V* of smooth skin. Something had drawn Tag to Alex Torres, like a magnetic force. She'd felt the attraction immediately that morning at the lab, and when the director touched her hand just now, it confirmed what Tag already knew in her gut. She'd met this woman before, maybe she'd even *loved* her. Dr. Torres knew it too.

Impulsively, Tag leaned in and kissed Dr. Torres lightly on the lips. Then she whispered: "Do you still want that shower?"

* * *

Underneath Alex Torres's hoodie was a lithe sculpture. Tag watched streams of water fall against the nape of the woman's neck and map the contours of her naked form. Under the spray of the shower, Tag traced the water's path with her mouth, her lips moving hungrily over Alex's stomach and hips, working her way to the neat point between her legs. The physicist rested a slippery thigh on Tag's shoulder. Tag felt a pleasant sting on her scalp as Alex gripped her hair. The director's moans echoed against the tile until they reached a shrill pitch. Balanced on her tiptoes, Alex's calf muscles hardened into marble posts and then vibrated dangerously. When it was over, Tag rose and the two women pressed their bodies together, standing nearly the same height so that their nipples slid across each other's, and their eyes lined up.

Tag nibbled on Alex's earlobe. "Who are you?" she asked.

The physicist just growled seductively, her hand slithering between them, moving lower. Then Tag felt a wonderful pressure as Alex's fingers explored her. Tag leaned against the wall, bucking, with her eyes shut tight. She recalled that same overpowering sensation. *Chen Wei—his solid weight pressing down, his hips grinding, rocking the bed in that Shanghai apartment like a canoe in open water.* Tag recognized the pressure inside of her, too, as Alex's fingers took on the familiar shape of the one she'd loved over and over. Her soul mate. *Corba Perella, Chen Wei, Gerald Cutter . . . Alex Torres. Could they all be connected?*

Alex pumped her arm. A deep throb pulsed in Tag's belly. She clawed at the physicist's back with her mouth open so wide that she'd swallow a gallon of water before the spasms stopped.

The women lingered in the shower until the stream began to lose its heat. Tag enjoyed the intimacy of standing naked beside Alex, but she also knew the white noise from the spray would mask their conversation from any FBI listening devices. Tag explained everything to Alex. The past-life memories she'd unearthed during her hypnotherapy sessions with Dr. Jacobson, the strange similarities she shared with Sophie Whitestone.

For a scientist governed by the tidy rules of mathematics, Alex responded with remarkable openness. "Quantum physicists are the first to recognize that we don't really know shit about the universe. We're philosophers by necessity, remember?"

"Maybe that's why I found you in this life. Your experiment could prove all of this. Do you really think you'll detect human consciousness in that giant underground machine you've built? Will you find Big C and prove that we never really die, but exist as some kind of infinite energy source?" Tag asked.

"I don't know, Vera. I really don't. We make wild bets in my field, spend a lot of money to test our theories, and sometimes we hit the jackpot. Sure, we could find Big C, but we could spit out a fat goose egg too," Alex said. "I urge you to hold on to some degree of skepticism, though, until the science proves otherwise. It's too easy to get swept up into our own fantasies of what's possible, and ignore evidence to the contrary. That said, if anything you've told me is actually true, it only supports just how important my experiment is. We can't let Caleb Miller, or anyone else, fuck it up."

* * *

After the shower, the women moved to the bed. The sheets enveloped them in soft, silky layers. They lay still at first, Alex's leg's coiled around Tag's waist. Their breathing synchronized.

"You're a part of me now," Alex said softly.

Tag smiled, thinking the woman was wrong. They'd *always* been one unified whole.

Alex used a fingernail to draw circles around Tag's right breast, causing the nipple to peak into a hard button. The gentle gesture stirred up the embers of lust still glowing inside Tag's chest. She mounted the physicist and felt the woman's hands glide over her body. Tag's chin pointed toward the ceiling as she sucked in every last molecule of oxygen in the room, feeding the hungry flames inside. The heat in her veins intensified as Alex touched her everywhere, and she reciprocated with her own probing fingertips. Tag's head fell to the side, and that's when she saw it, resting on top of the dresser, polished and black.

A music box—one made of Bolivian rosewood.

The light seeping in from the window was enough to make out the detail on the box's lid and its ornate brass latch.

The object sat in a blue square of light that seemed meant to celebrate its mystical significance. Was it the same box? Had it really traveled from Shanghai, China, to Batavia, Illinois? In Tag's vision, Rae Yin had revealed the music box to Chen Wei, her lover. Had he passed it to someone else? Or maybe Chen had hidden it, planning to retrieve the box after reincarnating as someone else—as Alex Torres, perhaps. It was a risky move for something so important. The box could've been lost forever. Unless a soul like Chen could control the details of his reincarnation, select a body for the next life.

Tag looked at Alex, who in the throes of ecstasy had bitten her own lip so hard she'd drawn a bead of blood. The woman was close to climax. She writhed underneath Tag's weight, but her gaze remained locked. *The shape of Alex's eyes, the bridge of her nose—yes, she does look like him. And she certainly* feels *like him.* And now, the presence of the music box wiped away any remaining doubt. *Yes! I remember now.*

Tag felt lightning shoot up her thighs into her rib cage. Electricity crackled up her spine and shocked her brain stem with a blinding flash. Underneath her, Alex gripped the mattress and howled as the two women reached the mountaintop simultaneously. At such high altitude, Tag absorbed bolt after bolt for what felt like a full minute. Through narrowed eyes, she stared at the wooden music box—the container that held the eternal secrets of the Sons of Elijah. The Capstone was inside it. Tag shook from the snapping voltage.

29

THE FARMHOUSE'S WIDE porch shone under a coat of fresh white paint, even though the wooden planks had to be a half-century old. They squeaked under Tag's feet, as if warning her to tread lightly or risk falling through a rotted-out patch, into the soggy, moldy section hidden underneath the deck. The entire home leaned slightly, the natural slope nudging guests outside. *Is this how scientists expel unwanted visitors?* Tag wondered. *With a subtle assist from physics?* But Tag wasn't an unwanted visitor, at least not last night. Dr. Torres—Alex—had invited her, welcomed her inside, opened up to her. Tag had never slept with a stranger before. But nothing about Alex had felt strange. *And her scent . . .*

Tag had awoken that morning between Alex's sheets. The bed was warm. And empty. She'd found a note taped to the bathroom mirror: *Early morning today. Please stay.*

Alex had made a full pot of coffee, something dark and nutty. Tag poured a cup and allowed gravity to guide her along the floor's slight pitch and out the front door. A panoramic prairie stretched out from the house. Wild grasses shuddered in waves. A single white oak towered over the field. A hawk was perched on its highest branch, fifty feet up. The bird's head flicked, and its sharp beak angled toward the ground as it scanned the grasslands for breakfast. Did an animal like that ever feel morally conflicted? *Certainly not with an empty belly,* Tag thought. It had a job to do, and that job was ripping the heads off mice. Tag had a responsibility to her job too. So why did she feel so guilty?

Because you know her. Because she made your legs quiver like that prairie grass. Because her body feels like home. Because she's not a stranger, she's . . . Gerald. That's what you don't want to think about, Hunny Bunny. Just like you don't want to think about that music box on the dresser. But you're hungry for the truth, and that hunger's pulsing in your belly. Your empty belly.

Tag flung the rest of her coffee into the yard. She marched back into the house, pushing against the invisible forces that wanted to keep her out. She returned to Alex's bedroom, moved to the dresser, and placed both palms on the lid of the music box. The Capstone was inside, she was certain. So many people had died to protect it; now it sat unguarded in a messy bedroom in Illinois. *What the hell is it anyway?* she wondered.

The Capstone is the key to life, and likewise, the key to life's undoing. Isn't that what Bishop Marti had told Ramon? But how does a disk of polished stone hold so much power over life itself?

In one motion, Tag could open the box, look inside, and then get the hell out of there, having satisfied her curiosity. But it wasn't curiosity keeping her sweaty hands on that box. It was that *hunger.*

Minutes later, Tag was behind the wheel of her Crown Vic, racing down the narrow road, away from the farmhouse. The latch on the music box jangled as it bounced in the passenger seat. Tag had pried it open easily, expecting some divine revelation or rush of ancient knowledge with the squeak of the brass hinges. A pocket of stale air had escaped from the box when she'd pulled back its lid. Tag had heard music too—resonant piano notes—that mechanically could not have come from the now hollowed-out container. The tune had filled Tag's ears like a whispered secret.

Unfortunately, what she'd found inside the box didn't bring clarity, only more confusion. The object hadn't seemed the least bit valuable. Still, Tag had felt compelled to take it. If she'd left it, she would never see it again, and she'd still feel so insatiable; of that Tag was certain.

With one hand on the wheel, piloting the beastly Crown Vic, Tag slapped the box's lid to stop that loose, rattling latch. In her first week working a real investigation, she'd already stolen two pieces of evidence. Tag would return to her apartment and shove the music box onto the top shelf of her closet, beside the floppy disk from Sophie's bedroom. Her little collection of contraband.

In her rearview mirror, Tag watched the hawk launch itself from the tip of the oak tree and dive soundlessly to the earth, its great wings spread, its beak open.

*   *   *

By the time Tag reached the clot of traffic slow-pumping its way into downtown Chicago, she'd decided to come clean about the music box. First, she'd call Alex and tell her that she'd taken it. A visceral compulsion had driven her to snatch it—that was the best explanation Tag could provide. It was the truth, and Alex would understand. *No, you klepto-freak, she won't understand. You're an officer of the law, and you stole her stuff. Remember how Alex reacted when she suspected someone had taken her cereal?*

Tag could turn around; drive back to Batavia; crunch down that gravel road, past the grazing buffalo; roll right up to the weird farmhouse that belonged somewhere in central Kansas; and place the wooden box right back on Alex's dresser. She could wipe off her fingerprints (like a bona fide criminal) and scoot. Dr. Torres—the beautiful, brilliant, fire-plug sex goddess—would never know Tag had taken it. And neither would Acting Special Agent in Charge Gina Butler.

Tag veered toward the freeway off ramp, and the Crown Vic hit a pothole. The music box's lid snapped. She reached for it. Her fingers felt the smooth wood. She wanted to lift the lid. *Just one more look.*

Her phone trilled, and she nearly swerved off the road. She looked at the screen. The number had a 630 area code— Chicago's western suburbs, including Batavia. It was Alex. She'd discovered the music box was missing. Tag silenced the ring and tossed the phone into the cup holder. She'd passed the point of no return now. She couldn't bring the box back. *You never wanted to do that anyway. You wanted to keep it for yourself. Put it on* your *dresser.*

She'd have to admit to Butler that she'd taken it. The boss would initiate an internal review, and surely that would unearth the stolen floppy disk too. It would mean the end of Tag's career. Maybe it was for the best. She pressed her sneaker into the gas pedal, and the Vic's V8 engine growled. The sooner Tag got to the field office, the sooner she could hand over the music box, along with her resignation, and get out of there before Butler's disappointed frown melted right off her face. Tag had always admired the woman's superior instincts, but Agent Butler had clearly made a mistake when she'd recruited Tag for the Bureau.

The car's meaty rumble vibrated inside Tag's gut. *Add speeding to the list of transgressions,* she thought. At least she'd avoid the worst offense: lying to the FBI. If there was one lesson she'd absorbed from her training, it was never lie to a colleague. They'd lock a person up for doing that.

The stoplight flicked red as Tag sailed through an intersection, going sixty-five. A flash of yellow stepped off the curb. It was an elderly woman in a floral muumuu. Tag threw her weight onto the brake and swerved into the oncoming lanes before jerking the wheel back just as a truck lopped off her side mirror. Her heartbeat pounded in her neck.

Shaken, Tag pulled into the parking lot of a medical building and killed the engine. She rested her forehead on the steering wheel and sucked in long breaths. When she finally looked up, something hooked her attention, and her gut growled again.

A woman emerged from the medical building. She stood underneath the block letters "Cortava Infusion Center" and scrambled the contents of her purse. She'd slicked her hair into a ponytail. It had grown out since Tag had seen her last. The woman's eyes met Tag's. Her nostrils twitched. Then the woman raced to a Chevy Malibu, fumbled with the door, started the engine, and zipped away. For a moment, Tag forgot about the stolen music box, the yellow-smocked granny, the image of Butler's melting lipstick frown, the smoldering garbage fire of her months-long FBI career. It all flew from her mind because she'd just seen something impossible. *Someone* impossible.

Chloe King, Tag's murdered roommate, was alive.

30

CHLOE HAD APPLIED for an apartment in Winnetka, giving her middle name, Aletta, and then used the same trick to register the Chevy Malibu. Tag probably hadn't even needed to check the Illinois DMV database to confirm this. "Aletta King" had posted plenty of useful details about her suspiciously nascent life on her private Instagram (that was not so private as far as Uncle Sam was concerned). That's where Tag learned about her former roommate's mother, who had been growing a riot of cancer cells in her colon for some time. Chloe had likely been visiting the Cortava Infusion Center to sit with her mom during an extended chemo drip.

After spotting Tag in the parking lot, a panicked Chloe had driven twenty miles to the Oakbrook Center, bought a brunette wig and an acid-washed jean jacket, and then chased the sun, pushing the Chevrolet to its limit for nearly four hours. Tag had followed her for the entire jaunty afternoon. The Crown Vic's low-gas indicator light had illuminated just as Chloe pulled into an IHOP parking lot fifteen miles outside Cedar Rapids. After a dip into the ladies' room,

Chloe emerged wearing the brown bob and tacky tangerine lipstick.

Posted in a well-shaded parking spot, Tag watched the restaurant window as Chloe attacked a short stack and drained a cup of coffee. Her former roommate probably thought she'd managed to slip away unnoticed, like a dollar-movie heroine running from an abusive husband. Tag waited to make her move until Chloe had filled her belly with the cheap breakfast food.

"I've always thought you'd look great with darker hair," Tag said, sliding into Chloe's side of the booth, blocking her escape. The young woman dropped her fork and nearly toppled a glass of OJ. "Do you mind if I have a sip?" Tag asked, stabilizing the glass. "Road trips always leave me so parched." She gulped, finishing with a dramatic *"Ahh."*

Chloe's hands trembled. "They paid for everything— you've got to understand what that meant to me . . . and to Mama." She slumped in the seat, eyes darting.

"Who? Who paid?"

Chloe's nose scrunched up.

"Listen, until this morning, I thought you'd been found dead in a bathtub more than a year ago. I'm so relieved you're alive, Chloe." Tag put a hand on her roommate's arm, and the woman seemed to relax a little. "But I don't understand any of this. Please tell me what's going on."

Chloe stared at the swirls of syrup on her plate, as if considering the risks of explaining further. Finally, she spoke. "About a month before I . . . went away, a man came by the apartment. You were at the gym, I think. You know I was behind on rent, and I'd just lost my job at the bike shop, and then my mom . . . The doctors caught it late, probably too late to operate, but they wanted to try anyway. She didn't have insurance or savings. What was I supposed to do? She would've died otherwise."

"The man," Tag said, "he offered to pay for your mom's surgery?"

Chloe nodded. "Not just the surgery—*everything*. He put her up in one of those assisted care homes where they have movie nights and Salisbury steak dinners on Fridays. I don't even *know* how much the chemo costs, but they're covering that too."

"And all you had to do was give up your entire life? Disappear? Why, Chloe? It makes no sense."

"Yeah, it was shady as hell. I'm not an idiot. People don't ask you to fall off the face of the planet for legit reasons, but I knew enough not to ask too many questions. It's not like they wanted me to hurt anyone. And the treatments—they probably saved my mom. She's not out of the woods yet, but she's getting stronger. Maybe another month and she'll—"

"What exactly did this man ask you to do?" Tag asked.

Chloe stabbed at her uneaten toast with the points of her fork. "The rules were simple. Invite some dude over—not the man who first approached me; this new guy was closer to my age—bang some shit around in the bedroom and moan a little, make it sound like a wild romp, you know? And then leave with him after you fell asleep."

"How did you know when I'd fallen asleep?"

"He hid a camera in your room, in the recessed light above your bed."

"Holy shit!"

"I know, it was fucked up, Tag. I'm so sorry." Chloe's eyes became shiny.

Tag was too angry to feel bad for her. Someone had paid Chloe to fake her own disappearance, her own *murder*. It was insanity. "Where did you go that night?" Tag asked.

"The young guy, he staged the bedroom. I'd given them a blood sample that afternoon, and he put some drops on the sheet. Then he did something to our lock, used this long tool that slipped underneath the apartment door to slide the barrel bolt after we left. That's when I started to figure this was about you. They wanted to set you up. I almost called the whole thing off."

Almost, Tag thought. *But you didn't. You would've let them pin your murder on me. And, stupid me, I thought we were friends.*

"Chloe, who was that man? Who did this?" Tag didn't need to hear the answer; she already knew.

"I never saw the younger guy after that night, but the older one—the one who pitched the whole idea in the first place—he checks up on me, tells me I'm doing a great job, that my country is thankful for my service. My *service,* he says. Can you believe that? It's all bullshit, I know."

"So he's with the government?"

Chloe held a napkin to her face to hide her lips. "The FBI," she whispered. "He never told me that, just said vague things like 'I work for Uncle Sam,' but I could tell that's where he was from. The feds all have the same arrogant swagger, you know? Like their badge adds an inch to their cock. Stay away from them, Tag."

A little late for that, Tag thought.

"They gave me a new name, new car, new apartment—although I had to move out to the burbs. I could get a job and come into the city to visit my mom once a week. Really, he just wanted me to lay low. If I contacted you in any way . . ." Chloe's voice hitched. "If you found out that I was alive, then it would all go up in smoke, he said. He'd arrest me—somehow he'd found out about that check I'd forged from my aunt's bank account while she was cruising in the Caribbean—and Mama wouldn't get her treatment. It was basically blackmail. I was furious, but you know what? It worked. Now the government has its hands around my throat, and I can't move an inch. But I don't care because Mama is going to survive. I did what I had to do."

It *was* blackmail, in the technical sense, and yes, it *did* work. Tag's New Agent Training curriculum had included detailed how-to instructional blocks on all flavors of coercion. Most people had done something in the gray zone between legal and illegal, and if they had any conscience at all, they felt pretty shitty about it. A rap on the front door from the FBI would send them into a tizzy, make them think they'd go straight to maximum security for tagging a stop sign in high school. These were generally good people who'd made a mistake, but sometimes they were also people who had information that the Bureau found useful. But what did the FBI want with Chloe King?

"They took your life away," Tag said. "They had no right."

"It's not forever. The older man said it was only for two years. Then everything could go back to normal. By then, Mama could be in remission, maybe cured. I'd give up *ten* years if it meant she could live another thirty or forty."

Chloe pressed the corner of a paper napkin against her bottom eyelids to soak up the tears welling there. After breakfast, she'd probably drive home, throw that stupid wig into the trash, and bury her face in the couch cushions. In the morning, she'd lose it all—the car, the apartment, the medical treatments for Mom—when the FBI found out. *And they will find out,* Tag vowed. She would demand answers. And Tag wouldn't feel a drop of remorse for what would happen to her ex-roomie. Chloe had struck a devil's bargain and then broken the rules. She deserved what came next. Her mom shouldn't have to pay the price, but that was Chloe's demon to wrestle, not Tag's.

"I'm so sorry, Tag. Please believe me. I was desperate." Chloe reached over and placed a hand on Tag's forearm. Her fingers felt like wet pieces of clay, clammy and dead. Tag was disgusted by her.

"The night you disappeared, that was the same night of my final art exhibit," Tag said. "A woman from the FBI approached me, said I should apply to be an agent. I told you about her when I got home. You encouraged me to do it. You knew the feds were planning to stage your disappearance that same night, and yet you *pushed* me to consider the job."

"It was part of the deal," Chloe said. "The man didn't tell me why, but he was very clear. Tell your roommate to trust the FBI, he said. When you came home with that agent's business card . . ." Chloe stared at her plate. "After I left, what did the FBI *do* to you?"

Tag wanted to slap Chloe so hard it would leave a tangerine smear across her ex-roommate's cheek. Instead, Tag slid out of the booth with her chin raised.

"What did the FBI do?" Tag repeated. "They hired me. And then that woman I'd met assigned me to the most important case the Chicago Field Office has had in three decades."

With a sharp pivot, Tag left the restaurant. Chloe was hopelessly naive, but she was right about one thing: the FBI had set Tag up. Gina Butler had planned it from the beginning.

THE TOILET FLUSHED and the stall door opened. Acting
Special Agent in Charge Gina Butler straightened her
skirt and smoothed the fabric over the curves of her hips. She
looked annoyed to see Tag leaning against the hand dryer.

"One of the perks of getting the big office for real will
be the private bathroom. Maybe then I'll be able to move
my bowels without people lining up for autographs." Butler
moved to the sink. "Although I am pleased to see that you
decided to show up for work, Agent Taggart. There's a
bomber on the loose, in case you'd forgotten, and it's your
name printed across the top of his case file. I'm beginning to
think that was a mistake."

"Not your only one," Tag retorted.

Butler's head snapped toward the junior agent. "Excuse me?"

"Well, for starters, you probably should've relocated
Chloe's mother too. The woman would've hollered about
having to find a new doctor, what with the cancer blooming
inside her gut, and all, but did she want the money or not?
And with Mom convalescing in the suburbs, Chloe wouldn't

have needed to travel into the city to sit with her during those long chemo-drip treatments. The Cortava Infusion Center is only five blocks from my apartment. Did you know that? Seems like an oversight to me. A *mistake*, perhaps."

Butler sucked in her cheeks. She studied herself in the mirror, angling her chin. "I've lost friends too. Things can get muddy when you're grieving. It's completely normal to think you've seen them picking out yogurt in the grocery store or walking a dog in the park. You probably—"

"I sat next to her, close enough to smell the plastic of her cheap wig. We had pancakes," Tag said. "Chloe King told me everything."

The acting SAC reapplied lipstick along her bottom lip. Her color was fire-engine red, not tangerine like Chloe's. Butler couldn't go on pretending she had nothing to do with Chloe's disappearance. "So now that Quantico playtime is over, you're getting a crash course on how things really get done around here."

"You *lied* to me." Tag's voice flew up an octave. She fought to suppress her rage. "You told me Chloe had been murdered. There was no suspicious boyfriend, no snake bite. You set the whole thing up. What kind of sick reason did you have for that?"

"Oh, Taggart. We're not the sick ones. But the psychopaths we're hunting—*they* are deeply disturbed. Thankfully, most are dum-dums who can't get out of bed without tripping over their own dicks. Those we snatch up easily. But the really nasty fellas, they can be damn clever. They do their deeds in plain sight, right under our noses, and we still can't catch them, not with around-the-clock surveillance or covert searches or confidential informants or any of the normal rigmarole. Those guys are sneaky fucks. So, we have to be even sneakier."

Tag folded her arms. "This is about Dr. Jacobson. You still think he's helping the Sons of Elijah."

"Dear girl. Dr. Jacobson *is* the Sons of Elijah. The ringleader himself. He feeds on the young and vulnerable, the mentally unstable people who go to him for help. He earns their trust and admiration to the point that they'd do anything for him. Jacobson is like a modern-day Charles Manson. He may not pull the trigger himself, but he loads the gun and thrusts it into the hands of a deranged groupie. Sophie Whitestone gave her life for Jacobson. Probably Gerald Cutter too; we just never found him. And Caleb Miller is Jacobson's next victim."

"It's not so simple to convince people to commit a suicide attack after a few months of therapy."

"You're right. Persuasion alone wouldn't necessarily work. That's why Jacobson uses drugs. Biotoxins, in fact. It's his area of expertise. He mashes up these . . . jungle plants and then does his black magic hypno-spell. It takes time, but he essentially rewires his victim's brain until they can't tell fantasy from reality," Butler explained.

Tag remembered Dr. Jacobson's story about the lecture he was supposed to give in Paris years ago. He'd mentioned those Amazonian shrubs and their—*what was it?*—psychoactive effects. They reconfigured the brain, he'd said. He'd thought the treatment could improve memory. *Improve memory or create false ones?* Tag felt chills slithering up her back.

"But toxicology would've—"

"There's not much to work with after a suicide bombing," Butler interrupted. "Jacobson knows what he's doing. Tell me, has he ever offered you anything to drink? When you're alone with him at his office? At his *home?*"

Tag hadn't reported the details of her visit to Dr. Jacobson's residence. Butler had ordered her to follow up with him, hadn't she? Butler had wanted her to find out what Jacobson knew about Sophie's sonogram of Caleb. *She didn't tell me to go to his house so late at night, though,* Tag thought. *She didn't tell me to drink his whiskey and lie down on his couch.*

"You had me followed," Tag said. "I went to Jacobson's home to elicit information about Caleb. Ordering the SSGs to tail me without my knowledge could've disrupted my op."

Acting SAC Butler turned to face Tag and clucked her tongue on the roof of her mouth. "Open your pretty brown eyes, Taggart. *You* are the op."

That slick, slithering chill coiled around Tag's neck. Butler glared at her with a piercing squint.

"Do you really believe the Federal Bureau of Investigation needs to recruit art students?" Butler asked. The bathroom door suddenly opened, and a woman entered—a gal Tag knew from Human Resources. Butler snapped her fingers, and the lady reversed back into the hallway. "You're a goddamn dangle. A wriggling worm on a hook."

Tag accidentally bit the inside of her cheek. She tasted sour blood. The memories of that night they first met flowed across her field of vision—Butler, the seductress in a tight evening gown, showering Tag with praise for her macabre exhibit. *And my art wasn't even really that good, was it?* Then had come the improbable proposal. *Join the Bureau, put those brushstrokes to work in law enforcement!* More strangely, on day one, Butler had assigned Tag to lead what would become the most critical case in decades—a case that the acting SAC had run personally until the new rookie reported for duty. *A perfectly normal transition, right?* And then there was Agent Joe Michelson, Tag's so-called partner, who didn't give a damn about actually working with her. *He's in on this. He's my babysitter. Michelson's been handling me like a ten-dollar informant. Was he the "older man" Chloe mentioned? The one who worked for "Uncle Sam" and thanked her for her "service"?* Why hadn't Tag seen it before?

"Mrs. Whitestone, Sophie's mother . . . she mentioned other girls," Tag said weakly, her thoughts racing in streaks. "There were . . . complaints, she said."

"Jacobson's got a thing for coeds. He targets them on campus, grooms them like any other predator would, except in his case, he's got thirty years of experience perfecting biochemical mind control. The university dismisses the complaints every time. Jacobson explains them away as idiosyncratic side effects of his research. His methods are atypical, he says. Too innovative for some patients to understand. Bottom line: the University of Chicago has a superstar on its payroll, and they aren't about to let a few confused teenagers fudge that up for them. Or Jacobson's ex-fiancée, for that matter."

"Dayella? Jacobson told me about her," Tag said, remembering the chilling story. "She fell from a hotel balcony in Paris."

"Fell? Or was she *pushed*?" Butler's red lips made a popping sound. "Oh, he didn't include that part in his little anecdote? He didn't tell you that the French Gendarmerie had him tied up in knots for three weeks after Dayella's tragic death? The police interviewed everyone on their floor. Turns out, the elderly couple staying in the hotel room next to theirs had heard shouting. *Angry* shouting."

"He told me that she'd fainted and lost her balance. The railing was damaged, and it broke away."

"A security camera mounted outside on a lamppost captured Dayella on the balcony, waving her arms at someone inside in the hotel room. They were arguing and Jacobson came at her, Taggart. That's what the French police thought, but they couldn't prove it. The CCTV footage was too grainy to see everything."

"Jacobson invited Dayella to Paris. They had planned to marry that upcoming spring," Tag said. "When he spoke of her, it really sounded like he'd loved her."

"Who knows? Maybe he did. But not as much as he loved his career. The Gendarmerie dug into Jacobson's emails. They think Dayella found out about one of his flings—a hot young thing in the freshman class. This girl was problematic, though. She was only seventeen. The university administration wouldn't have been able to turn a blind eye. If they'd found out, that is. These young girls were nothing more than sexual playthings to Seth Jacobson. Dayella confronted him, and then he killed her to keep her quiet. And now he's grooming you."

Tag remembered the painting she'd made of Jacobson and Sophie, nude and embracing. *And after the second hypnosis session, I awoke and found my shoes untied and switched on my feet . . . and Jacobson was so sweaty.* "I'm really not his type, you know."

"Like hell you're not. You're a square peg in a round hole, Taggart. You're smart and talented but totally lost. Most importantly, your special abilities, the psychic visions you claim to experience when painting, even if it's all bogus— you were wrong about a snake biting Chloe, after all—we knew you'd fascinate Jacobson. Plus, those experiences would make you more open to his methods. You are open, aren't you?" Butler asked, moving closer. "You've let him put you under. You've *seen* things. Haven't you? Tell me, Taggart. Do you think what you've seen is real?"

Tag backed away until her body pressed into the door. Her fingers found the handle. She wanted to bolt from the bathroom, race out of the building, gulp the blue air. The scenes flashed, one by one. The row of burning Cathars strung up at the base of Montségur like wriggling black pods, their skin peeling from the heat. Then the trucks with loud-speakers mounted to their roofs, passing under the apartment window in Shanghai, blaring propaganda in Mandarin—a language Tag had never learned, yet understood perfectly. Could Jacobson really have planted those images in her mind with nothing more than some ground-up leaves and smooth talking? What about the photo of Mr. Whitestone's red parka (*but a lot of men wear red, don't they—especially in the woods, to stand out against the snow?*) or Tag's completely new allergy to honey (*just an adverse reaction to Jacobson's tricky leaves, perhaps*)? Dr. Jacobson had planted the seeds of these visions, and Tag had watered them until they'd grown into thick stalks. She wasn't a federal investigator; she was a victim. And not just Jacobson's victim.

"I'm done talking," Tag said to Butler. "You're using me."

The acting SAC inched closer, crowding into Tag's space, and put her palm against the bathroom door, beside Tag's head. She brought her nose inches from Tag's. Butler's perfume smelled like that honey oil from the diner. "Oh no. You're in deep with him. Exactly where you need to be. I'm not using you. I've given you a gift. You are in a position to save thousands, maybe millions of lives. Sure, I may have crossed a line or two, but in thirty years the FBI had gotten nowhere with this case. Besides, I'm not the only one who's bent a few rules."

No doubt Michelson had told Butler about the floppy disk Tag had stolen from Sophie's closet. And there was also Alex's music box, still resting in the passenger seat of her Crown Vic.

Butler cocked her head and sniffed the nape of Tag's neck. "You're right about one thing. This psychopathic manipulation for personal gain, it's *always* something sexual." Butler's sticky lips brushed Tag's earlobe. "Who do you think is the real father of Sophie's child?"

"Jacobson? No, he isn't. The sonogram says Caleb *Cutter*. Sophie and Gerald—"

"A pregnant teen can scribble whatever she wants on a sonogram photo, but she can't change a baby's DNA."

"You already knew that Caleb was Sophie's son?" Tag asked. The continued betrayal felt like hot venom streaming through her veins.

"Seth Jacobson is a monster. He hunted Sophie Whitestone, tangled her mind into knots, impregnated her, and then compelled her to murder four hundred and thirty-seven people, killing herself in the process. What's worse, before her death, she'd managed to recruit at least four others who went on to terrorize the city with a rash of suicide bombings, reaching a body count in the thousands. Yes, you're a dangle, a lure meant to draw Jacobson out. So what? You're still an FBI agent, and I was telling the truth when I said you had potential. Jacobson's got his wide fish mouth around you, and with a firm yank we'll have our hook in him. So, shake it off, splash some water on those cheeks, and let's save the fucking world, Agent Taggart."

Butler pulled open the bathroom door. "Welcome to the *real* FBI," she said, and left.

Tag bent over the sink, listening to the fading click-clack of Gina Butler's high heels.

CHAPTER

32

THE BOY'S EYES were two flashlights running on fresh bat-
teries at full bright. He reached out to accept a hot dog
with both hands like it was a crystal scepter—some sacred tool
imbued with the magic of the place. He didn't seem to care
about the knot of people squeezing him, eager to buy their
own foot-long before Carl Hogan stepped up to the plate. The
boy had come to the Wrigley Field ballpark for Hogan too, no
doubt. People had said the Cubs' star hitter would break the
record for career home runs today. Even folks who didn't keep
a personal logbook of Hogan's batting and fielding stats tucked
under their pillow (as this kid most certainly did) appreciated
the majesty of history in the making. It filled the air with
crackling static. And when Hogan finally did take up his slug-
ger and square up in the batter's box, where he'd tap the toes
of his right foot three times into the finely ground red clay (as
he *always* did before a dinger), the surge would course through
the stands, causing every hair to stand stiff and salute.

With a ball cap pulled down to his eyebrows, a man wearing a backpack watched the young fan worm through the
crowd, away from the concession stand, prize in hand. The

boy aligned the hot dog with his small mouth. Just before the first bite, a large woman knocked into his elbow. A spurt of ketchup leapt from the dog onto his white T-shirt. It streaked the front, right down the middle. It looked like an incision a surgeon would make, just before cracking open a ribcage and poking at the pulsing muscle inside.

The lady groped around the inside of her handbag and produced an assortment of wet naps. Her efforts to remedy the ketchup tragedy only resulted in more gory smears, but the boy looked more concerned with the stream of fans flooding back into the stands. *Had the announcer said it? Had he said his name?* The large lady really ought to give the wet naps a rest and hand the poor lad a twenty-dollar bill for a new shirt. Maybe she had one of those in that fat purse. *How is it they're still letting people bring bags into places like this, stadiums packed with souls clinging to their earthly flesh?* the man thought. Someone could smuggle in something more harmful than moist towelettes from Red Lobster. Something that caused a *lot* of red smears.

The man walked to the nearest exit. It felt good to have the weight of the backpack off his shoulders. Now that backpack leaned up against a load-bearing concrete column just a few paces from the hot dog vendor's cart. The man looked up, and his eyes met with the glossy lens of a security camera. He made sure the looping mark on his neck was plainly visible; they'd be looking for it when they reviewed the tapes, just like they scrutinized the footage from the doorbell camera at the Chinatown restaurant. Even without the mark, the man was sure he stood out. Anyone watching must've thought he looked strange, swimming upstream, against the current of sweaty spectators, all rushing back to their seats as the announcer shouted, *"Here comes Hoooogan!"*

* * *

The lake brimmed with water that lapped over the shoreline path in places. The other runners searched for higher ground, but Tag splashed right through, soaking her sneakers. She hadn't jogged much before New Agent Training and had often found the idea of racing around downtown Chicago, dodging madcap Uber drivers and workaday office slaves, absurd. FBI recruits had to clock a seven-minute mile, though, so while at Quantico, Tag had laced up a pair of Nikes and hit the trails each morning, rain or shine. Out there, within the raw envelop, Tag had felt like an animal herself, so in tune with the natural organism. She could lean against a trunk, press her skin into the peeling bark, and melt into the wood grain.

In the city, the lakeshore was as close as she could get to that symbiotic sensation. When running, she never listened to music—it blocked out the sound of the smacking waves— and if her ankles dripped by the end of it, all the better.

She came up on Ohio Street Beach, a pocket of sand the city planners had trucked in for sunbathing and volleyball. Tag slowed to a walk and checked her watch. She'd hit six miles in forty minutes—a fast enough time to maintain her best fitness scores from the Academy, but unfortunately not long enough to clear her mind of the mounting dung pile from the day. At sunrise, she'd awoken still buzzed from a passionate night with Alex Torres. Then, seeing Chloe had changed everything. Her roommate—her friend—had betrayed her. Maybe Chloe had had a good reason, but that didn't numb the sting. And Butler's admission, that the FBI had only recruited Tag to use her as bait for Dr. Jacobson, had felt like a punch in the lung.

Bait or not, Tag had successfully completed her train- ing alongside everyone else in her New Agent class. She'd crushed the obstacle course, skillfully arrested phony bank robbers, learned the differences between *Mapp v. Ohio* and *New Jersey v. T.L.O.* She'd shaken the director's hand at grad- uation and exchanged her blue plastic gun for a bona fide Glock 9 mm. Special Agent Vera Taggart wasn't bait. She was goddamn FBI, just like Butler.

Except Butler couldn't solve the Sons of Elijah case, Tag thought. *I'm going to crack it open like a walnut. Because she's right about one thing: I* do *have unique abilities.*

Butler had lied to Tag about Chloe dying from a snake bite. Tag had painted her roommate tangled up in those asps, drawn her own conclusion, and then Butler had simply confirmed the snake-bite theory. Butler must've thought Tag was a fraud, like some daytime talk show psychic. Even Tag had felt a tinge of doubt when she saw her roommate alive. Now, however, Tag knew that her depiction of her roommate had been bang on. A snake *had* bitten Chloe, but this snake carried FBI credentials and wore fire-engine red lipstick to distract from her fangs.

Tag removed her shoes and felt the sand clump on her wet feet. A lakeside beach bar had set up one of those inflatable movie screens. The Cubs were playing, and a crowd of fans had congregated. A woman watching cupped her mouth. A child tugged on her pants, but the woman's eyes remained glued to the screen. Everyone seemed transfixed by it.

The team must be getting creamed, Tag thought.

But something felt off. Tag drew closer.

Projected onto the screen was the hulking Wrigley Field with its green steel beams and the retro sign tacked above the entrance that read "Home of Chicago Cubs." There were no shots of the infield, the pitcher's mound, the raving fans. Rather, the images showed the exterior of the stadium and the ribbons of people spilling from the doors onto Clark Street. The news crawl read: *Smoke fills main concourse at Wrigley . . . suspicious package found.*

"At least nineteen people have been taken to Thorek Memorial Hospital to be treated for smoke inhalation, but authorities don't believe anyone has died at this point," the female newscaster reported. "Still, as you know, Charlie, smoke inhalation can lead to serious—"

Tag reached for her phone just as it began buzzing in her pocket. She read the name on the screen.

"Joe, I'm seeing it now. Is it another bomb?" Tag asked.

"Dunno yet. CPD is poking at it with one of their robots. Our guys think it was just a smoke bomb, like the kind you can buy at a fireworks store," Agent Michelson answered.

Caleb knew how to make an effective bomb. He'd proven that in Chinatown. And judging by the stuff they'd found in his apartment, he'd planned to escalate his attacks, not resort to Halloween special effects. "So, it's not the Sons of Elijah," Tag reasoned.

"Oh, it is. Trust me. You'd better get down here. He only wants to talk to you."

"What? You caught him?" Tag nearly dropped the phone. With Caleb Miller in custody, this nightmare could be over. She could type up her final report, close the case, and request a transfer to Cleveland or Seattle. *If you aren't fired for stealing evidence, like that music box still in your car. You want to lift the lid and look inside. You want to see it again. But If you touch it—the thing that's the key to life's undoing—it'll sear your fingerprints right off.*

"CPD tackled him before he got even three blocks away. The dude was all over the security cameras. As soon as the backpack started coughing smoke, the computer spat out stills of suspects. It runs on some AI bullshit. The cops recognized him right away. The idiot should've used a time delay. That would've given him a longer head start. Maybe he wanted to get caught."

"What makes you say that?" Tag asked.

"The smoke," Michelson continued. "It came out in red billows. This was all about creating a spectacle, the sad sap's final attempt for attention."

Michelson's theory didn't sound right to Tag. "Caleb doesn't crave attention. He's burdened by shame and guilt. If anything, he shuns the limelight."

"Ho-ho. Not Caleb, hon. Let's rewind the tape and catch you up to speed."

"What do you mean?"

"CPD didn't arrest Caleb Miller for this," Michelson said. "It's Jacobson. I've got the doc sitting in Interrogation Room B right now. And like I said, he only wants to speak to you."

33

"I DON'T GET IT. He's supposed to be thirty thousand feet over the Atlantic right now, on a flight to the International Symposium on Parapsychology in London." Tag stood on the dark side of the two-way mirrored glass, studying Dr. Jacobson. The doctor slouched in a chair in the interrogation room. His cuffed hands were tethered to the tabletop with a steel chain. "What are the smudges on his neck?"

"Eyeliner," Michelson answered. "He'd drawn a purple infinity symbol right under his ear. Had a cheap hairpiece on under his hat too. Looked like he took shears to a lady's wig to shorten it, make it look like Caleb's hair."

"Caleb's?"

"Yeah. The doc was romping around right under the security cameras. He *wanted* us to spot him. And look at him now, grimacing like he's trying to pass a kidney stone. The guy's practically weeping. I say, let him pout. I'm getting a refill." He shook his empty coffee cup.

Tag ran a hand up the back of her head, confused. She hardly recognized the man in the room. Dr. Jacobson always conveyed an air of authority in his office. *And in his home, don't forget about that.* Now, he looked like someone's feeble grandpa, exhausted and vulnerable. Under the florescent lights, she could see his plastic surgery scars peeking out from his sideburns. Maybe the man who hobnobbed with movie stars and presidents, who signed his bestselling books with Sharpies in two-inch-tall lettering, was merely a persona. Perhaps this miserable man was the *real* Jacobson—the one who'd secretly led a deranged terrorist organization for decades, right under the FBI's nose. And the one who'd once impregnated his nineteen-year-old patient, Sophie Whitestone.

Tag thought about how she'd asked Jacobson to sleep with her while in a hypnotic trance. She had no memory of it, only that eerie recording of her voice speaking the revolting request. She'd sounded possessed.

Through the window, Tag examined the doctor carefully, one final scan before opening the door.

Dr. Jacobson looked up when Tag entered the interrogation room. "I suppose you're hoping for an explanation," he said.

"Are you prepared to give me one?" Tag asked. "Why aren't you in London?"

"I had more pressing matters to attend to here."

"The smoke bomb."

"Nothing more than a prank, I assure you," Jacobson explained. "You'll check my credit card transactions and see I bought it at a novelty shop in Downers Grove. It's practically harmless. Nothing more dangerous than standing downwind from a fireworks show. Perhaps the smoke will cause some lung irritation for those within close proximity, but with a mild steroid, that should clear right up. In any case, they want you to ask me about this because it seems like such a strange thing to do—career-ending, probably—but that's not what you really want to ask. It's not what you *really* want to know about."

"Did you know that Caleb Miller was your son?" Tag asked, standing over the table with her arms crossed.

Jacobson didn't flinch. "Yes, Special Agent Taggart. I knew that in the weeks before Sophie Whitestone's death, she had given birth to our son, Caleb."

In Tag's painting, Dr. Jacobson was cradling Sophie. His arms and legs were wrapped around her from behind. She'd painted them both stark naked, and as her brush spread peach and cream onto the canvas, revealing bare shoulders and smooth arms, Tag had assumed the nudity had something to do with Sophie's vulnerability. A metaphor, most likely. The young student had found comfort and protection in her psychiatrist, and in the course of her treatment, she had revealed her raw center to him. The forms had taken shape on Tag's canvas with dimples and shadows, and finally, with urgent strokes, until her own arm burned from holding the brush for so long. When Tag had completed the piece, she'd stood back and let the overhead light flood the glistening paint, casting a shine over the part where the two bodies met without a trace of innocence. That was when Tag had known that a deeper bond had formed between doctor and patient.

"She was in love," Jacobson continued.

Tag felt nauseous. Wasn't that always what narcissistic men like Jacobson thought, that women couldn't resist them? "I don't have to be a psychiatrist to know love from infatuation. Do you honestly believe that impressionable young woman had feelings for you, her therapist?"

"Not me," Dr. Jacobson corrected. "Gerald Cutter. Even I'd come to believe they were soul mates, cast and recast as a matched pair throughout the ages. Once, Gerald showed up to his session on the wrong day and bumped right into Sophie. How serendipitous that they'd found one another, both patients of my practice. Or maybe serendipity had nothing to do with it."

"You were jealous of him. You wanted Gerald out of the picture so you could have Sophie to yourself."

Dr. Jacobson shook his head. Bits of the hacked-up wig that had stuck to his hair snowed down onto the table. "No, no. That's not it at all. Sophie was devastated after Gerald's disappearance. They were like two halves of a pulsing star, bound by cosmic energy. In our final sessions, we'd uncovered lifetime after lifetime, and they'd always found one another. With Gerald gone, a piece of Sophie had turned cold, hardened. The idea of waiting for another incarnation to be with him again . . . she presented a different idea. A sort of Hail Mary. I sincerely doubted it would work, and it could've landed both of us in a great deal of trouble, but Sophie insisted. She wanted to—"

The interrogation room door opened and Agent Michelson swaggered in, a fresh coffee in hand. "Okay, Dr. Mindfuck. Time to give up Junior. You really thought you could save him? What, you'd play dress up and we'd think it was Caleb who dropped that bomb? So now he can hole up in some rest stop bathroom and carve more hieroglyphics into his neck and maybe burp the worm to fantasies of busting a hole in the fuckin' planet? Well, that's not how this Sons of My Asshole bullshit is going to go down, Doc. So, just tell us where he is, and maybe you'll get to see the sun again before that Botox wears off."

"Joe, what are you doing?" Tag asked.

Dr. Jacobson grinned in his chair.

Michelson leaned over the man. "What the hell are you smiling at?"

"He's a psychiatrist, Joe," Tag answered. "Good cop, bad cop isn't going to work."

Dr. Jacobson shrugged and opened his palms. The handcuff chains rattled. "I assure you, there's no need for theatrics."

"How about good cop, *sadistic* cop, then? Agent Taggart can pin you to the table while I pull down your panties and twist a banana into your crusty brown eye. Maybe I could slip you something to knock you out first. That's how you did it with those girls, right? When you drugged them and then raped them under hypnosis?"

Jacobson looked at Tag with almond eyes, downturned and dilated. "Those accusations were dismissed."

Tag wanted to believe the doctor, but she couldn't shake the dull, aching doubt in her stomach. It was time to confront him outright.

"Why did you remove my clothes?" she asked him. Dr. Jacobson blinked.

"The fuck?" Michelson said and turned to his partner. "You never told—"

"After I awoke from hypnosis—the second time, in your office—my boots were on the wrong feet and the laces were untied." Tag stared directly into the doctor's eyes. "You took them off."

"No, I—"

"What else did you take off?" Tag asked. "My pants? My underwear? Did you drug me too?" She tried to steady her voice. She didn't want Jacobson to sense her rising anger.

"I didn't touch you. You had an extreme reaction during the session. You kicked off your boots. I tried to elicit the stimulus of the emotion you were feeling, but you didn't share, and that was just fine. Sometimes patients need to guard themselves after such vivid recollections. But I knew you'd eventually learn about those women who'd accused me in the course of your investigation, if you hadn't already. And if I brought you out of hypnosis, and you saw that your shoes had . . . well, I just thought it best to avoid an unfortunate misunderstanding. You were already beginning to come out of your trance state, and I made a hasty decision in the moment to slip them back onto your feet. It was deceptive not to tell you what had happened. For that I am truly sorry."

"You believe this bullshit?" Michelson asked Tag.

She did. In her vision, a gang wearing ragged uniforms had brutally attacked her. She *had* kicked off her shoes while trying to defend herself. And Tag remembered the scratch on Jacobson's face when she awoke. He could've done it to himself, drawn that pink line across his cheek with the sharp point of his fingernail, but Tag knew he hadn't. *She'd* done it to him.

The vision had been violent and real. She hadn't understood what it meant at the time, but now she did. It was the first glimpse of those scenes from China, when the Red Guards attacked her outside the Jade Buddha Temple. She'd tried to fight them off, kicked at them, *scratched* them. And Dr. Jacobson was right; if she'd suspected that he'd undressed her during the session, she would've reported him immediately. Tag's experimental hypnosis sessions would've ended right there. She would not have gone any further, *seen* any more. And that was his role, wasn't it? To help her *see*. That's what he'd done for Sophie and Gerald too.

"I believe you," Tag finally said. "About the boots, that is. I don't know what happened with those other young women, but I know you didn't violate me. When it comes to Caleb Miller, you're lying. He's your son. You've protected him from the beginning, and that's what you're doing now. You know where he is." Tag touched the back of the doctor's hand, an intimate gesture that made the man straighten in his chair. "You know what Caleb's capable of. A lot of people could die if we don't find him."

Dr. Jacobson worked his tongue against the inside of his cheek. Finally, he said, "Come closer."

Tag looked at Michelson, who threw his hands up. She leaned in. The scent of Jacobson's aftershave filled her nostrils. She could feel his lips brushing against her cheek as he spoke. Tag's eyes widened more with each word. Her gums felt cold in her mouth.

Her partner looked at her expectantly. She backed away from the doctor, knocking into a chair, sending it scraping across the tile floor. She fixed her stare on the interrogation room's door handle, but she never actually felt her hand turn it. The following seconds blurred into a colorful smear. The next sensation Tag felt was the warm breeze against her skin as she sprinted to her car. She didn't notice Michelson moving in on the doctor, with his fist bunched into the shape of a sledgehammer.

34

E VEN WITH THE swishing of passing cars and the woman's
voice on the radio warning her to *stay off the beaches this
evening—it's gonna get nasty out there,* Tag could only hear
Dr. Jacobson's whispers, repeating in her mind.

"You've found each other again, just like before," he'd said.
*"You and Gerald. It's written all over your face. Go to him! Fin-
ish what you started."*

Tag thought of her night with Alex Torres, the scorch-
ing fire of the woman's touch as she gently pushed Tag's
kneecaps apart. The current snapping between their lips as
their mouths made a tight seal, so only a single breath passed
between their bodies. Tag had never felt so deeply connected
to another human being. Could Alex really be the reincarnated soul of Gerald Cutter? *That would make you Sophie,
Hunny Bunny. You realize that, don't you?*

Tag shook her head, but the thoughts only rattled around.
She didn't trust Jacobson . . . or Michelson or Butler or Chloe.
The only person on her side was Alex, and Tag had only just
met the woman.

Tag had to get out of that interrogation room, away from everyone. She just wanted to lock herself in her apartment and think.

The woman on the radio was now warning about *hail the size of jade stones.* Had she really said that? Jade? No, Tag must've imagined it. She scanned to another station and heard a blaring announcement. The sound was badly distorted. Someone was shouting in a foreign language. Chinese, maybe. It was the voice from the loudspeaker, the one that had bellowed propaganda outside Rae Yin's window. The shouting was so damn loud. She turned the volume down, but it did nothing. That voice on the radio only grew louder, more fervent.

Héngsăo yīqiè niúguǐshéshén!

Somehow Tag knew what the barking chant meant: *Sweep away all cow demons and snake spirits.* How could she understand Mandarin Chinese so clearly, as if her tongue had formed the words herself?

Her foot pressed into the gas pedal, sending the Crown Vic soaring down the freeway. Tag spun the radio's tune knob. The ardent chanting dissipated into snowy static.

She focused on the emptiness of the white noise. It sounded like a mother hushing her infant. A faint woman's voice humming sweetly. No, not a woman. It was a man's voice, murmuring, full of breath: *"You and Gerald, you and Gerald. You've found each other again."*

Tag beat her fists against the radio. The tune knob broke off, baring a winking red light underneath. She kept slamming her knuckles into the console until it hurt. The whispering only grew louder.

"Found each other again. Again, again, AGAIN!" it finally shouted. She wanted to scream and rip the thing out by its roots.

Tag swerved and nearly smashed into another car. Horns blared as she regained control of the mammoth sedan. She took a deep breath and then heard only empty static again. Tag had simply imagined the voice coming from the speakers.

It had been a stressful day, and her mind was lashing out. Up ahead, she saw the sign for the freeway off-ramp that would take her home. She reached out and flicked off the radio, silencing the low buzzing. A soft tinkling sound took its place. It was coming from Alex's music box, still on the passenger seat. Its lid had flipped open somehow. The thing had been singing the entire time.

> *Think only arms and heads to shatter,*
> *Better to die than let him conquer.*

* * *

With the music box tucked into the crook of her arm, its lid tightly shut now, Tag climbed the ten flights of stairs to her apartment. She'd avoided the elevator. The idea of it sticking between floors with her sealed inside, clutching the stolen item—a box trapped within a box—made the short points of her neck hairs twitch. She stabbed her house key at the lock, and it jumped from her hands and fell with a dead thud. Tag bent to pluck it from the wood floor, and her eyes flicked to the base of the door. There were scuff marks. Black ones, but not from the soles of shoes.

"He did something to the lock, used this tool to slide the barrel bolt after we left."

The marks were scrapes made by a retractable arm, Tag reasoned. The FBI agent who had collected Chloe the night of her disappearance had slipped a device underneath the door and used it to slide the barrel bolt. Tag had found it locked when she'd awoken, something that she'd assumed could only be accomplished from inside the apartment. *It was Butler's insurance policy,* Tag thought. *She arranged it.* If Tag had refused to cooperate, Agent Butler would've turned the investigation toward Tag—the obsessed, lesbian artist with a thing for gore.

Relocking the door was an ingenious detail, even if disgustingly manipulative. Butler was damn smart. Dr. Jacobson was smart too. One of them was after the truth, and the other was a dangerous liar. Tag needed to sort out which was which.

Still under her arm, the music box beckoned. *"Open me. Look inside again. Pick up that thing sitting in there on the bed of worn satin, feel its heat in your palm."*

Finally, Tag opened her apartment door, and a breath of hazy smoke puffed out. The place smelled like burning toast (*or burning bodies?*). She pulled her shirt collar over her nose and searched for the source. Billows of gray smoke seeped from underneath her closet door. She ran to the kitchen, wet a wad of paper towels and then used it to turn the closet's handle. On a canvas leaning against the wall, an oily Dr. Seth Jacobson clutched Sophie Whitestone. This wasn't the image she'd painted. Fire now consumed the figures on the canvas. It ate away at their flesh as they threw back their heads in frozen howls. A thick, black cloud filled the entire closet.

Tag slammed the door, dropping the music box, which began to sing again. The sour notes sprang forth like piano strings snapping. Tag pushed her fists into her eye sockets and held her breath.

When she opened her eyes, the smell, the smoke, and the eerie singsong tune had all disappeared. The closet door was cool to the touch. Tag opened it. The painting of Sophie and Dr. Jacobson was still there, but it wasn't burning anymore.

Tag ran her fingertips across the canvas, feeling the ridges in the paint. Even in the dim light, she could see that Jacobson's expression was warm and caring, not lecherous. And Sophie's parted lips and arched eyebrows did not express pleasure, but *relief.* The two forms, frozen in a moment of carnal passion, fortified one another, the way two parents would commiserate after the tragedy of losing a child. And they had lost someone—not a child, but someone just as vital to their circle. Gerald. *They gained someone too,* Tag thought. Through this forbidden union of flesh, they'd made Caleb.

Tag traced the connections of the lovers' arms and legs, making the shape of a lazy figure eight. An infinity symbol— the Sons of Elijah's chosen emblem. It signified their belief in rebirth and justified their grotesque acts of violence. *Is it really murder if the soul is immortal?*

Tag picked up the music box, slid it onto the highest shelf, and covered the damned object with a coat. Then she reached for a fresh canvas. She'd solve this grand puzzle the same way she always did. *Visualize the pieces, give them form and weight and edges, light them and position them, turn and angle the bits until they settle into place.* Tag set the blank square on her easel. To others, it may have looked like a white void, but already Tag could see wisps, like smoke. The square became a window. Once she began to paint, she wouldn't stop until she'd answered the most important question of all: Why had Sophie Whitestone set off that bomb twenty-eight years ago?

* * *

When she finished, Navy Pier's iconic Ferris wheel occupied most of the canvas's vertical space. Tag could almost hear the steel joints creaking as the gondolas swayed. On the adjacent building, large, round lightbulbs spelled out "Happy New Year." A swarm of people—mostly faceless shapes wearing all varieties of hats, scarves, and coats—filled the area around the big wheel. A clearing in the crowd had formed. A figure stood in the clearing with its arms outstretched, like the wrong end of a magnet repelling iron fillings.

Many eyewitnesses of Sophie's suicide bombing had identified the girl as a man. Just as most survivors described, Tag had painted the figure on Navy Pier wearing a long men's parka. Possibly, the oversized coat explained the gender mixup. Now, examining her finished work, Tag knew there was more to it. The investigators had missed something. The bomber that Tag had painted was indeed Sophie Whitestone, and she *did* look like a man. Or more accurately, a *boy*. A spindly teenager who'd not yet developed enough to fill his father's coat. And whose freshly shaved head stuck out of the collar like a white egg.

Sophie buzzed her hair before the attack, Tag realized. The explosion had destroyed her body, so investigators had no physical evidence of Sophie's appearance that night, only the recollections of bystanders. Everyone had missed the detail about her hair.

Not everyone. What had Sophie's mother said?

"Shame, young ladies shearing their locks. Sure sends a signal. Men don't like 'em butch."

Mrs. Whitestone knew what her daughter had done. The bristles running up the back of Tag's own neck had reminded the old woman of Sophie's decision to shave her head. Why had she done it? The answer stared back at Tag from the wet canvas.

She ran to the closet, uncovered the music box, and pulled it down from the shelf. *"Back so soon, Hunny Bunny? Not so easy to bury me underneath those coats, is it?"* the box teased. *"The Capstone is meant to be treasured, not neglected like a smelly scarf."*

Tag lifted the music box's lid. A smooth object rested inside. Tag pinched the cold thing and raised it to eye level for closer inspection.

Yes, it's the same shape, Tag thought. She brought the object—a small, flat rock—to her painting and held it up to the canvas. The stone's unique shape looked vaguely like the head of a lion with an upturned chin and a terrific mane. And there, painted on the back of Sophie's bald pate, was the same dark shape. A big purple birthmark with man-eating jaws.

The Capstone—if that's what the rock really was—felt heavy between Tag's fingers, even though it looked so inconsequential. She could open a window and flick it into the street, where a tire would knock it into a gutter. What great secret would be lost then? Did an entire village of Cathars really surrender to flames to keep this stone a secret? Did Sophie Whitestone from the Chicago suburbs really tie bricks of C-4 to her breasts and clear a patch of Navy Pier because of this simple charm?

Maybe the Capstone itself held no power. The object in Tag's hand probably wasn't even the original. Maybe it had been copper once, or even cloth. The material of the object didn't matter. It was the *shape*. Maybe the Capstone was a key, a form of identification.

Tag remembered something she'd read in Dr. Jacobson's book. *"The soul is separate from the body, and yet certain physical characteristics can carry from lifetime to lifetime,"* he'd written. Certain physical characteristics, like birthmarks. Gerald's wife Linda had had a birthmark on her arm that matched an injury from her past life as Jean-Lambert Tallien. And Sophie had one on the back of her head that matched the shape of the Capstone, Tag was certain of it. Did Rae Yin and Ramon Perella have it too? One soul, traveling through time. *And what about you, Vera Taggart? What have you got back there?*

Tag brushed against the grain of short, black hair on the back of her head. She studied the blotch on the canvas; for how long exactly, she couldn't be sure. In a blink, the canvas became Tag's bathroom mirror. Instead of the flat stone, she now held clippers in her hand. She'd worn her hair short for years, but she'd never taken it down to the scalp. *To see what's on the skin.* Finally, this could verify the visions she'd had under hypnosis. *And don't forget about those dreams, when Corba Perella mashed that red-hot stone into the back of her husband's head in the same spot as Sophie's birthmark. She'd branded Ramon so that she could identify him later, after he recycled into another body.*

Tag felt reality slipping away and paranoid delusion consuming her last remaining shred of sanity. She'd dissolve into a blubbering mess, thinking this way. *Like Sophie.* Had Dr. Jacobson used psychoactive biotoxins to trick her mind, as Agent Butler believed, or had the psychiatrist simply unlocked Tag's true memories of her own past lives?

She brought the clippers to the skin just above her collar and held them there. A few quick swipes and she'd know. *That's why Sophie did it too. She wanted to know if she'd see that lion grinning back at her.*

"*Just do it,*" a voice commanded. Ramon's voice. Then Rae Yin's.

Tag pressed the power button and the clippers hummed.

A moment later, tufts of hair gathered around Tag's feet on the bathroom floor. She pulled a hand mirror from a drawer and clutched it to her chest, right over her thumping heart.

You've gone this far. Don't you want to take a look?

Tag raised the mirror behind her, slowly.

She saw the birthmark clearly, roaring away between her ears.

35

Tag's phone buzzed. No, it clanged. *Like the bell in Montségur's belfry*. She dropped the hand mirror into the sink. When she reached for it, a bit of broken glass cut her fingertips. Meanwhile, the phone screamed, the awful sound ping-ponging off the bathroom walls until Tag touched the screen, leaving behind a red fingerprint.

"I just hear heavy breathing," a man's voice said. "Did I interrupt something?"

"Declan, it's you," Tag finally whispered. "What . . . what do you want?"

"Sheesh, you beg for my help, and then when I call with some sweet intel, I get this frosty greeting. Brrrr, Taggart. My testes are like ice cubes over here."

"You have intel? About Caleb's documents?" Tag felt her heart begin to slap against her ribcage all over again.

"Sure do. And listen fast, 'cause I got shit to do tonight."

"The Black and Blue Ball, right." Tag remembered. Half of the Chicago Division would be downtown at the gala tonight. "Okay, just tell me what you found out."

"What do you know about Project PUP?" Declan asked. "It stands for Proton Upgrade Program."

"Nothing."

"A while back, Fermilab secured a massive line item in the Department of Energy's annual budget. They'd planned to construct another accelerator and link it up to the existing one to create a chain. It would've doubled the power of their proton beam," Declan explained.

"But they never built it, I assume. Why?"

"Some old coot wouldn't sell his ranch. The lab needed at least five hundred acres to build the thing, but they had a very stubborn neighbor, apparently."

Tag remembered the herd of bison grazing in the pasture to the north of Wilson Hall. It used to be part of a working ranch, Alex had mentioned. "The accelerator tunnels are underground," Tag said. "What does it matter what's happening in the field above it?"

"The rancher claimed the radiation would sterilize his bulls. He hired some environmental lawyer; I've read the formal complaint—and the court's ruling. The dude actually won his lawsuit."

"So the lab just mothballed the project?"

"Yeah, but not until *after* they'd already broken ground. Fermilab's director at the time was convinced the bison guy was playing hardball, holding out for a bigger payday. Turns out he was just a pigheaded bastard. The construction team had finished three hundred meters of the five-hundred-meter tunnel before DOE pulled the plug. The *Chicago Tribune* exposed the whole wasteful affair, which then pretty much forced a congressional oversight committee to appoint an inspector general. Congress demanded that Fermilab account for every red cent spent on Project PUP."

"This was when, exactly?" Tag asked, rubbing her buzzed head. "I haven't heard anything about this."

"I'm not surprised. It's old news. All of this drama went down in the nineties."

Tag perked up. "Declan, what was the name of the accounting firm that Fermilab hired to conduct the audit?"

"Ah, you see where I'm going with this. Clever girl."

"Just give me the name."

"Cutter and Associates," Declan answered. "The principal accountant was Gerald Cutter."

Tag coughed to get the air moving back into her lungs. "Would Gerald have been privy to the construction plans? Would he have known where to find the access points to the new tunnel from above ground?"

"The audit touched every facet of Fermilab's operations. Gerald Cutter would've had access to everything. Back then, a lot of records were still in hard copy. His firm would've had stacks of boxes filled with paperwork."

"That's why Caleb's documents looked like digitized photocopies," Tag reasoned. "And why Dr. Torres said they were out of date. Gerald must have given them to Sophie, who then hid them away for her son."

"Did you say *son*?" Declan asked. "Holy shit, Tag. Caleb Miller is Sophie Whitestone's *son*?"

"Whatever Caleb is preparing to do at Fermilab, Sophie planned it decades ago, when Caleb was still an infant," Tag went on, ignoring him.

I've got to find Caleb, she thought. She didn't know when he would make his move, but something told her she didn't have much time.

*   *   *

In the mirror, the reflection of Tag's laptop screen hooked her attention. It was playing live news coverage, with the sound off. The crawling text read: *Marking the anniversary of the Sunset Limited tragedy.* The screen filled with shaky footage filmed from a news helicopter showing train cars bobbing in the Mobile River like toy models.

"I should have died that night."

Caleb had spoken these words during his final session with Dr. Jacobson. For some reason, this horrific rail accident haunted the man. Caleb couldn't possibly have experienced the crash himself, but he *believed* he had. *Delusional disorder,* Dr. Jacobson had called it. The milestone anniversary of the Sunset Limited derailment would carry significant meaning for Caleb. He probably relived the delusions every year. And the guilt. He'd feel the crushing weight of it, pressing into him until his skeleton snapped apart at the joints and he came completely undone. He had already come so close to his breaking point, perched on the railing of the DuSable Bridge. All he'd needed was a nudge.

The day's news feed alone would be enough to send Caleb reeling. Staring at the silent images of the smoking steel bones of the Big Bayou Canot bridge and the dark spots floating in the river below, Tag felt a wave of dread. Time was up. Caleb would attack Fermilab *tonight.*

Tag raced from her apartment. The cut on her fingertip from the broken mirror had stopped bleeding, but not before she'd smeared red streaks across her lips.

CHAPTER

36

"JOE!" TAG SHOUTED into her phone while roaring down Interstate 290. "There's another way to get into the Fermilab campus, and Caleb knows about it."

"Now hang on, kid. We've got half the CPD guarding that place. It's screwed up tighter than a nun on Christmas. There's no way that skinny dude's getting inside." Michelson's voice sounded distant. Every other word bled into a spit of static, and the rain drumming on Tag's windshield didn't help.

"Where are you? Are you at a bar?"

"You could say that." He blew a wet snort. "They're pouring generously at the Fairmont tonight. I'm at the Black and Blue Ball. Butler's about to be crowned queen of Chicagoland. She invited some of her—"

"Top performers. Yeah, I heard," Tag cut in. "Listen, I tried calling the CPD team leader onsite in Batavia but got his damn voicemail. I'm going out there now. We need to get an urgent message to him."

"Who? Jake? Save yourself the drive. He's right here with me, sucking on what I hope is a dill pickle. Hey, Jakey,"

Michelson called out over the background music and rolls of male laughter. "Drop that salty pecker and get over here, will ya? My partner's got a question for you."

"Not a *question*," Tag clarified with frustration. "Information about—"

"Taggy, baby," a man said. It was Officer Jacob Clayton, slipping over every consonant.

"What the hell, Clayton?" Tag couldn't contain her frustration. The police officer in charge of overseeing Fermilab security was yucking it up with Joe Michelson and half of the FBI Chicago Division in a hotel ballroom forty miles away.

"Relax, Batavia's handling business tonight," Officer Clayton explained.

"Batavia PD? You're kidding. That's what—a dozen cops? We have more college interns than that on the joint task force."

"I spoke with the Batavia chief less than—shit, what time is it, Joe?—an hour ago, max. He's got his cruisers posted up and down Pine Street and Wilson Road. If anyone rides up to the lab who doesn't belong, they'll scoop 'em up."

"Listen, Clayton," Tag started. "Caleb Miller's going to make his move tonight, and he's not going to roll up to the front gates. There's an access point to a network of tunnels. It's on the northern edge of campus, somewhere along the fence line bordering the bison pasture. It's probably sealed up, overgrown with weeds. The point is, Caleb knows where to find it."

Clayton coughed. "Okay, sure. I'll call the boys. We'll send out a patrol to canvas the fields. No prob."

Tag wanted to scream into the mouthpiece. "A volunteer cop with a Maglite isn't going to cut it. Don't you get it? Caleb knows we've been zeroing in on him, and he's been waiting for an opening. You pulled back security and threw open the barn door. You fucking mor—"

The connection cut out just as a branch of lightning split the sky.

Tag exhaled through pursed lips. With one hand on the wheel, she called Alex Torres for the fifth time and listened to the same cheerful voice on the recording: *Leave a message and I'll call you back, because yoooou* matter. Tag flipped her phone into the empty passenger seat, the one that should've been occupied by her partner. A terrorist was plotting a catastrophic attack, probably tonight, and somehow she was the only one who seemed to give a damn. Gina Butler had invited more than just her top performers to the gala; she'd tied up nearly every agent with a pulse. It was almost like she'd *wanted* to leave Fermilab unguarded.

* * *

Gina Butler emerged from the Fairmont bathroom smelling like white tea leaves. She stood nearly six feet tall in her stilettos, the pricey ones with the red bottoms. Bloody shoes, some singer had called them. Maybe Butler had stepped over a few bodies on her climb to the mainstage. *On, love. You stepped on those bodies. Pierced right through them with the knife point of your six-inch heel.* What male in her position hadn't done the same? No woman had ever served as the special agent in charge of the FBI's Chicago field office. Tonight, that would change. Butler would wipe that "Acting" garbage off her office door for good, and then she'd have her assistant polish the "SAC Gina R. Butler" that remained until the words shone brighter than a silver dollar.

Her promotion hadn't been a sure bet. Plenty of men had made the short list of candidates for Chicago's top post, and the FBI brass in Washington weren't known for their progressive staffing policies. The current director in particular had a reputation for filling key leadership vacancies with people who he felt looked the part, as if he ran central casting for a 1930s gangster film instead of a modern law enforcement agency. And the candidates who *looked* like SACs had names like Chuck and Jim and Rob. Left to his own devices, the director would've lined up his top picks and ordered them to drop trou so he could size them up the way men did in the old days: with a foot-long ruler.

Fortunately for Butler, the world had changed considerably, just in the last week alone. The Sons of Elijah, Chicago's very own homespun terrorist organization, had suddenly reemerged without warning. Images of the Chinatown bombing had horrified the city's residents, and then Dr. Jacobson's smoky follow-up at Wrigley Field had only ratcheted up the fear meter. Those kinds of criminal acts typically happened on the *more diverse* South Side, one reporter had pointed out. Funny how quickly wealthy people rallied around law enforcement when violence came rushing up to their own doorsteps. The rich and connected were scared as hell and needed a savior.

Over the past forty-eight hours, Butler had sat for interviews with every major news outlet, blog, and podcast. She'd delivered joint press conferences with the mayor and governor. She'd become the face of law and order. The *Washington Post* had even called her Chicago's Top Cop. Suddenly, she looked the part. So now, Butler would glide across the ballroom, her dress sparkling in the amber light of exquisite chandeliers, climb the stairs of the stage, and extend her soft, white tea–scented hand to the director of the FBI. And after her coronation, they'd all toast with champagne.

Butler supposed she owed Caleb Miller and the Sons of Elijah a debt of gratitude for catapulting her career over the finish line. Miller's body count had become her stairway to heaven, and she'd marched skyward in her fabulous footwear. *Bloody shoes, indeed.*

A SECOND-FLOOR WINDOW OF Dr. Alex Torres's farm-house shone like a golden cat eye. It was her bedroom, Tag knew. A fuzzy shadow moved behind the shade. Alex was home. The director of Fermilab must know every detail of that campus, Tag reasoned. If there really was an unfinished secondary accelerator with an access hatch somewhere in the prairie, Alex would know where to find it. Tag climbed the porch steps.

"What the hell are you talking about?" the physicist said a few minutes later, standing barefoot in the doorway, her words garbled by the toothbrush poking out of her mouth. She wore a Chicago Bulls jersey that dropped a few inches below her hips, but not much more. "And what did you do to your hair? It's super cute, by the way."

"There's a tunnel, for another accelerator. Congress scrapped the project in ninety-three," Tag explained, "but there's still a way to get in."

"In the field," Alex said, puzzled. "Under weeds and shit?"

Tag groaned. "Will you help me find it? Please?"

Alex worked the brush around in her mouth, and its handle wiggled like a chicken bone. She raised her eyebrows and slowly backed into the house. "Okay, goofball. Let me just throw on some boots . . . and maybe pants." She looked at the rainwater pouring from the gutters. "And maybe a slicker."

In minutes, the two women were bouncing down a gravel access road that skirted the northern perimeter of the laboratory campus in Tag's Crown Vic. The tires flung rocks into the vehicle's undercarriage. It sounded like machine-gun fire under their feet. The car's headlights reflected off pairs of green dots among the grass on the other side of a barbed wire fence. The bison.

"Okay, Max says you're right. Not that I doubted you," Alex reported. She tapped away on her phone, texting her assistant.

"Ask him for a map," Tag said, but before she could finish the request, Alex held up her phone to display a grainy photo of the lab's tunnel system. "How did he find that so fast?"

Alex shrugged. "If Max were slow, why would I have kept him around? We're on the right track to find your mystery hatch. It should be up here in about another—"

A hulking mass flashed into view on the road. Tag kicked her heel into the brake pedal. The Vic fishtailed, sending up splatters of mud. Alex pressed both palms into the dashboard to keep her forehead from colliding with the plastic. Tag cranked the emergency brake, and the vehicle did a wild half spin.

"You're going to roll it," Alex shouted. Tag suddenly couldn't remember if the physicist had buckled her seatbelt. If the car kept wheeling, the woman might be tossed through the windshield.

"I know what I'm doing," Tag said seconds before the Vic finally jerked to a stop. Both women watched in silence as a two-thousand-pound bull puttered back into the grass.

"Oh my fuck," Alex whispered, panting. "How did that thing even get in here?"

"Look." Tag pointed to the fence. A section of the barbed wire had been cut and pulled back to make an opening. "Caleb came through there."

* * *

Pink stripes rose on Caleb Miller's skin where spine-tipped bracts had scratched him. He'd found the hatch to the partially completed tunnel easily, but clearing it of the aggressive overgrowth had presented a challenge. The cuts on his neck and face stung, and Caleb wondered if he'd develop an angry rash. The pain didn't concern him, but any skin discoloration might cover the marking. It had taken more than scratches to make those twisting loops under his right ear.

He'd done it over a year ago, but sometimes he could still feel the hot tip of his switchblade slicing through his smooth skin. The candle's flame must not have thoroughly disinfected the knife because the cut had turned crimson overnight and oozed green pus. He'd waited three days, hoping it would heal on its own, until he'd awoken in a puddle of sweat and vomit. He'd gone to the ER, where the attending physician had refused to believe that Caleb hadn't attempted to take his own life. Slashes across a patient's carotid artery could only mean one thing, that doc's glower had said. What a damn fool. Caleb hadn't attempted suicide. Not when he'd chiseled that neck brand, anyway. And the marking didn't symbolize despair; quite the opposite. The permanent scar under his earlobe—the one the news reports had identified as an infinity symbol—served to remind Caleb of something much more important: hope. He needed that inspiration tonight if he had any chance of succeeding.

The tabloid melodrama wouldn't delude Agent Taggart. That woman had needle-sharp intuition, even if she was an inexperienced investigator. Caleb had no doubt that she'd learn about his past and snap the circuits together. With any luck, Taggart would match the figure eight scar with the one Sophie Whitestone had scrawled into her back flesh. Sophie would've needed help with that one, but from everything Caleb had heard, Mom had a knack for winning friends and influencing people. Some qualities were easily passed down to the next generation, like a sense of cosmic obligation . . . and the location of a storage unit, bursting with old files. Sophie had bequeathed him enough clues to find the trove of documents about particle accelerators and hidden hatches. *Among other useful secrets,* Caleb thought, zipping his jacket up to his Adam's apple.

Agent Taggart must've found those documents too. He'd burned the paperwork, but not before digitizing everything and hiding it all inside porn videos on his laptop. It would look like a genuine effort to conceal the information about the tunnels, but Caleb knew the FBI would crack the encryption. He'd counted on it.

Everything in this miserable, lonely life had led up to tonight. He'd found the soggy, mold-infested tubes leading to the world's largest neutrino detector, and with any luck, Agent Taggart would follow him inside. Like it or not, the woman was part of this story, maybe even the hero of it, if such an idealistic role existed.

Caleb was hoping Taggart would make an appearance. He'd even left the door open for her.

* * *

"Well, I guess that takes the mystery out of the question?" Alex said. "Loverboy's been here, all right." She pointed to a large metal disk sticking up in the grass.

"He left it open. Why would Caleb do that?" Tag asked, shouting over the rain, which was coming down in buckets now.

"No one's cracked the seal on that tunnel in ages. It probably smelled like Nefertiti's tomb. Maybe he just wanted to air it out," Alex reasoned.

"So, the tunnel is closed off? There's no way to get into the detector?"

Alex frowned. "I didn't say that, exactly. There's probably a hatch just like this one at the other end, but I have no idea if it's locked. I mean, no one thought to slap a Master Lock on *this* one, so . . ."

"We'll close the hatch, lock him in. I'll call for backup, and then we'll flush him out with tear gas." Tag reached for her phone.

"No, no, no. You put that away, Vera. I *cannot* have the Channel Five evening news crawling all over my lab," Alex said. "And if you call in the infantry, that's exactly what will happen. The whole fiasco would spook Washington, and they'd put a freeze on my experiment. It's launching tomorrow, remember? I won't let an angsty dude with delusions of grandeur eff all that up. If Caleb Miller really went in there, he's like a hamster in a tube. Let's just go in and drag him out by the tail."

Tag huffed. "Did they teach apprehending terrorists in physics school?"

"By physics school, you must mean *Harvard*. And no, but you do have a gun, right?" Alex asked. "There's a two-hundred-billion-dollar particle detector underneath our feet, and I'm not waiting for Sergeant Slapdick from Batavia PD to get his greasy hand off his gigglestick and drive down here."

Tag could hear the resolve in Alex's voice. The director wanted to protect her lab and, more importantly, her career-defining experiment. Still, there were standard operating procedures for circumstances such as these. A lone special agent wasn't supposed to burrow into a rabbit hole to chase down a mentally unstable man with violent intentions. Tag should call for backup, wait until the team secured all points of egress, and then let SWAT root out the perp.

And what? Just stand by and watch like Butler's pawn? That dreadful woman had never expected anything of Tag. When this was all over, Butler would probably transfer Tag to Training Division, where all of the bad guys were paid actors. Butler clearly didn't think Tag was capable of anything else. Maybe it was time to prove her wrong.

"Okay, we'll go after Caleb. Give me a minute to alert the team leader first." Tag used her jacket to shield her phone from the downpour and began to scroll for Clayton's number.

"Take your minute," Alex said, swinging her legs into the open hatch. She pulled a penlight from her pocket and shone it into the tunnel's black mouth, and with a scoot, she disappeared.

"*Shit,*" Tag said, and climbed into the hole.

*   *   *

Caleb found the mouth of the Ross Shaft with little trouble, even without help from his decades-old map of the tunnel system. Now, a metal freight elevator would lower him one mile into the heart of the earth.

Mining crews had worked for three years to excavate the shaft and then another five to carve out the cavernous cavity for the mammoth neutrino detector. Caleb had been a rudderless teenager when the work crews began chipping away the first layer of rock, and now, as a grown-up man with a grown-up mission, he was finally going to do something important with his life.

Caleb shifted the weight of the tactical vest underneath his jacket. He felt the flat bricks of C-4 press against his chest. They bulged like hard muscles. For once, he felt alive and powerful. He gripped the metal door of the cage elevator and slid it open with a grunt.

*   *   *

"Fudge." Alex wiped the limp coils of her wet hair from her face. "The cage has already descended. It takes six and a half minutes to get to the bottom and even longer to get back up, so this guy has had at least a fifteen-minute head start."

She pressed a green button, and a steel wheel ten feet high began turning. It looked like a colossal movie reel as it rotated, spooling a cable about two inches wide. The metal components of the elevator's hoist cables groaned. After a tediously long wait, the cage emerged from the shadows. Alex held the door for Tag, who tentatively stepped inside. The cage's floor was made of metal grating. Underneath Tag's boots, a black abyss stretched endlessly.

"This shaft is our superhighway," Alex explained. "The underground facility itself is sprawling, but everything must come and go through this elevator system."

After descending for a few seconds, Alex's penlight flickered and then went out. Darkness consumed them. Tag inhaled sharply.

"I'm just conserving the battery," Alex said.

"What's that sound? Something's leaking." She heard dribbling water all around them.

"The wooden support planks lining the shaft. We have to keep them wet." The elevator cage rattled. Tag felt a splash of water on her cheek.

"The only thing holding back tons of bedrock is rotting, wet wood?" Tag imagined the planks crumbling away as the earth swallowed them.

"It's not rotting. Wood only rots if it dries out and then gets wet again. So, we keep it wet at all times," Alex explained. "It's not difficult to do. This far underneath the natural water table, everything is saturated. Without our industrial pumps, this entire facility would flood."

In that moment, the full danger of the situation sank in. Tag would soon be stuck one mile underground with an unstable criminal who likely had a bomb powerful enough to crack the Midwest like an egg. Her only escape depended on a single steel wire lifting her out of a hole that apparently could flood at any time.

"What if it breaks?" Tag asked, watching the cable vibrate.

"The hoist rope? We hauled over eight hundred thousand tons of rock during the excavation with this bad boy. It can handle just about anything."

Still, Tag imagined that cord snapping and trapping them down there. They'd run out of oxygen or drown when the pumps failed and the water poured in. And that was if the killer creeping around the dark detector facility didn't murder them first. Every possible disaster scenario rushed through Tag's mind.

"You've got nothing to worry about," Alex added. "At least not when it comes to the cage elevator. I'm more concerned about time. My experiment is almost entirely automated, and the clock is ticking. Beginning at sunrise, the pipes surrounding the cryostats will begin to circulate liquid nitrogen. The cryogenic liquid is super cold—negative one hundred and ninety-eight degrees Celsius, to be exact. It's the only way to keep the argon in the detector in liquid form."

"Cryostats?" Tag asked, still staring into the bottomless pit.

"The cryostats house the detector components," Alex explained. "Essentially, they're big, garage-sized thermoses. We fill them with liquid argon, seal them up, and then fire neutrinos at them to record what happens. There's a ton more fancy physics to it, but I can tell from your face that you're thinking about something else."

Tag faced the Fermilab director. "If you wanted to cause the most damage down there, how would you do it? Try to think like a terrorist."

Alex didn't hesitate. "I'd set off a bomb inside one of the cryostats. The heat would instantly convert the liquid nitrogen circulating in the pipes and pumps to a gas. A gas under pressure with nowhere to go is bad news. The entire cryogenic system, including the swimming pool–sized storage tanks, would explode."

"That's what our intelligence analysts think too. So, how could Caleb Miller get a bomb into a cryostat? You said they're filled with liquid argon and sealed."

Alex bit her lip. "That asshole must know about the automations. That's why he came tonight. He's timed everything perfectly."

"What do you mean?" Tag could now see the faint light coming from the lab level below them.

"We built four cryostats, and we've brought them online in sequence over the past month. Cryostat Four is currently still empty; it's the last one to initialize. We have to cool it down before we can fill it with argon. At sunrise the pipes surrounding the chamber will begin pumping liquid nitrogen. It's the first step in the process."

"He's going to detonate his bomb inside Cryostat Four," Tag reasoned.

The lines and creases of Dr. Alex Torres young face darkened with genuine concern, possibly even fear. She touched Tag's arm. "Vera, we've got to stop this man. If he blows up that cryostat, he could do catastrophic damage. And I'm not just talking about my experiment." The metal cage came to a stop. Alex heaved open the elevator door with a practiced jerk. "You better make sure that gun is loaded," she said, and stepped into the corridor.

*   *   *

Caleb moved through a long white hallway, on autopilot. His plan's inertia propelled him now. He probably couldn't have stopped if he'd wanted to. Was this how soldiers felt when charging the enemy line, knowing they were sprinting headlong into certain death yet powerless to slow the forward momentum? That was how this entire life had felt, in fact. Like one big barreling rush toward this day, this moment.

Up ahead, the hallway split into four branches. At the juncture, painted arrows identified each passageway. Caleb started for the path on the far right, underneath the sign that read "Cryostat Four."

Before he took another step, a dull thud echoed throughout the facility. The cage elevator in the shaft had just docked at the sublevel. *She made it,* Caleb thought with satisfaction. In a moment, Special Agent Vera Taggart would fall into the same irreversible slipstream, powered by the pull of gravity and the invisible, tugging forces of the universe. She'd die alongside him, and they'd be the first of many millions to shed their fleshy husks.

Caleb checked his watch. He'd made good time but still had a thin margin of error. What if Taggart chose the wrong passageway at the junction? He hadn't considered the possibility. Ever since he'd met the woman on that bridge downtown, they'd seemed spiritually in sync. Still, he couldn't take the risk. His entire operation must come to a head in a specific chamber, here in the detector facility. As a precaution, Caleb marked the passageway. He heard the distinct clap of footsteps approaching.

A bolt of new energy surged inside his legs, and he began to run.

*　*　*

The red smear streaking the white wall was unmistakable. "Blood," Tag said. "He wanted us to know which way he went." She paused, studying the four hallways branching off in different directions.

"He cut himself to mark the wall? Sheesh, use a Sharpie, bro." Alex pressed a palm into her wrist, most likely imagining the slick feel of a blade running across her own skin.

The infinity symbol Caleb had scratched into his neck suggested he wasn't a stranger to self-mutilation. And with the way he'd swayed while standing on the railing of the DuSable Bridge, without an ounce of concern that his sneakers might slip off the metal bar, Caleb seemed to have a low regard for his own life.

No, not his life. His body, Tag thought. His body was only a temporary shell, a tool. The cuts on his neck and the blood stain on the wall were messages.

"I was wrong, then," Alex said. "The streak shows he's headed to Cryostat One. Look, there are blood drops on the tile too." She pointed to the passageway to the far left.

"Why would he go there?" Tag asked. "I thought you said Cryostat Four made the most sense for an explosion."

"I said it's the *best* place for a bomb, but not the *only* place. All of the cryogenic support systems are housed behind Cryostat One. He could blow up those pressurized pumps and filters and get a pretty good bang out of it."

"But destroying the support systems wouldn't achieve the same magnitude of explosion, would it? It wouldn't be large enough to trigger an earthquake."

"Probably not, but it would be enough to shut down my experiment, that's for sure. We'd have to replace that entire section of the facility, and that would take eighteen months, maybe longer."

It didn't make sense. Caleb had found the hidden hatch in the bison pasture. He'd expertly timed his infiltration of Fermilab to coincide with the automated cooling schedule of Cryostat Four and the Black and Blue Ball, when police coverage would be minimal. Why would he plan everything so carefully and then choose a location that would only inflict nominal damage?

"I hate to be the one who's always in a rush, but every second we stand here, that guy is getting closer to his target." Alex walked up to the wet smear of blood and swiped her finger through it. "We can't afford to be wrong about this. I'll head to Cryostat One, to the pumps, and you take Cryostat Four."

Alex spoke with the confident authority that Tag had always lacked. The director was accustomed to giving orders, especially when it came to her lab. Tag was an FBI special agent in pursuit of a suspected bomber, and all she could do was swivel her head back and forth from Caleb's blood art to the clean passageway leading to Cryostat Four.

"You're right," she said finally. "We have no choice. If we want to ensure that we'll catch him, we've got to split up." Even as she spoke the words, Tag wished she could reel them back into her mouth. She cared about Alex and couldn't imagine the thought of her confronting Caleb Miller alone and defenseless. She drew her Glock from its holster.

"Do you know how to use this?" Tag asked.

"Firing projectiles at top speed is kinda my thing, Vera."

Tag held out the gun. "If you find Caleb, just try to scare him. If that doesn't work—"

"I'll blow his motherfucking head off," Alex said, and gripped the Glock's handle. "But what about you? What if you find him at Cryostat Four? You'll be unarmed."

Tag inhaled deeply. "I've talked him down once before. I can do it again."

Alex reached out and grabbed the back of Tag's buzzed head. She pulled her in and kissed her hard on the lips. Then, in a breath, the physicist turned and raced down the passageway, following the drops of blood toward the cryogenic support system.

Tag felt a thousand needle pricks stabbing her arms and neck and face. Something felt terribly wrong. She wiped the sweat from her forehead and took off for Cryostat Four, alone and unarmed.

38

MICHELSON RAISED HIS champagne flute—an invitation
to clink glasses with Chicago's newly ordained Special
Agent in Charge Gina Butler. "How does it feel to be biggest
cock on the block?"

The woman ignored him and skipped to the customary
post-toast sip. "My mother always said it's poor form to gloat,
Joseph," Butler said.

"The way the director fawned over you on that stage, and
then your barn-burning speech about restoring law and order
to the Chicagoland, for a minute I thought you were about
to announce your bid for mayor. The press ate that shit up."

"I don't care about the press," Butler lied. "I'm just pleased
so many of you from the division were able to share in this
moment. This is an accomplishment for us all, Joe."

Michelson snorted. "That's why you invited so many of
us here tonight, isn't it? You wanted your squad leaders to see
the spectacle, to watch you get knighted by the king. Jesus,
Gina. Even with the official title, you're still worried the boys
won't respect you."

Butler didn't respond. She gazed out over the sea of tuxedos and bow ties, the broad shoulders and beards, all thumping around in shiny black shoes.

"Well, you're probably smart for doing it. I'm not just saying this 'cause I'm your buddy, but you did look like a bad bitch up there under those lights. Your shiny smile is going to be on the cover of the *Tribune* tomorrow—just watch. Unless Caleb Miller shits the bed again."

The mention of Chicago's most wanted suspect snapped Butler out of her reverie. She considered what the FBI director had whispered in her ear, just out of range of the stage microphones. *"You got your prize, Gina. Now you'd better have that fucker in steel cuffs before I land in Washington tomorrow afternoon."* Caleb Miller had served his purpose, and now it was time to cut him down.

"What's the latest intel?" she asked. "Has Dr. Jacobson given us anything useful yet?"

Michelson shrugged. "It's like trying to drown an Olympic swimmer in a bathtub. That man's a renowned psychiatrist. He knows every trick we've got. Solitary confinement, sleep deprivation—we even blasted Nickelback for three hours straight. After that, I lost my damn patience and split his wig with my knuckles. Maybe I went too far, but I know the medics can patch him up. Point is, nothing's broken him."

"Taggart is the key. Lock them in a cell together if you have to. He'll talk to her."

"I would, but our girl Tag's out digging through actual bullshit in a pasture somewhere near Fermilab. She thinks she'll find a hole to slip through."

"What's that, Michelson? You lookin' for someone to slip into your hole?" Officer Jacob Clayton clapped Michelson so hard on the back that the FBI agent's drink sloshed over the rim of his glass. A few drops speckled the carpet inches from Butler's shoes.

"Whoa, you almost made me spray the boss, asshole." Michelson playfully hooked an arm around Clayton's neck.

The CPD officer stuck out his tongue, pretending to choke. "The SAC here was just asking about Taggart. Did the fellas posted at the lab find anything on their walkabout?"

"That's what I came over to tell you," Clayton said. "My guys found Agent Taggart's car halfway up one of the access roads. The driver-side door was hanging open, and the keys were still inside."

"What? She left in a hurry, then," Michelson said.

"Looks like it. And she wasn't alone. Our surveillance cams caught her scooping up Dr. Torres around eight thirty. And get this, the girl has shaved her entire—"

"That was over an hour ago," Butler interjected. "She knows something. Maybe Jacobson passed her a message after all, some kind of code."

"Tag was blubbering about a hatch in the field," Clayton explained. He suddenly stood straighter and looked soberer. "Some kind of alternate access point."

Michelson cut in. "If Tag's onto something important, we'll run it down."

"I want you out there now, Joe." Butler took his champagne flute. "Best-case scenario, Taggart is actually chasing a productive lead."

Officer Clayton dashed away to rally his squad.

"What's the worst-case scenario?" Michelson asked.

Butler smoothed her eyelid, which had begun to flutter again. "She's involved." She threw back the rest of the champagne in her glass. "And if that's true, if Tag's helping Jacobson and Miller, I want you to take care of it."

Butler turned sharply and headed for the press pool, pearly whites on high beam.

39

EVERY CORRIDOR IN the underground labyrinth looked identical. After separating from Alex, Tag had worried that she'd get lost or just loop around to where she'd started. Fortunately, there was exceptional wayfinding signage at nearly every corner. Up ahead, a sign hanging from short chains indicated the entrance to Cryostat Four.

The door to the cryostat looked like it belonged on a submarine. It was shaped like an oval with a big wheel in its center. The hatch had no window, so Tag would have to enter the space blind. If she found Caleb inside, he would probably be armed with more than a bomb. And having made it this far, he would fight with the desperation of man on the precipice of achieving his grand goal. This wasn't the DuSable Bridge, where Caleb had spontaneously climbed the railing. He'd prepared meticulously to infiltrate the detector facility.

Tag would have to muster every ounce of wit to talk Caleb down. She had no weapon or leverage of any kind, just her words and hopefully a bit of earned trust after having saved the man's life once already. She'd work methodically and patiently to chip away at his resolve. She'd sit with him, hear him out. But she didn't have forever. The cryostat's automated cooling process would begin at sunrise, Alex had said. If Tag didn't get Caleb, and herself, out of there before morning, the liquid nitrogen coursing through the pipes around the cryostat would freeze them both to death. That was, of course, if Caleb didn't kill her first.

Tag turned the wheel on the hatch. The door opened easily, and she stepped inside Cryostat Four. She soon saw that she was standing in the center of an enormous cube that must have reached four stories high. Inside the cavernous space, it was difficult to believe that she was actually a mile underground. *It's like a ship in a bottle,* she'd explained to Butler. More like a spaceship. The walls weren't smooth, but lined with puffy square panels, each wrapped in gold foil. The shiny cells covered the ceiling too, surrounding her like a geometric honeycomb. The overhead florescent lights flickered, reflecting off the lustrous wall plates with bright bursts that created a disorienting, fun-house effect. The space was empty and eerily quiet. Tag touched one of the gold cells. It was already as hard as ice.

The lights buzzed and then shut off completely. For a brief moment, Tag was smothered in complete darkness. She felt like someone else was in the space with her. Her arms broke out into gooseflesh. *It's just the cold,* she thought.

Then the cyrostat's metal hatch slammed shut.

An emergency light switched on and bathed the chamber in blue hues that turned green when they bounced off the golden walls. Tag saw a figure standing on the opposite side of the cube.

"No matter where I go, you're always there, trying to save me," Caleb Miller said in a low-pitched growl. Tag's hand instinctively flew to her sidearm holster before she remembered that she'd given her gun to Alex. Caleb didn't know that, though.

"Wait!" Caleb shouted. He held up his empty palms. "I'm not here to hurt you. You know that."

"What *are* you doing here, Caleb?" Tag asked. She kept her hand at her hip, pretending to grip her gun. It had occurred to Tag that Caleb might not have come alone. He was the key to all of this, but for all Tag knew, there were others involved. If he could convince Dr. Jacobson to distract the authorities with a smoke bomb at Wrigley Field, then who else had he corrupted?

"You call me Caleb, and that's fine, I suppose. But you've known me by many other names," he said, taking a step closer.

A string of names zipped through Tag's mind—a collection of nefarious figures from Jacobson's book and her own hypnotic nightmares. *Ferrier, Tallien, Linda . . . Caleb. No, it's just more nonsense, implanted by Jacobson and his psychoactive cocktails. Caleb is a terrorist, plain and simple. Not a supervillain reborn.*

"You can feel the connection, can't you?" Caleb continued. "Our souls are inextricably linked. Lifetime after lifetime, we are drawn together, the opposite poles of two magnets. The world swirls around us in a halo, but we're always at the center. Two bright beings."

"I only met you this week." Tag's voice wavered, even though she tried to speak firmly. "You experienced a traumatic event on that bridge, and you think because I saved you that we have some sort of bond, but really, Caleb, I was just a stranger trying to help. Anyone would have—"

"No!" Caleb barked. His eyebrows formed an angry shape on his forehead. "Not *anyone*. I knew you were following me. I climbed that railing and pretended that I wanted to jump because I knew you'd stop me."

Tag blinked, recalling that bleak morning just a few days before. Caleb had seemed so despondent. If she hadn't intervened, the young man would've hurled himself skull-first into the Chicago River—she'd been sure of it. But had he faked the entire thing?

"What about now, Caleb. Is this real? Are you really planning to do something here, to hurt yourself?" *And hurt millions of others—don't forget about all of those poor souls.*

For a moment, the young man looked astonished. "You're still resisting the truth. After all of the time you've spent with Dr. Jacobson."

"He's part of this, isn't he?" Tag raised her hands to show that she wasn't a threat and inched closer.

"Of course, he is."

"He's the leader of the Sons of Elijah," Tag said bluntly.

"Oh God, no. The man's not even a member."

"But he helped you. The police apprehended Jacobson at Wrigley Field right after he set off his Halloween smoke bomb. He was trying to divert attention away from Fermilab."

"And let me guess: he would only agree to speak to you."

Tag didn't respond. She chewed the inside of her cheek.

"And what did he say?" Caleb took a step closer. His enlarged pupils shone in the dim blue light. "He told you to find me, didn't he?"

Tag grew weary of the guessing games. Caleb Miller had clearly devised an elaborate attack on Fermilab, and for some reason, he'd wanted Tag to be a part of it. He'd correctly assumed that she wouldn't follow the passageway that he'd smeared with blood—the ploy had seemed too contrived—and yet the streaks had still served Caleb's intended purpose: to get Tag alone. But why? Why was she so important, not just to Caleb, but to *everyone*? Gina Butler had used Tag to get close to Jacobson. Jacobson had refused to speak with anyone but her. And Caleb had lured her deep underground to witness his sadistic act of mass murder. Why was Tag's life so entwined with this goddamn cult—the Sons of Elijah? She felt the birthmark burning the back of her head.

"If Jacobson isn't a member of the Sons, he's still complicit. So let's begin there, Caleb. What does the doctor have to do with this?" Tag asked.

"Dr. Jacobson is a guide. He helps the members find each other. He plucks the Sons out of the obscurity of normal life and peels away the gauze covering their eyes. He helps them to remember. Jacobson did this for you, Taggart. At least, he tried. Do you really remember *nothing*?"

Tag's skull was on fire now. "I know about the Capstone," she admitted. "I have it." Tag pulled the object from her pocket. Caleb's lips curled up to his ears in an unnerving grin. Suddenly, Tag was back in the shadow of Montségur, watching helplessly as red flames licked the heels of the innocent men and women who'd defied Inquisitor Ferrier.

"That little rock is not the Capstone," Caleb explained.

"Then what the hell is it?"

"It's a key to a locked safe that holds the greatest treasure mankind has ever known. The real Capstone isn't even an object. It's a *secret* . . . or a curse, depending on how you look at it. To know about the Capstone is to know about yourself, Vera Taggart. *You* are that locked safe."

That's why he wants me here, Tag realized. *He thinks I possess some mystic knowledge of the ages.* Tag was nothing more than a mediocre artist and a mostly terrible FBI agent. She was nobody special. *And when Caleb finds that out, he'll kill me. Like Ferrier killed those Cathars.*

"Dr. Jacobson jangled the key inside the lock, but clearly it still needs a sharp crank of the wrist." Caleb unzipped his jacket and shrugged it off his shoulders. Rows of plastic explosive bricks plated his stomach and chest like a suit of armor. He craned his neck, pointing his chin up at the ceiling. The weird lighting made the scar under his ear look dark red, almost freshly carved.

Tag took a short, jerking breath. "Endless rebirth. That's what you believe. It's why you have no fear of dying. Cycle after cycle, you'll come back, just like the endless loop of that infinity symbol."

"Look closer, Vera. It's not an infinity symbol."

The back of Tag's head pulsed now, like something was pressing into it. She could almost hear her skin sizzling. The pain made Tag's eyes water. She blinked away the wet beads, staring at Caleb's neck. The man turned sideways and slowly bowed his head until the symbol rotated a quarter turn.

"It's an eight," Tag said.

The young man's eyebrows raised with surprise. *No, it's relief*, Tag realized.

"Yes!" Caleb shouted. "You remember. I knew you would. And now you must know why we're here. Both of us. You must realize how important this is."

"What does it mean? Why an eight?"

"Not just eight," Caleb said. "Concentrate."

Tag's mind swirled with colors and sounds and scents— the fragments of memories recombining. She heard whispers, the voice of an aging emperor revealing a shocking secret on his deathbed.

"Listen to me," Caleb continued. "This experiment that Dr. Torres is attempting, it's extremely dangerous. There is so much more at stake than you know. That woman must not be allowed to—"

A deep, mechanical thump came from behind the gold foil walls, followed by a hiss that traveled from one corner of the cryostat to the next, until the sound surrounded them. The temperature of the air plummeted. Tag cupped her elbows to keep them from shaking. Caleb's eyes glinted with raw pleasure.

"The cryogenic system is coming online. But it's too early," Tag said. "It's not supposed to switch on until sunrise."

"Who told you that? The pumps were all set to activate at midnight. The network of pipes surrounding this cryostat are now filling up with liquid nitrogen. Right on time," Caleb explained.

It was impossible. Alex had clearly said they had until sunrise before the cooling system initiated. Tag felt the hairs on her arms rise into spikes. She moved to the cryostat's sealed hatch, but the wheel wouldn't budge. She turned to look at Caleb, shivering now as the cold gnashed at her neck. Even through the cloud of condensation puffing from Caleb's mouth, Tag could see that grin of his. He'd planned all of this. Like a confused sheep, Tag had wandered right into the wolf's den, and he was ravenous.

Alex will come, Tag thought. She'd realize her mistake about the timing and race to Cryostat Four. She was the director of Fermilab; she must know how to open the hatch.

"How much time do we have?" Tag asked, her lips vibrating so rapidly that *have* came out like *haff.*

"Not long. But it's enough time for me to explain everything," Caleb answered.

*   *   *

"Jesus Christ, he must've burrowed through these weeds like a fucking groundhog." Officer Clayton spat into the pasture and continued to clear the tangle of grass away from the hole in the ground. A string of police cruisers had lined up behind Tag's parked Crown Victoria. A dozen CPD officers and FBI agents had spread out in the field, waving flashlights, searching for the portal to the abandoned underground accelerator tunnel.

"We found it," Special Agent Michelson shouted. "Over here." He gnawed on a stalk of dried grass, his thumbs hooked into his belt buckle.

"Bomb Squad is on its way. They'll send in a drone to check for explosives," Clayton explained.

"They'll never get a signal through all that rock. Intel says this tunnel goes down pretty damn deep. Besides, you know there's not time for all that fancy robot shit." Michelson removed his tuxedo jacket and pulled off his bow tie, draping both over Officer Clayton's shoulder.

"You're not seriously going in there alone," Clayton said.

Michelson shook his head in disgust. "I suppose that means you're not planning to join me." He crouched, threw both legs over the edge of the hole, and slipped inside.

*   *   *

"What did Dr. Torres tell you about her experiment?" Caleb asked. He seemed unfazed by the frost accumulating on his eyelashes.

"The Big C particle," Tag answered. "She's trying to discover human consciousness."

"Not just discover; she's trying to *measure* it. She wants to quantify consciousness." Caleb stepped forward with his arms out, almost like he wanted a hug. Tag cringed at the sight of the gnarled, purple scar on his neck. *An eight.* Then something sparked behind her eyes, like a match flaring.

Nolite propinquius venire! Don't get close!

"Not just eight. Eight *billion*," she whispered. "That's the secret? That's what the Sons of Elijah have spent centuries to protect? A number?"

"A very specific number, yes. One that we must never reach—the highest point, the culmination, the *Capstone* of humanity. Eight billion."

"I don't understand. What does it mean?"

"It's the precise number of human souls," Caleb answered.

Tag's mind raced. Suddenly she remembered kneeling in the mud, watching her wife, Corba, consumed by angry fire. Then she was on her back, staring up at the moon rising over the roofline of a temple, as the pointed tips of boots mashed into her ribs. And then she heard it: the scraping growl as the gondolas of a great Ferris wheel snapped free of their bolts.

So much death and sacrifice, all to safeguard this simple number. *And so much terror to obtain it,* Tag thought. She pictured the faces of Inquisitor Ferrier, Tallien, Zhang Boda—those pointed teeth and that disgusting black spot on their tongues. Who was this man, driven by obsession and malice? *No, not a man. A devil.*

She looked at Caleb. The packs of C-4 strapped to his body glowed blue-green like lizard scales. That devil lived, and he was here with her, trapped inside this ship in a bottle. And he was about to blow the whole damn thing apart.

"Then you already know," Tag said. "You finally learned the secret of the Sons of Elijah, and this is your plan? To murder millions of innocent people?"

"No, don't you understand? I didn't just learn of this. I've always known. *We've* always known. If you turned around to show me the back of your head, I know there'd be the mark of a lion there. Big and purple and regal. The mark of a guardian of the Capstone. I know it would be there, because *I* put it there." Caleb stepped forward again. Up close, he didn't look at all like Ferrier. His eyes weren't inky black and monstrous. They radiated hope and . . . love.

"*We* are those guardians, Vera Taggart," he continued. "Together, we've protected this secret. And together we've prevented the most dangerous cataclysm humankind could ever know. And now we must do it again."

Waves of emotion crashed over Tag. She was so confused. Maybe this man standing in front of her, holding her hands in his, wasn't the spirit of a bloodthirsty Inquisitor or a menacing Red Guard leader. Could Tag have been wrong about Caleb? Wrong about everything?

"What cataclysm?" she asked. "What are you trying to prevent?"

"You said it yourself. Eight billion. No more."

"If that's the total number of souls, then it must be the maximum number of *people*," Tag reasoned.

"People as we know them, yes."

"What happens when the world's population surpasses eight billion? We're nearly there, aren't we?" A chill colder than the cryostat's frozen air filled Tag's lungs. She finally understood. "That's why you want to set off that bomb. It's why you want to kill so many people. It's why Sophie and the others blew themselves up. Except their suicide attacks didn't do enough damage."

"We've tried unleashing disease and famine, and these worked for short bursts of time. But humanity always surges back. Only violence persists. As a form of population control, it's more effective than any plague. Even a small act of terror can spark decades of deadly conflict, if the conditions are right. There's no vaccine for fear and anger. This was Sophie's strategy, but she'd underestimated how numb the public had become to random acts of violence. She bought a little time, but the population has only continued to grow."

"You need something that really grabs the people's attention," Tag reasoned. "Something shocking with a much higher body count. Because—"

"Because if more than eight billion bodies walk the earth, there won't be enough souls to populate them all. Every new baby will be born soulless. These soulless creatures will belong to *it*. They will serve as soldiers in *its* army."

"The creature with the black-spotted tongue," Tag said, thinking of Ferrier and Zhang Boda.

Caleb nodded and brushed Tag's cheek. "So, you see, my love, we have no choice. We've tried for generations to prevent the population from reaching the maximum threshold, but train crashes and fires aren't enough anymore. We knew it would come to this eventually. We need to do something grander.

"That evil entity has learned much over the past century. It's grown more and more clever in its quest to obtain our secret. It already knows there is a finite number of human souls—as Zhang Boda, it tortured that much out of me— but it doesn't know what that number is. If this experiment succeeds, and consciousness is quantified, then our secret is lost. Humanity's greatest vulnerability will be revealed to our greatest enemy. If we destroy this detector, we'll keep that knowledge hidden, and we'll finally have a way to bring the number of bodies back down to a safe population."

"If you detonate that bomb down here, a lot of people will die. Innocent people." The thought made Tag's stomach churn.

"Yes, and over time, they will all be reborn into new bodies. Their souls will continue to grow and learn and love. That devil will have lost. All because of you."

Tag blinked. "Me?"

"Don't you see? It's always been you. I've played my part and supported you, but only you have had the courage to go against the Evil One. You've endured torture and brutal beatings, and you've persisted in the face of it all."

Tag felt a smooth object in her palm. Caleb had placed the bomb's detonator in her hand.

Her thumb hovered over the button. *Press it,* she thought. *He's telling the truth. This is bigger than you or him or Dr. Jacobson. The very soul of humanity is at stake. You've known all along that it would come to this. Just look at your art. Death is a part of you, and now you understand the reason. Death brings life. An endless loop, like an infinity symbol. No, like eight billion souls swirling among bodies, interchangeable hosts. Don't break the cycle. Caleb is not that devil, so that means the creature is still out there in some other toxic body. It's salivating, waiting for the body count on earth to reach eight billion . . . and one. Don't get close! Then it will raise its army of death. It will open its mouth and wait for the first innocent soul to slick down its throat, right past that rotting black splotch on its tongue.*

The wells forming on Tag's lower eyelids had completely frozen. She and Caleb both shook from the extreme cold. Liquid nitrogen gurgled inside the pipes. As the super-chilled fluid flowed, Tag felt her own blood thicken into a sticky sauce. She'd die in that lustrous golden room. The question remained: How many would die with her?

The pad of Tag's thumb slid delicately across the plastic detonator button. She could barely feel its slick surface in her blue corpse-hand. Then her thumb stiffened and began to apply pressure. *This is your destiny. Your responsibility. But if he's wrong . . .*

"Do it, Ramon. Have no fear as you reach the end of this life. I will find you again. I will be there when it counts," Caleb whispered. At least Tag thought it was Caleb speaking. His voice sounded high and feminine, like the voice of a woman in a stable, curled up under a bear skin. *He can't be her. Caleb can't be Corba.* Ramon's wife, Corba, had eventually lived as Chen Wei and then as Gerald Cutter. *My love, my eternal match.* Tag's mind flashed to the words written on Sophie's ultrasound image: *CUTTER, CALEB.*

She'd thought it was a proof that Caleb was really Gerald's son, but DNA had proven this was untrue. Caleb was Dr. Jacobson's son. So why had Sophie written that name?

Because it's the order that matters, Hunny Bunny. Cutter, then Caleb. It's not one name, but two. The same soul, occupying two bodies in sequence.

Could Caleb really be Gerald Cutter reborn? It would explain how he knew about the hidden accelerator tunnels. And why he'd lured Tag into the facility. Admittedly, Tag had felt a strong attachment to this man, and a responsibility to protect him, but she didn't love him. Did she? Well, she hadn't *made* love to him. She hadn't felt that perfect fit when two bodies mold into one. *Like last night at the farmhouse, in the shower and in the bed.* If Gerald had returned as Caleb, then who the hell was—

A gunshot cracked like an iceberg snapping in two. Caleb's body flew backward. The detonator was yanked out of Tag's hand by a cord attached to Caleb's vest. Blood spread out from the young man's back.

"Holy Hades! It's freaking freezing in here," a voice said from high above. "Did I get him? Vera, are you okay?"

Tag looked up to see a woman standing on a metal catwalk twenty feet above her. It was Alex, holding Tag's gun. The room swirled in gold foil and blue-green light and purple blood and gray clouds of condensation. She didn't feel herself fall, but Tag felt her temple smack the floor. She stared into the dead eyes of Caleb Miller, and she sensed her own heart slowing as the cold burrowed into her core.

"Oh, shit. Just stay with me, Vera. I'm coming right down," Alex shouted, but all Tag could hear were the shrill screams of heretics burning on the pyre.

*   *   *

"We've got it from here, boss. We'll roll her into the back and get her down the road," a deep voice said.

"Which hospital?" another man asked.

"Delnor, on Randall Road. The ER. She's not been shot, but her temperature has crashed. We've got to get her warmed up."

Tag heard a crinkling sound and felt someone tucking a thin material underneath her arms and legs. It was one of those thermal blankets they gave to refugees and marathon runners. The fabric crackled as her body shook on what she assumed was a gurney. When she opened her eyes, they filled with the flashing red lights of an ambulance.

"She lives." Michelson craned over her. "Don't worry—I'm not an angel. Just the poor shmuck who hauled your ass out of that hole."

Tag groaned and tried to sit up. The man with the deep voice, an EMT, gently squeezed her arm. "Hey-yo, you really need to lie back down, ma'am."

"Where's Caleb?" Tag asked, her words slurring as her frozen tongue refused to move.

"Somewhere much warmer, if you ask me," Michelson said. "His body, on the other hand, is still down there. Bomb Squad has to pick through the gore and make sure that C-4 doesn't blow the top off the American Midwest. They'll bring him up soon." A female EMT rolled another gurney passed them. "Speak of the devil," Michelson said.

"I've got to see him. I've got to look," Tag croaked, and sat up.

Michelson steadied her shoulders before she tumbled face-first into the gravel road. He whistled through his fingers.

"Hey, bring him back. Over here. Agent Taggart wants to pay her respects to the departed."

The female EMT flashed a surprised look and wheeled Caleb's body up to Tag. The techs had already zipped him into a body bag.

Tag stood and gripped the rail of the gurney for support. Her knees threatened to give out, but she had to check. If she zipped open that bag and saw a splotch on Caleb's chest, right above his breastbone, than she would know. That night in the stable, Ramon Perella had marked his wife, Corba, with the same purple lion that she'd branded into the back of his head. *And now it's on my head,* Tag thought. Corba's birthmark had been visible on Chen Wei's chest and on Gerald's chest in their lifetimes.

The ruddy splotch is the only physical constant, cycle after cycle.

And if she saw it on Caleb's chest, it would confirm that he'd been telling the truth. *The Capstone was a key, a form of identification. And only the members of the Sons of Elijah, the guardians of humankind's most precious secret, had it.*

The zipper croaked as she pulled it across the length of the shiny body bag. Tag could see Caleb's face now, ghost-white and serene. He wasn't wearing a shirt; the bomb squad must've cut it off when they'd removed the C-4. Blood speckled Caleb's neck, and Tag cringed at the thought of possibly needing to wipe away a dried stain to check for the mark. When the zipper reached the young man's waist, she saw that wouldn't be necessary. Then she pried open his mouth, just to be sure.

"Well, find what you were looking for?" Michelson asked.

Tag stopped shaking. She didn't feel cold anymore, just a dull, aching defeat. She lowered herself back onto her gurney and stared blankly at the night sky. "Where's Dr. Torres?" she asked.

"She and Officer Clayton went up to her office. She's debriefing him on what happened down there. You're lucky that woman is such a sharpshooter. Who knows what would've happened if she hadn't taken Caleb out."

Tag sighed. "Yes, I guess we'll never know."

She fixed her eyes on the moon, which was covered by gauzy clouds, but still bright and full. She knew if she closed her eyes, she'd only see the thing on Caleb's chest again. A gaping, bloody bullet hole and flaps of ripped skin, right above his breastbone, leaving behind nothing but red gore. If the mark of the Capstone had been there, it was now obliterated. His tongue had looked completely normal—no black death spot—but what did that prove? She wouldn't get any more answers from Caleb Miller. So Tag would stare at the moon and allow it's light to vanquish all the dark thoughts that had fogged her mind. As her eyes grew wide to match the glowing disk above, a breeze swept away the clouds. Finally, she was waking from the nightmare.

40

Raising the Sons of Elijah

by Dr. Seth Jacobson

Confession

IT'S MY FAULT, I suppose. As of the time I'm writing this chapter, you would be hard-pressed to find more than a handful of Americans who have not heard of the Sons of Elijah. *That's the Christian cult out of Chicago, right?* Nowadays, I rarely make it to sunset without hearing some version of that question. Of course, the answer is, resoundingly, no. As far as I know, neither Sophie Whitestone nor Gerald Cutter ever referred to themselves as the Sons of Elijah. That moniker, I confess, is fully attributable to me. Please, dear reader, permit me to correct the record, if only for posterity.

Shortly after Sophie's initial regression to her past life as Eusebius the Bishop, and once I'd overcome my own skepticism that her recollection could be authentic, I delved into the history of reincarnation. I'm embarrassed to admit that I had held all of the cliché preconceived notions, especially that transmigration of the soul from one body to the next was a concept strictly found in Buddhism and Hinduism. Throw in a few other flavors of Eastern mysticism, sure, but certainly no aspect of Christianity subscribed to such beliefs. And yet, during our hypnotherapy sessions, Sophie had recounted nuanced debates among high-ranking Catholic clergy about the validity of just such an idea. Should the Church adopt reincarnation as official doctrine or repudiate it as blasphemous? In fact, the esteemed members of Constantine's councils quarreled endlessly over this decision. However, the men could agree on one central point: whatever they decided would become truth.

I'd verified so many details from Sophie's memories as the bishop, I had no reason to doubt that these disputes had indeed occurred as she'd described them. And that would mean reincarnation may have been at the root of nearly every major human religion, before certain administrators in ancient Rome had simply decided to strike it from the script. A well-intentioned (if not an overly dedicated) Catholic myself, I did the obvious thing. I went to see a priest.

Father Rose smelled like anything but. When I stepped into his book-lined office, tucked into the basement of Chicago's Holy Name Cathedral, a malodorous scent crawled into my nostrils. It wasn't the woody smell of incense or the must of aged Bibles or anything even close to holy, and it nearly turned me right around.

"You'll have to forgive me. It is Tuesday, and on Tuesday I sup on onion stew and cornbread," he explained, sitting behind his desk. "Sister Martha's recipe is not famous for its impotence, but I make no apologies. The stuff is damn good, and the Good Lord is well aware of that fact."

The man cleaned his ear with the eraser end of a pencil. His white clerical collar sat curled up on his desk beside a plastic Big Gulp cup. His short arm reached for the drink, which he gripped with five stubby fingers that looked more like sausage links.

"I'm not doing confessions this late, though. Come back in the morning after I've had a chance to work this particularly vigorous batch of Martha's masterpiece out of my system."

Father Rose's unusual greeting should've repulsed me, but his frankness had quite the opposite effect. I needed an expert on religious history to cut through the bullshit (pardon my bluntness), and this fellow seemed to fit the bill.

"The archbishop moved me to the basement because of the flatulence," the priest continued. "Again, no apologies."

Yes, I thought, *this is just the man I need.* Without fully divulging the nature of my experiences with Sophie, I asked the priest about his understanding of reincarnation as a *Christian* philosophy. Was it really part of the whole deal until Christian elders voted it down in the first century to preserve their own power and control?

"You've seen my lectures, then. The ones I used to give at Northwestern," Father Rose said. Indeed, the man had created quite a stir for his pronouncements as a visiting religious scholar. I surmised the Vatican hadn't endorsed his views, which were undoubtedly the real reasons for the smelly basement office. I admitted that I hadn't attended any of his talks, but I explained that the trail to acquire knowledge on the topic of rebirth within the Christian faith had led directly to him.

"Then you've never heard about Elijah, I suppose. A virgin, as it were!" He propped his feet on his desk and pointed to a bookshelf behind me. "Grab that sucker, there. The one with Mr. Happy on it." I turned to see a black leather-bound Bible with a smiley face sticker stuck to its spine.

"Thanks, bud," Father Rose said when I handed it over. "The Old Testament always cheers me up when I'm suffering a fit of the winter doldrums. All that magical vengeance really lifts my spirit.

"Some folks thought Jesus was a stud, but he wasn't the first to razzle-dazzle the common folk. Long before Jesus, Elijah made food appear to feed a starving mother and her young son. When the boy later died anyway, Elijah brought him back to life. This is the first known reference to resurrection in Scripture, by the way. It's all in here," he professed, waving the Bible. "I don't know why so many folks skip over the good stuff."

"So what happened to him?" I asked. "What happened to Elijah?"

"He got into some major trouble with the King of Israel, Ahab. Elijah didn't like that Ahab promoted the worship of false gods. So he proposed a contest. Let's climb a big ol' mountain, he said. You bring your team of prophets and I'll bring mine. We'll build two altars and pray to our respective deities to light them on fire. The first flame wins. You can probably see where this is going."

"Elijah's altar actually burned?"

"Precipitating spontaneous combustion is practically a requirement for any bona fide miracle man. So, yes, Elijah's prayer brought the fire, which really ticked off old Ahab. Elijah escaped the king's wrath by fleeing the city and hiding in a cave. It's not the end of their feud, though. Elijah returned later to confront King Ahab about his corruption and blasphemy, a grab bag of no-nos. Long story short, our boy, Big E, had to scram again, so he went out like the pro prophet that he was."

"How's that?"

"He rode a chariot of fire, pulled by powerful white horses, right up into heaven," Father Rose answered.

I shook my head. "You really believe that?"

"I'm a Catholic priest; it's not the strangest thing I believe. Besides, who am I to know why God does what He does? I started going bald at, like, twenty-nine. Prayed every day to make it stop, but God just put more hair everywhere except where I really wanted it."

This unsettling visual aside, Father Rose's story enthralled me. Still, I didn't see how this particular character from the Old Testament related to Sophie's memories as Eusebius the Bishop. "If I'm jumping ahead, please, forgive me, Father—"

"No dice. I already told you, I'm off the clock when it comes to absolving folks." He laughed at his own joke. "All right, all right. You want to know what the hell this longbeard from ancient times has to do with reincarnation. Well, the answer is, just about everything. Elijah's miracles didn't just catch the eye of the king; the man had a whole mess of groupies. They called themselves the Sons of the Prophets. It was kind of like a school, and Elijah was its dean. And after Elijah galloped off into the sky, the Sons of the Prophets knew their leader had to be pretty important. Who else had entered heaven alive?" Finally, Father Rose opened the Bible and flipped the pages. "Read this," he said, and jutted out his arm.

"*Behold, I will send you Elijah the prophet before the coming of the great and dreadful day of the Lord,*'" I read. It was from the conclusion of the Book of Malachi.

"For centuries, people believed Elijah would return and that his arrival would signal the end of the world. Many of the Jews believed Jesus was actually the reincarnated soul of Elijah," Father Rose explained.

I had never heard this concept before. "How did Jesus respond to this . . . theory? Surely he would have had to address it."

"He deflected, gave the credit to John the Baptist." The priest pulled another Bible from his desk drawer: the New Testament. This volume also had a sticker on its spine, but it was a yellow frowny face. I didn't think it wise to inquire about the symbolism.

"Check this out," he said, and read a passage from Matthew.

> Truly I tell you, among those born of women no one has arisen greater than John the Baptist; yet the least in the kingdom of heaven is greater than he. From the days of John the Baptist until now the kingdom of heaven has suffered violence, and the violent take it by force. For all the prophets and the law prophesied until John came; and if you are willing to accept it, he is Elijah who is to come. Let anyone with ears listen!

"Jesus said that? Holy shit!" I said, forgetting where I was for a moment, and then covering my lips like a guilty choir boy.

"I take no offense, Doctor. And for the record, I vehemently agree. There may be nothing in this world more holy than a strong bowel movement," Father Rose returned, deadpan.

"Reincarnation wasn't just a minor part of Christianity's foundation, Jesus *himself* taught the concept to his followers." I was floored. The Catholic version of the afterlife that I'd learned in Sunday school—where the soul is judged and then routed to heaven, hell, or purgatory—made no room for the possibility of rebirth in another human body. Was it true that a gathering of old Roman bishops had erased Jesus's intended message about reincarnation from early Christian doctrine?

"It all depends on whether you believe in such spectacular things," Father Rose said, reading my mind. "Those verses certainly imply that Jesus believed a soul could return to live in a different body, at least in Elijah's case, but there are plenty of other Bible passages that completely contradict this idea. That's what makes this job such jolly good fun."

I couldn't quite tell if the priest intended this remark sarcastically, but I assumed that frowny face sticker on his Bible may have offered a clue.

"Priests and bishops, followers and nonbelievers, have all argued and debated over this stuff for millennia," Father Rose said. "Personally, I've studied the topic in great detail, looking not only at Scripture but also at the literature and popular stories of the time, many passed down orally. I've concluded that, yes, Jesus promoted reincarnation. Just like the provocative students who called themselves the Sons of the Prophets, perhaps you could call the followers of Jesus's teachings about reincarnation the Sons of Elijah."

So, there it is folks. The origin story. The name Sons of Elijah seemed perfectly fitting given my patient's stories about protecting and preserving the concept of reincarnation over centuries of violent persecution. The power-hungry Roman bishops, the atheist Red Guards of Communist China—they all shared a common, burning desire to stamp out the notion of rebirth.

I'd concluded that Sophie and Gerald believed they were fighting similar oppressive forces in modern times, just as they had in every past incarnation that they'd lived on this planet. And yet, I know there was still something more driving their desperate actions—a grander secret of monumental signifi-cance that they shared with no one outside of their group. Those oppressive forces wanted this secret too, and they pursued it with maniacal zeal. And yet, there is no evidence that anyone outside the Sons of Elijah ever learned what information they guarded so intently. Perhaps it really did have something to do with the ancient prophet from Israel. Perhaps this secret fore-told some of that magical vengeance Father Rose spoke of so endearingly. The end of the world, maybe.

Whatever Sophie and Gerald's secret may have been, they killed for it and, in Sophie's case, died for it. Others came after Sophie—a handful of followers she and Gerald had recruited to their cause, four to be exact. These men and women detonated suicide bombs too, always in crowded places like malls or theme parks. The Sons of Elijah killed thousands.

People often ask me: Are there others out there who know the secret? The attacks stopped years ago, but are the Sons of Elijah really gone? Did their secret die with them? Unless Gerald Cutter resurfaces someday, we may never know the truth. For now, the secret of the Sons of Elijah will rest until one day when it is resurrected in the mind of someone new.

If you believe in such spectacular things.

41

THE SOUR-SWEET smell of ammonia and stale air freshener lingered in the hospital hallways. Ahead was a set of double doors with two round windows that looked like the hollow eyes of a cadaver with its lids pinned back. A long black streak where rubber-capped gurneys had scuffed the paint made a crooked smile. The nurse walking beside Tag waved her arm to activate a motion sensor, and the face split down the middle as the doors swung open.

"They just put in these thingies. The hospital administration swears they're safer, but I've just about dislocated my shoulder getting the damn sensors to see me," the nurse said.

"You're taking me a different way," Tag noticed. "They've moved him?"

"Beds are scarce at the moment. A Greyhound bus overturned on the interstate last night. The driver fell asleep and drifted right off the shoulder, going about seventy. Wrecked it good."

Tag grimaced. She hadn't heard about the accident, having had a rather eventful night of her own. "Any fatalities?"

"Yup, sure were. I don't know if those mega buses even have seat belts, but someone will surely require them now. Six dead, but a heck of a lot more laid out downstairs with a mess of injuries. Anyway, that's why we had to move your guy up here. Private rooms are practically a luxury. I call them the VIP suites. Hardly appropriate accommodations for this particular patient, but I suppose we have no choice given the circumstances."

They passed a man with his nose pressed against a pane of glass, smiling and waving. A sign above the window read "Nursery."

The nurse whispered, "I wonder how these new parents would feel if they knew a convicted felon was being treated just steps away from their little bambinos."

"He hasn't been convicted of anything," Tag replied. "Technically, the DA hasn't even released the charges yet."

"Well, when they do, I'm sure they'll make us move him again. Somewhere away from the public. With any luck, we'll just be rid of him by then."

"Has his condition improved?" Tag asked.

"You could say that," the nurse answered. "This morning, he asked for a king's breakfast. Ate a three-egg omelet in about three bites. I told him not to gorge himself, especially on an empty stomach. But you know doctors; they don't like being on the receiving end of medical advice."

The women arrived at a door marked "2E, Private." Tag lifted her fist to knock.

"Don't bother with that. He won't be able to open the door himself." The nurse pulled a set of keys from her pocket. "Can't be too careful."

"You locked him inside?" Tag asked.

"Look, we're short on nurses just like we're short on rooms. I can't just rush back here every time Dr. Jekyll needs to uri-nate." The nurse's key ring held an impressive collection, and the woman cycled through them, jamming them into the lock one by one, searching for the correct one. "So, yeah, I asked the officers to remove his handcuffs. They agreed, but only if we secured the door. Larry's up here most of the time too. Although he must be on a smoke break."

Tag wasn't concerned about Dr. Jacobson attempting to escape police custody. After she'd raced out of the interrogation room, Michelson, true to his promise to play the sadistic cop, had left the psychiatrist in pretty bad shape. He'd shattered the man's cheekbone, at least three ribs, and a kneecap.

Still, Jacobson would recover from the beating, even if the life he'd known and cherished had already ended. He would never practice psychiatry again. He'd lose his tenured professorship, and even his publisher would probably drop him. Jacobson had thrown his life away when he set off that bomb at Wrigley Field, even if it did nothing but release red smoke. And for what? To abet Caleb Miller, his deranged son?

Or was Caleb more than that? Tag thought. *Was he an eternal guardian of the Sons of Elijah's secret—the stuff about eight billion souls?* Nonsense. The Sons were a myth, invented and propagated by Dr. Jacobson himself to exploit vulnerable people and advance his career. Tag's supposed visions of past lives in far-flung places had already begun to fade, and she could finally see them for what they were: drug-induced delusions. The FBI lab analyzed the array of potted plants in Jacobson's office and identified five breeds with known psychoactive properties. He'd served Tag tainted water, tea, whiskey. Her toxicology screening revealed her blood was swimming with the rare biotoxins. The only thing left to do was confront the asshole who'd put her through it all.

The door lock finally clicked. Tag reached for the handle, but the nurse stopped her.

"Before you see him, I must warn you," she said.

"I know about his injuries," Tag replied. "I've seen worse." Limbs stacked across one another like meaty logs, bits of bone glittering in pools of gore, the mangled steel of a Ferris wheel still groaning. *No! Those memories aren't real.* It was as if the closer she got to Dr. Jacobson, the stronger his spell became. She wouldn't let him manipulate her again. To think what she'd almost done . . .

"Are you all right?" the nurse asked.

"Yeah, I'm fine. I'll only be a minute. In and out."

"Right, okay. Well, I see you've got protection," the nurse said, eyeing Tag's sidearm, "so I'll leave you to him. Just, uh, holler when you need me to lock up."

The door inched open soundlessly. A sheer curtain had been drawn across the window, but it still let in enough light to cast long shadows. A silk ficus, an IV stand, a wastebasket— they all stretched across the floor as dark, shapeless blotches, desperate to escape through the open door. A lumpy figure sat in a wheelchair in front of the window, with its back to Tag. Dr. Jacobson didn't react to her entry.

"It's over, if you haven't already heard," Tag said. When the man didn't reply, she pressed on. "Caleb is dead. He spun a wild story about the Sons and you and . . . and Gerald. But he failed. Fermilab is safe and Dr. Torres successfully executed her experiment." Tag heard the dull scrape of her own teeth grinding together. The slick professor with the shiny hair and bronze skin had been reduced to a decrepit heap of slack flesh, and yet somehow the man still held power over her. He'd made her doubt her own sanity, question her morality, and then he'd driven her to the brink of committing an unspeakable act.

And you nearly did, didn't you, Hunny Bunny? The thought terrified Tag, and she knew why. *Because you* wanted *to. And maybe, Vera, maybe you still do.*

"You brainwashed that poor man," Tag spat. "You don't feel any sense of responsibility? Any remorse?"

Still nothing. Tag approached, determined to get a reaction, any reaction, from this man who had almost ruined her life. She gripped the handles of his wheelchair. At this slight touch, Dr. Jacobson's head fell limp to one side. Tag spotted something on the floor beside the doctor's foot—a molar, smooth and white. Except it wasn't a real tooth. It looked to be made of plastic, hollowed out and dotted with flecks of green, like Italian seasoning.

Plants are remarkable organisms. Some are powerful enough to kill a man with a single seed . . .

Tag turned Dr. Jacobson's wheelchair. The man's face was swollen. Beyond the disfigurement, the rims of his nostrils were blue, and his lips had ballooned to twice their normal size. The doctor's eyes were shut, but the thin membranes of his eyelids had become nearly transparent. She could see his glassy corneas underneath, like two black bugs caught in a web of hairline veins. Tag pressed a finger into Jacobson's neck, a stump of cold clay. She backed away, gathered the biggest gulp of air, and bellowed for the nurse.

*   *   *

Three hours folded up in a hospital waiting room chair had done sinister things to Tag's spine. With no word from the staff regarding Jacobson's condition, she'd started to leave, when a young medical intern had chased her into the parking lot. "His heart rate is strong now," she said. "We're flushing him with fluids, and he's responding." Tag couldn't believe they'd even detected a pulse in Dr. Jacobson. The way his head had snapped back and that doughy texture of his skin—he'd seemed long gone.

"He's awake?" Tag asked.

"Yes, but we're going to give him something to make him rest. I imagine you'll want this as evidence." The doctor held the fake tooth in the palm of her hand. "The crown snaps open on a hinge. He hid a rosary pea inside. It's a little red seed. We found bits of it on his tongue."

"And this rosary pea, it's poisonous?" Tag asked.

"We had to consult our resident pharmacologist. This particular pea contains something she called abrin. The seed's perfectly safe when intact, but bite down on one and . . . well, you saw what happens."

Tag should've ordered the hospital to place Dr. Jacobson under suicide watch. She hadn't considered the depths of the man's vanity. One look at his own shapeless face, all purple from Michelson's beating, and he'd probably snapped.

"Take me to him," Tag ordered.

"I don't think that's a good—"

"I'm not asking."

The intern nodded and headed into the building. Tag held the plastic molar up to the light for another look, then pocketed the strange object and followed behind the intern's flapping white coat.

Inside Jacobson's hospital room, a heart monitor kept time with short digital beeps. He grimaced underneath an oxygen mask. A nurse stopped him when he lifted an arm to remove it.

"It's all right," Tag said. "I just want you to listen." She turned to the medical staff. "May we have the room? Five minutes, max." Once they were alone, Tag removed a paperback from inside her jacket and threw it onto the hospital bed.

"*Raising the Sons of Elijah*," Tag said contemptuously. "More like *inventing* them. Was any of it true? The sessions with Sophie, her remembered lives? Did you drug her too?"

Jacobson pulled the mask under his chin. The faint hiss of oxygen matched the wheezes coming from the doctor's mouth. "I have tapes. Hours of—"

"Audio recordings are easily faked, just like everything else about you." Tag pinched the artificial molar between her fingers. "It's all a show. The bestsellers, the sold-out seminars, the expensive clothes and face lifts. Guess you'll need a few more of those now."

Jacobson's chin retreated into his neck, and his eyes became shiny. The last remark had hit below the belt, and Tag immediately regretted it. Even if his appearance now matched the monster inside, the man was still healing from a serious assault. And if he really had eaten a poisonous seed to avoid the trauma, then clearly his injuries were more than skin deep. Tag thought he probably deserved it—the dread and hopelessness that made him consider death the preferable option—but she didn't need to drive her heel into his wounds.

"You're right about one thing, but wrong about most others," Dr. Jacobson said. His chest heaved with every breath. "I wasn't completely honest in my book."

"Yeah, no shit."

"The final chapter," he said, panting, "is a lie. I wrote that I hadn't discovered the secret of the Sons. The Capstone."

Tag felt an itch crawl up her scalp. The birthmark on the back of her head was just a coincidence. That was the only plausible explanation, and not even a far-fetched one. People had all kinds of strange splotches on their skin. There was nothing special or peculiar about hers. *Except it matched the smooth stone from the music box . . .*

"There is no Capstone. That's just another myth you fabricated," Tag said.

Jacobson shook his head, took a hit of the oxygen, and then opened his mouth with a wet smack. "You may not want to believe me, or Caleb, but you don't need to. You hold the knowledge inside yourself. It's not stored within your brain—that's merely a gray sponge that may last another sixty or seventy years before it dries up, if you're lucky. This is knowledge that you hold somewhere else, and it never leaves you. It just gets covered up with moss and cobwebs now and then, but it's always there."

"You're saying I know that it's true in my *soul*." Tag crossed her arms, enraged at the man's arrogance. Even after his entire destructive fantasy had crashed down around him, he was still peddling these sappy aphorisms. "You're so concerned with spiritual healing, yet you pushed Sophie, Gerald, and Caleb to commit unspeakable acts. You squeezed inside their heads and twisted the screws until they became killers."

"I only wanted to save us; you must recognize that now. *"Nolite propinquius venire. Don't get close"*—the words that Sophie said the emperor Constantine had uttered on his deathbed. It was a warning. Constantine knew the truth. God had revealed it to him during a pilgrimage to Gesoriacum. And then the Sons of Elijah protected it for thousands of years. The body count here on Earth . . . it has a limit. And now we're getting too close. I had to do something, but now it's probably too late."

"Is that the real reason you went to Wrigley Field?" Tag said.

"Caleb thought I could convince you . . . to show you who you are . . . but something was holding you back. It still is. I had to get your attention."

"You abetted a terrorist. Caleb could have killed *millions* if he'd blown up the Fermilab detector. But now he'll never hurt anyone ever again. He's gone."

Dr. Jacobson's eyes glistened. "I fear you may be right. We can't bring him back like last time."

"What are you talking about?"

"I tried to explain, back at the FBI field office. Gerald disappeared after killing his wife, and Sophie was convinced he was dead. She believed there was a way to bring him back. I didn't think it would work, but she insisted. The guardians of the Capstone, like Sophie and Gerald, seem to have some degree of control over their reincarnations. She believed if she were to become pregnant . . ."

"She thought Gerald's soul would enter her baby and be reborn as her own child?" A knot hardened in Tag's stomach. "That's why I asked you, that first time you put me under hypnosis."

"You knew Caleb would have to die, and you wanted to ensure that you could bring him back again."

When Tag had listened to the recording of her session with Dr. Jacobson, she'd hardly recognized her own voice, begging him to sleep with her, to *impregnate* her. And he'd agreed immediately, almost as if he'd expected her to ask. Or worse: *made* her do it somehow. That had to be how he'd tricked those other women into having sex with him. Tag should've walked away from the case and never returned to Jacobson's office after that. At the very least, she should've reported him.

"It's revolting," she said.

The nurse entered the room. When the door swung open, it let in the faint cry of a newborn coming from the nursery down the hall. "I've got to change the patient's IV bag and check his vitals again. Be just a minute, and then you can come back in, Agent Taggart."

Tag nodded and zipped her jacket. "I'm finished here," she said, glaring at Jacobson.

"Wait, Vera. There's something I need to tell you." The psychiatrist's hoarse voice rose in pitch. Tag turned away. She was done listening to Dr. Seth Jacobson. She had heard enough of his lies.

"I died sitting in that wheelchair," the man continued. "The doctors and nurses revived me, and I'm grateful they did, but I did die."

Tag looked at the nurse, who nodded in agreement.

"It's rare that someone comes back after complete cardiac arrest and apnea," the nurse said. "We don't know how long his heart had stopped for. He's lucky not to have suffered more severe brain damage."

Tag snorted. "Yeah, our lucky guy." She started to leave.

"That's not the point," Dr. Jacobson called out, wheezing now. "Vera, do you know what happened after I died today?"

Tag had already stepped into the hallway when she heard his rasping scream: "Nothing! No white light. No overwhelming sense of peace. It was just horrid black emptiness. I saw *nothing*."

Tag was practically running now. She had to get away, out of range of Dr. Jacobson's gravitational pull. She flew past a series of closed doors, all private rooms like Jacobson's, she supposed. Maybe a few of those survivors from the Greyhound bus accident had ended up in one. *Maybe even the careless driver,* Tag thought. *Murderer's row.* Unformed thoughts streaked her mind. Ribbons streaming through her consciousness.

Bus wreck.

Train wreck.

The Sunset Limited splashing into the Mobile River.

Dr. Jacobson's voice: *What would you say if I told you the Sunset Limited derailed twenty years ago?*

A newscaster: *Marking the anniversary . . . of the tragedy. The thirtieth anniversary. Our hearts go out to the victims' families . . .*

Tag froze. The Sunset Limited had derailed *thirty* years ago; the TV news anchor had said so. That would have been 1993. But Dr. Jacobson had told Caleb the accident had happened *twenty* years ago, in 2003. Jacobson had argued that Caleb's memory from the train couldn't have been retained from a past life, because he'd been a child when the train tipped off that bridge in Alabama. But Jacobson was wrong. The Sunset Limited had actually crashed a decade earlier, the year *before* Caleb Miller was born.

Had Caleb really died on that train in a former life? Dr. Jacobson must have known the FBI was listening; he'd wanted to paint Caleb as a delusional wannabe. Possibly the entire recorded session that Tag had monitored from the van was staged. Dr. Jacobson and Caleb had acted out a preplanned script intended to—

To get my attention. That moment was the beginning. Dr. Jacobson had gotten his hooks into her and never let go.

"*Dr. Jacobson is a guide,*" Caleb had said. "*He helps the members find each other.*"

The more Tag considered it, the more she became convinced that Jacobson and Caleb had premeditated the conversation about the train crash for a specific purpose: to manipulate Tag. Then they'd manufactured a dramatic event—a distraught, mentally ill man about to end his own life—all to facilitate her daring rescue on the bridge. Tag recalled the look in Caleb's eyes when she'd climbed the railing beside him. It wasn't fear or despair. He'd looked hopeful. Caleb had expected the emotional intensity of the moment to trigger a realization in Tag. He'd expected her to realize that Dr. Jacobson had gotten the date of the train crash wrong, because Caleb believed Tag already *knew* the truth.

"This is knowledge that you hold somewhere else, and it never leaves you."

Fumbling in her jacket pocket, Tag pulled out her phone and stabbed at the screen. In a moment, a man's voice spoke.

"Looks like you saved the day, Taggart," Declan Walsh said. "Too bad the gray suits stinking up the Hoover Building will probably shred your creds after the internal review. You broke about a hundred protocols, but I'm not one to judge. Hell, you're kinda my new hero."

"Declan, I need another favor," Tag said. "The trove of documents we found on Caleb's laptop—I need you to look for something."

"Can you be more specific?" Declan asked. "There are more than ten thousand of those old scanned files crammed in there. We still haven't gone through it all."

"Search for 'Sunset Limited.'" Tag waited, listening to the clicks of Declan's keyboard.

"Yeah, holy shit, Tag. There's a hit."

"What is it?"

"Sunset Limited—that's a train right?"

"Yes," Tag responded eagerly. "What did you find? I need to know."

"It looks like a travel itinerary. Sunset Limited, New Orleans to Miami. It's from September 1993, so it couldn't have belonged to Caleb. He's only twenty-eight. Must be stolen, like the rest of this shit."

"What's the name on the itinerary?" Tag already knew the answer before Declan spoke it.

"It says Gerald Cutter," Declan replied. "Well, I'll be damned."

Tag disconnected the call. Yes, of course Caleb had died in that terrible train crash. He'd died because he'd *caused* the crash, when he'd lived as Gerald Cutter.

"We've tried for years to prevent the population from reaching the maximum threshold," Caleb had said. *"But train crashes and fires aren't enough anymore."*

"Oh God. What have I done?" Tag whispered.

The infant in the nursery was still wailing. There were no anxious parents peering through the window this time. There was just an empty hallway with a thin glass wall separating a litter of new humans from the crushing disappointments of the outside world. Inside, a nurse wiped down a stretch of counters with her back to the babies. A red-faced infant wailed and struggled against the blanket swaddling his small body. It was as if the nurse couldn't hear him—*it is a him, you can tell by the hat, they always put the boys in blue beanies*—or she could hear just fine but had learned to tune out sounds above a certain frequency years ago.

The baby's eyes squeezed into slits, and a bubble of snot formed at the tip of his nose. He was really working against that swaddle hold now, shifting his shoulders for leverage. And then, a small victory for the young man: an arm whipped out. He clawed at the air with stubby fingers, howling louder still, perhaps at the cruel realization that one liberated limb really hadn't done anything to improve his lot. He remained as helpless as ever—neck muscles too weak to lift his own head and a nervous system firing too haphazardly to coordinate such a sophisticated action anyway. And then there was the nurse, that absentminded, neglectful, negligent woman. Wiping and sorting, sorting and wiping.

Tag couldn't understand how someone could ignore that awful screeching. Urgent and squeaky, like a mouse caught in a trap. A rubber doorstop propped open the nursery door, just a crack—undoubtedly a security violation, but a rule easily dismissed by Nurse Sally Slapdash. The sour, dissonant notes of the baby boy's cries squeezed through that crack and went romping around the ward. They sounded more animal than human.

Tag couldn't stand the sound anymore. She rushed into the nursery and stood over the infant's clear plastic bassinet. She hadn't seen it from the hallway; maybe the glare on the window had obscured it from view.

"Excuse me. You can't be in here," the nurse said, suddenly interested in fulfilling her duties.

The baby's free arm waved in jerky swats. Tag grabbed it at the wrist.

"What are you doing? Let that child go!" the nurse yelled, but Tag ignored her. She gently pinched the infant's little chin so she could open his mouth just a bit wider.

There was no mistaking it. The boy had a black spot stamped on his tongue.

The room went cold. The boy's yowling changed from a long, grating wail into bouncing, pulsing swoops. *Laughter. He's laughing at me.* The infant's lips seemed to pull back into a toothless grin. The inky mark on his tongue jiggled with each convulsing laugh. Tag had seen that rotten spot before, in those dreams, when Inquisitor Ferrier had leaned in close, and again on Zhang Boda. *Those weren't the only times, were they? You saw that spot just this week, up close. On someone else—someone who wanted to stop Caleb even more than the FBI.*

"Let go of him!" the nurse shrieked again, and Tag did just that. She released the baby's chin and bumped into another bassinet. The unexpected jolt set its occupant—*pink hat this time*—into a similar uproar. Soon the entire nursey exploded with unharmonious bellows. Tag was surrounded by writhing seed pods, screaming against their restrictive blankets. She fought for breath. The unnerving chorus swelled. Even the nurse pressed her palms into her ears to block out the sound.

Tag carefully pulled open the baby girl's mouth and peered inside. Then she moved to the next bassinet, and the next, squeezing tiny chins, inspecting tiny tongues, one by one. Each one of the infants had an identical death blotch on its tongue, hooked and honed, like the reaper's scythe.

"There won't be enough souls to populate them all. Every new baby will be born soulless. These soulless creatures will belong to it."

Tag slowly raised her head. Her blurry eyes landed on a figure standing in the hallway, peering in through the large nursery window. It smirked victoriously, bared its pointed teeth, and then opened its black maw to display its own inky tongue. Even through the maddening cacophony, Tag could hear Dr. Alex Torres's demonic laugh through the glass.

ACKNOWLEDGMENTS

ONE IN THREE Americans believes their soul will be reborn in another body after death, according to the Pew Research Center. And yes, Pew asked this survey question alongside others about psychics and astrology as part of their study on New Age beliefs. While the data collected by this esteemed institution fascinated me, the categorization of reincarnation as anything close to "new" seemed off. For millennia, nearly every major religion on the planet has made room for beliefs regarding some version of transmigration of the soul.

But does it stop there, with *belief*? If Plato or da Vinci or my late grandmother who baked the best chocolate chip cookies still walked the earth in other bodies, shouldn't there be evidence? Wouldn't we be able to prove it?

Fortunately, thriller writers like me aren't the only ones asking these questions. This book wouldn't have been possible without the meticulous research of Dr. Ian Stevenson, the founder of the University of Virginia School of Medicine's Division of Perceptual Studies. For over four decades, Stevenson investigated purported cases of reincarnation. He met children with extraordinary skills or specific knowledge they couldn't realistically have obtained in their short lives.

One boy could name almost every street of a faraway village in India from memory, including remarkably detailed descriptions of obscure landmarks, shops, and local residents, having never traveled there himself. Up until his death in 2007, Dr. Stevenson documented and classified thousands of pieces of similar evidence to better understand the merits (or fallacies) of the concept of reincarnation.

Another notable psychiatrist has approached this mysterious topic from a different angle, but with equal diligence. An acclaimed physician, Dr. Brian Weiss discovered many of his patients could access inexplicable memories while under hypnosis. Initially a skeptic, he's now seen as a pioneer in the practice of past-life regression hypnotherapy, a process that enables patients to access supposed past-life trauma to help them overcome severe medical conditions, from addiction to PTSD.

After immersing myself in the astonishing work of Stevenson, Weiss, and many others, I set out to write a story that explored reincarnation not as a New Age *belief*, but as a natural phenomenon that science could explain. In fact, every reference to past lives, hypnotic regression, near-death experiences, psychic dreams, and déjà vu in this novel is based on a real case, documented by a reputable academic or medical professional. I am deeply grateful for these individuals and their contributions to this intriguing, if underappreciated, field of study.

In search of a plausible, although entirely fictitious, scientific explanation for souls passing from body to body, I turned to particle physics. Why not? Even Albert Einstein described quantum mechanics as "spooky," so this flavor of science fit my needs perfectly. I am grateful to renowned physicists Brian Greene and Leon Lederman for publishing an array of books that have made particle physics accessible to us mere mortals. Many thanks to Anna Hall of the University of Virginia Department of Experimental High Energy Physics for sharing her love of neutrinos and advising me on the finer points of Fermilab's DUNE experiment. I take full responsibility for errors (and any other fantastical details I probably just made up).

I'm eternally grateful for my literary agent, Elizabeth Winick Rubinstein. Also, I want to thank the teams at McIntosh & Otis and Crooked Lane Books, including Zoë Bodzas, Matt Martz, Jessica Renheim, Katie McGuire, Melissa Rechter, Madeline Rathle, Rebecca Nelson, and Melanie Sun. Thanks go to Alicia Johnson, master photographer (and miracle worker), for making me look way younger in publicity photos, and to Stacy Cunningham for help with the Latin translations. I sincerely appreciate my former colleagues at the FBI for their efficient review of the manuscript. And finally, thank you Kelly, Naya, and Ameya for cheering me on every step of the way.